W9-AVS-780

MUM'S THE WORD

"Offers everything Cannell's fans have come to expect . . . a wonderfully dotty cast of characters, an unerring sense of the absurd, and witty dialogue and insights."
—*The Denver Post*

"Witty."—*Daily News,* New York

THE WIDOWS CLUB

"A thoroughly entertaining novel."—*Cosmopolitan*

"Romps along with a judicious blend of suspense, frivolity, and eccentric characters."—*Booklist*

DOWN THE GARDEN PATH

"Carries on the lovely lunacy in which Dorothy Cannell excels; I had an absolutely marvelous time with it."
—Elizabeth Peters

"Sparkling wit and outlandish characters."
—*Chicago Sun-Times*

THE THIN WOMAN

"Cannell makes a delicious debut; discriminatory whodunit fans will want more of her inventions."
—*Publishers Weekly*

"A likable debut—combining fairy-tale romance, treasure hunts, and a homicidal mania."—*Kirkus Reviews*

OTHER BOOKS BY DOROTHY CANNELL

The Thin Woman
Down the Garden Path
The Widows Club
Mum's the Word
Femmes Fatal
How to Murder Your Mother-in-Law

And
God Save the Queen!

HOW *to* MURDER THE MAN *of* YOUR DREAMS

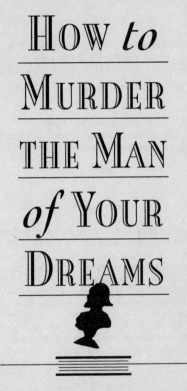

Dorothy Cannell

BANTAM BOOKS
New York Toronto London Sydney Auckland

This edition contains the complete text
of the original hardcover edition.
NOT ONE WORD HAS BEEN OMITTED.

HOW TO MURDER THE MAN OF YOUR DREAMS
A Bantam Book

PUBLISHING HISTORY
Bantam hardcover edition published October 1995
Bantam paperback edition / November 1996

ISBN 0-553-57360-8

Published simultaneously in the United States and Canada

Bantam Books are published by Bantam Books, a division of Bantam
Doubleday Dell Publishing Group, Inc. Its trademark, consisting of
the words "Bantam Books" and the portrayal of a rooster, is
Registered in U.S. Patent and Trademark Office and in other
countries. Marca Registrada. Bantam Books, 1540 Broadway, New
York, New York 10036.

PRINTED IN THE UNITED STATES OF AMERICA

OPM   10 9 8 7 6 5 4

To my friend Norma Larson,
for all the reasons why.

Many thanks to my friends at the Peoria Public Library for their generous support. An extra bouquet of gratitude to Maggie Nelson and Jean Shrier for providing me with information on the library ghost, without which ingredient this book wouldn't have been half as much fun to write.

Also I wish to thank my son Jason for leading me step-by-step through the dark labyrinths of my first grown-up word processor.

HOW TO
MURDER
THE MAN
OF YOUR
DREAMS

PROLOGUE

No one in the village suspected that Miss Bunch had a man in her life. She never spoke about him, let alone made contact with him while at her place of work. But often on returning home at night to her narrow house in Mackerel Lane, Miss Bunch would hurry to let the dog out into the back garden. After fetching him back in for his supper she would sit down to her own plain meal. Glad to be done with the dishes, she would comb her hair in the mirror above the tiny fireplace, because even a stout, no-nonsense woman wants to make the most of herself for the one who holds the key to her heart. Then she would sit down in her easy chair, pick up a volume that she had left lying open on the lamp table, and breathlessly turn a page. Within moments she would hear his footsteps. He was with her once again, murmuring endearments in his deep, caressing voice and instantly putting her loneliness to flight.

Sometimes he wore a cloak lined with moonlight, a Regency rake in a curly-brimmed hat with silver spurs on his mirror-bright boots. On other visits, his saturnine features were obscured by a highwayman's mask and his vibrant hair constrained by a carelessly knotted riband. At his throat cascaded a jabot of finest French lace and in his breeches' pocket lay a strand of purloined pearls. Occasionally he came as an Arabian sheikh with a penchant for stirring up sandstorms in his desert domain. A man who could change the course of history by the raising of one dark, sardonic eyebrow and whose smile would melt the snows of Kilimanjaro.

Throughout all the years of their relationship, Miss Bunch had known him in a myriad of guises and by many different names. But one thing never changed. He was the most faithful of lovers, forever waiting in the shadowy corners of her mind until they might next be together. And the only blight upon her secret happiness had come in recent days, when the big black dog would whimper pitifully while attempting to burrow under her chair.

Chapter

1

The Chitterton Fells library is a friendly Tudor building on the corner of Market Street and Spittle Lane. A week rarely goes by when I don't go there at least once. Even when I am not caught up with my reading I like to visit old favourites on the shelves—rather as if they are dear ones now living in a nursing home—to let them know Ellie Haskell hasn't forgotten them. So I am in a position to report that our library plays host to an inviting selection of well-dusted books, a marble bust of William Shakespeare, and a curmudgeonly ghost.

The story bandied about our seaside village is that Hector Rigglesworth, a widower and tea salesman by trade, did when on the brink of death at the tail end of the nineteenth century curse the library and vow to haunt its stacks until a just vengeance was achieved in reparation for his earthly suffering.

According to our librarian, the malcontent Mr. Rigglesworth was father to seven spinster daughters, all of whom remained under his roof, growing more querulous by the hour. The girls, as they were known in the village even after their hair had collectively turned grey, had never lacked for suitors when young. But, alas, a man never appeared on the doorstep of Tall Chimneys who was not found wanting in one particular or another. The curate blew his nose in public, the bank clerk had a twitch, the police constable guffawed, and so it went on, until Hector Rigglesworth reached the unassailable conclusion that his daughters' heads had been filled with romantic rubbish as a result of the books they were forever borrowing from the library.

What flesh-and-blood man could compete on an equal footing with swashbucklers or Regency beaus? So, as the seven girls changed from promising to menopausal, Hector Rigglesworth toiled up- and downstairs with endless cups of tea or tended to the housewifely duties that had fallen to his lot—the maid having married one of the rejected suitors. Poor Mr. Rigglesworth. He grew increasingly embittered. His burden was made the heavier during his declining years by being routinely dispatched to the library to collect the breathlessly awaited novels by favoured authors. The girls, understandably, were unable to go themselves in case the likes of Mr. Rochester or Mr. Darcy should show up with a special license and a couple of railway tickets to Gretna Green.

It was after heading home to Tall Chimneys through the puddling rain on a dreary May afternoon (it had been an unreasonably wet month) that the beleaguered papa suffered a bout of pneumonia and in his final ramblings (as witnessed by the doctor in attendance) did speak the words that were to echo grimly down the years:

"I, Hector Rigglesworth, being of sound mind, do lay my curse upon Chitterton Fells Library. May dry rot and woodworm prove its ruination and, as a further manifestation of ill will, my spirit shall roam its rooms and corridors until the day comes when I am avenged."

Inevitably there were people—most commonly of the male persuasion—who regarded the Rigglesworth legend as mere twaddle. These naysayers were not afraid to enter the library when the moon was full and crows gathered in a black cloud upon the bleached boughs of the blighted oak. It bothered them not if the tree's tendrils were wont to tap eerily upon the window of the second-floor reading room. But, surprisingly, support for the Rigglesworth ghost was found among the purportedly sane. Brigadier Lester-Smith who, at sixty-five, was by no means in his dotage, had publicly wagered his pension that the spirit had been present at many a Thursday-night meeting of the Library League.

The brigadier, adhering rigidly to the principle that punctuality is the eleventh commandment, was always first to arrive for these meetings, which were held in the reading room. He had taken upon himself the responsibility of percolating the coffee and setting out the cups and saucers. He had even on one occasion brought with him a packet of ginger nuts. This treat had been much appreciated by the group—excepting Mr. Gladstone Spike (our clergy-woman's husband) who more often than not turned up with one of his feathery-light sponge cakes.

It is my understanding that in years gone by, before the advent of the wireless, let alone the television set, the Library League had numbered as many as thirty persons. Nowadays Brigadier Lester-Smith might optimistically expect to find himself in the company of seven fellow members on a Thursday night, including myself.

On a wintry evening in what was supposed to be spring, he rounded the corner to the Spittle Lane entrance, only to collide with me as I was about to mount the library steps. The impact knocked me off balance, causing me to drop the stack of books I was carrying. Nothing short of an army tank could have made a dent in the brigadier's ramrod posture, however.

He was a sturdily built man with a fresh complexion, a steady gaze, and crinkly hair, with enough red still showing among the grey to pass for ginger in the glow from the street lamp. His khaki raincoat was of a military cut, its belt being threaded squarely through the buckle with the end tucked through not one but *both* loops. As always, he carried a leather briefcase (rumour had it the brigadier took it to bed with him) and it was polished to a mirror gloss, equal to that of his shoes. A quick peek at my own reflection was not consoling. Most of my hair had escaped from its French twist. I was minus an earring and the string from a baby's bib dangled from my pocket. Even worse, I was certain I had picked up weight since leaving home. Why else would I need to scan *both* the brigadier's shoes to get a good look at myself?

"My excuses, Mrs. Haskell." His voice was as precisely tailored as the rest of him. "I'm afraid I wasn't watching my step. My mind was already inside the library."

"It was my fault." I stood dithering with a foot half on, half off the bottom step, while one of the books did a belated bounce onto the pavement, as if no longer sure whether it was coming or going. "I was concerned I was going to be late, but that can't be the case, not with you arriving at the same time." I looked askance at my watch, which should on several prior occasions have been subjected to a polygraph test.

"How's the husband, Mrs. Haskell?" the brigadier asked kindly as he gingerly set down his briefcase on the pavement and picked up my books.

"Ben?" I spoke the name as if suddenly remembering a letter I had forgotten to post. "He's fine. Busy as always: But that's the way it goes with the restaurant business." It wasn't that I didn't adore my princely spouse, you understand, but what with the children and the shopping, to say nothing of my civic responsibilities, there tended to be hours on end when I did not think of him except as a dinner to be prepared, or a bundle of shirts to be collected from the laundry. But all that would change when the Swiss au pair arrived.

"And how are the little ones, Mrs. Haskell?"

"Abbey and Tam are my pride and joy!" The glow I shed upon my kind inquisitor was of a higher wattage than the street lamps.

"Being an old bachelor, I can't begin to think how you cope with twins." The brigadier's cheeks flushed a peachy pink as the wind made a sudden charge around the corner. It also started to rain at the same moment, a slow drop at a time, as if testing our patience. Handing me the neatly aligned stack of books, Brigadier Lester-Smith picked up his briefcase and checked it for scuff marks. "I hope you are finding things a little easier now that your offspring are getting up in years."

"They're halfway through the terrible twos." I was unable to conceal my pride as we marched up the brick steps in time to the quickening beat of rain upon the rooftops. "Tam's all boy and Abbey thinks she is too. Don't worry, Brigadier Lester-Smith: They're not having to fend for themselves tonight," I hastened to add in case he was picturing my delightful progeny whiling away the evening with a couple of cigars and a bottle of port. "Ben had to work tonight at Abigail's. But Mrs. Malloy, who helps me out a couple of days a week, agreed to watch them until I get home. Usually I can count on my cousin to baby-sit if he isn't working the evening shift with Ben. But Freddy left yesterday for a fortnight's holiday touring Scotland and Wales on his motorbike. He took Jonas with him." I pushed open the library door with my free hand while miraculously maintaining a steady hold on the books and my smile.

"Jonas Phipps?" The brigadier raised a gingery eyebrow. "Your gardener? But surely, the man's even longer in the tooth than I am."

"Mr. Phipps has a wild streak in him." I adroitly avoided slamming the door and knocking off the brigadier's nose. "The prospect of camping out and eating off tin plates for days on end, to say nothing of sleeping in his clothes, undid every one of the values I have been at pains to instill. The only thing that might have dissuaded Jonas from hopping on the back of Freddy's motorbike was my mentioning that Ben and I have decided to hire a mother's helper. But I refused to resort to bribery. And, to be frank, I am not sure that even the thought of inviting her to admire the prize roses on his bedroom wallpaper would have kept Jonas from donning his goggles and black leather jacket."

"Looking to cut quite a dash, by the sound of it." Brigadier Lester-Smith followed me into the library vestibule.

"Mrs. Malloy certainly thought so! She told him he could put Karisma out of a job if he would just let the hair on his head grow and shave the scruff on his chest."

"Karis-who?"

"Him!" I plucked a book from my pile and held it out to the bewildered brigadier as he drew the door shut behind us. "Behold the face that has launched billions of romance novels." Being a woman of some refinement, I did not draw attention to the way Karisma filled out his loincloth.

"You're saying he and the woman in that extraordinarily convoluted embrace are real people, not some artist's idea of what the characters in the book look like?" Brigadier Lester-Smith appeared awestruck, as well he might. The heroine of *The Last Temple Virgin*, by Zinnia Parrish, was clothed in little more than her virtue as she swooned in the arms of the gods' gift to women. Her breasts were round and smooth as wine goblets, her lips soft and dewy as rose petals after a rainstorm, her hair a rippling waterfall, her eyes smoky with desire. But who wouldn't look like that, including Ellie Haskell, if given the opportunity to recline upon Karisma's sun-bronzed chest and gaze enraptured upon his glorious physiognomy? So close that one's eyelashes entwined with his! So near that his heart pumped the lucky female's lifeblood and set her pulses throbbing with forbidden passion.

"We all have to make a living," the brigadier said doubtfully as we stood in the shadowy vestibule lit by one minuscule lightbulb dangling from a cord high above our heads.

"There is more to Karisma than raw sex appeal," I assured him. "My husband, if you will excuse the boast, has the kind of dark good looks that turns heads in Marks & Spencer. But never in a million years could I picture Ben on a book jacket. He lacks that untamed . . . *unmarried* look, for starters." I shuffled through my stack of books while my companion completed the all-consuming task of sponging the raindrops from his briefcase. When he was done and his handkerchief refolded and hung neatly over his belt to dry, I held out *Where Eagles Fear to Fly*. "Karisma has such incredible versatility. He can be anyone, anything the camera asks him to be!" I knew I was babbling away like a mindless brook, but a stay-at-home mum is occasionally overwhelmed by the need to show herself conversant with current events. "See for yourself why the tabloids hail him as the king of the male cover models!" I held out another book, a paperback this time, brilliantly packaged with foil and raised letters.

The brigadier made a well-bred endeavour to show interest. "Fascinating, Mrs. Haskell! The castle in the background puts me very much in mind of Merlin's Court."

I accepted the compliment and kept to myself the belief that my home had far more going for it by way of turrets and battlements than the one on the cover. "Here we have Karisma," I said. "Behold him at one with the elements. He is the uncharted sea, the unbridled wind, the promise of sunrise upon the horizon. He is the Earl of Polmorgan—his hair streaming like victory's banner. A nobleman ousted from the ancestral home by the cruel machinations of his impecunious stepmother and forced to turn smuggler along the Cornish coast. His innate gallantry dictates that he provide for the lovely young woman who was his father's ward. She has gone into a decline after being forced into marriage with an odious man who terrified her on the wedding night by unsheathing his sword and . . ."

Brigadier Lester-Smith took advantage of the emotional break in my voice to interject hastily, "It must take him a month of Sundays to dry his hair. And speaking of time marching on, Mrs. Haskell, I do think we should be making our way upstairs to the reading room. The other members of the league expect me to have the coffee on the perk, and the minutes from the last meeting"—he patted his briefcase—"laid out on the table, ready for review." Crossing the mosaic tile in two measured steps, the brigadier opened the door into the library proper.

The arrangement inside was unapologetically oldfashioned. No little turnstiles by which to enter and exit and send one into a tailspin. No revolving magazine racks. No magnifying mirrors installed for the purpose of assisting in the apprehension of book nabbers. No computers pretending to mind their own business even as they secreted away information on the reading habits of each and every library-card holder.

The brigadier and I might have been standing on the threshold of a household library, the kind guaranteed to lend just the right touch of snob appeal to a gentleman's country retreat. There were no other patrons about because it was after closing hour. And by some quirk of shadow and light the free-standing bookcases turned the room—partitioned by archways—into a maze that would appear to have been set up for the express amusement of his lordship's children. Two or three worn leather chairs were drawn conversationally around an oak table positioned in front of the leaded windows overlooking Spittle Lane. A pair of hunting prints echoed the muted tones of the Jacobean-patterned curtains. A hammered brass screen stood guard in front of the stone fireplace. The marble bust of Shakespeare sat on a pedestal above the archway leading into the nonfiction area, which in turn opened onto the children's section.

Perhaps, on second thought, the fact that the books were not uniformly bound in gold-tooled leather did hint that this was not a private collection. There was also the reception desk—the size of Amelia Earhart's practice runway—to clinch one's suspicions that we were in a lending institution.

Miss Bunch, our stalwart librarian, lived at that desk. Rumour had it that she had been born there—fully grown, already stout, red-faced, and with her hair cropped to an uncompromising bob. I had it on good authority (from Mrs. Malloy) that Miss Bunch did not possess a first name. Doubtless her parents had instantly realized the impropriety of attempting to become too familiar with their offspring.

My knees had a tendency to knock on those occasions when I approached Miss Bunch at her desk—my arms loaded with books whose overdue status would momentarily be calculated down to a percentage of a second. Being an accomplished coward, I had on occasion brought along a doctor's certificate to excuse my disregard for timely returns, but this evening I did not feel the full force of Miss Bunch's bull's-eye stare as I tiptoed forward with my eight volumes of riveting romance novels. My engrossing conversation with Brigadier Lester-Smith had blinded me to the obvious.

For tonight our librarian was conspicuous by her absence.

"Surprising!" The brigadier glanced from me to the door marked Private and shook his head. No need for him to expound. The concept of Miss Bunch abandoning her post in order to indulge in a cup of tea and a cream bun or—heaven forbid, go to the loo—was not open to discussion. Miss Bunch would have handed in her date stamp sooner than exhibit such human frailty. That she might be

stacking books in the far reaches of nonfiction was equally
unlikely. A time for every job was Miss Bunch's sacred
maxim. Books were always returned to their allotted
shelves between the hours of ten A.M. and noon.

"I expect she went upstairs to turn on the lights for us
in the reading room," I said while scanning the room uneasily out of the corner of my eye. Surely it was the patter
of rain on the windows and the ghoulish gurgle of the
wind that made the library seem suddenly forlorn?

"You cannot be serious, Mrs. Haskell." Brigadier
Lester-Smith looked suitably grave. "Turning on the lights,
along with plugging in the percolator, has always been my
job. I do not imagine that for all her industriousness, Miss
Bunch would overstep that particular line."

It was my opinion that Miss Bunch would do precisely
as she chose in her own library, but I kept mum as I
planted my books on the eerily deserted desk. For the moment I was freed from the obligation of confessing that I
had left an indelible coffee cup ring on page 342 of *Speak
Her Name Softly* by the prolific Zinnia Parrish. So with
my mind determinedly focused on the evening's meeting, I
stood behind the brigadier as he opened the door that gave
access to the staircase.

"After you, Mrs. Haskell."

My gasp made us both jump.

Misunderstanding my reaction, the brigadier's cheeks
turned a peachy pink that complemented his fading ginger
hair nicely as he hastily made his apologies. "You'll have
to forgive me, Mrs. Haskell; being an old-fashioned chap I
forget once in a while that what used to pass for common
courtesy is now perceived as an insult to all womankind."

"Forget the fallout from women's lib!" With a trembling finger I pointed towards the N–O fiction section of
the book stacks. "Brigadier, surely you see . . . there on
the floor . . . way down at the end of that aisle . . ."
The wind chose that moment to emit a death rattle that
vibrated the walls along with the windowpanes. "We have
a body in the library."

A blatant case of hyperbole! What we had was a leg.
No, make that a foot. But was it unreasonable to assume
that a body was in some way involved—out of sight,
around the corner of the stack?

"A shadow, Mrs. Haskell, nothing more."

"I tell you . . ."

"If you'll excuse my saying so, Mrs. Haskell, you've been reading too many thrillers." This said, with gentlemanly restraint Brigadier Lester-Smith did me the honour of setting down his briefcase on the desk.

"It's such a cliché, isn't it?" I followed him with lagging steps and galloping heart as, clearly bent on humouring me, he headed into the wooden maze. The foot I was sure I'd seen would prove to be nothing more ominous than a book left carelessly on the floor by a library patron. The brigadier's steps quickened even as I decided I had made a complete imbecile of myself. Doubtless before he could pick up said volume and return it to its rightful place on the shelf, Miss Bunch would appear from Nonfiction to announce that the guilty patron would be forthwith stripped of his or her library card and sentenced to two weeks' community service in card catalogue.

There was in fact a book—its pages flung wide in careless abandon on the floor. And a few inches away was an object that unmistakably constituted a foot, encased in a serviceable brogue. The wind drew a shuddering breath as the brigadier spoke our librarian's name in startled greeting.

"Miss Bunch, are you feeling out of sorts?" He had tracked around the end of the aisle and now dropped to his immaculate knees beside the librarian who lay sprawled face-up on the floor in her bottle-green skirt and matching jersey. She was, as always, a stout, florid-faced woman with a combative gleam in her glassy stare. "Brace yourself, Mrs. Haskell," the brigadier said, and I obediently swayed against the stacks. "Miss Bunch has crossed the finishing line." He spoke as a man who, though having routinely faced the grim implacability of death in his army textbooks, was opposed to using a certain four-letter word in the presence of the opposite sex.

"Dead? Perhaps she will come out of it." A crisis invariably brings out the idiot in me. "It's not as if her throat has been cut from ear to ear, or her head caved in with a blunt instrument."

"Possibly a heart attack, Mrs. Haskell."

"Surely not!" I warded off the suggestion with the

hand I wasn't using to wipe my eyes. "I'm convinced Miss
Bunch would never give way like that, not on the job. She
has an irreproachable work ethic. And an unerring sense
of what is appropriate. I will never forget the drumming
she gave me when she discovered I had jotted down a
phone number on the flyleaf of *A Midsummer Night's
Scream*. In pencil, mind you! And," I blithered, "it wasn't
as though it were the number of a male-escort service."

Clearly Miss Bunch's bulging eyes were beginning to
get to me, for nothing short of extreme stress would have
caused me to let slip the words "male escort." We all have
our little secrets. Mine was that I had acquired Ben Haskell for a husband after renting him for a family-reunion
weekend from Eligibility Escorts. Overweight, underloved,
I had been seized by a wild impulse to indulge in something more daring than a new frock with which to impress
my assorted relatives, especially my diabolically beautiful
cousin Vanessa. Eligibility was owned and managed by
Mrs. Swabucher, an elderly lady given to powder-pink
hats and a fondness for Belgian chocolates. Believe me,
there was nothing sleazy about her operation. No bullet
holes in her office door, no naughty magazines on the desk
or disgruntled clients being fed into the shredder. How
could I go wrong when the man who turned up at my door
to escort me to Merlin's Court was the breathtakingly
handsome Bentley T. Haskell?

When we were first married I wouldn't have lost more
than a few hours' sleep had word leaked out about Eligibility Escorts. Love would have weathered the gossip. But
now there were the twins to be considered. How awful it
would be if my children failed to get into the nursery
school of their choice because Ben and I lacked credibility
as parents. And, not to take myself too seriously, I did
have to consider my civic responsibilities, along with my
recent decision to return to work, on a part-time basis, as
an interior designer.

"Mrs. Haskell?" Brigadier Lester-Smith brought me
back to the matter—or rather the corpse—at hand. "Are
you feeling faint, my dear?"

"I'm steady as a rock," I lied. "Why don't you go and
ring for an ambulance while I wait here with Miss Bunch?
I know it's silly, but I don't like abandoning her to the

unholy glee of Hector Rigglesworth. Listen"—I held up a hand—"do you hear him laughing?"

"The wind," Brigadier Lester-Smith replied without undue conviction. "We mustn't let our imaginations run riot. It is true that upon occasion I have sensed a *presence* while on these premises but . . ." He paused as I took a step backwards, sending the book lying on the floor skidding across the aisle.

"You were saying?" I picked up the volume without looking at the title and absently dusted it off on my raincoat sleeve.

"Only, Mrs. Haskell, that whilst I might suspect Mr. Rigglesworth of such malicious pranks as unplugging the percolator or helping himself to a couple of ginger nuts while my back was turned, I cannot believe a gentleman of the old school, whether living or dead, would find poor Miss Bunch's . . . present predicament a laughing matter."

"The man was *soured* on women." I lowered my voice and looked around uneasily. "Look at this book, Brigadier. Can you deny the possibility that Mr. Rigglesworth lured Miss Bunch into the stacks by means of an ominous rustling and then caused this book to fly off the shelf and hit her a fatal wallop on the head?"

"Murder, Mrs. Haskell, is a serious accusation against a man who is not available to defend himself." Brigadier Lester-Smith tightened his raincoat belt in a grim attempt at holding his emotions in check. "I am sure Miss Bunch is the victim of a stroke or a heart attack, and the fact that tonight is the hundredth anniversary of Hector Rigglesworth's demise is no more than an unhappy coincidence."

This revelation brought a gasp to my lips. I was about to babble away about circumstantial evidence, when I felt the floor vibrate under my feet and, whether from a momentary dizziness or not, saw a section of books quiver as if revving themselves up to let fly. "You're absolutely right, Brigadier," I made haste to say, "life is filled with coincidence. And people die all the time without ghostly assistance. Poor Mr. Rigglesworth, he did not have things easy in life and should not be maligned in death." Avoiding Miss Bunch's icy glare, I took comfort in having avoided the avalanche. Then I felt it—another reverberation. But

before I could leap into the brigadier's arms, I realized that
the library door had swung open and closed.

Footsteps heralded the arrival of our fellow members
of the Library League. Mrs. Dovedale's pleasant musical
voice was heard in conversation with the vicar's husband.

"How kind of you to bring one of your lovely sponge
cakes. And not from a packet, if I know you, Mr. Spike."

"That's all well and good, Mrs. Dovedale," came Mr.
Poucher's dour response. "But I for one come to these
meetings to feed my mind, not my belly."

"Oh, go on, you old grouchy-pouch!" That was the
irrepressible Bunty Wiseman. "You'll be wolfing down
your slice of cake and licking the cream off your fingers
along with the rest of us."

My mouth watered, a purely nervous reaction.

"I'd better go and give them the bad news." Brigadier
Lester-Smith soldiered his way towards the assembled
voices.

Alas for Miss Bunch, I thought sadly. She was an institution and the library would never be the same without
her. But did she leave anyone to mourn her? The rain wept
steadily against the windows, but no loud burst of sobs
arose in response to the brigadier's announcement.

Sir Robert Pomeroy did say "Bloody bad show!" But
he spoiled the effect by adding, "I suppose this means the
meeting's off for this evening. What! What! A bit of a
shame really, seeing I was hoping to present my suggestions for improving the parking situation."

"He doesn't mean to be callous," I whispered to Miss
Bunch in the futile hope of softening her up. There could
be no doubt they were in shock, every one of them, including timid Sylvia Babcock, who had taken time out from
her honeymoon to be here, rather than risk censure for
seconding fewer motions than any league member, past or
present. Any moment now the penny would drop with a
monumental clang. Someone surely would voice the possibility of Hector Rigglesworth taking a ghostly hand in
Miss Bunch's demise. The significance of the date would
be bandied about. And the fact that the book I had found
lying on the floor within inches of the body was titled *The
Dream Lover* would forever ensure her place in local lore.

Chapter

2

"I'm sorry you couldn't get away from the restaurant to attend the funeral, dear." Ben and I sat in the rose-and-peacock drawing room at the close of a long but fulfilling day. "But for your absence, it couldn't have been more perfect. The rain never let up for a moment and we stood around the grave in a huddle of black umbrellas, just the way you see on the films. Only in those cases"—I leaned back, weary but replete, in the Queen Anne chair—"on the screen, that is, the person being buried is usually an extremely shady character who had managed to lead a double life while never missing a manicure appointment. But somehow, even in the chill of the moment, I could not picture Miss Bunch as a denizen of the underworld. Particularly as it has been determined that she died of natural causes."

"You can't be sure Miss Bunch was a model citizen." Ben shook his head at my naïveté. "My father always told me to beware of a woman with a forty-four-inch bust."

"There was a man in an upturned raincoat lurking behind a tombstone," I conceded. "And I'll admit I did find myself wondering if he might have fathered the child Miss Bunch conceived while a novitiate at the Convent of Perpetual Penance, the one she was forced to hand over into the keeping of the head gardener's wife."

"Ellie, you're making this up."

"I'm afraid so." I settled more comfortably in my chair. "The poor man was skulking around St. Anselm's churchyard, thinking he was in the pet cemetery at the other end of Chitterton Fells. Seemingly, he had come to pay his last respects to his aunt Edith's basset hound. As for Miss Bunch, I don't suppose she was ever inside a convent, let alone a man's pajamas." I lowered my voice, even though the twins had been upstairs in bed for over an hour. "Her life made for rather a tame eulogy."

"You're far too trusting, Ellie." Ben prowled over to the window and drew the curtains against the gathering night. He was looking endearingly spousal in the apron he had worn to bathe the twins—his shirt-sleeves rolled up to the elbow and his black hair tousled. "It is entirely like you to have been taken in by Miss Bunch's bottle-green cardigans and bolster bosom." He scooped up Tobias the cat and returned to the sofa. "But what do you know about her *inner* self?" Two cups of coffee after dinner and Ben tends to wax philosophical. "The sad truth, sweetheart," he said, "is that most of us remain an enigma even to ourselves."

"Oh, I don't know! You and I understand each other inside and out, dear. But it could be we're the lucky ones." It was impossible to prevent complacency creeping into my voice, given the coziness of the room and the certainty of Ben's affection. It had been ages since we had a good row. Thank God! The days flowed one into the other without any of the old silliness that used to get in the way. No more floods of tears from me if he forgot the anniversary of the day we met. No more sulking from him if I raved about Mr. Spike's sponge cakes. Yes, life was good. So good in fact that death lost all credibility, dwindling away to an old wives' tale that was only occasionally used these days to scare little children into good behaviour.

"Was it a big funeral?" Ben's voice interrupted my happy contemplation of the Chinese vases on the mantelpiece. I'd washed them along with polishing the silver and replacing the lightbulbs in the brass wall lamps before setting out for the service. The goad to my rear had been my intention to invite the mourners back to the house for tea or sherry, but it turned out that no one had the time to spare.

"The church wasn't exactly packed," I replied. "Only the Library League came. But all in all it was a very nice send-off for Miss Bunch. Eudora made an extremely kind reference to how well Miss Bunch managed the reference desk." I did not mention it was difficult for our lady vicar to elaborate when she, Eudora, is not a member of the library and Miss Bunch did not attend St. Anselm's except occasionally for Easter or Christmas.

"Surely the woman had friends." Setting Tobias Cat down on the floor, Ben stood up and stretched with a purposeful languor that signalled to me he was about to suggest that this meeting be adjourned to the bedroom.

"I don't think she had any special pals." I was on my feet, gathering up the coffee cups and looking around the room for cushions to be plumped up, or tapestry table runners to be straightened. "She had a dog, which one of the neighbours took in on a temporary basis. But the poor thing will probably have to be put down if no one volunteers to adopt it."

Tobias converted a grin into a yawn as I looked down at him.

"And don't tell me not to get any ideas, Ben . . ."

"I wasn't going to say anything of the sort." He strode towards me and stood gazing into my eyes in a manner that caused the coffee spoons to rattle on their saucers. "It will perhaps come as no surprise, sweetheart, that I returned home early this evening in hope that you might come up with one of your entrancing ideas."

He gathered me to him at great risk to crockery and silverware. Unbidden, the uneasy thought occurred that he had been taking a peek at my latest library book. Surely the dashing Sir Gavin Galbraithe had spoken in much the same terms to Hester Rosewood on the night he had offered to deflower her on the billiard table. But no, it was as ridiculous to imagine Ben thumbing through a romance novel as it was to imagine Brigadier Lester-Smith or Mr. Gladstone Spike writing purple prose.

"Darling." I exercised a wife's prerogative to misunderstand her mate. "I have no ideas, enchanting or otherwise, for spiriting Miss Bunch's orphaned pooch into this house. From what I hear, he is a great lumbering animal who would eat the twins as soon as look at them. I am, when all is said and done, a mother first and—"

"And what?" Ben removed the coffee cups from my hands as if they were a major barrier to full communication. "What comes next after the house, the Library League, the Hearthside Guild, and all your other volunteer commitments?"

"A return to work as an interior designer." If I sounded defiant, it was because I was remembering how bitterly thwarted Hester Rosewood had felt when Sir Gavin had insisted she retire from her duties as governess to his spirited children, Avignon and Runnymede. "Ben, darling, it's not that I don't love being a homemaker. But you know how very much I want to establish a clientele and get back into the thick of window treatments and what's new in sofa tables."

"I do know." Ben's eyebrows drew together in a black bar over his nose, reminding me of the days when he used to get seriously cross with me. "If you remember, I was the one who suggested we engage an au pair to free you up for a major career move."

"Part-time," I assured him. "But at the moment even that is academic, considering neither of the au pairs we have yet interviewed was anywhere near up to snuff."

"Agreed," Ben said. "I could picture both those females hanging the twins out of an upstairs window by their heels if they didn't finish their morning porridge. But at least we have Mrs. Malloy two days a week."

"True. And if she hadn't agreed to come in this afternoon and watch the twins, I don't know what I would have done. But never mind." I smiled. "Mrs. M. will think of a way for me to show my appreciation."

"Meantime"—Ben stacked one cup and saucer on top of the other—"you're going to sit down and write her a thank-you note."

"I hadn't planned to." I stared at him in surprise. "Do you think I should?"

"It occurred to me, sweetheart, that you must have important matters claiming your attention, seeing I'm getting the distinct impression you aren't planning on coming up to bed for a while."

"Well"—I firmly dismissed the eerie verbal resemblance to Sir Gavin and took the coffee cups back from him—"I do have to rinse these out, and while I'm at the sink I might just as well wash my hair, and then I'll have to wait for it to dry."

"You don't have to hang it on the line, do you?" Ben's smile had an edge to it that could readily be explained by his being seriously fatigued. He worked long days at Abigail's, and I would have been a complete trollop to take him up on his generous hints that we re-consummate our marriage.

"The hair dryer gives me split ends," I told him gently.

"Completely unacceptable." With a quirk of his left eyebrow, he left me.

"Sleep tight," I called after him as he went out into the hall on his way up to bed.

I loved my kitchen at night. The Aga cooker was ensconced like a benevolent patriarch, basking in the friendly gleam of the copper bowls hanging from the iron rack and the smiling faces of the plates on the Welsh dresser. The rocking chair before the open hearth proffered a welcoming lap. The plants in the greenhouse window took on the mysterious appeal of a miniature jungle where Tobias could prowl as undisputed king. And I was queen of all this quiet. A quiet that was presently enhanced, not spoiled, by the kettle coming to a boil. No need for me to cup my hand over its whistling snout. On this, as on all other nights, it kept its voice down to a throaty purr.

While waiting for the tea to infuse in the pot, I crept upstairs, past my bedroom door, and along the gallery to the twins' room with its blue-and-yellow nursery-rhyme decorating scheme. Guided by the pale gleam from the man-in-the-moon night-light, I tiptoed from one junior bed to the other, smoothing Tam's tousled hair back from his brow, bending to press a whisper of a kiss on Abbey's chubby fist. Happiness flooded through me, a happiness tinged with sadness for Miss Bunch, whose real life would appear to have been lived at the library and whose death had brought no more than polite regret. Picking up Peter Rabbit and tucking him in beside Tam, I stood wondering what my darlings dreamed about, before retreating down to the kitchen.

Having poured my cup of tea, I opened the pantry, gathered up the tin of digestive biscuits, and returned to the drawing room. For a person who had been a fat child and a less-than-skinny adult, nothing could have been more deliciously sinful than a period of uninterrupted intimacy with a food that was neither green nor lean. It wasn't that Ben watched what I ate, or sized me up before and after I sat down to a meal. Guilt was the bogeyman who stood behind me at the table, wincing each time I reached for a second helping of shepherd's pie or reminding me that eating dessert is no longer deemed politically correct. But in the still of the night the bogeyman retreated into the shadows. Then I could forget that there are people in this world (such as my unrepentantly gorgeous cousin Vanessa) who can eat a baker's dozen of doughnuts in one scoff and still span their waist with two fingers.

Lolling back on the sofa, with a clutch of digestives in one hand and my cup of tea comfortingly alongside, I relished the moment of unutterable peace before picking up my library book and reentering the world of Hester Rosewood, spirited governess and determined virgin.

Shame on me! I have to confess that virginity was never something I had prized unduly, considering everyone gets to be one at least for a while. It was always something I'd hoped I would outgrow, along with my childhood tendency to bronchitis. But the time had come when I'd begun to feel I was saddled with the condition for life, unless I overcame my terror of horses, took up riding, and was lucky enough to fall off the saddle. By the time Ben appeared on the scene, in my late twenties, I was convinced I was walking around with the scarlet letter V on my forehead for all the world to see.

Opening *Her Master's Voice* at the page I had left off reading, my life, my world, fell away as I entered the world of Hester Rosewood. I walked with her at dead of night towards the churchyard, and when we passed through the lichgate, we merged so that I became Hester of the eighteen-inch waist and deceptively demure bosom. It was my heart that pounded with mounting fear that Sir Gavin would follow the lantern's wavering gleam and demand my immediate return to Darkmoor House. It was my soul that cried out for him in the silence that told me he would not come, because his invalid wife would be staging one of her deliriums.

> *Somewhere within the branches of one of the looming elms an owl hooted, a sound both forlorn and predatory. Was I a fool to flee the man I worshipped with every fibre of my being? Could I bear to return to Cousin Bertha's dreary house, knowing my pulse would never again quicken at the sound of my beloved's footsteps on the stairs?*

Out in the hall the grandfather clock doled out twelve somber strokes. My hall, my clock. And the telephone that now rang once . . . twice . . . had to be my telephone because such intrusions did not exist in the world of Hester Rosewood. Whoever could be ringing up at this hour? Closing my book with a disgruntled sigh, I climbed off the sofa, took a sip of tea, now as cold as the graveyard, and braced myself for Ben's voice calling over the banister that my cousin Freddy was on the line and eager to give me a harrowing account of his camping holiday with Jonas. Freddy, being a confirmed night-owl, never worries about disrupting other people's sleep. There was not the least reason for me to panic that Jonas had broken his leg climbing into his sleeping bag, or had been attacked by a swarm of killer bees released into the woods by a mad scientist. Without resorting to running—never one of my favourite indoor sports—I crossed to the door, only to be met with deathly silence. No heavy thump, indicating that Ben had passed out cold on hearing ominous news, whatever its specifics. No urgent voice demanding I get upstairs on the double. Whether the caller had dialed a wrong number or was one of Ben's employees at Abigail's requesting instructions on how to reprogram the dishwasher, there was no reason for me to turn off the drawing room light and abandon Hester Rosewood to the gloom of the graveyard.

Ben probably hadn't noticed that I wasn't in bed yet. If I knew him, he had rolled over in a tangle of sheets, fumbled sleepily for the phone, mumbled some sort of semi-coherent response into the receiver, and, immediately after hanging up, burrowed back into sleep. For me to go up now and risk jolting him awake just wouldn't be fair. Far better to finish up the last of the digestive biscuits, while seeing poor Hester safely out of the churchyard. Things were looking dark indeed for her when I reopened the book.

> *"You shiver, my dear Miss Rosewood."* He reached out a hand to peel open the button at my throat. *"Let me warm you with my caress. Your skin has the soft glow of moonlight and your breath is as sweetly intoxicating as the night air."* A muscle tensed in Sir Gavin's jaw as he surveyed me from his great height with dark and slumberous eyes. His voice grew dangerously deep when he said: *"Did you think I would let you go, my dear delight?"* His eyes never leaving my face, he removed his clothing a slow button at a time, to reveal a body so magnificent in the glory of its manhood that I had to bite down on my lip in order to hold back a scream of ecstasy that verged on reverence.
>
> *"Please desist, sir."* I stepped back from his embrace and strove valiantly to remember I was a bishop's niece. *"I want to look at you, to revel in your broad chest, to glory in your firm flanks, rippling muscles, and splendid calves. Let me feast my eyes on the vigorous thrust of your man . . . ly jaw."*

Somewhere on the outskirts of my mind a bell was pealing with an urgency that brought me off the sofa with sufficient speed that I dropped my book smack down on the floor. Still in the throes of Sir Gavin's embrace, I was convinced for a horrific ten seconds that his invalid wife was pulling on the bell rope in a frenzy of jealousy that bade ill for virginal Hester Rosewood's continued employment at Darkmoor House.

Who could be ringing the doorbell at one-thirty in the morning?

If I'd been thinking straight, I would have armed myself with the poker before going out into the hall, or have waited for Ben to come stumbling bleary-eyed down the stairs. As it was, I exercised merely enough sense to feel uneasy as I approached the front door. My hair had come straggling out of its French twist, and my face was flushed from the exertion of turning the pages.

"Who's there?"

"Let me in!" Fists pounded on the door. The voice was hysterical.

"I'm afraid I did not catch your name." In the act of reaching to draw back the bolt, my hand froze. Whoever it was could be a full-fledged maniac in the manner of Sir Gavin's wife. Or at the very least, an Avon lady grimly bent on making her daily quota of lipstick sales.

"God in heaven!" A scream ricocheted through the door, already bulging from the force of increased pounding. "Another moment and it will be too late! I will be torn to shreds by the beast with the head of a grizzly bear!"

"Hold on!" It wasn't the midnight visitor's sobbing pronouncement that the creature had devoured one of her legs and was proceeding to polish off her real leather handbag that persuaded me to open up. What did the trick was the unmistakable sound of a deep-throated growl, followed by an evil belch.

My fumbling hands fought with the bolt. A woman hurtled into the hall, almost knocking me out in the process and rocking the twin suits of armour back against the staircase.

"Quick! Quick! Do not let him in!" The woman crouched down on the flagstone floor and swiftly made the sign of the cross. Her hand trembled so badly, it missed her forehead by a mile. Too late! As I debated whether to climb over her or dodge sideways in order to slam the door shut, a form—blacker than the angel of death—glided into the hall, leapt up the staircase, then doubled back to sit still and silent as the grave a few inches from my feet.

"It's a dog!" I informed the stranger who had slithered up against the door and bumped it shut with her rump, effectively closing us in with our four-legged adversary. "Not an especially handsome dog; although"—I took one look at the animal's fiery orbs and made haste to add—"handsome is as handsome does."

As if in appreciation of this verbal bouquet, the animal promptly lay down, nose on his enormous paws, and began to pant in a way that stretched his mouth into a smile wide enough to swallow a dinner plate.

"He comes after me, from behind a tombstone in the churchyard." The woman had mustered the physical and emotional wherewithal to rise to her knees and again make the sign of the cross, in patent hope of banishing the huge canine back from whence he came. "And when I scream and start to run, he chases me all the way down the road to this house. One minute he nips at my heels, the next time he makes the circles around me like I am a sheep he has to round up into the pen. That was not nice of him." Her accent was not from these parts.

A foreigner? Perhaps from some village in Transylvania where phantom dogs routinely set upon unwary travellers? My mind raced from this possibility to the realization that the poor woman might have come to serious grief. In her panic she could have blundered off the road and over the cliff, which in places sheered down to where the sea came slathering up over the rocks. Thank God she had made it safely to our gates and had reached the house before expiring of terror.

"He is the devil in dog's fur." The woman resisted my attempt to raise her to an upright position.

"We mustn't jump to conclusions." I went to stand over the dog, who cocked a hopeful ear and looked at me with the eyes of one ready and eager to be redeemed from a life of frightening helpless females out of their wits. I'm not a doggy person, mainly because Tobias Cat wouldn't have approved, but I've never been unduly nervous around dogs. "Look, he's wearing a collar with a tag. Hold tight a minute." I smiled reassuringly over my shoulder before bending down to lift the brass disk away from the furry throat and read the inscription.

"My goodness!" I exclaimed.

"His name is Lucifer?" The woman pressed a hand to her mouth.

"No, Heathcliff!" I said. "Which means . . ."

"What?" she demanded fearfully.

"That he belongs, or, I should say, *belonged* to our local librarian. Poor Miss Bunch died of a rare virus that shuts down the heart. Sometimes the victim suffers flu-like symptoms, but just as often there are no warning signs. It was a shock, particularly, I am sure, for Heathcliff here." I went on softly, very much aware that the dog had lowered his head onto his paws and was uttering a series of infinitely sad woofs like a dirge. "Miss Bunch was buried today in St. Anselm's churchyard, and this sad little orphan must have escaped from the people who were temporarily housing him and followed his mistress to her final resting place."

"Her ghost! I saw it, walking on feet that do not touch the ground, between the tombstones. A woman—dressed in black from the head to the feet. She wears a veil that flutters like a big cobweb in the wind. And she twists her bony hands and she talks to herself." My female visitor was pallid with terror.

"A tall, thin woman with stooped shoulders?" I asked.

"This is so."

"That wasn't Miss Bunch. She was only of medium height and quite stout. I think you must have seen Ione Tunbridge, one of our local characters. She's close to eighty now and has haunted, in a manner of speaking, St. Anselm's since the day her bridegroom failed to turn up at the church for the wedding ceremony." While speaking, I began to wonder if I had somehow become trapped within the pages of *Her Master's Voice* as a punishment for scoffing so many digestive biscuits. Was I doomed to wander from one melodrama to another throughout eternity?

"Miss Tunbridge hasn't left her house in daylight in nearly sixty years," I bumbled on, "but every so often she is spotted, between dusk and daylight, wandering around the churchyard. These days St. Anselm's is locked at night, so she can no longer get inside to kneel before the altar . . . waiting for the sound of her bridegroom's footsteps hastening down the nave to explain what had caused him to be more than half a century late showing up with the ring."

"Men! They are a bad kettle of apples." The woman was finally getting to her feet and I was relieved to see the physical damage done to her by Heathcliff was not as bad as she had made out when pounding her fists through my front door. Her handbag appeared to be intact apart from the broken strap, and she wasn't minus either of her legs.

The dog did rise up on his haunches when she stood, but there was nothing bristling about his posture. Instead, he extended a conciliatory paw while assuming an expression of tongue-lolling meekness worthy of a much-misunderstood canine, one fully prepared to let bygones be bygones.

"I behave like a chicken with three heads, Frau Haskell," said the woman. "It is a miracle I do not wake up your husband and set your entire household on its ear hole."

"You were in fear of your life," I assured her. Until that moment I had seen her in bits and blobs—a face blurred by terror, a pair of hands warding off the inevitability of annihilation. Now that the hall had changed back from one of the chillier chambers of Darkmoor House to its old friendly self, I was rather surprised by what I saw. Here was a plumpish woman who appeared to be approaching sixty, whose salt-and-pepper hair was braided into shoulder-length plaits, tied at the ends with ribboned bows as big as poppies. She wore a Swiss miss costume complete with dirndl and embroidered apron, white stockings, and buckled shoes. Hoping she hadn't noticed my rude stare, I added hastily, "You have the advantage of me. You know my name, while I . . . ?"

"Me?" Our midnight intruder gripped her handbag with both hands and her knees gave way so that she appeared to wobble a curtsy. "I am Gerta, your new au pair girl."

Chapter

3

"I refuse to have that creature in this house!"

My husband leapt out of bed before I had added the finishing touches to my explanation of the situation. Ben is rarely at his best at two in the morning, but even so there was no need for him to pace up and down in front of the bedroom fireplace, his eyes blazing, his black hair tousled from repeatedly raking his fingers through it. Any minute now he would be demanding to know who was the master of Merlin's Court! Meanwhile the pheasants on the wallpaper were all aflutter.

"Darling, you're being unreasonable!" I trotted around him as he circled the hearth rug. "We agreed . . ."

"We did indeed!" Ben stopped dead in his tracks. In turning to face me, he almost tripped over his pajama legs, which were a couple of inches taller than he and which, having perversely refused to shrink in the wash, needed hemming. Yanking on the cord, he tied it into a ferocious knot. "I told you, Ellie, in no uncertain terms this evening that I am not prepared to provide a home for Miss Bunch's orphan dog!"

I sat down on the bed with a bump and pressed a hand to my throbbing head. "He's the sweetest little pup in the world, although timid to a fault! But I thought we were talking about Gerta!"

"And she's not the German shepherd?"

"No! She's the au pair!" There was no point, I decided, in further complicating matters by explaining that Heathcliff had made no bones about his lack of pedigree. "You really are the limit, Ben. Have you paid any attention to what I've been saying for the last five minutes?"

"To every word, give or take a few, of the woman's heartrending story." Striding over to the window, Ben pulled the wine velvet curtains more tightly closed, either to relieve his feelings or to prevent the moon getting up to any peeping Tom tricks. "The woman came to this country from Switzerland some ten years ago, in the company of her husband. The two of them owned and operated a café in Putney, one of those places specializing in mango-flavoured cappuccino and hand-churned yogurt. Two days ago the husband announced he had fallen for the sloe-eyed harpy who runs the used-clothing shop down the street—"

"The harpy," I reminded him sternly, "is a six-foot ex-rugger player by the name of Robert Meyers and, as Gerta tearily explained it, she never stood a chance when Robert offered to arm-wrestle her for the man in their lives. The result was the poor woman found herself out in the street with nothing to show for her married life but the clothes on her back—which happened to be her alpine work uniform—and a packet of mocha deluxe coffee beans to go. Not a pretty story."

"Love can be a cutthroat business." Ben pried himself away from the mantelpiece and came to sit beside me on the bed. "It was fortunate Gerta had enough loose change in her purse to ring up her friend Jill, who, in addition to taking her in for the night, mentioned that her former flatmate, one Ellie Haskell, was looking for an au pair." Cupping my face in his hands, he pressed a kiss against my lips, which were by now pretty much numb with exhaustion, and murmured, "Do I get top marks for paying attention?"

"Yes, dear; but I'm not handing out any prizes tonight." Flopping back against the pillows, I did wonder if I might be leading my husband on by permitting him a glimpse of leg as he rolled me, like an unwieldy strudel, under the bedclothes. Even so, I'm ashamed to say it was the possibility of eating lots of hand-thrown apple strudel in the days ahead that quickened my pulses as Ben climbed in beside me and switched off the table lamp.

Turning on my side and repositioning Ben's hand around my waist, I thought about Jill, who in addition to being my ex-flatmate was also Cousin Freddy's girlfriend when they remembered to get in touch with each other. It was typical of her to extend a helping hand to Gerta. It was also typical that Jill had waited until midnight to telephone and inform us she was sending along an au pair who desperately needed the job, was of sound moral character, and could yodel like a dream. Jill's was the phone call that had sounded while I was in the throes of Sir Gavin's expert seduction.

I swallowed a yawn. If Gerta had shown any signs of being a homicidal maniac, Jill—who not only refuses to smash bugs but endeavours to find good homes for them— would not have landed us with the woman. Naturally, it would be wise to check out the references Gerta had provided. But I was optimistic that she would prove to be a treasure. She had been determinedly cheerful when Heathcliff trailed after us up the stairs, appeared delighted with her room, was eager to take a look at the twins, but understanding when I suggested we defer the introductions till the morning. Having lent her one of my nighties and a dressing gown, I had bidden her good night without wondering once if I should lock her door from the outside.

Our doggy visitor, however, was another matter. After feeding him two bowls of cat food under the watchful eye of Tobias Cat, who had scaled the Welsh dresser in the kitchen and was threatening a nervous breakdown, I had let Heathcliff out into the garden and, shortly thereafter, shut him away in the cupboard under the stairs. So far we had heard no howls of protest or sounds of his body slamming against the door with the reckless disregard for property typical of a policeman on a drug bust.

"That dog's being awfully quiet." Ben shifted up onto his elbow to lean over me just as I was sinking into soft clouds of sleep.

"I'm sure Miss Bunch had him well trained," I murmured while stuffing my head under the pillow.

"Well, don't go getting any ideas of using your feminine charms to get me to change my mind about keeping the hound." My husband lay back down and wrapped an arm and a leg around me. "It's true that I am at times unable to resist the soft touch of your hands upon my quivering manhood but . . ."

There it came again, the suspicion that he had been secretly leafing through my stash of romantic fiction. But that was ridiculous. Ben's idea of a real page-turner was a cookery book featuring an unexpurgated account of how to debone a chicken with one hand.

"Darling," I mumbled from under the pillow. "We both need to get some sleep."

"You're right," agreed my spouse, taking back his arm and his leg, "what else do we go to bed for?"

"Pleasant dreams!" Finally coming up for air, I settled myself for four or, optimistically, five hours of shut-eye. It was my understanding that people require less sleep as they grow older, and with another birthday looming up in a couple of days I could doubtless get away with burning the candle at both ends. Even so, I wouldn't be worth much in the morning if I didn't nod off soon. Within minutes Ben's rhythmic breathing told he had drifted into slumber, but there went my mind—chasing its own tale in the dark.

I went from thinking about Miss Bunch cooped up in her coffin with little or no elbow room, to wondering if Bunty Wiseman would ever get back with her ex-husband. Was Brigadier Lester-Smith a bachelor by choice or had he suffered a disappointment in love? And then there were those other members of the Library League—Sir Robert Pomeroy and Mrs. Dovedale, both of whom were recently widowed. Once or twice at our meetings I had wondered whether there was anything significant in the way their eyes would meet during the reading of the minutes. As for crotchety Mr. Poucher, it was hard to imagine any woman raking her fingernails down his back and begging him to walk out on his mother. Other than myself, the only married member of the league was Sylvia Babcock, who a fortnight previously had tied the knot with our milkman. That prophetess of doom—otherwise known as my faithful daily—Mrs. Malloy had declared the Babcock union would never last. For one thing Mr. B. was a passionate lover—of dogs, that is. And Sylvia, a nervy type, had stipulated that there would be no four-legged creatures bringing germs into her tidy home.

I must have fallen asleep without realizing how I got there, because suddenly I was in a chaise and four, being swept away into the night by a cloaked driver.

"Karisma!" The cry came from deep within my soul.

"I thought I was Sir Gavin." His laughter was at once sardonic and deeply sensual.

"Sometimes you are," I whispered. "You appear on the pages of romance novels in many guises, but it is always you I see—your face, the incomparable cheekbones, the dizzying depths of your eyes, the heroic nose, and that perfect mouth, so exquisitely tender even at its most predatory! I could rhapsodize all night about your tawny hair that I yearn to unleash in all its voluminous splendour, your magnificent body unequaled since the Greek gods ceased parading around in little more than their laurel wreaths. . . ."

I reached out my hands to him and found myself alone in a whirling blackness, the only one to hear the demonic chortling that I knew emanated from the ghost of Hector Rigglesworth. He who had put the coffin lid on Miss Bunch's career was there on the outskirts of my dream. And he had brought with him the hound of hell, a beast who, with fangs bared, leapt through the window of the phantom carriage to knock the breath out of my body.

"My God!" Ben bolted up in bed, fumbled for the bedside lamp, and, in the blaze of light that flooded the room, sat blinking down at the two-ton bear rug that had spread itself over me from toes to chin. "You told me you had shut that damn dog in the cupboard under the stairs." My husband's accusing finger vibrated between me and Heathcliff.

"I forgot we were dealing with an escape artist." I struggled to sit up and got half my face licked off in the process. "He wouldn't be here if Miss Bunch's neighbours, who took him in originally, had been able to prevent his making a bolt for it."

"Lucky them!" Ben yanked at the bedspread, which gave a mighty rip under the weight of the unbudgeable Heathcliff. "Why don't you open the window, Ellie, and pretend to look the other way while he makes a leap for freedom? If it will help, I'll knot the sheets into a rope and attach it to the ledge; or you might point out to him that there is a perfectly good drainpipe he could shin down."

Far from taking offence at these remarks, Heathcliff smiled broadly, in appreciation of what he clearly took for a jest. Unreeling his bottomless tongue, he slopped a series of licks on Ben's clenched hand.

"Look how he's taken to you!" My benign response to the intruder was due to an overwhelming relief that he was real, not some figment of my dream. Perhaps in future I would have to give up my late-night reading if, like cheese, it provoked a tendency to nightmares. But for now I must focus on getting massive Heathcliff off the bed before the springs flattened out and Ben threatened him with vivisection.

"I don't care what you do with the beast, Ellie, so long as he isn't here when I get home from work."

"Yes, dear!" In endeavouring to drag the dog off the bed, first by the collar, then by the ears, I sent my husband slithering onto the floor in a cacophony of curses that would have been the death of his Roman Catholic mother.

"If he eats one of the children, I will be extremely upset." So saying, Ben struggled to his feet and took out his annoyance on the poor alarm clock, which was only doing what it was supposed to do in giving a raucous buzz to inform us that it was now six A.M. precisely. Sucking on the fist he had used to pound on the button, the man who hated anything on four legs stomped off to the bathroom.

I looked unhappily down at Heathcliff. The dog had seen fit to climb off the bed and attack the cord of my dressing gown while I attempted to slip into the garment that had seen better days. "I'm sorry, but you will have to go!"

My heart ached. But duty to my husband and children was brought home when, with you-know-who trailing behind me, I descended into the hall to find the vacuum cleaner had been dragged out from the cupboard under the stairs. The hapless victim (showing signs of having put up the fight of its life) lay sprawled on its back, for all the world like a victim of Jack the Ripper, a gaping hole in its cloth stomach and its dusty innards scattered across the flagstones. And if that weren't bad enough, a chair had been knocked sideways and one of its legs chewed off to the knee. The vase that once stood on the trestle table was now a handful of mosaic shards which Heathcliff side-stepped without an embarrassed glance as he followed me on lighthearted paws into the kitchen.

Luckily he had failed to open this door. And I will say he acceded with good grace to my frowning enjoinder that he endeavour not to destroy anything else in the next five minutes. Stretching out in front of the fireplace, he assumed the prayerful pose of a Buddhist monk. But I kept a watchful eye on him as I filled the kettle and set it on the Aga. It soon hissed to the boil in perfect imitation of Tobias, who, still perched atop the Welsh dresser, fixed the invader with a laser stare aimed to annihilate. I had just heated the teapot and set out cups and saucers, when a knock sounded at the garden door.

Ever eager to be of service, Heathcliff took a ten-foot leap, got the handle between his jaws, and would have yanked the door off its hinges if it had not at that moment opened inward, effectively knocking him back on his haunches.

"Morning, Mrs. Haskell."

"Why, good morning, Mr. Babcock!" I stood clutching the teapot, quite taken aback—not by the milkman's informality in walking into the kitchen, he quite often behaved in this chummy way—but because I had believed him to be still on his honeymoon with Sylvia from the Library League.

"Six pints same as usual?" Mr. Babcock was a big, beefy man with a stomach that would have done a pregnant woman proud. He went jangling past me with his hand crate and deposited the bottles on the kitchen table. "Got yourself a new dog, I see." He looked down at Heathcliff with an admiring eye that did not dim when the cur gave a lunge, accompanied by a leonine growl, and began tearing at his shoelaces. "He's a caution, all right! What do you call him?"

"Ivan the Terrible."

"That's a bit of a mouthful, isn't it?" Whether Mr. Babcock was speaking to me or the dog, who was now chewing on his trouser legs, was unclear, but I quickly explained that the sad little orphan had belonged to Miss

Bunch, who had christened him Heathcliff, and that he wouldn't be with us long.

"Are you saying the poor lad'll try and do away with himself?" Mr. Babcock made a gallant attempt to bend down and pat the bereaved, but was prohibited by the rolls of fat holding up his trousers.

"What I meant to say"—I got busy pouring Mr. Babcock a cup of tea and trying to remember if he took four or five spoonfuls of sugar—"is that it is impossible for us to keep Heathcliff. He would be forever bowling Abbey and Tam over and otherwise upsetting the applecart. But let's talk about you, Mr. Babcock. I was expecting to have to make do with your temporary replacement for another few days. Aren't you still on your honeymoon?"

"You could say I am, officially speaking." The milkman accepted the cup and saucer I handed him and stood fiddling with the spoon. "But as they say, a bloke can take only so much of a good thing. So this morning I tells the new missus that I'm off for a breather—of fresh air."

"Yes," I said, "well, do sit down, Mr. Babcock, and enjoy your tea, if you can spare the time."

"Don't mind if I do, thanks very much." He settled himself on a chair at the kitchen table and held up his cup in salute. "Bottoms up, Mrs. Haskell . . . as the actress said to the bishop!"

Accepting this little joke from where it came—a man still officially on honeymoon—I was about to ask if Mr. B. would like a digestive biscuit, when I remembered I had left the nearly depleted tin in the drawing room the previous night. If I knew Heathcliff, he had polished off every last remaining crumb. Watching Mr. Babcock take a deep swallow of tea, I was horrified to see his lips constrict in a paroxysm of pain.

"Too much sugar?"

"It's not that . . ." He drew in a sharp breath that made his pale eyes bulge.

"Then it's Heathcliff!" Already I was picturing the court case wherein his lordship the judge listened unmoved to my panicked attempts to explain that I was not responsible for the foibles of the canine in question and sentenced me to a lifetime behind bars. "Has he helped himself to a bite out of your leg, Mr. Babcock?"

"No, it's naught to do with this little fellow." The milkman attempted a smile that turned into a grimace. "It's just that I get these pains in my chest sometimes. Nothing but a bit of indigestion that goes as quick as it comes. A spoonful of bicarbonate mixed in with half a cup of milk always fixes me up a treat."

"Are you sure you haven't been overdoing things, Mr. Babcock?" I immediately realized the impertinence of posing such a question to a brand-new bridegroom.

"It's more likely I haven't been getting enough exercise," he informed me valiantly.

"Oh, dear!" I buried my face over my teacup.

"Ever since my old dog, Rex—a real corker Rex was—died on me last spring, I haven't been getting out for walks like I once did, and that's a fact, true as I'm sitting here, Mrs. Haskell."

"What a shame."

"And I'm the sort that's not myself without a dog at my heels."

"Really?" I was glad to see that Mr. Babcock appeared to have recovered from his little bout, but uncertain how to respond to the hopeful look he was now bestowing on our Hound of the Chittervilles.

"As I understand it, Mrs. Haskell, you're on the lookout for a permanent home for Cliffy here."

"I'd certainly hate to think of him panhandling on the street," I agreed warily. "But I can't foist him on you, Mr. Babcock. For one thing, he's a walking demolition squad, and secondly, in talking to Sylvia at the library, I got the distinct impression she doesn't like dogs."

"Don't you believe it." The milkman poured some of his tea into the saucer and held it out to the animal with a besotted smile. "Women talk that kind of rubbish, but I've never known one that wasn't a softie for a hard-luck story. Believe you me, the missus will be dotty about this young man here five minutes after I walk him in the door."

Remembering his new bride, I had my doubts. "You're not afraid Sylvia will order you both out of the house and be on the phone to a locksmith before you can start apologizing?" This scenario appeared tame to me as I watched Heathcliff crunch down on the porcelain saucer.

"Don't you worry, Mrs. Haskell!"

Easy for Mr. Babcock to say! I couldn't help but worry about my next meeting with Sylvia. She was the sort who burst into tears if a fly buzzed in her vicinity, who was forever poking at her hair to make sure that every pin curl stayed in place. But on the other hand, it would be marvelous to greet Ben with the news that Heathcliff was already on his way to a new home.

"Are you sure, Mr. Babcock, you're doing the right thing?" Even as I spoke I was rummaging around in one of the drawers for a piece of cord to tie around the dog's thick leather collar.

"We've got some good years ahead of us, him and me." Draining his cup, Mr. Babcock took the makeshift lead from my hands and tied a solid knot before picking up the milk crate with his free hand and heading with his new soulmate for the garden door. "I feel like a bit of a grave robber, I do. But I hope that librarian woman, if she's looking down from above, knows this little lad will be well looked after."

"You're a life-saver, Mr. Babcock," I gushed heartily.

Thus I stood waving as man and dog set off across the courtyard. Just before climbing into the milk van, Heathcliff looked back at me, cocked his head as if to say "So long, chum" (or was that *chump?*), bared his teeth in a smile and . . . that was that. Closing the door, I collected the dustpan and broom and had just finished sweeping up the broken vase in the hall and setting the chair back on its remaining three legs, when Gerta came downstairs with the twins tugging on her alpine skirts.

"Good morning to you, Frau Haskell." With the sunlight bursting in through the windows to gild the hair plaited around her head, our new au pair looked like a conventional nanny. I guessed her age to be between fifty and sixty, with a strawberries-and-cream complexion that any young girl might have envied. "You see, I meet the little lambkins?"

"Why we got a new mummy?" Tam came trotting across the flagstones to grasp me around the knees and peer up at me with a face that was growing uncannily like his father's. The same blue-green eyes, the same silky thick lashes and tumbled dark hair.

"She's not your new mummy, darling!" I scooped my

son up into my arms and pressed my face against his peachy-soft cheek. "Her name is Gerta and she's going to help me look after you."

"We like him. Don't us, Tam?" Abbey's curls shone like sunbeams as she took hold of the other woman's hand and jigged up and down.

"Her, darling," I said. "Gerta is a 'her,' and I'm so glad you're pleased she's come to stay with us for a while."

"This morning, Frau Haskell, I give you names and addresses of the references you contact, does that satisfy!"

"There's no rush," I said, "seeing that our mutual friend Jill recommended you so highly."

"You must check me up!" Gerta shook her head with enough vehemence to knock one of her plaits down and set it swinging like a bell rope. "These days it does not do to be too trusting. For all you know, I could be a bad can of worms."

"I doubt that." Ben's voice broke in upon us as he came down the stairs. He looked like a study in black and white in his dark suit and crisply starched shirt.

"You are one of the few kind men in this world, Herr Haskell!" Gerta's gratitude showed in her glowing eyes as she pinned up the errant plait. I was immediately flooded with a profound satisfaction. Two lives salvaged as the result of the Haskells' intervention. Ben and I were undoubtedly quite a team.

And moments later I was assured of our domestic bliss when he bent to kiss my lips as I finished telling him how Heathcliff had landed on all four paws in finding a new home. "You're a miracle worker, Ellie. Why don't you walk out with me to the car and we'll talk about how you would like to celebrate your birthday tomorrow?"

"Darling, I would love to"—I handed Tam into his arms—"but I think I just heard Mrs. Malloy coming in the back way. Gerta will go with you so the twins can say bye-bye to Daddy. See you tonight, Ben."

Typical husband! He stood rooted to the spot in mute reproach as I whisked around and headed down the hall. Even as I entered the kitchen, I knew he still hadn't moved and that Abbey, sensing the moment was less than idyllic, had stopped jigging up and down. What Ben didn't understand was that I had to explain Gerta to Mrs. Malloy. My faithful daily was liable to get her powdered nose out of joint upon learning I would now have less need to impose on her good offices.

"Morning, Mrs. H!" The words were dourly spoken and I immediately jumped to the conclusion that I had been found out already.

"It is a nice day." I resisted the cowardly impulse to babble on about the lovely month of May. Mrs. Malloy is famed among her colleagues and clientele as a woman who takes no back chat from anyone. So far I had not entirely mastered the knack of holding my own with her. Part of her mystique was linked to the fact that she invariably turned up for work in a fur coat and sequinned toque, with her feet squeezed into impossibly tiny shoes with rhinestone clips and four-inch heels. "Nobody talks down to me when I'm on me stilts," Mrs. M. had informed me balefully on the morning she conducted the interview set up by her to determine whether I met her standards of employment. And it was weeks into our "trial marriage" before I saw a friendly gleam flicker in her neon-lidded, heavily mascaraed eyes, let alone a smile make a crack in the rouge she laid on with a trowel.

She certainly was not smiling now as she removed her chapeau to reveal the full glory of her jet-black hair with its trademark two inches of white roots. "This is the life, Mrs. H." She tossed the hat on the kitchen table, along with her supply bag, in which she kept a bottle of gin for emergencies, such as buffing up a piece of badly tarnished silver. "One bloody upset after another."

Common sense should have told me she couldn't have got wind of Gerta's arrival on the scene, but while scurrying over to check whether the tea was still warm in the pot so that I might ply her with a cup, I began apologizing for having had the temerity to hire an au pair without first consulting her.

"A what do you call her?" Mrs. Malloy started to raise a painted eyebrow, wearily gave up the attempt, and sank onto the rocking chair in front of the hearth.

"It's a fancy name for a nanny." I narrowly missed tripping over her black fishnet legs in my haste to place the teacup in her hands.

"What? One of those foreign ones?" She said the "F"

word with obvious distaste. "Some young girl who can't get out two words of English without *parlez-vous*ing, who's got bright-yellow hair down to her backside and has to be shown how to turn on the kitchen tap?"

"This one is *very* nice!" Glancing up at Tobias, who had still not forgiven Gerta for bringing a dog into the house, I dared him to meow a contradiction. "She's a little older than the usual au pair."

"That won't stop her!" Mrs. Malloy smacked her glossy butterfly lips in grim satisfaction.

"Stop her from what?" I attempted a laugh. "Making off with the children?"

"Making eyes at your husband is more like." She set the cup down in the saucer with a rattle that I could see was due to the fact that her hands were shaking. "But I'm not here to judge you, Mrs. H., we've all sinned. And I've never been one to throw stones . . . even before I found out . . ."

"Whatever is the matter?" I grabbed the cup away from her before she could drop it and watched in distress as she dabbed at her eyes with the cuff of her black taffeta sleeve.

"Now, don't you go getting worked up, Mrs. H., I'm the one what has to live with the shame. I'm the one who will be pointed at in the street when word gets out."

"Word about what?" I was bewildered.

"That I'm . . ." A sob went down the wrong way.

"Yes?" I prodded when she started breathing again.

"That I'm expecting."

"Expecting what?" My mind gyrated wildly between the possibility of a visitor from Mars, to a summons to meet the Queen.

"The same thing any woman means when she says she's expecting." Mrs. Malloy reared up her black-and-white head and fixed her raccoon eyes on my face. "A kid on the way, that's what I'm talking about! The flesh of me loins, the fruit of my lapse from grace in the back seat of a Rover."

"Isn't it possible you're mistaken?" Dragging a chair away from the kitchen table, I dropped down on it with a wallop that reverberated right through my skull. Mrs. Malloy was in her early sixties.

"Mistaken?" She looked at me as if I had lost my mind. "How can I be bloody well mistaken, when the lad's coming up for forty? Sometimes I worry about you, Mrs. H., you're off in cloud cuckoo land half the time. What I've been trying to tell you is that I'm expecting a visit from George—the son nobody here knows about, because he was grown and gone when I moved to Chitterton Fells and I never thought to mention him. An unnatural mother, that's what the muckrakers will call me."

"Surely not."

Mrs. Malloy ignored my attempt to soothe. "Haven't heard a dicky bird from George in years. Then last night I get a phone call from him. Seems he's getting married to a very posh young lady and the two of them want to come down here for a kiss and cuddle from the old mum."

"Well, I think that's lovely."

"You won't be singing that tune much longer," Mrs. Malloy said icily, "not when I tell you the name of George's fiancée."

"What difference can it make to me who she is?" I began bustling about, laying the Beatrix Potter china for the twins' breakfast. "Buck up, Mrs. Malloy. You're getting yourself upset over what should be a happy event. You're not losing a son, you're gaining a daughter."

"It's *you* what's going to be upset, Mrs. H.!" She tottered onto her high-heeled feet, squared her padded shoulders, and looked me straight in the eye. "I've been trying to break it to you gently; but I suppose it's best to say it straight out and watch you fall apart. My son George has got himself engaged to your cousin Vanessa."

Chapter

4

Mrs. Malloy must surely have had a few nips of gin before coming to Merlin's Court. Her son George could not possibly be betrothed to my nemesis! To my indecently gorgeous cousin! She who had been a thorn in my flesh since we first met at the age of six and she asked me whether I was a boy or a girl.

Vanessa, the successful fashion model and quintessential femme fatale, had only once in her life looked at me with a flicker of envy in her luminous, sherry-coloured eyes. That was on the glorious occasion when I announced my engagement to Ben. But she had very quickly weaseled around that weakness by informing me that a man of Ben's looks and charm could be marrying me only for my money.

It was hard for me not to blame Mrs. Malloy for the hideous turn of events that would land Vanessa on my doorstep after a halcyon period of absence.

"According to George," his aggrieved parent said as she plunked the kettle down on the cooker, emptying half its contents in a shower that watered the plants in the greenhouse window, "they met at some party or other in London. It was love at first sight."

"Your son must be a real catch." I stared morosely out into the garden, where Gerta was playing chasing games with Abbey and Tam, the object of which appeared to be who could fall over fastest. It should have been a day-brightener, given my now-jaundiced view of life, that she hadn't absconded with my children to parts unknown for the fell purpose of holding them captive until they learned how to yodel. But I had trouble working my face up into a smile. At the back of my mind was the conviction that if Mrs. Malloy had kept a closer eye on her offspring, Vanessa could never have got her claws into him.

"George isn't what you'd call handsome." Mrs. M. unearthed a bottle of gin from the supply bag and poured a slug into her tea. "When he was a few months old I took him to a plastic surgeon, but there wasn't nothing as could be done short of turning his face inside out. The poor little bugger took after his father, who if I remember rightly was my second . . . or it could have been my third . . . husband." On this mournful pronouncement, Mrs. Malloy came over to the table with the teacups and flopped onto a chair. "I changed George's surname to coincide with mine when I got married for the last time, and this is the thanks I get for doing right by the lad. He gets himself engaged to a woman who's bound to look down her snooty nose at me."

Here was an interesting thought. Why would Vanessa, the ultimate snob, have stooped to such a misalliance? Her mother, my aunt Astrid—of the gold pince-nez and the pedigree of a prize Pekingese—would hardly be falling over herself to place the announcement in *The Times*.

"If Vanessa isn't marrying George for his looks"—I picked up a teacup and stood tinkering with the spoon—"he must have sex appeal to spare."

"Not so as I ever noticed." Mrs. Malloy pursed her butterfly lips, the better to blow on her tea. "What he does have is cash. Pots of it!"

"Really?" The unpleasant image presented itself of Vanessa appearing on the doorstep of Merlin's Court with an engagement ring the size of the Rock of Gibraltar on her finger.

"I have to give George his due"—Mrs. Malloy poured another swig of gin into her teacup—"he's done well for himself, all right. Him and a friend opened an exercise equipment business some years back and he's been raking in the lolly ever since. The last time I had a Christmas card from George he mentioned as how he was about to open his third factory."

"Vanessa finds that sort of thing incredibly sexy. She loves nothing better than to skip barefoot through a forest of crisp, crackling fifty-pound notes and to inhale the sensual fragrance of Avarice upon the wind while the birds in the trees tweet 'Spend! Spend! Spend!' " I failed in my attempt to speak lightly.

"Well, you certainly know how to put the finishing touches on my happiness." Mrs. Malloy dabbed at her eyes with a purple hankie and gusted a sigh that toppled Tobias off the Welsh dresser. "No, don't say another word, Mrs. H., it's clear you blame me for giving George ideas above his station and—"

"Rubbish." I took the teacup out of her hands and endeavoured to hold them steady. "I'm being absolutely hateful about all this. The fact that Vanessa and I never got along doesn't mean she won't make your son a marvelous wife and that you won't come to love her dearly as a daughter-in-law."

"That'll be the day!" Mrs. Malloy was forced to resort again to the purple hankie. "The time I met her at your wedding, the woman treated me like I was the hired help."

"That's the way she treats everyone," I soothed, "but let's hope she makes an exception with George and that the fire he has ignited in her heart will thaw the ice in her veins. Everyone has their good points, and I'm sure that if I rack my brains all day and all night, I will remember some instance of Vanessa's lovableness."

"You're breaking my heart!" Mrs. Malloy returned the hankie to the pocket of her black taffeta frock and pressed a hand loaded with rings against her substantial bosom. "This is my punishment for keeping quiet about George."

"We all have our little secrets." I turned away and began filling up the sink with hot, sudsy water. Watching one of the saucers float upon the surface like a survivor from a shipwreck, I thought about Eligibility Escorts and how much I would dislike having the commercial aspect of my first meeting with Ben surface. The fact that he never cashed the check I wrote for the privilege of having him escort me to the family reunion at Merlin's Court and pass me doting looks guaranteed to turn Vanessa as green as the watercress in the sandwiches wouldn't stop the tongues from wagging in Chitterton Fells. And wasn't it possible that in the process, the certainty of Ben's loving me devotedly would become tarnished?

Trying to shake off my unease along with the suds from my hands, I told myself that the likelihood of my past catching up with me was infinitesimal. And then it hit me, like a spray of soapy water, that in the space of the last dozen or so hours I had been made aware of the inexorable link between what was and what is.

First there had been the arrival of Gerta, at the behest of my former flatmate Jill, and now there was Vanessa, not actually on my doorstep, but soon to arrive in an ebony swoop of mink coat. Stepping back from the ominous *gloog-gloog* of the sink emptying itself, I wrung my hands on the dish towel and wondered: Was it too far-fetched to picture myself colliding with Mrs. Swabucher, the owner of Eligibility Escorts, in the village High Street? Mrs. Swabucher, with her hair tinted a delicate shade of rose to match her tulle-swirled hats, was a figure impossible to miss. Who wouldn't gawk, were this miracle of corseting and cosmetics to stop traffic by dashing across the road, with a speed that belied her advancing years, to envelop me in her flamingo-pink feather boa and cry: "Ellie Haskell! How could I forget you—the success story of all time at Eligibility Escorts! And how is that lovely young man you rented for a weekend and ended up marrying?"

A chill invaded the kitchen to worm its way into my soul, but the cause was innocent enough. Gerta had come in through the garden door with Abbey and Tam in tow. And a merry little trio they made! Abbey dancing around the woman as if she were a pine tree straight from the mountain slopes and Tam squealing gleefully as he jigged up and down.

"Gerta, I show you my choo-choo train!"

"Soon, my little munchkin! But first we have the breakfast of cereal that goes popsy-daisy!"

"Ja!" shrieked my darlings.

It was a joy to realize my offspring were both so well

adjusted that they did not feel the need to rush over to me and bury their shy little faces in my skirts. Gerta was proving to be a treasure. She did not even turn white as her frilly apron when Tobias pounced out of nowhere to take a shortcut through her legs to the hall door, and a friendly smile appeared on her apple-dumpling face when I introduced Mrs. Malloy.

"It is a pleasure to meet you!" Gerta's knees buckled into a curtsy of sorts, due to the twins swinging Tarzan-fashion on her arms. And, taking this obeisance as her due, Mrs. Malloy put her best smile forward.

"At least you speak English, not some heathen gobble-dygook; so as long as you don't go forgetting who's senior around here, we should muck along all right."

"Thank you." Gerta lost a few of the points she had gained by adding, "Mrs. Mop."

"Malloy," I said quickly.

"It is a good name. And I do mean to do the good job in my work here. Never do these little children know my life is ruined by my so-wicked husband, who forgets the joy I give him with my apple strudel." Gerta blinked tears from her eyes and smoothed down her apron in a business-like fashion. "This is the new day starting! Now I stuff my broken heart down my jumper and get busy. How do you like, Frau Haskell, if after I feed the munchkins I let them help me make the Geneva butter cake and my yodel-hey-hey torte with the chocolate and black cherries and the kirsch and the clotted cream?"

Oh, my heavens! What evil had I admitted to my home? I felt my waistline expand as I pictured weeks of being subjected to such caloric barbarism. Was there any way to safely rid myself of this demon nanny?

Unaware of my alarm, the twins settled happily down at the kitchen table and Gerta got out a bottle of milk from the fridge, whereupon Mrs. Malloy apologized for its not being fresh-squeezed, seeing as how we had stopped keeping cows after one of them attacked the postman. Sensing that I might make myself more useful elsewhere, I went upstairs, wallowed in a nice hot bath, got dressed, made my bed, and on going to straighten up the nursery found it all shipshape. After which I proceeded to spend an industrious half-hour wondering what on earth to do with the rest of my day.

When I last looked, there had been a basket of ironing to be done, but something told me that Mrs. Malloy, not to be outdone by Gerta's Teutonic efficiency, would already be dashing away with the smoothing iron. And I had no doubt she would have the floors mopped and the furniture polished with Johnson's Lavender Wax by the time I headed downstairs. In other words, the inevitable rivalry between the two women bade fair to put me out of a job.

My plans to return to work part-time as a free-lance decorator were still in the aspiration stage. As of that moment I had no clients waiting with bated breath for me to order them to toss their present furniture on the fire and make ready for a totally new look. So, faint heart, I told myself sternly, get started on your advertising campaign. Is it too much to ask that you go and order a dozen business cards? Reaching into the wardrobe for a cardigan, I remembered something: The Reverend Eudora Spike had mentioned the other day that she would appreciate my help in selecting a new wardrobe for her bedroom, and she had also done some hemming and hawing about having the sitting room sofa reupholstered. Which led to my wondering whether Vanessa's perfect figure might be due in part to having had her bust reinforced with foam rubber.

Feeling somewhat cheered, I decided against the business cards in favour of popping over to the vicarage to discuss the wardrobe and sofa with Eudora, while at the same time getting in a moan about my lethally lovely cousin. Undaunted by the fact that the mirror, having nothing better to do than stand around all day, was only too eager to point out my physical shortcomings, I headed downstairs in a rush. More haste less speed, as it turned out, because when I heard the scream I had to grab hold of the banister to keep myself from pitching headlong the rest of the way.

Was the house on fire? Had Tam eaten his cereal bowl or had Abbey, convinced she would never learn to yodel, crawled away from home? Racing towards the scream—which seemed to be fueled by one of those long-life batteries—I found myself breathless in the study. Thank God the twins appeared whole and healthy. They were seated on the floor watching entranced as Mrs. Malloy and Gerta faced off against each other in front of the telly. Gerta was the one doing the screaming, in German, or Swiss, from the guttural sound of it, and when the two of them turned to see me in the doorway, she scuttled towards me with hands locked in prayer.

"Frau Haskell, you come not too soon a minute."

"Whatever is the matter?" I looked from her to Mrs. Malloy, whose face was a thundercloud of righteous wrath.

"I bring the children in this room because they want to watch *What the Dino Saw* on the television"—Gerta struggled to speak calmly—"and I ask Mrs. Mop if we bother her dusting—"

"To which I says, if memory serves me right"—Mrs. Malloy's black taffeta bosom inflated to mammoth proportions as she addressed herself strictly to me—"that if it was all the same as made no mind with Frau Goatherd here, I'd appreciate being allowed to watch the upcoming interview with the man of my dreams."

"You don't mean . . . ?" Clasping a hand to my tumultuous heart, I came close to swooning and was forced to steady myself by grabbing hold of the desk. "You can't mean . . . *Karisma*?"

"That was his name!" Gerta evinced relief that I was as shocked as she. "They show the picture of him on the screen before I turn off the television, snip, snap, stop! It is not right, I tell Mrs. Mop, for the munchkins to see this black leather man with too much hair on his head and none on his chest. I read about this Karisma in *News of the World*. He gives the bad ideas to women. He makes them think he is the Prince Charming."

"And what's wrong with that?" Mrs. Malloy folded her arms, thus inflating her bosom still further.

"Frau Haskell"—Gerta's plaits were unravelling along with the rest of her—"perhaps I was wrong to scream, but I cannot make her turn off the television and I know you'd not want for the little Abbey here"—she pointed a trembling finger to where my daughter sat on the floor happily hitting her brother on the head with a plastic brick—"to grow up thinking the prince will come along one day and pick her up on his sheet-white horse."

"No, of course I don't want Abbey to be reared with that sort of mind-set," I said stoutly. "But what would be so bad about her Prince Charming galloping up in a Rolls, if—that is, he were to let her drive?"

Gerta could not hide her dismay. Her face fell like a soufflé taken out of the oven too soon.

"Look, ducky"—Mrs. Malloy mellowed sufficiently to bestow a kindly smile on her vanquished opponent—"it stands out a mile you've had it up to the eyeballs with men. But Karisma's not like the rest of them. He's as close to human as the buggers get. Go on, see for yourself."

So saying, she switched the telly back on; and I had to sit down before my knees gave way when the cover of *All Passion Spent* flashed before my dazzled eyes. An off-screen female voice informed us that for this novel Karisma had posed as an Apache brave, standing on a solitary rock with his marvelous hair cascading over the woman draped in languorous delight over his bronzed arm. Did the announcer think we were blind? Did she think the likes of Mrs. Malloy and I needed a tour guide in order to appreciate this Marvel of Modern Male?

"Pretty man!" Abbey proved herself my daughter by her delighted squeal, but I was not without the makings of responsible parenthood.

"Perhaps it would be a good idea," I suggested to Gerta, "for you to take the children outside. This really isn't suitable viewing for them."

"What Mrs. H. means," Mrs. Malloy kindly interpreted, "is she doesn't want the kiddies to see her like this with tears rolling down her flushed face. As for me, I don't usually get this emotional"—she wiped her eyes—"over a man's bare chest."

"He shave it!" Gerta gathered Tam into her arms and reached out a hand for Abbey, who showed no eagerness to be budged.

"When you've got muscles like his, I say flaunt 'em." In another moment Mrs. Malloy would have her hands all over the television screen.

"It is unnatural, it is sick, it is against what the Bible teaches. I know it is not my place to say this to you, Frau Haskell, but I have to live inside myself." Before bundling the children out the door, Gerta gave me a look that expressed more clearly than words her fear that I was the Demon Mummy.

With the study mercifully ours alone, Mrs. Malloy and I perched on the edge of our seats, biting down on our lips to keep from moaning when the man himself—not the cover shot—appeared on the screen.

"Welcome, Karisma." The interviewer, an attractive blond woman in a black suit and pearls, sat resolutely back in her chair. The intensity of her gaze, however, was not one-hundred-percent professional. "Welcome to *Good Morning U.K.*" She dragged her eyes away from him to face the camera. "For those viewers just tuning in, I am Joan Richards. And today I have with me in the studio the man hailed as every woman's ultimate fantasy."

"Thank you, Joan." Karisma shook back his tousled mane and smiled his heart-stopping smile.

Miss Richards pressed a hand to her throat and quickly converted the gesture into playing with her pearls. "Karisma—you have the most amazing hair. Do you have to work at it?"

"Every day of my life." Karisma spoke with a sincerity that was impossible to resist, especially when it was accompanied by that thrilling hint of a continental inflection. "It is not true I was born beautiful. My hair"—he slid his fingers through it so that it spilled in sensual splendour through his hand—"it looks like this, because always I use the body-building shampoo. It is a discipline with me, but one I embrace with my entire soul . . . because I *lorve* women. All women. Everywhere."

"There are women from Land's End to John o' Groat's"—Mrs. Malloy gripped the arms of her chair—"who are having orgasms right this very minute."

"Well, don't you have one." I glared at her. "I'd like to be able to hear what he's saying."

"Karisma, I understand"—Ms. Richards spoke brightly over the ping-pinging of her pearls dropping off her neck onto the studio floor—"that you left Spain as a teenager because your father wanted you to be a bull-fighter."

"I lorve animals."

"And how do you feel about your critics?"

"I *lorve* them. For someone like me"—Karisma

shrugged his black leather shoulders and spread his hands in a gesture that was as beautiful as it was expressive—"there is no bad publicity."

"Then you were not offended . . ." Ms. Richards reached out to touch his knee, but swiftly came to her professional senses. "Then you were not the least bit upset by the tabloid article that accused you of being the only man alive who would pick up his dinner plate in order to look at his reflection in it?"

"A newspaper's job is to sell newspapers."

"And yours, Karisma?"

"To adore women, to make every one of them know that she is a treasure to be caressed and cherished for-ever-more." That way he had of rolling his r's and making every syllable sing would have made him irresistible even had he not appeared to be looking into my eyes alone, so that I was drawn into their wondrous depths, down labyrinths of pleasure . . .

Unfortunately Mrs. Malloy had to ruin the moment by falling back in her chair, flinging wide her arms, and crying out, "Take me, Karisma, take me—I'm yours!" Talk about reducing the sublime to the ridiculous!

I missed most of what he had to say about *Desire,* his new fragrance for women, and his latest exercise video.

"Your calendar is a lunar sensation." Ms. Richards had undone the top button of her suit jacket and was fanning herself with her hand. "Any fears of over-exposure?"

The month of June appeared on screen. It featured a glistening Karisma stepping out of a swimming pool in a strip of bathing trunks that molded itself to his incomparable proportions.

"You are not concerned"—Ms. Richards tore her attention from the calendar image and returned to her guest and the viewing audience—"that you are a passing sensation and that one day, perhaps sooner than later, you may be replaced as the king of the romance cover models?"

The camera closed in, for the kill it seemed to me, on Karisma's face. His response was the continental shrug and a smile that did not quite reach his eyes.

Ms. Richards laughed, to indicate that she was teasing. "I understand you have a birthday coming up and, whilst thirty-four isn't exactly over the hill, isn't it possible that you may be passed over in favour of a younger man—with a new look—for the cover of *A Knight to Remember,* the eagerly awaited sequel to the late Azalea Twilight's *Crossing the Moat?*"

"What will be, so it is!" Karisma stilled my beating heart, with that continental throb in his voice and the smile that once more lit up his magnificent eyes. "I am here, I have a good time and lorve women. What more can I say? I do not speak English so good."

"You speak it a bloody sight better than most foreigners, my darling." Mrs. Malloy directed a virulent glance at the door in blatant hope that Gerta had her ear pressed to the keyhole. Shame on her! She did not pale under her rouge when the au pair walked into the room.

"Frau Haskell!" Gerta had flour all down her front and on the tips of the plait that looked as if she had been using it for a pastry brush. "You are wanted on the telephone."

"If it's my husband, please tell him I will ring him back when"—I shifted my chair closer to the television—"when I have finished rearranging the furniture in here."

"No. It is a brigand . . ."

"A what?"

"A brigand, Lester-Smith."

"Bother!" My decision to go and speak to my fellow Library League member was made when Karisma vanished from the screen to be replaced by a dancing teabag with spider-leg eyelashes, stumpy legs ending in impossible red shoes, and a smile that went up or down as the puppeteer kettle pulled on the string.

It wasn't easy to come down to earth after the transcendent experience of being in the same room with the man of my dreams, but I endeavoured to pay attention to what Gerta was saying when I followed her into the hall and across the flagstones and square of Persian carpet to the telephone.

"Frau Haskell, it was not my place to make a big stink bomb about what you choose to watch on television."

"You were quite right, Gerta, to monitor the children's viewing." I reached for the phone on the trestle table, but she got to it first and dusted off the receiver with her apron before presenting it to me—coated like a chicken leg in flour.

"Then you don't turn me out into the street?"

I covered the mouthpiece with my hand. "Of course not."

"Then"—her smile filled up all her worry lines so that her face became plump and smooth—"I go back to the kitchen now, Frau Haskell, and tell the children the story about the old clockmaker and the snow elves, while I finish making my special beef stew—just how my wicked husband used to like. It is not easy for me, Frau Haskell, thinking of him in Putney with Mr. Meyers, both of them so laughing and so gay."

"Very difficult," I said.

"It is a small revenge that never again will Ernst taste my stew made rich and thick with gingersnaps."

Feeling my waist thicken as she bustled down the hall, I spoke into the phone. "Sorry to keep you waiting, Brigadier Lester-Smith—"

"I do hope, Mrs. Haskell, that I'm not catching you at an awkward moment?"

"Absolutely nothing that won't keep." I resolutely banished Karisma to the dark recesses of my mind. "Is there something you need me to do in the way of Library League business?"

"It's about Miss Bunch."

I guessed immediately what he was going to say. The police hadn't been taken in by all the medical mumbo-jumbo of death from natural causes. They were convinced she had met her end by foul means and an order to exhume the body would shortly be forthcoming.

"It all came as quite a shock." Brigadier Lester-Smith sounded suitably glum.

"Of course."

"It's going to mean quite an upheaval."

"Before the earth has even settled over her grave," I agreed.

"You could have knocked me down without the aid of a shovel, Mrs. Haskell, when her solicitor, Mr. Lionel Wiseman, rang me up yesterday after I got back from the funeral and broke the news that Miss Bunch had left me

what modest amount of money she possessed, along with
her little house on Mackerel Lane."

"But that's wonderful," I enthused. Or was it? "You
sound a little worried, Brigadier." Did the police suspect
him of doing in Miss Bunch for the sake of what sounded
like a tidy inheritance?

"There is one small problem . . ."

"Yes." I hoped he was not about to say anything that
could possibly be construed as incriminating.

"Miss Bunch also bequeathed me her dog."

"Oh, help!" I fixed my eyes on the statue of St. Francis
of Assisi that occupied the niche above my head and im-
plored this protector of four-legged creatures to bear in
mind that I had acted in what I believed to be Heathcliff's
best interest. "You have discovered the dog is missing and
are absolutely heartbroken, Brigadier."

"Missing?" The voice on the other end of the phone
brightened up considerably. "Are you sure? I've been wondering what to do with the animal, because I've never been
one for pets—all that dog hair over my trousers, and I was
wondering if you might like to have him—for the kiddies."

"That's very kind of you," I said, "but Heathcliff is
awfully big. And when he showed up here last night, like a
great black thundercloud, I realized that were I to let him
stay, I would have to get rid of most of the furniture and at
least one of the children."

"Turned up at your house, Mrs. Haskell?"

"Without so much as phoning first; but it's all right,
Brigadier Lester-Smith. I pried Gerta, our new au pair, out
from his slathering jaws and palmed him off on Mr. Babcock, the milkman, this morning."

"I don't know how to thank you." The heartfelt sigh
that came through the receiver blew my hair all over my
face, and I sensed that had the brigadier not been a bachelor of the old school, he would have expressed a desire to
kiss me. "Would Mr. Babcock be the gentleman who married Sylvia from the Library League a week or so ago?"

"That's him. And we had better keep our fingers
crossed that he can love-talk his bride into keeping the
woof-woof. I have to take them their wedding present, and
when I do I'll report back to you on how things are going."

"That is most kind of you, Mrs. Haskell, so kind that I hesitate to ask another favour of you." Brigadier Lester-Smith paused to gather up his courage. "I had a look over Miss Bunch's house this morning and I did not feel that I could live in harmony with her choice of furnishing. Not that I imply any criticism, you understand that, Mrs. Haskell."

"We all have our own taste."

"Exactly!" He latched onto my statement as if I had said something intensely profound. "Being a man, I like simplicity and function. Furniture that makes sense. But at the same time I do realize that certain touches, not what you would call frilly, are needed to turn a house into a home. And I was wondering if you, Mrs. Haskell, would be willing to take a look at the house and provide me with some professional advice."

My first client! If I had not been a respectably married woman I might have expressed a desire to kiss the brigadier the next time I was alone with him in the library reading room. "I will be delighted to help you in any way I can," I said as my mind filled with visions of a navy-blue sofa piped in a rich burgundy—which colour might be repeated in the leather chairs and perhaps the wallpaper border. . . .

"This is good of you, Mrs. Haskell! You must be sure and charge me your usual fee."

"Minus a friendly discount!"

"How very kind! Would tomorrow be too soon for you to take a look at the house? I need also to mention, Mrs. Haskell, that I talked to Sir Robert Pomeroy when I met him at the barber's this morning, and we decided we should get all the members together for a special meeting of the Library League tomorrow afternoon at one o'clock. There is nothing in the bylaws to prohibit our assembling at a time other than our regularly scheduled meeting date, and Sir Robert and I thought the Library League should get started immediately on planning a memorial to Miss Bunch."

"What a lovely idea."

"Sir Robert came up with the suggestion of commissioning a bronze statue of our dear departed librarian to be placed at the front entrance."

"You don't think that a simple brass plaque might do nicely?" I asked. But not surprisingly, Brigadier Lester-Smith, having come into her money, was not prepared to screw the lady to the wall and be done with it.

"I imagine there'll have to be some sort of fund-raiser," he said. "We'll talk about all that at the meeting tomorrow. And afterwards, perhaps you could take a look at the house on Mackerel Lane."

It wasn't until I had hung up the phone that I wondered if Miss Bunch had made the brigadier her heir because he always returned his library books on time.

Chapter

5

"A bronze statue of Miss Bunch!" The string mop in Mrs. Malloy's hand did double duty as an exclamation point as she held it above her bucket in the kitchen. "What bright spark came up with that idea? Don't tell me, Mrs. H.: It had to be a man! Common decency tells you it isn't right to make a public spectacle of what was, as far as we know, a respectable woman. It's a crying shame, that's what it is—setting her up to be pooped on by birds and leered at by every passing Tom, Dick, and Harry."

It was my feeling that Mrs. Malloy was jealous of any woman but herself being put on a pedestal, but all I said was, "She'll be fully clothed, right down to her brogue or, rather, her bronze shoes. The Library League would never vote for a nude. We're a very conservative group. I don't think there's one amongst us that reads poetry that doesn't rhyme."

"I wouldn't call Bunty Wiseman straight-laced." Mrs. Malloy planted her mop in the sink as if it were a tree with a lot of stringy roots, to be watered when she emptied the bucket. "You may have blocked it all out, Mrs. H., but I for one haven't forgotten how Ms. Miniskirt brought Chitterton Fells to its knees when she was running Fully Female."

Clearing away the remains of the three course lunch

Gerta had fed the twins before taking them upstairs for their naps, I shuddered at Mrs. Malloy's reminder of our enrollment in the health club from hell. Far from discovering my full physical and emotional potential as a sensual woman, I had felt lucky to get out alive. But Bunty had paid the highest price. By the time Fully Female's doors closed, she had lost her husband, Lionel Wiseman (Miss Bunch's solicitor), to a woman who got her exercise climbing into bed with other women's husbands. The Hollywood-style Wiseman home was sold for a hotel. And Bunty was left with little but the leotard on her back. During the past year, she had gamely worked at a series of part-time jobs, but, as she pointed out, people weren't queuing up to hire an ex–chorus girl turned failed businesswoman.

"Go on, Mrs. H., stick up for Bunty Wiseman."

"She is a friend of mine." I put the Beatrix Potter crockery in the sink as Mrs. Malloy stowed the bucket and mop in the broom cupboard. "And she's been a great new recruit for the Library League; in fact, I am hoping she will take over as secretary when my term is up."

"Proper back-breaking work."

"I'll have you know that last month I sent out at least two get well cards to former league members, as well as purchasing and gift-wrapping Sylvia Babcock's wedding present, which I shall personally deliver."

"And now I suppose you'll be on the phone day and night, begging people to pitch in by crocheting doilies and what have you for this fund-raiser for Miss Bunch's memorial." Mrs. Malloy helped herself to some of the stew Gerta had left on the cooker and teetered on her six-inch heels over to the table. There she further vented her feelings with the pepper pot before picking up her knife and fork.

"I don't think we'll have another bring-and-buy sale," I conceded. "The last one the Library League put on was not a roaring success. If I remember rightly, we raised only five pounds."

"And the only reason there was that much"—Mrs. M. polished off her plate with a piece of bread to save on the washing up—"was that you went crackers and bought that pair of tin swords and the two whacking big sieves with the leather handles."

"They were fencing guards, but you're right, they did resemble the medieval equivalent of a colander. Ben was quite chuffed until he realized his mistake. But I certainly don't think I overpaid. The foils and the guards came from Pomeroy Manor and no doubt figured in some very romantic swashbuckling."

While putting away the children's dishes, I pictured one of Sir Robert's ancestors—a handsome wastrel in form-fitting breeches and gleaming Hessian boots—tossing a foil to a muslin-clad miss with golden ringlets, and exclaiming, "En garde, my dear Arabella, time for a little foreplay!"

Trust Mrs. Malloy to break the mood. Getting to her feet, she said, "If you ask me, Mrs. H., you'll save yourself and the rest of the Library League a lot of bloomin' aggravation if you pick up one of those life-size inflatable dolls from a dirty-joke shop. I'm sure as how Bunty Wiseman can tell you where to go. Then you spray the dolly Lolita with bronze paint, and Bob's your uncle, you've got your statue of Miss Bunch."

"I hardly think that would be suitable," I was saying, when the garden door opened and my husband, of all impossible people, walked into the kitchen. Ben never came home at lunchtime. But there he was, looking far too real, with his tie loosened and his suit jacket unbuttoned, to be a figment of my overwrought imagination.

"Men!" Mrs. Malloy eyed him darkly as he walked brazenly across her newly washed floor. "I could have told you, Mrs. H., you was making a horrible mistake bringing that Swiss temptress into this house. She may be old enough to be his mother, but she's a new broom when all is said and done. The next thing we'll know, she'll be tying the master here to the bedpost with those braids of hers, and the two of them will be yodeling their heads off."

"You have an incorrigibly evil mind, Mrs. Malloy." Ben's scowl was at odds with the smile he gave her. "You've never forgiven me for resisting your attempts to lure me into the pantry while my wife's back was turned. And you're jealous because I've come home in the middle of the day to spirit Ellie away in the car parked, for a fast

getaway, within inches of the door. Come, my darling!"
He held out his hands.

"Who, me?" I glanced wildly around the kitchen as if
expecting another Ellie Haskell to step forward into the
limelight, coquettishly twirling her dishcloth.

"I'm taking you out for lunch." Ben crossed the room
in two strides and, placing a husbandly arm around my
shoulders, propelled me towards the garden door, which
Mrs. Malloy with a poor attempt at servility was holding
open.

"But I can't—" I resisted my husband's attempt to
kidnap me by trying to duck under his elbow. "I can't
leave without saying good-bye to Abbey and Tam—"

"Oh, go on with you." Mrs. Malloy shook her black-
and-white head in disgust. "You'll be back before they're
up from their naps. And with Mistress Gerta goo-gooing
all over them, they probably wouldn't miss you anyway."

"She made all that stew and her feelings may be hurt if
we go out for a meal . . ."

"And your insides may suffer if you eat what's in that
saucepan. I was hungry, so I didn't let the taste put me off.
But"—she pressed a hand to her stomach—"I'm beginning
to think I made a mistake not fixing meself a sandwich.
And it wouldn't surprise me one bit if that husband of hers
called the marriage quits because he couldn't take another
bout of indigestion, not because he found out he preferred
men."

"But I don't have my handbag," I fretted as Ben
marched me down the steps into the courtyard.

"You won't need it."

"And I'm not wearing restaurant shoes."

"We're not going to Abigail's."

"No?" My feet had to skip in order to keep up with
his as we crossed the moat bridge.

"We're going on a picnic, Ellie; doesn't that sound
romantic?"

In theory, yes! In theory, a picnic takes place on the
one perfect day of the English year. What clouds do appear in the limpid blue sky are light and airy as shut-
tlecocks being playfully batted about by the warm breeze,
while a big orange sun beams its approval. This, however,
was most definitely not that day of days. The wind that

unravelled my hair and attempted to choke me with it was chilly in the extreme. And every breath I took tasted of rain. The trees had been flattened into giant badminton rackets that flung the birds into the air and sent them pinging to the end of the garden and back again. My attempt at a smile was literally whipped off my face as we stepped onto the gravel drive, where the car sat huddled in shivering discomfort. Poor thing! It was old and had for years been subject to every infirmity known to anything on four wheels.

"Your chariot awaits, my lady!" Ben opened the door with a flourish and stood with unabated enjoyment as the wind ran its fingers with wild abandon through his black hair and I slithered onto the passenger seat. "Are we having fun yet?" he inquired.

It was ridiculous to ascribe a diabolical gleam to his blue-green eyes and a sinister spring to his gait as he nipped around the car and climbed into the driver's seat. And it was wrong of me to hope that the engine would gasp its last breath and the headlights roll back into their sockets.

"Don't you think we should bring Abbey and Tam?" I ventured. "They'd have so much fun on a picnic." Whilst I would have a chance of keeping warm chasing after them as they escaped from the travelling rug spread out on the damp grass.

"We can bring the twins another time." Ben stared at me, dumbfounded. "Ellie, what is the matter with you? I thought you would be pleased that I abandoned work at lunchtime, one of my busiest times of the day, to spend quality time with you."

"Oh, darling, I *am* pleased." I reached over to kiss him on the cheek. "It's just that I feel a little guilty, despite what Mrs. Malloy said, about walking out of the house when Gerta has gone to such a lot of trouble cooking that stew."

"We can eat it for dinner." Ben, whose preference is to serve beef in slices so rare a vet might have some hope of reviving the poor cow, did not look enthusiastic.

"Of course we can." I squeezed his knee. "The only other thing holding me back from fully getting into the spirit of your picnic is that I do have to go along to the vicarage this afternoon to give Eudora some advice on re-decorating."

"Then I'll drop you off there on the way back. Any other problems we haven't discussed?" Ben started up the car without any of the doors flying off and buzzed down the drive, through the gates. Before I could finish buckling my seat belt, we were out on the Cliff Road, heading in the direction of the village. "You weren't expecting a gentleman friend, Ellie, when I turned up to ruin everything?"

"Of course not. You are the only man in my life and always have been," I assured him.

This was not strictly true. There had been the Marquise of Marshington, the Duke of Darrow, any number of earls and a handful of viscounts, along with all the Sir Somebodies. And I wasn't ashamed of my past. These men had been there, in my single days, to rescue me from the lonely bed-sitter and the tin of sardines I was doomed to share with my cat Tobias. They had escorted me to Bath assemblies and masquerade balls attended by the Prince Regent and to picnics where the sun always shone and the blue of the sky was as pure as a virgin's heart. Would it have been fair, would it have been *moral* to send these gallants packing when Ben appeared, somewhat belatedly, on the scene?

My husband smiled at me, apparently taking my silence as a sign that I was enjoying the view from the car window. And I tried, really I did, to appreciate the cackling of the wind as it shoved us off the narrow road and tried to send us over the cliff's edge to somersault down onto the murderous crags below. As we turned a corner I caught a glimpse of the sea, frothing and foaming, as if smacking its lips at the prospect of devouring us, car and all, at a gulp.

We drove a couple of miles and shortly before reaching the village turned onto a winding lane that was fringed on either side by the sort of thickets that would be a highwayman's dream. We were practically alongside the house before I saw it. It was a wonderfully macabre old place, with a secretive look to its long, narrow windows. And I was utterly enchanted until I noticed the multitude of chimneys and read the lettering on the ramshackle gate.

"Good heavens!" I grabbed Ben's arm so tightly that

the car swerved—clipping off a sizable chunk of the hedge which stood badly in need of such pruning. "That's Tall Chimneys, the one-time abode of Hector Rigglesworth."

"Who?" Ben backed the car up and proceeded on down the lane without giving me further time to gawk.

"The man who haunts the library, the ghost who, in the opinion of Brigadier Lester-Smith, frightened Miss Bunch to death."

"I thought she died from a virus."

"So she did, but in this case one can read between the lines of the autopsy report. A malevolent force was at work and his name was Hector Rigglesworth." I shuddered. Ben had drawn the car to a standstill beside a stretch of grass ringed by trees and with a solitary beech tree standing patiently in the middle, like a gnarled old butler awaiting his instructions.

"Here we are, sweetheart." Ben exited the car with lithe grace and went round to the boot to collect the picnic basket. Rejoining me as I stepped from the road onto the grass, he asked, "What do you think?"

"It's rather . . ." I was going to say *drafty*, but as such tends to be a condition of the outdoors, I belatedly remembered to be enthusiastic. "It is rather *lovely*. And how odd to think that in all the time I have lived at Merlin's Court, I have never been down this lane."

Following Ben towards the beech tree, I glanced over my shoulder. I could see a chimney and what was probably an attic window of Hector Rigglesworth's house. Was I imagining it, or was that a face pressed against the pane? Endeavouring to shake off the unease that gripped me, I struggled to focus on the delights of the moment.

"How's this for the perfect picnic spot?" Ben set down the basket. And I tried not to notice that he did not have a travelling rug tucked under his arm, ready to unroll and lay at my feet. Or a hot water bottle. Shame on me! So what if the grass was damp and I developed sciatica? I suddenly remembered Vanessa and how she had once fielded our cousin Freddy's suggestion that she ought to try a camping holiday, with the response that, as far as she was concerned, roughing it was black-and-white TV. Heaven forbid that I should develop her pampered-puss mind-set.

"You couldn't have chosen a more idyllic place." I knelt down and felt my knees turn green, while Ben began the business of unloading packages and plates, to the rustling annoyance of the beech tree, which clearly did not think me up to snuff without a parasol, or that the tablecloth Ben was spreading out on the grass made up for the missing travelling rug. "Darling," I said, "I've been meaning to tell you . . ." A raindrop plopped on my nose.

"What's that?" Ben scanned the sky, bulging with wooly grey clouds, and with a wary eye continued unwrapping with increased speed.

"Nothing earthshaking," I replied as a rumble of thunder caused a couple of knives and forks to scuttle under the tablecloth which had been blown up by the wind. "Only that I got the strangest bit of news this morning. Mrs. Malloy told me that her son—"

"I didn't know she had one."

"Well, she does. And it seems he's going to marry Vanessa."

"What a very small world!" Ben held his hair down with a plate as he laid out the serviettes and caught both of them one-handed as they attempted to blow away.

"It turns out"—I shuffled on my knees after the escaping salt and pepper shakers—"that George Malloy has done rather well for himself financially."

"Even so, I'd have expected our lovely Vanessa to hold out for a chap with a title as well as money."

"My thinking exactly."

"We'll have to drink a toast to the engaged couple." Ben, having secured the tablecloth with a hefty rock at each corner, was rummaging frantically in the picnic basket. "You won't believe this, Ellie! I can't find the corkscrew!"

It was a wonder to me that he could find the hand stretched out in front of him in the drizzling rain, but I mopped my face with my serviette and said brightly that it really didn't matter.

"Of course it matters." Ben sounded as thoroughly exasperated with me as with the situation. "I brought wine"—he held up the bottle—"and, by damn, we are going to drink it." Stumbling to his feet, he rooted around the trunk of the disgruntled beech and returned to the tablecloth with a stout-looking twig that snapped in two the moment he jammed it into the cork.

"Here, let me try." I picked up a knife, took the bottle from him, broke off the top of the cork, and began stabbing away at the remainder until it broke into chunks that ended up in the drink.

Ben firmly removed the bottle from my hands. "I don't like my wine chewy." He poured us each a glass and attempted to convert his grimace into a grin to show a determined party spirit. "Drink up, my darling, before it's two-thirds water."

"You could not have foreseen the rain," I soothed.

"I could have looked out the window."

"Never mind." Resolutely I sat down on the grass and promptly felt my underwear shrink two sizes. "Let's make that toast, Ben." I tapped my glass to his as he squatted gingerly down across the tablecloth from me. "To Vanessa and George!"

"May they be as happy as we are!"

"At this very minute!" I agreed, taking a sip of sauterne and almost choking on a chunk of cork. My resulting croak was echoed by several crows perched in ungainly malevolence on a bough halfway up the beech tree. Hugging my cardigan around me, I tried to push away the feeling of foreboding that came with the memory of Vanessa telling me, when we were children and saw a bunch of black crows in a tree, that their infernal cawing meant somebody was going to die. My affectionate cousin had been suggesting that my days were numbered, and here I still was; but even so . . . I reached for something to put in my mouth to keep my teeth from chattering.

"You remember, don't you, Ellie?"

"That old saying about the crows?" I should not have been surprised that a husband could read his wife's mind.

"No, the food!" His smile wavered in the mist that had mercifully replaced the rain. "Don't you recognize it?"

I stared at the assortment of dishes. Of course I recognized lobster and green salad and crusty brown rolls when I saw them, but I wasn't getting the point of the picture.

"Our first picnic!" Ben ran his fingers through his damp hair, instantly bringing the curl back to life in a way many a woman would have envied. "Surely you remember on that occasion I prepared this same lobster dish—stewed in white wine, chilled to icy perfection, and dressed with capers and my own special mayonnaise."

"It is coming back to me. . . ."

"I can hear myself as if it were yesterday, Ellie, explaining that the mystery ingredient of the rolls was a tablespoon of treacle added to the yeast base. And I remember your exclamations of delight over the salad with its lemon and sweet vermouth dressing."

"I do recall vaguely . . ."

"There is nothing the least vague about it!" Perhaps the shadows cast by the beech tree were responsible for the darkening of my husband's face. "The dressing may be subtle, but it is never insipid. The secret is in the tossing, which must be extraordinarily gentle so as not to bruise the spinach or the baby oak leaf lettuce."

"Did I say *vaguely?*" I shook my head at such stupidity. My tongue must have slipped on my wet lips. I looked meaningfully up at the clouds. If they dropped any lower, they'd be sitting on our heads like knitted hats. "I meant to say that I *vividly* recalled that first picnic. We had it . . . outdoors, didn't we?"

"Under the beech tree in the garden at Merlin's Court."

"That's right!" I beamed, hoping the sun would follow my example, but, cowardlike, it remained resolutely wrapped up in its dirty grey woolies.

"Unfortunately the garden was an impossibility this time." Ben began spooning lobster onto our plates and garnishing it with radish rosettes and cucumber leaves. "I was thwarted, sweetheart, by the image of Gerta tying red and yellow streamers to the trunk of the tree, and she and the twins dancing around the maypole, while you and I were trying to relive our memories. Then I remembered seeing this place with the beech, so strikingly similar to the one at Merlin's Court."

"You've thought of everything!" I scooted around the wet tablecloth to nestle up close to him. For several moments the warmth of my love for this man, whom I did not deserve, drove back the chilly damp. We ate in a companionable silence, broken only intermittently by the crows' unmelodious chorus. The rolls were not quite as crusty as usual. But I did not mind and Ben made no apologies for them. It would seem that his sensitivities as a chef had been totally subliminated by his ardour as a husband.

The mist had cleared but, even had it turned into a pea-souper, it could not have masked his mounting passion. His eyes had darkened to a glittering emerald green and a muscle tensed in his jaw as, with intensity of purpose, he removed my half-finished plate from my hand, set it down slowly but surely on the tablecloth, and brought his lips down on mine in a kiss that would have lit a fire within me but for the weather conditions. As it was, it smouldered nicely, and I made no effort to resist as he drew me back to lie upon the grass.

"Alone at last, sweetheart!" His hand caressed my cheek and my throat with feathery delicacy before moving ever lower. Who knows how far things might have gone? Alas, when I turned my head in the throes of a warm rush of pleasure, I interrupted his heavy breathing with a horrified shriek.

"Stop!" I struggled to sit up and immediately fell back down, cracking my head on the wine bottle that had inconsiderately rolled off the tablecloth. "Ben, we can't do this!" I was making frantic attempts to button my cardigan back to respectability. "We are being watched."

"Nonsense!" He made a grab for me, but I managed to elude him and stagger to my feet.

"I tell you"—I pointed a finger at the upper portions of Tall Chimneys showing through the trees—"I can see someone at the top window. It's . . . it's a woman in a black frock, with long hair—or maybe she's wearing a veil."

"Then it's not the ghost of Hector Rigglesworth. Or did you forget to tell me that he was a transvestite?"

"Legend does not say anything to that effect." I took a couple of steps towards the thicket separating us from the house, hoping for a clearer view of the apparition. "Besides, as far as I know, he restricts his hauntings to the Chitterton Fells library. Doesn't it seem more likely that this is one of the seven daughters watching from the window for the man of her dreams to come driving up in his curricle?"

"What I think is that you're not making any sense."

Ben spoke with ill-concealed irritability while making no attempt to get to his feet. "It is either a real live woman at that window, or you are seeing a shadow caused by the way the curtain is looped."

Indeed, when I looked again, the figure at the window was gone. Perhaps I had imagined her, or perhaps she was one of the present-day occupants of Tall Chimneys. It did not matter. There was no way for me to recapture the moment of passion with my husband. And he was, I thought defensively, partly to blame for continuing to lie prone on the grass, hands folded on his chest, as if awaiting interment. Suddenly I could not think of a more unsettling spot for a picnic, let alone lovemaking. It was clear to me that an unspeakable evil lurked within the walls of Tall Chimneys. An evil that reached out to permeate the thicket and even the island of green grass on which I stood shivering.

"I have the creepiest feeling that beech tree could tell some harrowing stories of what it has seen and heard in its time," I told Ben. "Who knows? Perhaps one of the seven Rigglesworth daughters occasionally interrupted her reading of romance novels to trudge out into the gloom of night and bury an unsuitable suitor? One who tried to make a virtue out of his warts and the fact that he never took a bath. There are men who won't take no for an answer—even when a slammed door is staring them in the face."

"I think I get the message." Ben shot to his feet and began repacking the basket with a ruthless disregard for the life span of china and glass. "All it will take to put a lid on this ill-fated adventure"—he banged one down on the butter dish—"is for us to hear a spectral hound howling among the trees."

Foolish man! It was made hideously apparent that one did not sneer at the forces present on this unhallowed spot, for we immediately heard a series of unearthly woofs. Before I could grab up the two broken pieces of twig that Ben had used in his attempt to uncork the wine and form a cross with which to protect myself, a huge animal—more wolf than dog—came careening onto the grass. Fur bristling, stalactite fangs exposed, the monster rushed towards us in a blur of black—and attempted to crawl, whimpering, under the tablecloth.

"Why, blow me down!" Mr. Babcock stepped out of the lane and onto the grass. "If it isn't Mr. and Mrs. Haskell!"

"And isn't that Heathcliff?" Ben glumly addressed the tablecloth that was lumbering around his feet.

"Your missus very kindly gave the dog to me this morning." The milkman sounded decidedly nervous. "And already we've become such mates, you wouldn't believe! You don't want him back, do you?"

"You must be joking!" My husband was looking at me with rekindled affection.

"Speaking of spouses . . . is Sylvia happy about the new addition to the family?" I inquired.

"That's one I can't answer." Mr. Babcock scratched his ear. "To tell the truth, I got the wind up thinking about how she might react to Cliffy here, so when I finished my rounds I decided to take him on a bit of a walk. And believe you me, he was walking to heel as nice as you please, when all of a sudden like he went all to pieces. It happened just when we came up to that house back there—the one that looks like it's haunted. And spooked he was all right. The poor lad!" Mr. Babcock's beefy face looked the worse for worry as he puffed across the grass towards the tablecloth that was chasing its tail in increasingly frenzied circles.

"Heathcliff was Miss Bunch's dog," I reminded Ben. "Surely, my love, that must make even a skeptic like you stop and think that there may be more to Tall Chimneys and the Rigglesworth legend than meets the mortal eye. . . ."

Chapter

6

When Ben dropped me off at the vicarage some ten minutes later, I experienced the rapturous relief of being returned to the sanity of the everyday world after journeying to the dark on the other side. Whether Ben was in equally good spirits was questionable. But I hoped that his soul would be restored when he entered the kitchen at Abigail's and saw the last of the picnic basket.

As I entered the churchyard gates I made a vow to unearth my lacy sea-green nightie when I got home, and to brush my hair a hundred strokes before getting into bed for the night. A husband deserved to be pampered, and I would not succumb to the temptation of sitting up till the small hours to finish reading *Her Master's Voice*. My aunt Astrid, Vanessa's mother, was known to say grimly that she had never once refused her husband. I could only imagine what she would think of my slipshod approach to marital duty.

I had to laugh at myself as I wended my way down the mossy path that angled left towards the Norman church with its narrow stained glass windows, and right towards the early Victorian vicarage. Making love with Ben could never seriously be viewed as a duty—it was just that I was always hoping for the perfect moment, when I would be several pounds thinner, and the children would be older and less likely to interrupt at the crucial moment, and I would finally be caught up with the ironing.

Perhaps, I thought, nipping along faster so that the wind wouldn't catch hold of me and spin me around like a top, perhaps I would have a word with Eudora and see if she thought my fondness for romance novels bordered on an addiction that might have a negative impact on my marriage, and whether I should attempt to quit cold turkey or just try to cut back.

What I didn't think about was Miss Bunch's freshly dug grave, lying in the dark green shade of the weeping willow.

"Hello, Ellie!" Eudora opened the front door as I mounted the last of the stone steps which the wear of countless footsteps had scooped out to resemble a headsman's block. "I saw you from the sitting room window and thought I'd save you ringing the bell. Gladstone is in the study working on the *Clarion Call*, otherwise known as the parish bulletin, and you know how men are," Eudora laughed fondly, "it doesn't take much to break their concentration."

"I certainly wouldn't want to disturb him!" Smiling my understanding, I tiptoed into the hall with its dark brown varnish and pictures of various Archbishops of Canterbury on the walls, and closed the door as silently as I could behind me. "Gladstone has done a marvelous job since he took over the bulletin. Quite honestly," I whispered, "before his day I never got much further than the first paragraph, but he has made it into a real page-turner. His reporting of the Babcock wedding in last week's issue brought tears to my eyes. The description of Sylvia wafting down the aisle on a rose-scented cloud, with the sun framing her radiant face like a golden halo . . ."

"Yes, well, I did think Gladstone might have done better to leave that last bit out." Eudora led me into the sitting room. The painting mounted above the fireplace was of a sailing ship glued on top of an unbudgeable wave. The china in the glass-fronted cabinet was a common-or-garden rose pattern. The brown sofa and fireside chairs sagged comfortably like women with middle-age spread who breathed sighs of relief at being finally, and irrevocably, freed from their corsets. It was a room where nothing matched and harmony was the result. And it suited St. Anselm's clergywoman perfectly.

Eudora was a substantial woman—not fat or even plump, just solidly built. A woman inclined to beige twin sets and a single strand of pearls with her tweed skirts and good shoes. Recently our vicar had begun to wear her greying hair in a softer style, emphasizing the natural curl, so that it no longer resembled a serviceable felt hat. And I noticed that today Eudora was wearing a new pair of glasses whose speckled frames picked up the colour of her hazel eyes.

"It really is nice to see you, Ellie." She plumped up a cushion and arranged it at a more inviting angle on the easy chair to the left of the fireside. "Make yourself comfortable and we'll have a good chat." Turning away from me, she shifted a sheaf of legal-looking papers to the middle of the coffee table and set the Delft vase of daffodils on top of them. "There! That gives you more elbow room . . ." She laughed a little self-consciously. It was unlike her to fuss. There had been only one time when I had seen Eudora seriously discomposed, when her mother-in-law came to visit for several weeks with dire results. "So tell me, Ellie"—she sat down across from me—"are you here to help me redecorate?"

"That sounds a bit drastic," I faltered. "Weren't you just thinking about a new bedroom wardrobe?"

"Originally, yes. But you know how one thing leads to another. And now that spring is here"—she looked around the room—"everything suddenly looks so shabby. The wallpaper has faded so badly, you can hardly see the pattern, and the furniture, well—you can see for yourself, Ellie."

"I don't see too much wrong." I shifted to the edge of my chair and the springs gave a heartfelt groan as if fully aware that their end was near.

"Perhaps I'm just ready for a change." Eudora seemed to be eyeing the paperback novel on the coffee table with Karisma on the cover. It was impossible for me not to recognize those torrents of windblown hair and bulging biceps, even when viewed from the wrong way round. "Life doesn't stand still, and if we don't make some effort to keep up—" She broke off. "Well, I certainly don't want to turn into a fuddy-duddy."

"You could never be anything of the sort," I said fondly. "You're an extremely up-to-date woman."

"Obviously I am in some ways." Eudora's smile was unreadable as she turned the novel facedown on the table and then pressed her hands, as if to steady them, on her tweed skirt. "My work has for a long time left Gladstone saddled with the traditional 'wifely' role. The cooking and the shopping, that sort of thing! Such a dear! So often in my shadow in our parish life! Is it any surprise that he wants his own identity? That he should branch out in a way that might strike some of the good people of St. Anselm's as somewhat shocking?"

"You mean that he wants to redecorate the vicarage?"

"No!" Eudora sounded thoroughly flustered. "That was entirely my idea. I was talking about Gladstone having taken up knitting. People can, even the best of them, be a little catty. And it would hurt his feelings terribly if, for instance, the members of the Library League were to make little jokes."

"I'm sure no one thinks anything negative," I said. "The fact that a man likes to knit or embroider hardly implies he has a hormone imbalance. If I knew how to do either, I would certainly teach Tam and Abbey."

"You'll have to send them over to Gladstone for lessons." Eudora's smile looked frayed around the edges, and I began to be a little worried about her, especially when she continued. "I sincerely trust, Ellie, that no one will consider him an unsuitable influence, when word gets out that he . . ." Her voice cracked. "That he also enjoys darning."

I started to speak, but my eyes were drawn to the window and the view of the graveyard, with its weary regiment of tombstones waiting for the Last Judgement's trumpet call to relieve them of their posts. Did this ever-present reminder of the grim implacability of death breed dark fancies? Was Eudora in need of a change of scene rather than a change of furniture? I was wondering how to approach the subject, when she sat back in her chair and readjusted her glasses so that immediately her face was her own again. Sound and cheerful. Could it be that I was the one who was off balance and therefore getting a distorted view of things? Had I been more affected than I realized by the shock of practically stumbling over Miss Bunch's body in the library?

"So, Ellie!" Eudora seemed at ease now with me and life in general. "Before we start discussing the decorating, you must tell me how things are with you."

It was tempting to spill the beans about Vanessa's engagement to George Malloy, but I managed to exercise heroic restraint. My cousin's imminent arrival in Chitterton Fells was not in the scheme of things a major tragedy. Knowing Vanessa, she would breeze into Merlin's Court on a cloud of expensive perfume, warn me not to look at her diamond ring with the naked eye, while bragging about her latest modeling assignment for Felini Senghini. And say she noticed I had taken to wearing a size forty-long bra since the birth of the twins. I would adjust. Besides, it should be Mrs. Malloy's privilege to make the gladsome announcement.

And it no longer made sense to bring up the subject of my reading habits. The book on the coffee table—which revealed that Eudora, too, succumbed to the temptations of a romance novel—made nonsense of my concern that I might be jeopardizing my marriage. I was not a romance novel junkie. I could quit anytime I chose.

"My life is fine," I told Eudora while putting on my professional thinking cap. What this room called for was a decorating plan that would not prove a death sentence to every piece of furniture now looking at me with abject reproach. I was toying with the idea of re-covering the sofa in a houndstooth pattern and finding a new shade in hunter green for the standard lamp, when the telephone on the side table by Eudora's chair rang. Excusing herself, she picked up the receiver and was speaking in a lowered voice to the caller, when her husband walked into the room.

Gladstone Spike was silver-haired, and slender in build, with the stooped shoulders of a much taller man. His demeanour was particularly gentle, and upon first meeting him I had thought it ironic that he looked so much the traditional vicar, when it was his wife who was in the clergy. Today, as he invariably did, Gladstone wore a grey cardigan, one which I had no doubt he had knitted himself.

"Hello, Ellie! Am I intruding?" He hesitated in the doorway, glancing from me to his wife, who was still on the phone. "I can always go away, you know"—his pale grey eyes twinkled—"and not come back until you give the all-clear!"

"Eudora and I were having a chat about the redecorating," I explained.

"Ah, lovely!" He crossed the floor silently on his slippered feet and settled himself on the sofa, hands crossed primly on his knees. "You're the expert on such matters, Ellie, but if I may make the suggestion, I do think that some ruffles and lots of pink, I'm particularly fond of fuchsia, would make for a very nice change."

"Well . . ." My heart sank.

"And what do you think, my dear—and do be frank—of a heart-shaped mirror in a gilt frame to hang above the mantelpiece?"

God was good. Before I was forced to answer, Eudora hung up the phone and, standing, blurted out to her husband, "Gladstone, that was the surgeon, Mr. Sundrani, on the phone. He's going on holiday to India and won't be able to do your operation until he gets back next month." She looked extremely upset.

"That is a nuisance, my dear." Mr. Spike's face turned the fuchsia of which he was so fond as he avoided my eyes and fussed with his trouser knees. "But I suppose I can be patient in waiting a little longer." He attempted a valiant smile.

"Your parents should have taken care of the matter when you were a baby." Clearly, Eudora was so rattled that she failed to notice she had embarrassed her husband. From the look and sound of her, she was also oblivious to *my* presence. "If they'd had the emotional stamina to make the appropriate decision, you wouldn't now be facing invasive surgery."

"Is there any other kind, my dear?"

"This one has particular repercussions to a married couple." Eudora pulled off her glasses, blinked wildly, and rammed them back on her nose. "I'm not blaming you, Gladstone. This isn't your fault and I do realize that you are the major sufferer, but sometimes all I can see is a future of your sleeping in the guest bedroom . . ." Smothering a sob with a trembling hand, Eudora rushed out into the hall, leaving her husband and me to the loud ticking of the mantelpiece clock.

Gladstone hummed a few bars from a hymn and tapped out the melody on the table at his side, while I avoided his eyes. "I'd better go and make her a nice cup of tea." He stood up after an emotion-packed few moments. "Why don't you go after her, Ellie, and continue your chat about doing up the house? I know she wants a new wardrobe for"—the next word caught in his throat—"our bedroom."

"Perhaps it would be better if I left. . . ."

"Not at all!" Gladstone sounded quite panicked by the idea of my abandoning ship. "Eudora needs cheering up, and sad to say I'm not for the job. What with one thing and another"—he bowed his head over his steepled fingers—"I'm being something of a trial, in more ways than one, at present."

My first instinct was to tell him I was sorry about the operation. But because I could hazard a guess as to what it entailed, and could appreciate his acute embarrassment, it seemed best to merely press his shoulder in passing before slipping quietly out the door in search of his wife.

After mounting the stairs, whose third and fifth steps creaked loudly enough to waken the dead in the churchyard, I found Eudora on the rectangular landing. It was an area made somewhat dark by the olive-green wallpaper and by the closely knit row of oak doors. But a narrow window at one end admitted enough pale light for me to see that Eudora's eyes were reddened from crying.

"Please accept my apology, Ellie, for my dreadful behaviour." She rubbed at her forehead with two fingers, as if trying to ease an intolerable ache. "I don't, for the life of me, know what made me go to pieces like that. Gladstone is so dear and good. For years he has consistently put my work—my needs—ahead of his own. It is the epitome of selfishness for me to let my fears of an impending change in our lives come between us. And to blow up at him about the operation, in front of you, was inexcusable!"

I put my arm around her. "You love him. And when

we are worried about those dearest to us, we sometimes turn the tables and blame them for putting us through grief on their account."

Eudora squeezed my hand. "No, I was thinking only of myself. I wished that he'd taken care of the matter years ago, when it was clear he had a problem. And I lashed out at him because I was resentful of a choice he is fully entitled to make. He has the right to his own identity."

I couldn't see how the impending operation would make an entirely new man of Gladstone; but that perhaps showed how little I knew of the miracles of modern surgery. What I did suggest was that Eudora might feel better if she went downstairs immediately and talked to her husband. But she said she preferred to give herself five or ten minutes in which to pull herself together.

"It won't do Gladstone any good to see me looking like this." She tugged at her sleeves and stood up straight. "A woman of my age and build doesn't look the least enchanting when she's been snivelling. So why don't you and I, Ellie, march into the bedroom and see how you can advise me regarding making some changes? The wardrobe isn't the only problem, as you will see."

"Are you sure you're up to this?" I asked and, upon receiving her nod, followed Eudora through the door at the end of the landing.

"Well, what do you think?" She switched on the light, to reveal a good-size room with a fireplace on the wall facing the circa World War II bed. "The wallpaper"—she pointed at the rambling red roses—"was here when we came, and I know it clashes horribly with the yellow bedspread. What do you think about our getting a duvet, Ellie? I like the idea of the easy bed-making, but I'm concerned that the down filling might irritate my allergies."

"Ben and I have a duvet with a synthetic filling," I told her, "because Ben was worried about real down, with his ticklish nose. Luckily I don't have a problem. You'd have to hold a feather under my nose for the purpose of checking whether I was still breathing to make me sneeze. But there are really wonderful substitutes these days, and if you decide you want to keep the rose wallpaper and curtains for a while, a white eyelet duvet cover would work very nicely." My voice sounded a little too loud, as if I were talking to ward off the gloom that enveloped Eudora as visibly as the mist gathering outside the window.

"No, I think I'd like to change everything in the room except the fireplace." She laughed unsteadily with the result that she had to resettle her glasses on her nose. "And maybe we should rip that out."

"You may want to wait before doing anything major." I watched uneasily as my friend gravitated between the dressing table and a tallboy. "It is usually better to make decorating decisions when you are in reasonably good spirits. Otherwise you could end up with black wallpaper and a coffin for a coffee table."

"You're not going to make money this way, Ellie."

"And I don't want to see you waste yours," I told her.

"For once in our lives, Gladstone and I have it to spend." She looked thoroughly miserable as she said this. "Our daughter is married and settled in Australia, and Gladstone and I have always lived frugally. And . . . given the circumstances"—she shook herself like a dog coming out of water—"well, it seemed time to have a bit of a splurge. But you're quite right, Ellie, perhaps it would be better to wait until our lives settle back down."

"Let me have a think about the wardrobe." I eyed the present one with mixed feelings. It was rather a nice late Victorian piece which, if refinished and its front panels painted with a pastoral scene of sheep grazing under twin trees, would provide a handsome accompaniment to an iron four-poster and complementary side tables. But if Eudora really wanted a change of wardrobe, I had several ideas in mind. "Why don't I work up a variety of plans for here and the sitting room," I suggested, "and get back in touch with you in about a week, or even next month, when Gladstone has had his surgery and you're feeling more on top of things?"

"That does sound the more sensible approach." My friend smiled at me with determined cheerfulness. "Now, why don't you go down and ask Gladstone to put the kettle on for a cup of tea." She laid the hairbrush she had been fiddling with back on the dressing table. "And tell him I'll join you both in a few moments."

"I really should be getting home."

"Don't leave without a cup of tea and a slice of the sponge cake Gladstone made this morning." Eudora walked with me out onto the landing. "I'll be down as soon as I've washed my face and dabbed a bit of powder around my eyes."

"Don't rush."

I gave her a hug before heading down the stairs. A glance at my watch as I stood on the fourth step from the bottom showed that the stupid thing had stopped at one-thirty. I was peering at the hall clock on the wall across from the banisters, when the telephone in the sitting room rang once. Before I could finish resetting my watch, I heard Gladstone Spike's voice. Through the open door it sounded a little breathless and high-pitched.

"Ah, lovely! Yours is the one voice I needed to hear! No one but you could possibly understand how much I want to be done with this business of being a woman in a man's body."

Good heavens! My hand went to my mouth, but otherwise I was immobilized. Even had I been able to get my legs going, I couldn't risk the stair creaking. And only think what agonies of embarrassment poor Gladstone would experience on realizing I had overheard his painful revelation!

"I've determined that I can't keep up the pretense any longer," he was now saying in a quavering voice. "But my dear wife is naturally very worried about how some of her congregation will react when I reveal that I am a woman. Eudora doesn't like the name Zinnia, too flowery for her, but I never could see myself as an Alice or a Ruth."

While Gladstone Spike listened to the response from the other end of the line, I quaked at the prospect of being caught eavesdropping on the stairs by Eudora heading down from the bathroom. The poor woman already had enough to bear, with her husband about to end his gender confusion by having a sex-change operation. She didn't need to discover I was a snoop. Upon hiring an interior decorator, it is always understood that cupboard doors would be opened and some embarrassing contents revealed. But the domestic chaos in this house should remain private for as long as possible. When the tabloids got hold of the scoop, I could only imagine the headlines: *Congre-*

gation Chattering in Chitterton Fells. The Vicar Is a Woman, Now So Is Her Husband!

My heart broke for both Eudora and Gladstone! What an agonizing situation in which to find themselves! No wonder she was entirely to pieces! I would have been a basket case if Ben had announced that he wanted to be Benita; but at the same time I wouldn't want him to live out his life in emotional torment, when a snip here and there could free him up to be the female of his fantasies.

And apparently Eudora did not plan on abandoning Gladstone. She had spoken about his moving into the guest bedroom, not out of the vicarage. I pictured them both in future years—him, or I should say, Zinnia, knitting a shell-pink bed jacket while Eudora sat on the other side of the fireplace, reading. No wonder St. Anselm's lady vicar had taken up romance novels as an outlet for her needs as a woman. . . .

Suddenly I heard something. A heart-stopping silence. Gladstone must be off the phone. Swiftly I got my legs in gear. I was making my way down the last couple of steps, when he came out into the hall.

Blushing all the way down to my toes, I gabbled that Eudora had sent me to tell him that she would be down in a moment for a cup of tea.

"Ah, lovely." Gladstone eyed me mildly. The man in the grey cardigan and carpet slippers, a husband in a thousand, one would have thought. And so I reflected sadly, as I envisioned the tabloids, indeed he was. "I just got off the phone with a friend of mine who also writes"—he was clearly making this up as he went along—"for his church bulletin."

"How very nice," I stammered, "for you to have someone with whom you can pour your heart out. Would you be awfully kind"—I edged towards the front door—"and explain to Eudora that I have to hurry home? I don't like to leave Gerta, our new nanny, for too long on her first day. She's already under a lot of stress because her marriage recently broke up. Her husband left her for another man."

The words were out before I could bite them back. Great! I thought savagely, now Gladstone will think I'm a narrow-minded busybody! Just the sort to start wagging my vicious tongue the minute he gets out of hospital after his operation.

"Life is not easy." He shook his head as he followed me to the door. "Eudora and I will remember these troubled people in our prayers."

"You are such a dear." Impulsively, I planted a kiss on his cheek before heading down the steps onto the garden path. I was wiping away a tear when he called out to me.

"Don't forget, Ellie"—he sounded much more cheery—"the Library League meeting tomorrow at one in the afternoon. It's important we all be there to begin making plans to raise money for Miss Bunch's memorial."

"I won't be late!" Waving an unsteady hand in farewell, I headed into the churchyard feeling as though I were in a fog, even though the mist had lifted. A superb human being, that was Gladstone Spike, whether man or woman. And I had learned my lesson. Any problems I had weren't worth thinking about, let alone mentioning. I would go home and read a fairy story to Abbey and Tam about people who live happily ever after. No, perhaps not, I decided as I went through the lichgate and out onto Cliff Road. Gerta might decide to sit in on the story-telling and be reminded that her Prince Charming had run off with Cinderfella. But, hopefully, one day Gerta, too, would be ready to believe in the miracle of second chances. And so perhaps would Eudora and Gladstone—or should I say Zinnia?

Remembering a novel I had read recently titled *Love Springs Eternal,* the walk home passed quickly. With a smile tacked on my face I crossed the moat bridge and went up the steps to the garden door.

Gerta was in the kitchen, which smelled comfortingly of ginger and cloves; and if that wasn't enough to lift my spirits, the twins were happily engaged in building a tower of marvelously abstract design on the rug in front of the Aga.

"Hello," I said brightly, and received a shock. The face Gerta turned to me was exceedingly bleak. Her cheeks had gone from plump to hollow, and her plaits swished ominously as she came towards me.

"Oh, dear!" I exclaimed, closing the door behind me before I could take the coward's way out and bolt back outside. "You're upset because I left the house without leaving you any instructions. It was thoughtless, I know, but Mrs. Malloy promised to explain that my husband and I were taking advantage of the wonderful luxury of having you here by going on a picnic. . . ." I faltered guiltily.

"Mrs. Mop went home two long hours ago." Gerta pointed at the clock as if expecting it to corroborate her words. "And I and the munchkins am all alone." She was now trembling so violently, she had to sit down in the rocking chair with a thump that almost sent her over backwards. "We are all alone in the study room where is the television, when we hear someone come in that way." She directed a finger in the general vicinity of the garden door. "I think it is you, Frau Haskell. And I say to the children—'Oopsy daisy! We go and tell Mumma what a happy time we have all together.' "

"Then what happened?" I stared in bafflement at the twins, and Abbey lifted her head of barley-sugar curls to say with suitable pathos, "Tam hitted me."

"Me didn't!" Her brother knocked over the wooden tower to emphasize his denial, and I had to scoop up my little girl before she ruined her organdy and pink ribbon image by bopping him over the head with a red block.

"I think Abbey is telling the fairy tale." Gerta was twisting her plaits into a rope under her chin, thus running great risk of choking herself.

"Who was it you heard coming into the house?" I demanded desperately. "Was it Mrs. Mop—I mean Mrs. Malloy—returning because she had forgotten her handbag?"

"No! When I go out into the hall I see this intruder in black trousers and the raincoat with the collar turned up to the chin and the hat with the lid pulled down over the eyes walking bold as brass lamps into the big sitting room. It is not your husband. I know Herr Haskell from his walk. This is a burglar, I understand that because my mind always works like *snap*!" Gerta demonstrated the quickness of her thinking with her finger and thumb. "I know even before I see him pick up the candlesticks on the mantel shelf and check for to see if they are silver."

"Good heavens!" I caught Abbey as she slid through my arms. "Whatever did you do?"

"I push the munchkins back in the study room and shut the door." Gerta had a little more colour in her cheeks as she warmed to her tale. "Then I tipsy-toe over to where the statue of St. Francis is on the shelf in the hall." Here she paused to cross herself. "Such a good saint he is; I know he will help save me from the wicked one, who still has the back to me."

"Go on!" I was beginning to feel numb, partly because Abbey was pinching my cheeks, and with my eyes watering it was difficult to keep Gerta's face in focus.

"I creep up behind the wicked one who would steal from my so-good employees. And I hit him bang on the head with St. Francis. To give myself strength I think about my husband and how I would like to kill him dead, with lots of blood and a smashed-up skull. And the burglar he fell without making a beep. With the face down on the floor."

"Tam hitted me." Abbey spoke with her rosebud lips pressed up against my nose, and I realized that she had heard Gerta's account before and had made up her own variation. With herself as the damsel in distress.

"You were incredibly brave, Gerta," I said. "What did the police say when they arrived?"

"What?" Our au pair looked at me blankly. "I did not telephone them! To do so would, I think, be making myself too much in charge. I close the door and push the big table from the hall in front of it. And since all this time I have not heard any sound from that room."

No, I thought, because in all probability the burglar had long since come round from that tap on the head with a plaster of Paris statue and had legged it out the window. Putting Abbey down on the floor, I determined that I would go outside and take a peek through the latticed panes so as to relieve Gerta's mind before I rang the constable. At that moment, however, the pounding started, setting the copper bowls clanging into each other on the iron rack suspended from the ceiling over the cooker. Abbey and Tam paid no attention, but Tobias Cat promptly shinned up the Welsh dresser, and Gerta cannoned into my arms. An outraged voice yelled with unladylike menace, "Ellie, I always suspected you *hated* me, but I never thought you would go to such lengths to make me feel unwelcome when I decided to honour you with a visit."

"The burglar?" Gerta staggered backwards.

"That's one name for her," I replied in hollow accents as I went out into the hall to open the lion's den. "There is only one woman in the world who would find it fashionably amusing to dress like a mobster, and who wouldn't hesitate to breeze into my house without so much as knocking and immediately check out the hallmark on my silver candlesticks. That woman is my cousin Vanessa."

Chapter

7

It is not a crime to forget someone's birthday, especially when the someone is yourself. When Ben walked into the kitchen the following morning, looking quite fetching in his charcoal grey suit, and said "Many happy returns, sweetheart," I thought for one harrowing moment that he was wishing upon me a series of repeat performances of Vanessa's arrival in our midst. It is hardly surprising that I was not thinking clearly.

On being freed from her imprisonment in our drawing room, my cousin had staged a dramatic and, admittedly, graceful swoon on the flagstones in the hall. Presumably fashion models, considering all the perils of tripping as they swan down the runway, are taught how to fall without injury. And I don't believe for an instant she added another bump to the one she already had on her head. Upon coming to, Vanessa demanded that Gerta be handed over to the authorities on a charge of assault and battery. She also suggested that I place the children in the nearest orphanage because their squealing was driving her right up the wall. Unfortunately it did not drive her out of the house.

It finally dawned on me that Ben was wishing me many happy returns of the anniversary of my birth, but it was difficult to bubble over with elation at being another year older when I thought of Vanessa snuggled up in the tower bedroom. My cousin was wearing my best green nightie with the sea-foam lace because, as she explained, she had left the London flat she shared with her mother in such haste that she had failed to bring so much as a toothbrush. Naturally, I had been loath to invite her ridicule by offering her one of my cotton nighties. Too domesticated for words, would have been her verdict. Vanessa had further managed to rattle my rib cage, before she finished the glass of brandy she had demanded to settle her nerves, by asking me if I had misplaced my eyelashes.

"God's in His heaven," Ben said after bestowing a birthday kiss on my lips, "and I suppose Vanessa is still in her bed."

"For the moment all is right with the world." I picked up the coffeepot and poured us each a cup. "One of my cousin's better points is that she and mornings have never hit it off. I expect that George Malloy will wake up one day and realize he hasn't seen his wife in daylight in thirty years. But I imagine that will be the least of his complaints."

"Don't you think you're being a little hard on her?" Ben raised an interrogative eyebrow as he took the cup and saucer I handed him. "I know Vanessa can be a witch, but maybe you should go easy on her, considering her mother threw a fit over the engagement and ordered her out of the flat."

I stirred my coffee vigorously enough to remove the pattern from the inside of the cup. "Next you'll be telling me that Vanessa came down to Merlin's Court because she has a burning desire to become pals with her future mother-in-law! Let me remind you"—I wagged my spoon at him—"that on Vanessa's last visit here she described Mrs. Malloy as having less breeding than a cart horse."

"Your cousin is a snob." Ben poured himself a refill. "But you have to admit she hasn't let her fiancé's lack of blue blood stop her from marrying him, despite her mother's objections. Sounds to me as if she may love the bloke. And she'll want to please him by making friends with Mrs. Malloy."

"I'll believe that," I said nastily, "when I wear a smaller size frock than Vanessa."

"Let's forget about her for now." Ben glanced at the wall clock whose hands were moving relentlessly towards seven-thirty, the time he usually left for the restaurant. "Gerta will be bringing the twins downstairs soon, so why don't we treasure these few moments alone?" He set his cup in the sink before crossing to the alcove by the garden door and coming back to me with a festively wrapped box that was too big to contain a piece of jewelry other than a crown. "I'll put this on the table and when I say ready, steady, go, you can start tearing off the paper."

"Why, thank you, darling." I gave him a kiss before setting to work with my bare hands. Scissors never stepped forward to offer their services in our house. "This is wonderful. Exactly what I wanted!"

"I thought you'd be pleased." Ben turned my present at a better angle so that the sunlight could highlight its mechanical perfections. I was now the proud owner of a cappuccino machine. "You'll see that it comes not only with a booklet of instructions but a videotape titled *Introduction to Cappuccino Making*."

"Do I also have to take evening classes?" I asked in an attempt to make light of the mounting intimidation I experienced when confronted by the battery of buttons and the handle which, in all likelihood, would send the machine into orbit if turned the wrong way.

"It really is child's play to operate." Ben stroked my hair fondly but fortunately did not kiss me, or he might have realized my lips were trembling. For me, plugging in the Hoover has always been a life-threatening procedure. And I never touch a lightbulb with the naked hand even when it is still in its box.

"This part looks easy." I studied the two cappuccino cups and saucers that came as part of the package.

"Think of our future evenings together." Fortunately Ben noticed only that the clock said seven-thirty and lifted his jacket from the back of a chair. "First the delicious foreplay of grinding the beans and savouring the intoxicating aroma. Then the two of us sitting together after dinner, sipping our cappuccino and foaming at the lips if the telephone should ring and destroy the magic moment."

"I can't wait." I followed him to the door. "Thank you, darling, for a wonderful present."

"Oh, one more thing, Ellie—" He turned to me, apparently struck by a brilliant idea. "Why don't you come down to Abigail's at six this evening and we'll have dinner? I'd take you somewhere else, but I can't think of a place"—he quirked a mocking eyebrow—"where the food is half as good as mine."

"That sounds nice." I picked a piece of thread off the shoulder of his jacket. "But wouldn't it be better to eat at home with the twins? You could bring something from the restaurant to make it a special treat."

"We'll get home early and have cake with Abbey and Tam." Ben was heading down the steps as he spoke. "You have to go down to Chitterton Fells to the library meeting, so why not make an afternoon of it—go shopping and then meet me at Abigail's? The reason we have Gerta is to make it easier for you to get out of the house."

"I'll be there, darling!" I said, and, after closing the door on his retreating back, gathered up the cappuccino box and the wrapping paper and put them in the tidy bin. A fancy lace-trimmed nightie and matching peignoir, to replace the ones I would be lucky to get back from Vanessa, would have been easy to operate. But all gifts can't be romantic, I reminded myself as I began getting the twins' breakfast ready.

The reason I hadn't wanted to leave Abbey and Tam for the evening was that with Gerta assuming the responsibility of getting them up and dressed in the mornings, I was beginning to feel I was missing out on huge chunks of their day, including my role as keeper of the twins' bath. Would Gerta understand the importance to Tam of sitting at the tap end? And would Abbey hesitate to explain that the rubber duck got a dusting with baby powder after being dried with the towel?

Part of my problem, I reflected as I stirred the orange juice I had taken from the fridge, was that as of yet I had only two clients interested in my services as an interior decorator. Or could it be that I liked being a full-time, hands-on mum, one who really didn't relish someone else taking a prominent role in raising my children? I certainly wasn't worried about Gerta's competence because she had mistaken Vanessa for a burglar and in the upset of that moment pictured herself caving in her husband's head with the statue of St. Francis.

Lots of perfectly nice women fantasize about murdering their errant spouses, and no one could have looked less homicidal than Gerta when she now appeared in the kitchen, still wearing her alpine outfit, with Abbey and Tam toddling in her wake. I had offered to lend her some clothes, but she'd told me there was no need. She had washed her undies in the bathroom basin and dried them with the hair dryer.

"Please, Gerta," I told her now, "make as much use as you wish of the washing machine and tumble dryer. Ben and I want you to treat this as your home."

"You are good, Frau Haskell. It is the wonder you don't throw me out the house on both ears because of the mistake I make with your beautiful cousin."

"She should have knocked instead of walking into the house and scaring you out of your wits." I did not add that I myself had often wished to give Vanessa a conk on the head. My heart was full, along with my arms, when Abbey and Tam rushed up to me as if I were their long-lost mother. "You deserve a bonus, Gerta, for risking your life to protect the children. And I'm going to write you a cheque so that you can go shopping for a change of clothes."

"No, Frau Haskell!" A tear slid down her plump cheek and she dabbed it away with the back of her hand. "I don't deserve for you to be so good to me."

"Now, don't argue." I sat and lifted first Tam, then Abbey onto my lap. "Why not go into Chitterton Fells this morning and rig yourself up? I won't have to leave for my meeting at the library until around twelve-thirty."

"My husband can send my clothes," she sniffed, "if he is not too busy making the kissy-face with the new love of his life, Mr. Meyers."

"In the meantime"—I smiled at her—"you are to go shopping. There is a bus stop a few yards from St. Anselm's Church." For a moment I thought I had put her off by bringing back memories of her first night here, when she had seen the spectral figure of the Virgin Bride in the churchyard and had been chased by the black dog to the front door of Merlin's Court. But it appeared that Gerta had either blocked out the memory or that a bright blue sky made for a daylight world in which further meetings with evil incarnate seemed unlikely.

Mr. Babcock had deposited the usual six pints of milk before I came downstairs, so I was still left guessing as to how his new bride had reacted to the arrival of Heathcliff. While Gerta and I were getting the twins into their booster seats at the table, I wondered whether I should take the Babcocks' wedding present with me this afternoon and give it to Sylvia at the meeting, but decided it would be more appropriate to take it to their house tomorrow. She had been pressing me to stop by for a cup of tea, but until now it had been difficult on account of the twins. Sylvia, who was afraid of the air she breathed, might have leapt onto a chair and screamed bloody murder if she saw a child in her front room.

The morning passed at a happily plodding pace, with Abbey and Tam playing peaceably with their toys and Gerta insisting she would not leave until she had helped me tidy up, this not being one of the days when Mrs. Malloy came to rule the roost with her iron mop. But when ten-thirty rolled around, Gerta admitted she would need to catch the next bus into the village if she were to have enough time to buy a deodorant at Boots, let alone anything else, and be back in time for me to keep my appointment at the library.

Just as the hall clock began to strike eleven, in came Vanessa looking like the goddess of spring in my sea-green peignoir set. My cousin has always been one of those horrid females who, although half-dead from getting only ten or eleven hours' sleep, manages to look utterly ravishing. It's the fault of all that titian hair, the creamy skin—with the blush of rose on the perfect cheekbones—and those marvelous sherry-coloured eyes that look all the more sultry when smudged with sleep.

"For pity's sake, Ellie." She pressed her pearl-pink fingertips to her forehead. "Can't you shut up that blasted clock? I'm too exhausted to have a headache this early in the morning."

"Here, have a cup of tea." I stepped around Abbey and Tam to hand her the one I had been about to drink. "It's not quite time for anything stronger."

"Such as poison?" My cousin smiled sweetly at me as she trailed, in drifts of green gauze and lace, to sink gracefully onto a chair. "Yes, darling, I can read you like a book. The sort with the foot-high letters that little what's-his-name is looking at." She pointed gingerly at Tam, as if afraid he would leap up from the floor and bite off her finger. "I know you positively loathe having me here, disrupting all this charming domesticity. *My God!* What is that nasty-looking contraption? Some new gadget to let you take your own blood pressure if you get a bit worked up when you're making jam and it won't jell?"

"It's a coffeepot," I said frigidly.

"And I suppose darling Bentley gave it to you for your birthday or for some equally special reason." Vanessa turned her chair away from Abbey, who stood staring at her with blue eyes wide in her cherub face. "I don't blame you, Ellie—really I don't, for wishing I were anywhere but here. I actually feel guilty because that army tank of a woman didn't finish me off! You've always been just the teensy-weeniest bit jealous of me, and who can blame you?" She smoothed the lace at her peerless throat. "And I suppose at times I have rubbed it in a bit that I got *all* the looks in the family. But," she added kindly, "I have always admitted that you have the nicer nature."

"Thank you!"

"And that is why, darling, when Mummy threw the most awful fit about my marrying George Malloy, screaming herself into hysterics and turning violet, I thought okay, I will go down to Merlin's Court. Ellie will forget the past when she learns that my one remaining parent has cast me off. Ellie will take me to her matronly bosom. And I will know that I am not without a family."

"You have George," I reminded her.

"Yes, and see how he adores me!" Vanessa held out her left hand to dazzle me again with the brilliance of her obscenely sized diamond solitaire. "Big as some mirrors, isn't it?"

"You can use it for touching up your makeup," I said with my eyes on Abbey, who was still standing immobile, a scant six inches from my cousin.

"Did God turn that child into a pillar of salt"—Vanessa drew in her shoulders—"or did she come that way?"

"Pretty lady." Abbey took an entranced step closer and placed a chubby hand on my cousin's gauzy knee. "Is you a fairy?"

"Oh, my goodness!" Vanessa amazed me by reaching out her arms and gathering my daughter onto her lap. And when she looked at me, her eyes were made the more lustrous by the shine of tears. "What a precious, priceless little creature! Why didn't I realize before that she looks like me? When I was a child, my hair was just this shade of gold as little Ashley's. Or is it Allison? Whatever! She most definitely has my divine nose!"

Tam, determined not to stand in his sister's limelight, immediately dropped his picture book with a plop and raced over to Vanessa, crying "Me loves you too!"

"Dear, intelligent little boy!" Vanessa sat with chiffon arms wrapped around my children. "Oh, I was right to come where I can recover from the turmoil of Mummy's tirade."

"And get to know Mrs. Malloy." I tried not to look at my offspring as if they were a pair of turncoats.

"Oh, yes! My future mother-in-law!" Vanessa kissed the tops of the twins' heads. "But there doesn't have to be any rush. I'm sure I'll see her when she comes here to clean, and we're bound to have a little chat, especially if she starts vacuuming outside my bedroom door at some ungodly hour. I'm certain she's a lovely woman, just thrilled out of her simple wits to know that her son is going to marry"—Vanessa tapped Abbey coyly on the cheek—"a fairy princess."

This called for a strong cup of tea. Pouring myself one, I banished the evil thought that my cousin might no longer be getting the plum modeling jobs, making marriage an excellent career move. "You must be very much in love with George Malloy," I ventured kindly.

"Darling, you're such a romantic! I'm enormously fond of him. He's well-off and really quite presentable. I like being with him. We have good times. And he came along in the nick of . . . I mean at the right time. But as for my being madly, agonizingly nuts about George Malloy, good heavens no! And don't look at me like that, Ellie. I wouldn't be doing the man any favours by being all goo-

goo-eyed in love with him. That sort of full-blown emotion can't ever last. Not if you intend to stay married."

"You're wrong." I took a sip of tea, but it was so stewed, I couldn't take the bitter taste and poured it down the sink.

"Look at you and Ben." Vanessa spoke over the top of Tam's dark head as he stood on her knee to kiss her damask cheek. "He has to be one of the handsomest, sexiest men alive, but are you floating around in a state of permanent rapture, counting every moment lost that you cannot be in his arms? No! Your mind is mostly on higher things, like being the perfect mummy to these adorable kiddies and keeping the wheels of dull domesticity turning. And that's just as well, Ellie, because one day Ben will be old and grey and it will be hard for you to remember what there ever was about him to set your pulses racing."

"Thanks for the warning," I said.

"Don't mention it." Vanessa, looking like the Madonna with an extra child, smiled angelically. "With dear George I'm not setting myself up to wish him underground when he gets the gout and can't get up the stairs without puffing. I realize that romantic love should be reserved for the men one has loved in days of moonlight and roses. 'Age shall not weary them, nor the years condemn,' or whatever the mournful saying is! The men we once thought we couldn't live without remain enshrined in our hearts, never growing a day older or steadily more tiresome when they can't remember where they put their dentures."

"Well"—I held my empty teacup aloft—"here's hoping you and George will be very happy in your own special way. When may I hope to meet your fiancé?"

"Goodness only knows, darling!" Vanessa put the twins down on the floor, stood up, and stretched her arms in lovely languor. "I telephoned Georgie Porgie last night and he felt quite wretched about Mummy being so beastly, but he can't come rushing down here today because he's up to his eyes with work at his factory."

"And what is it he manufactures?"

"Exercise machines. That's how I met him."

"You collided with him on your stationary bike?"

"George needed a model for his advertising campaign." Vanessa studied a fingernail that would appear to have disgraced itself by acquiring a chip in its pearl-pink varnish. "I applied for and got the job. Simple as that."

"It certainly beats working for *Vogue*," I replied with my eyes on the clock. It was almost time for me to get the twins' lunches prepared, after which I would have quite a rush getting myself ready to go to the library meeting. It wouldn't do to keep Brigadier Lester-Smith and the rest of the league members drumming their pencils on the table. We would need every ounce of available brain power to come up with a means of raising the necessary for Miss Bunch's memorial.

"It suddenly strikes me, Ellie"—Vanessa drifted about the room with the twins each holding up their end of her peignoir train—"something, or, I should say, *someone* is missing in this house."

"Gerta went shopping for some odds and ends."

"I wasn't thinking about her." My cousin pressed a hand to the back of her head, where no doubt the bump she had received from her assailant still lingered. "What's lacking is that old curmudgeon—Judas the gardener."

"Jonas is off on a camping trip with Freddy."

"Our cousin with the ponytail and the tattoo and the skull-and-crossbones earring?" Vanessa swayed artistically. "Would you believe I get amnesia where he is concerned."

"He remembers you." I took another look at the clock that appeared to be chasing its tail in ever faster circles. "When Freddy telephoned last night and I told him you were here, he promised that he and Jonas would forget about their nettle rash and lie low in the woods for a while."

"How sweet, considering I may be here for *ages*!" Vanessa swung around to face me, with the result that Abbey and Tam released her skirts and sat smack down on the floor. "I've been thinking that it would work out perfectly for me to be married at St. Anselm's."

"Really?" I almost landed on the floor beside the twins.

"Ellie, I don't have a church of my own, so why shouldn't I borrow yours for the day?" She might have been talking about the nightie she was wearing. "It would put Mummy's nose out of joint. We would have the reception here at Merlin's Court, with Ben doing the catering, and Gerta, the human hand grenade, getting stuck with all the washing up. What could be more heavenly than me in miles and miles of white satin and French lace, sweeping down the stairs of the ancestral home? A vision of misty-eyed beauty to be witnessed only once in a dozen lifetimes."

With a bedazzled Abbey and Tam clapping their hands in time to the wedding march playing inside their heads, it was perhaps unnoticeable that I was not one hundred percent enthusiastic. "There is one thing you need to know, Vanessa. St. Anselm's Church has rather an unhappy history in the nuptials department."

"Because you and Ben were married there?"

"Because of the Virgin Bride, and the wedding that didn't take place some sixty years ago. The story is that the groom forgot to show up or was unavoidably detained. And his lovelorn lady went off her rocker as a result. She's still alive, in her eighties, and has been spotted on numerous occasions after dusk. Only the other night Gerta saw her keeping her doleful vigil."

Setting a saucepan of Gerta's stew down on the Aga, I hoped I had convinced Vanessa that the Virgin Bride's bitter unhappiness was bound to have permeated every inch of St. Anselm's Church and cursed the once-hallowed ground on which it stood. Meaning my cousin would rather die than be married within two hundred miles of the site lest she meet with some awful fate in the years to come—my eyes went to the cappuccino machine—such as receiving a coffeepot from George on her birthday.

"You've just proved the point of what I was saying earlier," Vanessa said without a tremble in her voice. "It's a thousand times easier to remain madly in love, even into one's dotage, with a man who fails to show up at the altar than it is to experience enduring passion for a husband with whom one lives alongside year in and year out in various stages of physical and emotional disintegration. Thanks for the warning, darling Ellie, but I think I'll ring up the vicar this afternoon and discuss suitable dates for my wedding to George Malloy."

Was there no escape from the grisly prospect of being

saddled with the job of attending Vanessa at every fitting for her bridal gown, and having to watch the dressmaker swallow a mouthful of pins upon realizing she was beholding the stuff of legends? An eighteen-inch waist. It did cross my mind to tell my cousin that Eudora Spike was in the midst of a crisis in her own marriage and might not be in the mood to talk with any great enthusiasm about the blessed state of matrimony. But as I vigorously stirred the stew to keep it from scorching on the bottom, I couldn't bring myself to betray a single word of what I had discovered regarding Gladstone Spike's impending sex-change operation. It would be bad enough when the time came for people like Vanessa to make vulgar jokes about his having a coming-out ball . . . now that he didn't have the ones he received at birth.

"Ellie, you're standing too close to the cooker, your face looks like it's on fire," my cousin kindly informed me. "Thank God, George understands that buttering a piece of toast is all the cooking I'm prepared to do when we are married. And how I wish Mummy would be happy that he's got pots of money and would overlook the fact that he earned every penny without even the saving grace of a proper education."

Knowing Aunt Astrid, a woman composed of whalebone corsets and an iron tongue, I had little hope of her ever having an egalitarian conversion and every fear she might even now be issuing a royal summons for a taxi, intent upon making a matriarchal raid on Merlin's Court. Had I believed for a minute that Aunt A. would succeed in whisking Vanessa away to be deprogrammed by a pioneer in the field of class-defection disorders, I would have welcomed the old battle-axe with open arms. But I knew my cousin well enough to realize she would not be budged an inch were she truly hell-bent on marrying George Malloy.

Vanessa went out into the hall with the avowed intention of gazing soulfully at the staircase which one day soon she would descend in all her bridal glory. While preventing the twins from trotting after her, at the risk of missing their lunch, I reflected that it was typical of my cousin to have failed to wish me happy birthday. Admittedly she had a lot on her mind, but I knew that the date was engraved on her mind because it was the one on which she had first appeared in *Beauty Magazine*. What did surprise me was that Mrs. Malloy had not rung me up to sing "Happy Birthday to You" in a voice guaranteed to make a songbird cringe. Was she in a snit because she had heard from George that her future daughter-in-law was at Merlin's Court and the carriage had not been sent round to convey her here with all pomp and circumstance?

I felt guilty over this neglect as I got Abbey and Tam into their booster seats. And resentful in knowing that Vanessa was unlikely to lift a finger that afternoon to phone Mrs. Malloy. But I didn't have time to wallow, because Gerta came in through the kitchen door, her salt-and-pepper plaits uncoiled in her haste and a carrier bag from Marks & Spencer in her hand.

"I am late, Frau Haskell?"

"No, you're back at exactly the right moment," I assured her. "I hope you had a successful shopping spree."

"Yes! But I am careful in what I buy." She took off her coat. "From now on, with no husband anywhere I look, I have to keep the werewolf from the door."

"If you'll give the twins their stew, and some fruit to follow, I'll go and get ready for my meeting." Handing her the serving spoon, I hurried upstairs and saw Vanessa flit into the bathroom in a silken drift of sea green. She would spend an hour making up her face, which didn't require any improvement to be a work of art, while I needed to scrap everything I owned in the way of body parts and would have to make do with putting on my turquoise frock that looked as if it expected to be taken out to dinner and twisting my hair into a French pleat.

There was, through no one's fault but my own, not a spare minute to pinch a little colour into my cheeks. But I did remember to put two notepads into my handbag. One for the Library League meeting, and the other to be used for recording measurements and creative inspirations when I went to look at the house Brigadier Lester-Smith had inherited.

The day was blue but decidedly chilly. Even so, I kept the car window down as I drove down Cliff Road and into the village. I was hoping that a good dose of fresh air would unclog my brain, thus enabling me to come up with some terrific idea for a fund-raising event that would en-able the league to commission a bronze statue worthy of the woman who had given her life to the Chitterton Fells library. I hadn't thought of anything beyond the ubiquitous raffle when I parked the car—illegally—in the alley to the rear of the library.

I went in through the back door marked Employees Only, which entered onto the narrow hall with the toilet on one side and the stairs leading up to the reading room on the other. A glance at my watch as I took two steps at a time showed me I was one minute late.

"Sorry," I panted to Brigadier Lester-Smith, who held the door open for me, "I hope I didn't keep the coffee . . . I mean everyone waiting."

They were all there. Gladstone Spike sat at the table with his knitting in his hands. The new bride, Sylvia Babcock, had every pin curl in place. Mrs. Dovedale handed around a plate of sponge cake. Mr. Poucher looked his usual disgruntled self. Sir Robert Pomeroy was saying "What! what!" in response to something someone had said, or just because he felt like it. And my friend Bunty Wiseman, the blond bombshell, looked wickedly sexy in earrings that were longer than her black leather miniskirt. She whipped over to me on heels that were almost as high as Mrs. Malloy's, and dragged me into the room.

"Ellie, you have to help me convince some of these fuddy-duddies that my idea for a fund-raiser is *brilliant* beyond belief!" Bunty had grabbed hold of me and I was afraid to speak for fear she would hug me tighter and I would become impaled on one of her dangerously pointed breasts. "Maybe I'm dreaming the impossible dream but I have this feeling that if we asked nicely, he would come!"

"Who?" I gasped, looking around at the other members of the league in hopes of enlightenment.

"Karisma!" Bunty breathed triumphantly.

Chapter

8

My fantasy life was on a collision course with reality! I didn't know whether to burst into song, the way people do at the slightest provocation in musicals, or to tell Bunty she had another think coming if she imagined I would risk going into a lifelong trance as the result of being in the same room as Karisma. But surely I was getting all worked up over nothing! The king of the cover models must be booked from now until doomsday with public appearances. He undoubtedly had a business manager who monitored every invitation he received to breathe in public. And why would Karisma want to come to Chitterton Fells? We were charming enough in a chocolate-box sort of way, but so were hundreds of other villages.

No wonder my thoughts were in a whirl! Bunty was waltzing me in ever faster circles, as if we were Ginger Rogers and Fred Astaire. "You do think it's a knock-dead idea?" she demanded, and released me with a final spin that sent me into Brigadier Lester-Smith's arms. "When I saw Karisma interviewed on the telly yesterday morning, I decided I'd gladly go without sex for the rest of my wicked life in exchange"—orgasmic sigh—"for being able to touch the hem of that God-like man's trousers!"

"Most intriguing." Brigadier Lester-Smith let go of me before his blush finished burning a hole in my back.

"And then"—Bunty blew him a kiss—"you telephoned, Brigadier, and told me about how you thought it would be nice for the Library League to put up a statue of Miss Bunch, and really I'd have been a complete idiot *not* to have thought of Karisma as the perfect way to raise the lolly!" Her smile included the others, who were hovering around like extras in a movie, eager to be directed in their minuscule roles. "Is there anyone here who wouldn't pay up like a shot for the once-in-a-lifetime chance of spending five seconds in Karisma's heavenly arms?"

Gladstone Spike stopped knitting and looked thoughtful, but Sir Robert said, "Can't say as I would, what! what! But I do see your point, my dear young lady. Even an old codger like me has heard about Karisma. The streets will be standing-room-only with panting women if we can bring the chap here to Chitterton Fells. M'daughter-in-law, Pamela, is always mooning on about him, as if she didn't have a husband who, if he's a chip off the old block"—Sir Robert gave a jocular laugh—"is quite the lady's man."

Mrs. Dovedale, whom I suspected of having a crush on the recently widowed baronet, twinkled at him. "The trouble is that I don't see what on earth would make this young man, who's riding a wave of amazing public adulation, agree to come to our little library."

"I don't rightly know why I come here." Mr. Poucher, a man as grey and glum as a fog on the Yorkshire moors, gave a disgusted snort. "And I don't know why we need to put up a statue of Old Bunch. Bloomin' daft, that's what I call it."

Bunty ignored this. "I say Karisma will jump at the chance to help us out with our fund-raiser." Her baby-blue eyes dancing, she placed her hands on her black leather hips and wiggled provocatively.

Gladstone Spike dropped a stitch. "Why?"

"Because, you dear little man"—Bunty stretched her pause into a sunbeam smile—"of the *library ghost*!"

Sylvia Babcock gave a nervous start as if the icy hand of Hector Rigglesworth had descended on her shoulder. "Oh, but do you think Karisma, who has fought all those duels and gone over white-water rapids on a banana skin, would believe in ghosts?"

"It would not make him less a man, Mrs. Babcock, if he were to concede the possibility of the impossible." Brigadier Lester-Smith looked at me from under his gingery eyebrows; the healthy pink had faded from his cheeks. I knew he was remembering the two of us standing over Miss Bunch's body, while something that might—or might not—have been the wind whooped with ghoulish glee at the library window. Yes, Brigadier! We both believed in the darkest corners of our minds that Miss Bunch had died of unnatural causes. I could not forget the book we had found lying on the floor beside her body. And, given the ominous significance of its title, could I in all good conscience wish for Karisma, the embodiment of the Dream Lover, to set one manly foot within the Chitterton Fells library?

Mrs. Dovedale pulled out a chair and sat down at the long table next to Gladstone Spike, who was concentrating on picking up his dropped stitch. "I do think we have a drawing card. It's a long shot, I'll admit, but Karisma's publicity people might just think it a bit of a lark to have him visit a library that was cursed one hundred years ago this month by the Man Who Hated Romantic Novels."

"You really are giving me the shivers." Sylvia Babcock looked ready to leap into Mr. Poucher's arms, and he responded with a grunt that expressed what he thought of Mrs. Dovedale's idea. I was about to say that it would be wrong to risk subjecting Karisma to the wrath of a ghost who clearly needed to talk to a psychiatrist about his irrational obsession, when Gladstone Spike put down his knitting.

"My dear friends." He began, sounding rather like his wife speaking from the pulpit. His voice escalated to a high note that caused me to wonder if the hormones he was taking in preparation for his sex-change operation had suddenly kicked in. "Do we wish to pander to the primitive superstitions, to which even the most God-fearing are sometimes prey? It is my opinion"—he picked up his knitting again—"that inviting this man, lovely as I am sure he is, would be a grave mistake."

"Tommyrot!" Sir Robert blew out his lips so that his moustache touched his nose, and thumped one fist on top of the other. "Don't believe in ghosts! No one with a brain between the ears could believe in such rubbishing nonsense. There's always been talk of a ghost at Pomeroy Manor—goes by the name of the Wailing Woman, or the Woman in White, never could remember! Houses are supposed to be haunted. Gives them a bit of the old snob appeal. Same as a maze on the grounds, only better, because you don't have all the ruddy upkeep. I say let's milk the legend of Hector Rigglesworth for all its spectator—or, if you like, *specter*—value. We need to raise the money for the memorial, and this Karisma chap will get some very nice publicity."

"Well said, Sir Robert!" Mrs. Dovedale, the woman who ran the corner grocery shop, blushed a smile at him and he, the peer of the realm, responded with a gallant bow. They had known each other from the days when they were children. Mrs. D. had told me once that he had quite often come into the shop, when her father stood behind the counter, to buy a paper cone of sweets in the holidays when he was home from boarding school. And she had thought him as splendid and unreachable as the tins of biscuits on the topmost shelf. Looking at him now, I wondered if Sir Robert had ever felt a youthful interest in the pretty girl Mrs. Dovedale must once have been. Had he wished that the difference in their stations in life did not prohibit the blossoming of a love that would lend a rainbow radiance to their entire lives?

"What do you think, Ellie?" asked Bunty.

"About Karisma?" I blinked to bring the room back into focus. "I believe we should put the matter up for vote."

"An entirely proper approach, Mrs. Haskell," agreed Brigadier Lester-Smith. He was invariably at his crispest when the world was restored to the sanity of bylaws and the amendments thereof. He moved to the head of the table, where his highly polished briefcase awaited him. "If I may suggest that we all be seated, I will read the minutes of the last meeting, and if they are accepted as read, ask for a motion from the floor."

"There are no minutes from the last meeting." Bunty plopped impatiently down in her chair. "Miss Bunch croaking put the kibosh on our fun and games."

"I meant the meeting *prior* to that unhappy evening."

The brigadier snapped open his briefcase with the sound of a gunshot, causing Sylvia Babcock to cringe as she subsided into her chair. How, I wondered, avoiding her eye, was she coping with Heathcliff, the bête noire?

"Forget the rubbishing minutes!" Sir Robert took his seat across from me. "I say, let's get on to the business at hand, what! what!"

"I make a motion"—Mrs. Dovedale leaned her bosom, possibly unintentionally, towards him—"that the Chitterton Fells Library League invite Karisma to attend, in a fund-raising capacity, the memorial benefit for Miss Bunch."

"And I second the motion," groused Mr. Poucher, "so we can take a vote and I can head back to the farm and milk the cow before my aged mother turns blue at having to drink her tea black."

Brigadier Lester-Smith picked up a sharply pointed pencil with which to record the outcome. "May I please have a show of hands from all those in favour?"

"I'm not sure how to vote." Sylvia Babcock inched up a finger to indicate her indecision. "I've got to say I'd like to meet Karisma, but I hate crowds, they scare me to pieces."

"What doesn't scare the living daylights out of you?" Mr. Poucher, along with everyone at the table excepting Gladstone Spike and myself, had his hand in the "aye" position. And I could feel an irresistible tingling of the fingers. What Sir Robert had said about ghosts had struck home. I was one of those susceptible human beings who did not so much believe, as like to pretend they believed, in the terrors of the supernatural because it added a bit of spice to life. Without the possibility of unearthly intervention by Hector Rigglesworth, my having been present at the death of Miss Bunch would have lacked the mystique with which I had subsequently endowed that sad event. Everyone loves a ghost story, and I, with Brigadier Lester-Smith, had succumbed to the temptation to figure in the saga of the library ghost. It wasn't a crime to want to make myself feel important in the local scheme of things. Any more than it was a crime that no one had sung "Happy Birthday" when I came into the reading room this afternoon, even though such events were recorded on the league calendar. Trying not to feel peevish, I studied the brigadier's upraised hand.

"I vote yes," I said impulsively through a dizzying haze of excitement at the prospect of meeting in the not-too-distant, radiantly rosy future, the man who was every woman's fantasy come to life. For I knew he would come. His acceptance of our invitation was written in the stars that shone in my eyes. Karisma would ride into my life in a snow-white limousine, trailing clouds of glory. His tousled mane of hair would highlight his noble cheekbones. His achingly kissable mouth would ease into a smile that would light up his fine eyes when he caught his first glimpse of me standing modestly in the background, my hair escaping from its chignon to frame a face made instantly beautiful. "My angel," he would whisper, the words wrenched from the very depths of his being, "where have you been all my life?"

"The motion is carried on the basis that we have only one dissenter." Brigadier Lester-Smith looked disappointedly down the table at Gladstone Spike, who had not ceased clicking away with his needles during the vote.

"I understand, old girl—" Sir Robert hastily corrected himself. "I mean, old chap! Being married to a clergywoman, you probably don't think much of Karisma or the penny-dreadful love stories for which he struts his stuff. Pretty torrid reading some of them, what! what! Picked up one the other day that m'daughter-in-law had her nose in all evening. By some woman called Parrish, if I remember rightly, with a fa-de-da first name such as Dahlia or the like. But I don't suppose names like Doris or Dorothy sell those kind of books! The one I thumbed through, just to see what had Pamela all fired up, was steamy enough to make m'moustache curl! The Count of God-Knows-Where was doing things to his lady love under the silk sheets that I prefer not discuss in mixed company."

Mrs. Dovedale shook her head and attempted to look shocked. "They are not all like that, truly, Sir Robert. The Regency romances I read are always about young ladies of quality who are pitifully unprepared for the revelations of the wedding night and often flee in terror when the groom presents them with something other than a rose."

Brigadier Lester-Smith, the perennial bachelor, blushed to the roots of his greying ginger hair; and Gladstone Spike finally spoke. "It is lovely of you"—here he smiled at Sir Robert and Mrs. Dovedale—"to be concerned about my feelings. But it is not a distaste for these novels that makes it impossible for me to vote along with the rest of you. There are personal reasons for my decision. May we leave it at that?" His face had turned decidedly pale and his fingers shook as he returned to his knitting. Of course Gladstone did not want to find himself caught up in an event that would bring swarms of reporters and cameramen to Chitterton Fells within weeks, or days, of his returning from hospital a new woman. But, sadly, there were other interests than his at stake. The Chitterton Fells Library League had voiced almost unanimously their desire to take extraordinary steps to honour the deserving Miss Bunch with a statue that would take Nelson down a peg on his column.

"And now"—Bunty Wiseman, who had been basking in the success of her Brilliant Suggestion, leapt up on her high heels—"why don't we have Ellie take the bull by the horns and telephone Karisma's publicity people and make all the arrangements?"

I gaped at her. "You don't mean *now*?"

"No time like the present, what! what!" Sir Robert came round to clap me on the back, almost sending my chair under the table.

"But why *me*?"

"You're the league secretary," said Mr. Poucher. "Stands to reason you get the dirty job of grovelling on the phone."

"But"—I was turning alternately hot and cold—"I wouldn't have a clue how to get hold of the number. . . ."

"Then I must be lots smarter than you." Bunty grinned impishly at me. "Because I already have it. This morning I rang up several of the publishers that put out books with Karisma on the cover. And finally a nice woman decided to do her good deed for the day and gave me the number."

"Congratulations," I stammered. "But honestly, Bunty, I don't think I could make the call without fainting!

What if Karisma happened to be in the office and answered the phone *himself*? No, really"—I looked imploringly at the rest of the league—"I can't do it."

"Then I'll pretend I'm you." Bunty clattered over to the desk by the window and picked up the phone. "Saying I'm Mrs. Bentley Haskell of Merlin's Court will have a lot more clout than if I ring up as myself."

"Such misrepresentation could be in violation of the bylaws." Brigadier Lester-Smith took the charter from his briefcase and began flipping pages with such zeal that the sound became a roar inside my head. Mr. Poucher began grumbling about his cows and his mother. Sylvia Babcock knocked over her coffee cup, and Gladstone Spike was knitting very loudly. Bunty gave the okay sign by circling her finger and thumb, indicating that someone had answered on the other end of the line. But I couldn't hear anything more than the words *"Chitterton Fells library . . . would be extremely honoured by . . . humanitarian gesture."*

After what seemed an eternity, Bunty put down the receiver. She turned to face us with a stunned look on her face.

"Well?" Several voices spoke as one.

"Karisma . . ."

"Yes?" I dragged myself out of my chair and took a couple of steps forward. Bunty looked as if she would crumple into a heap on the floor if anyone breathed on her.

"He won't be coming to Chitterton Fells." Her voice cracked. "The woman I spoke to was very polite, but she said Karisma is fully booked for publicity purposes at this time. I tried my spiel about the library ghost, but it was obvious she wasn't interested. Well, pals, so much for my brilliant idea!" I'd never seen Bunty look so heartbroken.

The only one who could get his tongue round his voice at this tragic moment was Gladstone Spike. Wrapping his knitting around the needles, he said, "I hope, Mrs. Wiseman, that you will believe I speak with all sincerity when saying how sorry I am for your disappointment. But sometimes life does know best. . . ."

"If your sermon's over," Mr. Poucher interrupted nastily, "I say we adjourn this meeting. It's coming on for three o'clock and I'm not in the mood to talk about crocheting pot holders or to listen to the half-baked ideas the lot of you now think would be a way of raising the necessary for Miss Bunch."

"I regret that I may have raised false hopes." The brigadier hastily turned the break in his voice into a cough. "The words of a former teacher of mine come back to me at this moment. Miss Woodcock told our class: 'Aim for the sky and you will reach the top of the oak tree, aim for the top of the oak tree and you will grovel on the ground.' We"—he looked about the room with watery eyes— "aimed for the sky in our hopes of seeing the woman who did battle in the trenches of the card catalogue system cast in bronze, but we are left grovelling on the ground." The loud snapping sound made when he closed his briefcase echoed with a lamentable finality. Bunty Wiseman excused herself on a sob, to skitter from the room.

"We can raise the money somehow." But Sylvia Babcock spoke without much hope.

"And I'm the King of Siam!" Mr. Poucher thumped his grubby old hat on his head and plodded through the gloom he helped spread around like manure to the door.

"No use shirking facts: A statue would cost a packet." Sir Robert stroked his moustache in the hope, I imagine, that the gesture made him look like an elder statesman. "As I understand it, we have five pounds and fourpence in the piggy bank."

"An engraved brass plaque," added Mrs. Dovedale, "would be a very nice tribute to Miss Bunch."

True! But given our grandiose plans, it was a monumental comedown. One by one the Library League members headed down the stairs and along the narrow hall to exit through the Employees Only door into the alley. Who could wish to see Miss Bunch's replacement at the front desk? Who could look at the fine box without remembering with smarting eyes her creed that an overdue book made one a crook? Brigadier Lester-Smith and I made up the rear of our group, and when we stood outside in the chill of the afternoon, he asked if I still wished to take a look at the house bequeathed to him by the woman whose memory he had sought so valiantly to honour.

"Of course I want to see it." Impulsively I took his

arm, at the risk of putting a crease in his raincoat sleeve. "We can take my car. And on the way you can tell me whether you are thinking about investing in new furniture or more along the lines of sprucing the place up with fresh paint and wallpaper."

"Since my retirement, I've always lived in furnished rooms, Mrs. Haskell. I don't even have much in the way of the odds and ends—cushions and hooked rugs, those sort of things—that make a place a home."

"I can understand that," I said as we climbed aboard my car and I started up the engine. "One of the advantages of not being married is that it's easier to pick up and move to new digs. So why encumber yourself with unnecessary possessions?" Remembering my visit to the vicarage yesterday and how I had tried to discourage Eudora from making major furniture purchases for the sitting room, I abruptly realized that if I didn't change my ways in advising clients, I was unlikely to make any money worth pocketing.

The brigadier adjusted his seat belt and set his briefcase down on the floor as I drove out of the alley and onto Market Street. "Mrs. Haskell," he said grimly, "I fear I have been guilty of seriously misleading you."

"You don't want to hire me as a decorator?" I nipped around a lorry, only to find myself behind a bus that pulled up at a stop to let off more passengers than ever crammed into the Ark.

The brigadier plucked at the knife-edged pleats of his trousers. "Indeed, Mrs. Haskell, I want your advice on the house Miss Bunch left me. But I wonder if you will wish to back out when I tell you that I have been living a lie since coming to Chitterton Fells."

"We all have our little secrets." I took a peek at his hair, which I had always thought impressively thick for a man in his sixties. No, of course that wasn't it! The bus started moving and I bumped along after it in the wrong gear. Oh, the poor man! He was going to confess that he wasn't a brigadier at all. Moved by the need to ease his embarrassment, I could picture myself spilling the beans about how I had met Ben through the kind offices of Mrs. Swabucher at Eligibility Escorts.

"When we first met," the brigadier addressed his

knees, "I steered you to the conclusion that I have never been married. I did the same thing with all my other acquaintances in Chitterton Fells. The truth is, however, that many years ago I entered a marriage that ended as quickly as it began."

"My goodness!" My laugh went down the wrong way when I swerved to avoid a woman weighed down with shopping bags who stepped off the curb almost under my wheels. "Why would you make a deep dark secret of that?"

"It's an extremely painful memory."

"Oh, do forgive me!" Dropping my hands from the wheel, I inadvertently rounded the corner onto Sea Gull Lane as I turned a contrite face towards him.

"It took me years to put the experience behind me."

"Please, Brigadier Lester-Smith, don't upset yourself by talking about it."

"But I wish to tell you, Mrs. Haskell." Brigadier Lester-Smith raised his head and spoke in a firmer voice. "Our shared experience of discovering Miss Bunch's corpse has created a very special bond between us. Indeed, after witnessing your womanly combination of strength and compassion on that occasion, I have not been able to think of you as I did before. The bond between us transcends our mutual involvement in the Library League."

Oh, dear! Was the poor man going to reveal he had fallen head over heels in love with me?

"You have become a . . . friend, Mrs. Haskell!"

"Thank you!" I floated past a bicycle on a wave of relief.

"And, therefore, I would like to tell you about my wedding night."

"Really?" The car wheels came down to earth with a bump.

"I had met Evangeline when I spent a weekend with a soldier friend of mine in Pebblewell. She was acquainted with one of his sisters and—you know how these things happen, one tennis party led to another, and within two months Evangeline and I were engaged. Our romantic moments together included no more than hand-holding and the occasional chaste kiss."

"Quite proper," I said.

"She was a very modest girl, Mrs. Haskell, and being deeply in love with her, I kept a stiff rein on my passion. We were married in November on an unfortunately bleak and stormy day, and upon arriving at our honeymoon hotel in Brighton, I delayed the moment when we made ready for bed for fear that the ominous rolls of thunder would make it difficult for Evangeline to relax. I anticipated that she might be nervous when the moment for our coming together as man and wife arrived, but I never dreamed she would react with terror and—if I may be frank with you, Mrs. Haskell—utter revulsion when I—"

"Bared your soul?" I kept my eyes on the road.

"She went into hysterics!" The brigadier's eyes turned glassy at the memory. "Roused the entire hotel! Someone broke down the door and people poured into our room before I could even grab up my briefcase and make some attempt to cover myself! The shouting was unbelievable! People hurled the vilest of epithets at me! I was called a loathsome monster and a ravager of women. And then Lady Heidelman, whom we had met at dinner, hit me over the head with her walking stick, and when I recovered consciousness, Evangeline was gone. I did not see her again until we met, with a clergyman and solicitor present, to discuss the annulment."

"What a heartbreaking experience!"

"The emotional scars have never faded." Brigadier Lester-Smith pressed a folded handkerchief to his lips. "It all came back to me in waves of shame and sorrow when Mrs. Dovedale spoke this afternoon of the romance novels she reads, where the bride, having no idea what the wedding night entailed, flees into the tempest-tossed night."

"Have you," I asked gently, "never thought of marrying again?"

"I wouldn't risk it, Mrs. Haskell!"

"Do you know what became of Evangeline?" I had drawn the car alongside the curb which fronted the little house on Herring Street.

"Our paths have never crossed since our marriage was dissolved." He sighed, then endeavoured to speak cheerfully. "And so we come back to the present. What do you think of my new abode, Mrs. Haskell?"

In truth, it was a nondescript terraced house identical

to the one Mrs. Malloy occupied several doors down the road, except that hers had acquired some character by the liberal application of purple paint and a community of brilliantly coloured garden gnomes. But who knew what wonders Miss Bunch may have worked in the interior of her house?

"I think we have to make it your home," I assured the brigadier.

"I wonder," he mused, "if it might not be better for you to go inside without me. That way your impressions will not be influenced by mine and you will feel more free to come up with decorating suggestions. Also, I'm sure you have . . . plans for this evening and would like to get done here as early as possible."

My suspicion was that, given all he had just told me, he was feeling somewhat embarrassed and wanted to go off by himself. So I took the key he handed me, and when assured that he did not have far to walk to his rooms, said good-bye. I went in through the gate to the handkerchief garden and up the crazy-paving path to let myself in at the front door.

The halls in these little houses were so narrow that in Mrs. Malloy's you had to walk sideways in order not to bruise your hips on the coat stand or knock over the china poodle that served for a door stop. Here there was nothing but the staircase and beige walls, not even a carpet runner on the floor or a shade for the naked bulb that came starkly to life when I flicked the switch. Removing the notebook in a businesslike manner from my handbag, I decided to begin upstairs.

A quick tour revealed that Miss Bunch's decorating habits ranged from using a pink sponge for a soap-dish in the bathroom to covering her bed with a curtain with its hooks still in the tape. There were no pictures on the walls, no photographs anywhere in sight, nothing to tidy away, and very little to dust. I went back downstairs, torn between excitement at bringing this sad little house to life and a wistfulness for the emptiness of Miss Bunch's solitary existence.

The kitchen was exactly what the upstairs led me to expect: bottle-green paint, a bare table and one chair, and a gas cooker that looked as if it had forgotten why God gave it a pilot light. There was only one heartwarming touch—Heathcliff's dog bowl sitting in front of the sink. How, I wondered as I went back into the hall, would Miss Bunch feel about my having given him to the Babcocks? Not that I had high hopes, given the excessive timidity of Sylvia Babcock, Heathcliff would last long with her.

The tiny back room of Heathcliff's former home looked out onto a garden that was no longer than its clothesline and was paved in concrete, apart from a narrow border along the bottom that was lined with bushes. The view inside was equally bare, just a sideboard and a drop-leaf table on opposite walls. My expectations of the front sitting room were minimal. I was scribbling away in my notebook, already seeing the house as it could look if Brigadier Lester-Smith were prepared to spend a little money and think in terms of ivory paint with primary accents of teal and burgundy, when I pushed open the door and was stopped dead in my tracks.

The sitting room in which I stood was a miniature version of the Chitterton Fells library. Oak ceiling beams, Jacobean-patterned curtains at the window, and two framed hunting prints on the wall facing the minuscule fireplace helped create the dizzying sense of déjà vu. There was even a bust of Shakespeare mounted on a pedestal. And everywhere I looked there were books. On shelves, on tables, on the two easy chairs, and on the floor. The only striking difference from Miss Bunch's workaday domain was that here organization was obviously not key. On the shelves, biographies rubbed shoulders with novels. True crime was interspersed with books of poetry. And several volumes lay open, as though they were old acquaintances who had walked into the house to sit at their ease as they shared thoughts, remembrances, laughter, and tears with each other as well as with the lady of the house.

Tears filled my eyes at the realization she had not been a woman alone in the world. She'd had countless friends to give warmth and joy to her life. The fact that I was here to measure walls and windows and plot a new décor for the brigadier completely slipped from my mind. I picked up a biography of Elizabeth Barrett Browning, lying open on a footstool, but there was no need to regret that Miss Bunch had never come home to finish it. She had read it many times before. I went from book to book, shelf to shelf, with no awareness of time ticking away on the mantel clock. And once again I saw something that made me stop: *Her Master's Voice,* squeezed in between *Crime and Punishment* and *A Brief History of the World.*

Taking out the worn paperback volume with Karisma in all his untamed splendour on its cover, I got all teary-eyed. Miss Bunch and I had all along been sisters under the skin. As if an unseen force was at work, the book fell open to the very page where I had left off reading on the night Gerta arrived at Merlin's Court. Abandoning my notebook, I settled down in the easy chair to the right of the fireplace and was immediately swept up in the nineteenth-century world of Hester Rosewood and the diabolically gorgeous Sir Gavin.

> *"My angel," he rasped through lips vibrating with the torment of his passion, "I love you as I have never loved any other woman I have sought to take as my mistress. Deny me no longer the sight of your milk-white body! Let me strip away every last vestige of your clothing so that I may feast my eyes upon the exquisite swell of your breasts and . . ."*

Sir Gavin turned back the silk sheets as I turned a page. Hester's mounting desire for the rake whose hands and lips found her points of least resistance seeped through the pores of the paper, scorching my hand as I reached the bottom of yet another page. Would his petulant wife succeed in destroying their love? Would the allegations that Sir Gavin was not the true heir to the title, but was instead the son of the local innkeeper, cast a permanent shadow over Darkmoor House?

I had reached the last chapter and a happy ending was in sight when the mantelpiece clock chimed, and when I looked up into its smiling face, I experienced a chill equal to the one I had felt when Hester was thrust into the dungeon by the vengeful wife and told not to expect room service. It couldn't be—but it was! Seven-thirty! And I was supposed to have met Ben for dinner at Abigail's at six!

Dropping *Her Master's Voice* like a hot coal, I

grabbed up my handbag, forgot all about the notebook, and raced out of the house to the car. Usually it started up before I could finish turning the key in the ignition. But tonight of all times, the beastly vehicle turned balky, and I had to pound on the steering wheel and kick the pedals before the engine responded with an injured growl. I was off, but barely moving—trapped in traffic that seemed to be sleepwalking. At last I made it around the corner of Market Street. I drove at a quickening pace around the village square. Thank God! a parking place only yards from Abigail's entrance.

What would Ben be thinking? I agonized as I dashed up the steps and stood to catch my breath for half a second under the green and gold awning. Would he be picturing me in a ditch with my head caved in? A fate I thoroughly deserved, I decided as I pushed open the door and entered the restaurant foyer with its eighteenth-century rent table serving as a reception desk and the gilt-framed portraits on the Regency-striped walls.

There was no one—not so much as a scurrying waiter—within view, but I could hear people speaking in the main dining room. I hurried in that direction. The voices fell silent as I stepped through the doorway. The room was full of gaily coloured balloons and faces—familiar faces! Everyone from the Library League, other friends, such as Frizzy Taffer and her husband, Tom, and Pamela Pomeroy and Deirdre Jones from my Lamaze class. And, my eyes blinked, I saw Vanessa over in the far corner with Abbey in her arms. Next to her stood Gerta, holding Tam!

"Surprise!" someone said in a voice that was as flat as champagne from which all the bubbles have evaporated.

Ben stepped out of the press of people to hand me a glass. "Happy birthday, Ellie." He was smiling, but his eyes were those of a man who has had an arrow plunged in his heart.

Chapter

9

Ben wasn't talking to me. This may have been because it was four A.M. and he was sound asleep with his face burrowed into the pillow, but guilt caused me to read hostility and wounded feelings into every inhale and exhale.

At the restaurant I had apologized until my lips were numb. And he had been extremely nice about my not arriving until the beef tenderloin was as rubbery as the deflated balloons. He assured me the fiasco was entirely his fault, that surprise parties were juvenile stuff and he should have taken into account that I was a woman newly returned to the workforce, with an entirely new set of priorities. He comprehended completely that I had felt obliged to inspect each stripe on the brigadier's wallpaper with my industrial spyglass. And goodness only knew how many times I had to flush the toilet before convincing myself that the plumbing was up to snuff.

Ben had stopped harping on about how utterly he understood only when poor Brigadier Lester-Smith nervously scooped up a knife from one of the linen-clad tables and appeared ready and willing to cut his own throat in atonement for having been the unwitting cause of ruining the celebration. I'm sure at that moment the wretched man wished devoutly that Miss Bunch had never left him the blasted house in her will. But his agitation did stop Ben in his tracks before I was brought to my knees under the weight of all that unrelenting husbandly benevolence. Gerta handed Abbey and Tam over to me, and the twins squealed with delight at being reunited with the mother who had vanished into the afternoon sunlight without a backward glance. After that, the party picked up momentum.

My friends and acquaintances surged around me, most of them saying "hello" and "good-bye" in the same breath. Did I feel like an archvillainess! And I could have had such a lovely time being fêted! Here came Mrs. Dovedale, Bunty Wiseman, and Sir Robert Pomeroy, all of them explaining at once that the Babcocks weren't able to come because they couldn't leave the dog, or was it that the dog wouldn't let them leave the house? And Mr. Poucher hadn't come for two reasons—he couldn't leave his mother and he loathed parties. How silly, because this had been such a super get-together and they all hated to cut the evening short, but . . . The "buts" were still buzzing in my ears and Abbey and Tam were dragging on my arms until I felt like a mother gorilla, when I saw my chums Frizzy Taffer and Jacqueline Diamond coming towards me.

My eyes blurred with tears as the point sank in—with the brutal precision of a six-inch blade—that Ben was a prince among husbands and I was a lamentable excuse for a wife.

"You really don't deserve him, darling!" Vanessa, the toast of all eyes, in a sleeveless, backless, virtually frontless green taffeta frock, whispered this home truth in my ear. And her words continued to beat upon my guilty conscience as I now lay in bed with a spouse who refused to talk even in his sleep and a clock ticking relentlessly towards dawn. A dawn when Ben would pick up where he had left off in being relentlessly understanding and obdurately affectionate until I was driven screaming from the house in the manner of a Gothic heroine in urgent need of a cliff from which to take a flying leap into oblivion.

My eyelids flickered and I saw my foot inch its way out of the sheet to dangle purposefully above the floor. No! I fought for physical and emotional control, thrusting my shoulders into the mattress and straightening my spine, until I felt like a trampoline that could have bounced a half dozen or so gymnasts off the ceiling. I would *not* sneak out of bed, pick up a novel (preferably one by Zinnia Parrish), and sneak with it into the bathroom!

For last night I had learned the bitter truth. I was a romance novel addict, incapable at stopping at one page. And if I didn't make a change in my lifestyle I would have more than a ruined surprise birthday party on my conscience. I'd end up losing everything that had meaning for me—my family, my home, my self-respect. My mind shied away from the image it projected of an unwashed hag, hair hanging in snakes, stumbling around a refuse pit, searching among the rubble for a tattered paperback with Karisma's egg-stained face on the cover. No! It wouldn't happen because I knew I had a problem, and I'd deal with it one day at a time. But—my foot quivered and inched towards the floor—one day was as good as another and tomorrow was yet another day. Surely there was no point in rushing things. I'd be so much more successful at beating this thing in the long run if I started from solid ground, having worked up my momentum. Quitting cold turkey wasn't the answer. In fact I'd surely find I'd do best by cutting back, one novel at a time.

My eyes turned back to Ben as I gathered up my night dress, so as to prevent any telltale rustling, and tiptoed towards the door. He looked so dear, so unsuspecting in the depths of sleep. His black hair rumpled and his long eyelashes fanned out upon his cheek. A sob caught in my throat and I raced out onto the landing, without a glance at the bookcase, and along to the bathroom. Opening the door, I leaned against it for several tormented minutes before turning on the shower and stripping off my night dress. The bracing beat of cold water did a good job of restoring me to common sense, and I had just stepped out and was reaching for a towel when the door opened and Vanessa stuck in her titian head.

"Posing for *National Geographic*, Ellie?"

"If they need a headhunter for the centerfold!" I glared at her.

"You do look cute when you frown." She smiled sweetly. "The lines on your forehead match your stretch marks."

"If you'll kindly excuse me"—I flexed my toothbrush with a view to scrubbing the smirk off her beauteous face—"I would appreciate a few moments' privacy before beginning the day."

"Oh, all right." Vanessa peered over my shoulder into the mirror to groom an already perfect eyebrow with a coral fingernail. "But don't waste time trying to make yourself look gorgeous, it doesn't do to tangle with Mother Nature when she seems to have had it in for you from the beginning. Just *teasing*, Ellie darling!" My cousin backed strategically towards the door. "I've got coffee in the kitchen to warm us up before we set out. . . ." Her voice trailed gracefully away as she disappeared.

Set out? Where did the silly twit plan on going at five o'clock in the morning? Despite myself, I hurried through brushing my teeth. Curiosity nearly killed the cat when I tripped on Tobias outside the bathroom door and almost sent him flying over the banister rail. But five minutes later I entered the kitchen to find Vanessa looking as if she were doing a TV advert for a cappuccino machine. My birthday present cappuccino machine.

"What a cross face, darling!" Vanessa presented a perfect profile as she filled two itsy-bitsy cups with the steaming brew, floated a dollop of foam on both, and set a coffee spoon tinkling in each saucer. "Anyone would think I climbed in the marriage bed with you and poor Ben, and here I was trying to be housewifely and helpful!"

It would have been inexcusably childish of me to have stood there stamping my feet while I pointed out that she had played with my machine before I had a chance to take it apart and try to figure out how the wretched thing worked. It would have been excessive to tell Vanessa that I felt violated, that she had taken away a piece of myself that I could never get back. So I lied and told her that if I looked cross, it was because I was dying for a cup of frothy coffee.

"Cheers!" I clinked cups with her and took a sip which drained my china thimble and left me with a foam moustache.

"Delicious, if I do say so myself." My cousin perched on the table, golden legs swinging gracefully below her gauzy olive-green skirt, her head tilted so that her hair tumbled away from the creamy column of her throat in a mass of rippling waves that managed to trap every bit of light in the room and turn it from copper to bronze and back again.

"You said something about setting out for somewhere." I licked off my cappuccino moustache under cover of my saucer and felt better. It's amazing how a half teaspoon of foam can help bridge the before-breakfast gap.

"Yes, darling, but don't let's rush." Vanessa clasped her demitasse to her incomparable bosom and radiated soulfulness. "My life until recently has been such a rat race. Metaphorically speaking, one might say I have spent my existence in relentless pursuit of the perfect cup of cappuccino!"

"Oh, yes?"

"I've been shallow, Ellie, more interested in froth than in substance." She dipped a fingertip into the puffy cloud on top of her cup and drew out a wisp of white which she wiggled in front of me before touching it to her coral lips. "But I promise you, darling, I'm a new woman since George Malloy came into my life."

"Congratulations." I set my Thumbelina cup and saucer down in the sink.

"Yes." Her eyes sparkled like Harvey's Bristol Cream sherry in a crystal glass. "Now I shall have it all—beauty, taste, and fibre."

"You could market yourself as a new brand of cereal," I told her fondly.

"How can I convince you that I have changed to the point that my own mother—may her fox furs rot on their hangers—would not recognize me? Would it do the trick"—with silken ease Vanessa slid off the table—"if I told you that I am about to drag you off to church?"

"To St. Anselm's?"

"It's where I plan to be married." She brushed past me on her way to the garden door. "Sure, I would prefer that the family kirk was Westminster Abbey and the Duke of Edinburgh and Prince Charles were squabbling over which of them should have the privilege of giving me away, but I've become a realist, Ellie."

"But why on earth do we have to go at this hour?"

"Because I've been lying awake half the night picturing the ceremony through a dreamy haze of white lace and I can't wait another minute to practice my grand entrance."

"And you want me along so I can hum 'Here Comes the Bride'?"

"I was hoping you could play the organ. You have to have some talents I don't know about."

"The church will be locked at this hour."

"Then we'll wake up the vicar. If her boss is on call at all hours, I don't see why she shouldn't be." Vanessa tossed a raincoat at me, and by the time I had grabbed it up off the floor and stopped the door from slamming into me, she was already halfway across the courtyard.

It wasn't raining, but it was certainly chilly enough for a coat. A sharp wind was coming in off the sea as we passed through the iron gates onto Cliff Road into the dawn. Vanessa's tawny hair was the only splash of colour in what would otherwise have been a black-and-white movie scene. And as I plodded after her, still trying to get my arms into the raincoat sleeves, my imagination produced Karisma waiting for her inside the lichgate of the church. His seventeenth-century pirate's shirt was as white and billowing as the sails of the ship that waited for him in Smuggler's Cove. His expression was as bleak and impenetrable as St. Anselm's tower until he turned and in the flicker of a blackbird's wings she was in his arms, their flowing locks entangled, their lips entwined, and they were one breath, one heartbeat, one soul.

"You came, my entrancing firebrand." He lifted his magnificent head but did not release her from his imprisoning arms. "No one—not your tyrannical mother nor the King's men—shall part us. We will be wed before the cock crows."

"It's not a very big church," Vanessa said, cruelly interrupting my fantasy.

"It's big enough for the Chitterton Fells congregation," I said tartly as I followed her through the lichgate and up the path that wended its mossy way between the churchyard, with its sleepy-eyed regiment of tombstones, and the rag-and-tangle vicarage garden.

"Oh, I'm sure it's fine for your little Sunday get-togethers." My cousin tucked her arm into mine. Probably practicing walking down the aisle with George Malloy. "But, Ellie darling, I don't plan to have a *small* wedding. I'm not so selfish that I would deny all my friends and relations the pleasure of witnessing the splendour that is *moi*." She paused as we rounded the bend in the path to face the church. "Something old, something new, something borrowed . . . oh, heavens, I've just realized something ghastly! I don't have any women friends—we always seem to clash the way those navy-blue shoes of yours do with that brown raincoat. Would it be a frightful imposition, Ellie, if I asked to borrow some of your friends, just for the day?"

"All right"—I tried not to sound begrudging—"but you have to promise to return them in mint condition."

"I'm not sure I'm frightfully keen on the bell tower." Vanessa looked heavenward. "It's hopelessly dated, don't you think?"

"It is dated, 1131," I said, "and no, I don't think Eudora Spike would agree to take it down and store it in the crypt until after your wedding." I had climbed the first steps towards the heavy oak doors of St. Anselm's, when my cousin gave a bloodcurdling screech behind me.

"Oh, my God!" she cried, causing me to assume that one of the bushes hedging the wall beneath the stained glass windows had burst into flame. And when I turned, it was to discover Vanessa gesticulating towards the shrubbery. "Someone's there! I saw a hand," she exclaimed, "a surreptitious, black-gloved hand, creep around that corner over there."

"You're imagining things."

"I guess so." Vanessa closed her eyes—carefully, so as not to crease her eyelashes—and followed me up the steps. "But let's get inside the church before some ghoul from the graveyard tries to put the moves on me."

"It is locked, my dears."

"What?" In latching on to my cousin's arm I caused both of us to stumble and slither on our behinds down onto the path. There a woman dressed all in black, from her unwieldy pre–World War I hat with its fluttering veil to her button boots, stood looking at us with a perplexed expression. She was an old lady, eighty if she were a day; but her hazel eyes were as bright as a girl's and her tissue-paper skin still held a hint of rosy blush.

"Forgive my impetuosity in accosting you." She extended a pair of black-gloved hands towards Vanessa, who dragged me to my feet and pushed me to the fore. "It is a sad state of affairs when a church locks its doors at night."

"There's the fear of vandalism . . ." I stammered as is my wont when finding myself face-to-face with a local legend.

"What misguided thinking." The ancient Lady in Black smiled as if in wistful memory of a kinder age. "The church that claims to welcome sinners should embrace the hooligan."

"Possibly, but I see no harm in drawing the line at people who buy clothes off the rack." Vanessa shuddered.

"Lay not up treasure upon earth, is that not what the Bible teaches? One would hope the clergy would apply that little rule to silver chalices and other religious what-nots along with other worldly goods." Our new acquaintance tossed her bonneted head, providing me with a flash of how Vanessa might look and act as an octogenarian. "But never fret, my dear young ladies." Here she gave a girlish giggle. "It so happens that I was here one night and saw where the silly old verger hid the spare key. And I have it here." She reached into her coat pocket and produced said object.

"I don't think we should creep into St. Anselm's while Reverend Spike is tucked unsuspecting in bed," I objected, picturing myself being drummed out of the Hearthside Guild. "We'll come back at a more appropriate time and . . ."

"Cowardy, cowardy custard, Ellie can't cut the mustard," Vanessa chanted rudely. "Go rabbiting home if you wish, but I'm going up those steps with our delightful new friend. If I'm to be married here—"

"A wedding!" The Lady in Black spoke with a choke in her voice. "I was to have been married here when I was a dreamy-eyed girl of unsurpassed beauty and sparkling wit. My bridal gown was an angelic confection of ivory silk and lace imported from Paris. My bouquet was of apple blossom to match the wreath that was to encircle my raven tresses, but, alas, my handsome groom failed to arrive at the church and I was destined to stand alone at the altar with my hand pressed to my broken heart while the organist played on and . . . on. . . ."

"How sad," Vanessa said insincerely, standing impatiently at the church door as I blinked away my tears and gave the tiny black-gloved hand a consoling squeeze before following the trailing skirts up the steps.

"Would you?" The Lady in Black gave me the key. Her forlorn sigh echoed the heavy groan as the door swung inward and the three of us stepped into the musty gloom.

"Let there be light!" My cousin pressed a hand to the wall and was miraculously rewarded for her irreverence by immediately locating a switch. Forbearing to loiter in the entryway, with its long table stacked with inspirational booklets and several collection boxes posted prominently on the walls, Vanessa entered the nave as though she knew exactly where she was going. And that was another miracle, considering there wasn't a tour guide at her elbow.

"Oh, God!" she exclaimed, taking Him to task. "You really need to think about moving. Or at least doing some major redecorating."

"I think St. Anselm's is perfect." I stood behind her in the aisle, flanked on either side by rows of time-worn pews. "Some of these windows date back to the fourteenth century and even the Victorian stained glass is less garish than most of its kind. And look at the altar rail! The carving is exquisite."

"How well I know!" The Lady in Black spoke over my shoulder. "I remember how on that fateful day my eyes remained riveted for what seemed an eternity on a wooden rose with a chip in its heart."

"Would anybody mind frightfully," Vanessa said, "if we try to remain focused on my wedding? I don't want to be selfish," she fibbed, "but at any moment horrid hordes of schoolchildren could burst in upon us intent on making brass rubbings for Christmas cards and I won't be able to think straight. You understand, don't you?" She smiled sweetly at the Lady in Black.

"Absolutely, my dear," came the sighing reply. "I

haven't been able to keep anything straight for sixty years, a sad price to pay for girlish hopes and dreams."

Vanessa shot me a glance that dared me to produce a hankie from my raincoat pocket and dab at my eyes. Then she paraded down the aisle as if it were a modeling ramp. The sun paid suitable homage by providing her with a gossamer train of gold upon which the Lady in Black and I trod as gingerly as if it cost eighty pounds a yard.

My cousin spun around.

"These pews will have to be moved!"

"Why didn't I think of that?" I said.

"The aisle is far too narrow. I won't be able to take a step without scrunching my dress or snagging my veil when someone sticks his nose out of the pew." Somehow Vanessa managed to resemble one of the titian-haired angels on the stained glass windows while uttering this snippy remark. "And I don't much care for those brass vases on the altar. They look like something Aladdin's mother would have bought for a song from the bazaar."

"Perhaps we should also get rid of the baptismal font," I suggested, "unless you think it might come in handy as a punch bowl. And"—my eyes roved the stone walls—"I'm sure Reverend Spike would go for a Laura Ashley paper with matching curtains at the windows."

"There's no need to be snide, Ellie." Vanessa shook back her luxuriant hair, swayed gracefully, and reached for the edge of a pew. "I'm feeling a bit off colour. This getting up early is for the birds, and I'd think even they'd get tired of it."

Before I could profess sympathy, however, she glided away in the direction of the vestry, where I guessed she would spend a soulful few moments picturing herself signing the registry while George Malloy hovered beside her, giving thanks to God for blessing him with amazing good fortune.

The Lady in Black tugged at my sleeve. "I haven't told you my name," she said. "I am Ione Tunbridge, and you"—she leaned closer as I started to speak—"you are Ellie Haskell. I have my ways of knowing such things. And I'll tell you a little secret, dear: I was in the churchyard on your wedding day. Even though I am in the main a recluse, I can never resist hovering among the tombstones on such heart-stirring occasions, and I saw the look of abject despair on your face as you came through the lichgate."

"I was late," I said, resisting the urge to take a step back from her clutching hand and the smell of mouldy face powder that was making me feel queasy. "I was thirty minutes late for my wedding," I continued in a rush reminiscent of the day in question. "The cat ate my veil and the taxi didn't turn up and I was terrified that Ben would get tired of waiting for me and I'd end up at the altar all alone. . . ." My voice petered out as I realized I'd been tactless in the extreme.

But Miss Tunbridge's expression was all sympathy. "Men!" Her breath came in an almost visible wisp of stale air escaping under a door that hadn't been opened in half a century. "I felt a bond with you, Ellie Haskell, on your bridal morn. And then the other day, when I looked out of the attic window and saw you being forced to picnic on the wet grass with your dark, forbidding husband, my spirit cried out to yours: Hit the insufferable tyrant over the head with the wine bottle. Spear his heart with the butter knife. Free yourself for a life of unwedded bliss." Her face was ashen with fierce emotion.

If I'd been a wife worthy of my wedding ring, I would have protested fiercely that Ben was an angel equal to any of those carved on the altar rail, and that I loved him madly, but true to form, I fastened on the fascinating discovery.

"You live at Tall Chimneys!" I exclaimed. "The house that was once the residence of Hector Rigglesworth and his seven daughters. Excuse my curiosity, but do you believe the stories that he haunts the Chitterton Fells library? Have you ever sensed his repressive presence prowling around your home?" I might have gone rambling on in this fashion if Vanessa had not returned at that moment from scouting out the vestry to stand inches away from me and Ione Tunbridge. Her pensive eyes were on the magnificent crucifix mounted behind the pulpit.

"That'll have to go, Ellie! Call me shallow, but it is a bit of a downer!"

My appalled gasp wasn't the only reaction to my cousin's blasphemy. For at that instant the lights went out, indicating God had moved swiftly to cast my cousin and those unfortunate enough to be standing in her presence into outer darkness. In the midst of a squeal I backed clumsily into a pew. A hand brushed mine; Ione's whisper trickled inside my ear: "You must come and see me, Ellie Haskell. You remind me of a dear friend I had when I was a young girl and the world was my meadow."

Her icy breath was gone from my ear, and when the lights came back on there was no sign of Ione Tunbridge. Coming down the aisle was Gladstone Spike wearing a hand-knitted cardigan and dusky grey trousers. His silver hair was tousled.

"Good morning," he said over steepled fingers, his voice a little higher than I remembered it. "I saw the lights and thought they had been accidentally left on last night, so I came in, switched them off, and then heard movements. Are you ladies waiting to see my wife?" He glanced at his pocket watch and looked momentarily perplexed before returning it to the breast pocket of his cardigan. "Could it be, Ellie, that you misunderstood Eudora, not realizing it was her intention to meet you here at five in the evening?"

"We didn't have an appointment." Vanessa favoured him with a bewitching smile, something she might not have done if she had known Gladstone Spike was soon to become one of the girls. "When I told my cousin Ellie that I couldn't sleep and was dying to take a look inside the church where I plan to be married, she suggested we walk over here on the chance that the door would be unlocked. Luckily, that proved to be the case."

She told this outrageous lie without a blush. Indeed, she looked decidedly pale as she eased down onto the edge of a pew. Bother! Ione Tunbridge was nowhere in sight, and I wasn't up to denouncing my cousin as a crafty minx who'd always enjoyed watching me squirm. My stomach was rumbling, and all I wanted to do was get home and make some scrambled eggs and toast before Gerta—who, sad to say, had proved to be an even worse cook than Mrs. Malloy had indicated—got busy on a batch of scones that would have done for doorstops.

"I also was unable to sleep the night through," Gladstone Spike confessed. "It's a problem that's been plaguing me for several weeks, and I often spend the small hours doing a bit of knitting or whipping up a sponge cake. But on this occasion I decided upon taking a walk around the grounds. I am, or, rather"—he cleared his throat—"Eudora and I are expecting a guest this weekend, someone of particular significance to our future, and it did occur to me, Ellie, as I passed the blackcurrant bushes, that Ben might be willing to share with me his recipe for summer pudding."

"He'll be delighted," I said. "Seriously, Gladstone, it's a pity Ben couldn't have married *you*, considering the two of you share this grand passion for cooking." My mind, in shying away from the suspicion that the Spikes' weekend guest would be the doctor who had something to do with the surgery that would make most men wince, had blundered into making this grotesquely stupid statement.

"We would make quite a team." Gladstone's eyes twinkled, suggesting he took the joke at face value, unless . . . My heart missed a whole string of beats as I followed his gaze and saw my husband striding down the aisle towards us. Instead of wondering what brought Ben here, I reassessed that twinkle and thanked God that Eudora was not present to witness it and possibly misinterpret.

"Ellie!" My spouse had eyes only for me. Reaching me in full stride, Ben growled menacingly, "Do you deliberately set out to drive me to distraction? I woke in a cold sweat to find you weren't in bed. After ransacking the house for any sign of you, I was forced to invade the privacy of Gerta's bedroom and after quieting her hysteria, I asked her to take care of the twins for as long as it took me to return with or without you."

"You shouldn't have panicked . . . ," I faltered. Vanessa was watching us with great interest.

"The least you could have done was leave a note pinned to my pajamas. I was convinced you'd left me because you've been seeing another man. You haven't been your usual affectionate self lately, Ellie, and there was that business of your being late for your birthday party. Something fishy there. Could it be you have a thing for Brigadier Lester-Smith—the urbane older man?" Ben drew a furious breath. "That's what I was asking myself as I dashed over to the vicarage to have a word with Eudora in case you had confided in her as your spiritual advisor. And then I saw the lights in the church. What's going on here?"

He now directed his fiery gaze upon Gladstone Spike as if suspecting the man of luring me to the church with the intent of using foul means to pry a recipe from me.

But before either the vicar's husband or I could explain matters, Vanessa rose unsteadily from the pew on which she had been sitting, pressed a hand to her ivory brow, took a couple of faltering steps, whispered that she felt faint, and proceeded to pitch gracefully into my husband's arms, which had opened to receive her.

Before I could blink, Ben lifted her up so that her face was cradled against his shoulder and the rippling river of her hair spilled in tawny torrents over his jacket sleeve. What a picture they made—he darkly handsome and appropriately impassive, she a wilted lily powerless for the moment to determine her own fate. A picture worthy of being reproduced on the cover of a romance novel. And I was not the only one to be both stunned and captivated by the image. Gladstone Spike was staring at my husband as if he had just seen the man of his dreams.

Chapter

10

The devil made me do something really wicked. When I got home I abandoned Abbey and Tam to Gerta's care, went upstairs, and climbed into my bed that was neither too hard, nor too soft, but just right. The clock on the mantelpiece pointed out that it was six-thirty A.M., far too early in the day for a nap. And my conscience did its best to make me feel guilty by reminding me that Ben had left for work immediately after carrying Vanessa up to her room and gently depositing her on the bed. I could hardly expect him to toss her one-handed through the doorway, could I? Women don't faint at the drop of a hat these days, so naturally he had been concerned about her, even though she insisted it was nothing and did not need to see a doctor.

Pulling the sheet over my head, I snuggled into the downy softness of the pillow. Forty winks would set me up for the day. I'd be a better mother to the twins if I made up for the night's lack of sleep. And this evening I would cook a special dinner for Ben. It would be just the two of us . . . and Gerta, seeing it would be positively Gothic not to include her, I decided as the wallpaper blurred and the wardrobe drifted upon the horizon like a lighthouse swathed in fog. What horrible weather for May, I thought fuzzily as hailstones pelted the window.

I would have been able to ignore them if the telephone had not started ringing with inconsiderate persistence. Stuffing a pillow in each ear did not save me. By the time the great communicator had finally shut up, I had staggered to my feet and saw a shower of pebbles hit the window. The sun blazing through the window ridiculed the possibility that God had decided to enliven His day by intoning "Let there be hail!" No! Someone, some oafish person, was outside the house, scooping up gravel from the drive and tossing it heavenward by the fistful in hopes of rousing me from slumber. Gerta, I thought crossly, would prove to be the culprit. She undoubtedly had the twins outside and wanted to know if it was all right to let Abbey undress her doll and expose Sunshine's plastic bottom to some passing sex offender.

Summoning up a smile liable to strike terror in my children's hearts, I pulled back the curtains, opened the window, and shouted down, "Hold your fire! I'm unarmed and prepared to come quietly."

How wrong can a woman be? The person staring up at me was a man I had never seen before in my life. A stocky, red-haired man who dropped his upraised hands and stood rubbing them together while giving an earsplitting whistle that should have brought the local constabulary on the run.

"There's my lass! A sight for sore eyes and"—I could see his Adam's apple throb—"what a pair of knockers!"

"Get out of my garden, you pervert!" I almost suffocated in wrapping the heavy velvet curtain mummy-fashion around me so that only a wedge of my face was left to feed his bestial ardour. "If you're not gone by the time I count to one, I'll phone the police!"

"You're something else, girl!" The red-headed fiend chuckled with evil relish and spread wide his arms. "Always one for a bit of a tease. Come on, Nessie, jump into me arms and tell me you missed your old Georgie Porgie!"

"Nessie?" I rolled the name around on my tongue, indifferent to the fact that I was showing more of my neck than was seemly. "Nessie—as in short for Vanessa?" This nasty encounter had turned out to be a classic case of mistaken identity. "I'm sorry, you've been knocking on the wrong window. I'm her cousin Ellie, but don't be embarrassed: I'm flattered you saw a family resemblance. Probably just the sun in your eyes, but never mind, I'm pleased to meet you, Mr. Malloy."

"I feel a right blithering idiot." He gave a gulp that carried all the way up to my window. "I figured the room, yours, that is, had to be Nessie's, seeing it was the only one with the curtains still drawn. She's a great one for getting her beauty sleep, is my little lass."

"Vanessa's a prize in all respects." The insincerity sat lightly upon my lips. "Her bedroom is on the other side of the house, but don't give any of this another thought." I avoided looking down at my . . . knockers. "Your attempt to surprise her was lovely and romantic and I'm only sorry she didn't get to play Juliet to your Romeo."

"You're being a proper brick, Mrs. Haskell." George Malloy wiped a hand over his sweaty face. "But there's no two ways about it, I should have behaved meself and come knocking on the front door like a gent. Me mum will have my hide for this, let me tell you. She's already given me an earful on how I'm mucking things up between you and her. And I can see it is a mite awkward, what with me marrying Nessie and Mum charring for her cousin."

"Your mother rules the roost here at Merlin's Court," I informed him, "but I do see she might decide it would be best to drop me from her list of clients. But that's not your fault. So cheer up! I'll nip downstairs and open the kitchen door for you."

Flopping down on the bed in my skirt and blouse had made me into a reprehensibly rumpled hostess, but I doubted George Malloy would notice. And even if he did, it wouldn't matter. His Nessie would have explained that in addition to her own, she had been the beneficiary of my share of the family looks. Nessie! I couldn't keep from laughing as I hurried down the stairs. How common! would have been Aunt Astrid's verdict. The sort of name that belonged to a servant girl who had grown up skipping rope in the back streets of a Catherine Cookson novel. That Vanessa, her showcase daughter, should be brought so low must have been a pain in the royal rear. Nessie! And yet the way George Malloy had said the name sounded as tender as the morning light that poured in through the garden door as I opened up to let him inside.

"Hello," I said. "Come in and make yourself at home."

"I'll take you up on that kind invite." He removed his hands from his pockets and crossed the threshold to stand wiping his feet as if he were on a treadmill.

"Gerta, who takes care of our twins, must be giving them their baths, and Vanessa is still in bed." Seen at close quarters, George Malloy's looks did not improve to the point where I felt I need apologize for not being a raving beauty or wonder why Mrs. Malloy had not insisted on displaying her sonny boy's photos in every house where she worked. George was short and verging on stout, and the owner of one of those mass-produced faces that you know did not cost his parents an arm and a leg. His red hair faded to the ginger of a nice but ordinary cat.

Speaking of cats, Tobias, who considers himself a prince among felines, wore a disparaging smirk as he surveyed our guest from the top of the Welsh dresser, but I had begun to warm to George.

"I'll be blowed," he said, "I'd know you was related to Nessie if I was to spot you in Charing Cross station."

"You would?" I pulled a chair away from the table and watched him settle himself by crossing first one leg then the other before deciding upon putting both stubby feet on the floor.

"You've got that same sunny look, that same nice smile. If you'll excuse me being so familiar, Mrs. Haskell."

"Ellie," I said warmly. "After all, we are going to be cousins."

"Over my dead body!"

This less-than-familial statement was given an exclamation point by the slamming of the garden door. Mrs. Malloy, her black head resembling a thundercloud, clattered towards us on heels that were even higher than usual, indicating that this morning she intended to dust the high spots. Mrs. M. had made it clear from the get-go that she did not do ladders.

"I've nothing in particular against you, Mrs. H., other than you've shown rotten taste in picking your relations." She dumped the supply bag down on the table, almost knocking her son down as he attempted to rise from his chair. "No use giving me them puppy-dog eyes, George!

I'd as soon as dig me own grave as see you married to that toffee-nosed wench." The aggrieved mother heaved a sigh that blew Tobias across the room. "Always treated me like the dirt in me dustpan, she has. If she had one shred of proper feeling, she'd have picked up the telephone and asked me how I felt about taking her on as a daughter-in-law."

"Nessie's shy." George, perched an uncomfortable two inches above his chair, defended his betrothed.

"She's been that way since she was a child," I lied. "Vanessa always worried that her looks might create the mistaken impression that she bordered upon being shallow."

"Are people talking about me as usual?"

My cousin could always pick the moment to make an entrance. Now she glided into the room, a vision of loveliness to behold in my former negligee. But Mrs. Malloy, unlike her son, whose eyes lit up with joy as he leapt to his feet, did not look noticeably smitten. Indeed, she appeared in need of a tumbler full of gin as Vanessa swept towards her with lace-edged arms outstretched.

"Mummy! May I call you that? I feel so *incredibly* close to you, the woman who gave my darling George life."

"She's a wonder, is my Nessie," George murmured worshipfully.

Mrs. Malloy's purple lips paled as Vanessa planted a kiss several inches to the right of the powdered cheek. "Don't go getting ideas I suffered the tortures of the damned giving birth to me one and only. Fact is, he popped out like a champagne cork. You can call it luck if you like, though I've sometimes thought different, that the midwife was across the room at the time, having a smoke, and caught him before he landed in the saucepan of boiling water."

"I'm glad you shared that story with us," I said.

"Isn't it sweet!" Vanessa rippled nails long enough to dissect frogs through her hair, so that it cascaded in a sun-burnished waterfall over her gleaming shoulders. "Oh, what bliss to belong to both of you, to be at the centre of my own little family. . . ." She extended one hand to

George and the other to Mrs. Malloy, who immediately began fiddling in the supply bag.

"You're bringing tears to me eyes, duck." Out whipped the bottle of cleaning fluid that was mostly gin. "But we both know the only reason you're marrying my George is because he's made himself a pot of money. If it wasn't for that . . ." Mrs. Malloy poured herself a capful of fortification and sipped it down with her little finger genteelly elevated. "If it wasn't for the lolly, you wouldn't have looked twice at George if you'd run him down in the street."

"Now, Mum, I won't have none of that." The fruit of her loins intervened on behalf of his betrothed, who promptly wilted into his outstretched arms and would no doubt have rested her petal cheek upon his manly shoulder had he not been considerably the shorter of the two. "I don't mean to start a rumpus, but I'll not have anyone, including you, Mum, upsetting Nessie. She's been through enough heartache what with her own mother turning her out on account of me."

"Mummy refused to believe that I *adore* you, my darling." Vanessa pressed impassioned lips to his; I hastily busied myself filling the kettle rather than witness this nice man being played like a harmonica. "And it does hurt, because Mummy and I were always such chums, borrowing each other's fur coats and jewelry like a couple of giddy schoolgirls. And now with this rift with Mummy I feel like an orphan." A wisp of a sigh that I found hard to equate with Aunt Astrid—who always looked to me as though she had douched with vinegar and water once too often.

The moan that pulsed through the room came not from Vanessa but the kettle, which had a clogged whistle and was given to such outbursts. While I set out cups and saucers, George Malloy cradled his beloved against his stalwart chest.

"There, there, lass, you've got me for good and all, and if Mum doesn't come round to accepting you as me chosen wife, she'll be the loser."

"Meaning you'll stop sending me a few quid for me birthday so I'm reduced to going out charring for a living," said Mrs. Malloy as if she were currently employed in another line of work. "Very well." And with that, she screwed the cap back on the bottle of gin with an air of finality which had me convinced she was going to pick up her supply bag and march out of the house, never to return.

"Very well, what?" George eyed her grimly.

Mrs. M. drew back her black taffeta shoulders and stood as if facing the firing squad. "I'm not saying things will work out, mind you, between me and Orphan Annie, but if you're set on marrying her, I'm prepared to take her on as a daughter-in-law. Strictly on approval, you understand. A six-month trial basis is what I have in mind."

"Whatever you say, Mummy Malloy!" Unlocking her arms from her betrothed's neck, Vanessa spun around in gauzy swirls of silk and sea-foam lace to express her gratitude to her future mum-in-law with a fluttering of the eyelashes and a demure smile. She lifted her teacup with a flourish. "How about a toast, to love in all its many guises?"

Personally I would have preferred my favourite toast with lots of butter and lashings of marmalade. Never mind. I joined in the clinking of cups with good grace and even managed a protest when Mrs. Malloy said she had better get down to work, seeing she was going to have to fork out some of her hard-earned cash for a new frock for the nuptials.

"Take the day off," I urged her. "Why don't the three of you go out to lunch, at Abigail's if you like, compliments of the house?"

"Thank you, Mrs. H."—she gave me a telling glance from under her neon lids—"but I'd just as soon the young couple went off for a bit on their own. I'm sure they've got plenty to talk about that's not for my ears."

George beamed his appreciation of his parent's newfound sensitivity. "Come to think of it, Mum, I do want a word or two in Nessie's ear hole about the Airobyc. The new suspension exercise bicycle that'll be going into production next month at the factory," he explained. "If I do say so myself, it's a right nifty concept, the bike being supported four feet off the ground on a steel frame to provide a feeling of weightlessness and free-floating. And I need to ask me favourite model here if she's ready to get back in the saddle for our advertising campaign."

The smile Vanessa gave him was somewhat lackluster. And I could see her point, presuming she would be doing what she'd let slip George had hired her for at the beginning of their working relationship. Those famed "before" and "after" shots, which by means of some havey-cavey camerawork would bloat her up and slim her back down in ten seconds flat, in hopes of luring thousands of the desperately overweight into purchasing the Airobyc with its no-money-back guarantee in order to achieve the same miraculous results.

I expected my cousin to swan upstairs and spend the better part of the day getting dressed for her tête-à-tête with George. Instead, she went out with him into the garden, a diaphanous daphne who I had no doubt would get George to shift gears from bicycle to wedding bells before they had crossed the moat bridge.

"So that's that." Mrs. Malloy closed the door on them and with faltering steps made her way to a chair where she settled herself like a deposed queen in a Greek tragedy. "I'll take a cold cloth for me poor aching head, Mrs. H., if you'd be so kind. . . ."

"Coming up," I said, soaking a tea towel under cold water and wringing it out over an outraged Tobias, who was in the sink, trying to get a suntan through the open window. I draped the folded linen strip in proper Florence Nightingale fashion on Mrs. Malloy's forehead. "How's that?" I asked, and saw tears gush down her cheeks, creating a mud slide of her makeup. Naturally I assumed she was touched to the quick by my ministrations.

"You've got the buggering thing too wet!" she exclaimed. And I watched, powerless, as her pencilled eyebrows washed out in the flood.

"I'm sorry," I said, looking at the clock and wondering when Gerta would bring the twins down for their breakfast.

"Well, I suppose you was only trying to help me drown me sorrows. Who'd have kids, Mrs. H.? When they're little they break every bit of furniture in sight and when they grow up they break our hearts." Mrs. Malloy lifted her legs in their black fishnet hose so I could prop a stool under them. "My George married to that woman, it doesn't bear thinking about! But what's a mother to do? He's over twenty-one, when all is said and done."

"And"—it was an heroic attempt on my part to be charitable—"I believe he really does love Vanessa."

"Perverted, isn't it?" Mrs. M. shuddered, and the tea cloth fell into a dreary heap on the floor.

I picked it up and went over to the sink. "You have to think about your son's happiness. And telling yourself he could have done a lot worse might sweeten the pill."

"You're right for once, Mrs. H."—a brave smile— "the way the world's going, my George could have got mixed up with some bit of fluff just out of the clink for murdering her last ten fiancés and presently working for an escort service."

"Exactly," I said through stiff lips as the specter of my initial meeting with Ben hovered in the air between us, and I had to keep my arms firmly at my sides to stop from shooshing it away. Mrs. Malloy hadn't meant anything personal by her remark. She didn't know that I had met my husband through Eligibility Escorts; nobody in Chitterton Fells had any idea, least of all Vanessa, and I would have killed before letting her find out.

"What's got you so red in the face, Mrs. H.?"

"Nothing . . . I mean the sun, it's going to be a scorcher of a day." Before I could continue with the weather forecast, the hall door opened with hurricane force, and Gerta appeared with the twins at her feet like bows on the tail of a kite. It took a full minute for me to work out whether she was talking in English or Swiss, partly because the words were all jumbled up but mainly because Abbey and Tam were climbing all over me as if they had not seen me since the day of their birth.

"Say that again, Gerta?" I addressed the plaits wrapped around her head, which was all I could see with a twin standing on each knee.

"I have telephoned the police station, Frau Haskell."

"You did what?" Abbey fell through my legs and was rescued by Mrs. Malloy, who would no doubt charge me an extra pound for the favour.

"Such a terrible shock . . ." Gerta leaned against the table, incapable for the moment of continuing and, with

Tam half choking me, all I could think was that she had discovered a bar of soap missing from the bathroom and suspected foul play. "We have a *madman* on the premises, Frau Haskell!"

"Don't talk so daft." Mrs. Malloy retreated with Abbey into the broom cupboard. "Mr. H. is at work. I saw him going into the restaurant when I was waiting for me bus."

"Not him." Gerta shook her head so violently that her plaits swung loose from their moorings. "I talk about the crazy man I see from the nursery window, sitting on that low branch of the big tree, with his hands out in front of him and his foots going up and down like he is on the bicycle. And all the time he talking to someone who isn't anywhere to be seen, 'his angel' I hear him say when I go to fall out the window."

"That would be Mrs. Malloy's son," I said before the proud mother could emerge from the broom cupboard to defend his honour by administering forty whacks with the mop. "George would have been demonstrating the capabilities of the stationary bike he is manufacturing to Vanessa, who must have wandered out of your view for the moment."

"Again I upset the apple cake!" Gerta bundled her plaits back in place with trembling hands. "I am the crazy one, that is what you will be thinking, Frau Haskell. First I think your cousin for a burglar and now I make this mistake." A tear trickled down her cheek and, with the sensitivity that so often lurks within the soul of the small, dark, silent type, Tam toddled over and gave her knees a hug.

"Why don't I ring the police," I said, "and suggest this is not the most convenient time for a visit and perhaps they could come another day." I escaped into the hall.

The policewoman who answered my call said, with enough acid in her voice to burn more holes in the receiver, that but for the previous call from this number coming in while the tea break was in full swing, someone would have been sent rushing to the scene. My apologies for the false alarm went down like a stale currant bun, and I hung up the receiver, torn between relief that I hadn't been ordered to do thirty days' community service and irritation with Gerta.

It was only by reminding myself that she was understandably prone to view all men as beasts as a result of her broken marriage that I was able to stick a smile on my face when I returned to the kitchen to find Gerta in her apron at the working surface, pounding her rolling pin into a circle of dough that already looked more suited for a sewer cover than a pie. My spirits were not lifted by the morose ballad she was singing about a false-hearted goatherd who callously played the accordion in a meadow of wildflowers while his damsel fair drowned herself in a mountain stream. The twins had retreated under the table and had their hands over each other's ears, and one look at Mrs. Malloy's face made me think seriously of joining them.

"If that woman don't shut her gob, this flaming minute"—my much-put-upon daily help turned off the tap and lifted her bucket out of the sink—"I'll stick her head in this here pail and hold her down till she don't think drowning's something to bloody sing about."

"Leave that to me," I said hastily as Gerta began another verse in which the goatherd ended up shaped like his accordion after an encounter with the father of the fair corpse. "I mean . . . I'll take care of things here in the kitchen, Mrs. Malloy, while you go and get started on the other rooms."

"I wouldn't charge extra for doing the woman in!" Shaking her head at my inability to see reason, she teetered out of the room, slopping water from the bucket in her wake, which succeeded in bringing Abbey and Tam out from the table so they could chase after the soap bubbles. Luckily, by the time I had captured my unholy terrors and got them settled in their booster chairs with promises of breakfast on the way, Gerta had concluded her aria.

"That Mrs. Mop, she *hates* me!"

"No, no, she doesn't." I shuffled a bowl of cereal in front of Tam and restrained Abbey from climbing onto the table, where the sugar bowl beckoned. "She's just a little edgy today, what with her son getting engaged and almost getting arr—" Biting my tongue, I produced my daughter's breakfast, told both children to "eat up," and then realized neither had a spoon. This omission remedied, I focused on Gerta, whose tears poured like water from a measuring jug onto the pastry, necessitating the use of more flour, in sufficient quantity to whiten the air in the kitchen and turn my children into a couple of snowmen.

"I am a *big* nuisance to you, Frau Haskell!"

"Don't be silly," I said with all the conviction I could muster. "You're an absolute boon, your cooking is out of this world, and the children love you!"

"Me do!" Abbey provided emphasis by banging her spoon on the table and crowing with delight. Tam, bless him, was too busy turning his bowl upside down, with horribly messy results, to express his monumental affection for Gerta, but when the flour had settled, she looked more cheerful.

"Then you don't send me backpacking into the streets?"

"Of course not," I said.

"For you, Frau Haskell and the little munchkins"—she hoisted up the pastry and squashed it back into a ball—"I work my fingers to the bones. I will make the strudel and the dumplings and the—"

"You mustn't spoil us—" Removing Tam's bowl from his sticky hands, I fought down an attack of indigestion.

"Nothing I do is too much!" Gerta beamed at me as she got busy with the rolling pin. "The rest of my life I spend in your service, for what pennies you choose to throw at me. When I am an old woman with the white hairs and the bent back, I will still be in this happy house, taking care of the great-grandchildren when they come for the visit, cooking for you and cleaning for you and answering the telephone—" She stopped. The rolling pin spun out of her hands and landed with a wallop on the floor within inches of Tobias Cat, who with a gleeful flick of his tail chased it under the Welsh dresser.

"What's wrong, Gerta?"

"You will let Mrs. Mop kill me! And I will not say a word to stop you. When you go up the stairs for your sleep this morning, the telephone gave a ring and it is a woman speaking. She said her name was . . ."

"Yes?" I prodded.

"I don't remember all of it." Gerta pressed her hands to her head and turned white on the spot.

"The first name?" I encouraged her.

"I remember the first letter." She brightened. "Her name it began with the *S*, that I will swear on your grave."

Wiping off Tam's face, then the table, I racked my brain and brandished a name in the air: "Sylvia? Does that sound right? Sylvia Babcock?"

"That could be it."

"Well, never mind." I scooped the twins out of their seats and watched them scurry over to the toy basket in the alcove. "She's bound to ring back."

"But not before lunch."

"That doesn't matter." I laughed. "I can stand the suspense until our mystery caller's identity is revealed."

"But I have not explained, Frau Haskell." Gerta jumped half out of her apron when Tam bounced a red ball in her direction. "The woman say she will wait to meet you in Herr Haskell's restaurant. For lunch."

My heart plummeted. The woman had to be Sylvia and she had chosen to meet me in a public place rather than at her house or mine so that when she burst into tears and begged me to take Miss Bunch's dog back before she had a nervous breakdown, I would be unable to refuse, or risk looking like a monster in the eyes of everyone.

"She say lunch at noon, Frau Haskell," Gerta added helpfully.

Bother! It was now eleven-thirty. There was nothing I could do for the moment but thank Gerta for the message. Being saddled with Heathcliff again while I tried to find him another foster home was hardly a fate worse than death. Ben would not be pleased, but marriage is not meant to be a never-ending round of merriment. Seemingly George Malloy had not yet grasped this concept; when the garden door opened he followed Vanessa jauntily into the kitchen, his face almost as red as his hair and glowing like the sun.

I introduced him to Gerta, who made a quick exit on the grounds that she needed to take the twins up to the potty. Then for five minutes I listened to the besotted fellow extol my cousin's social acumen in arranging their wedding, which would include a reception at Merlin's Court for five hundred of her very, very closest friends, featuring a sit-down dinner with Ben doing the food and

Mrs. Malloy and I in charge of the washing up. While I endeavoured to look enthusiastic and murmur the right noises, Vanessa stood like a Royal Doulton figure in her pale green negligee, with a posy of flowers in her china-white hands. And suddenly lunch with Sylvia Babcock, with whom I had never been great chums, became the most enchanting of prospects.

So at eleven forty-five I left the house with her wedding present tucked under my arm and drove off, confident that Abbey and Tam would be fed and put down for their naps, and reasonably hopeful that I would not return to find Mrs. Malloy had plugged Gerta into a light socket. Passing St. Anselm's Church, I glimpsed someone moving among the shrubbery in the vicarage garden. It proved to be Eudora. She looked listless and beige in a skirt and cardigan that seemed superfluous, given the heat.

Parking the car outside Abigail's, I felt a little guilty that I had not stopped to pass the time of day with Eudora, although what one could say to cheer up a woman whose husband was about to undergo a sex-change operation I had no idea. To become the talk of the tabloids, I thought as I mounted the steps and passed under the green and gold awning and into the restaurant, would be hell on earth for anyone except a publicity-starved celebrity. And even that sort of fame must grow thin. Something I did not have to worry about, I was reminded by the gilt-framed mirror behind the reception desk. I was reflecting that Ben would be well-advised to get rid of the evil-looking glass before it put any other patrons off their lunch by reminding them they already had pounds to lose, when Ben himself came through the main dining room doorway. He strode towards me, eyes alight and hands outstretched.

"Ellie! What a wonderful surprise. No one told me you were coming." He looked towards the young woman at the desk, whose striped frock so perfectly matched the Regency-period wallpaper that I had mistaken her for a standard lamp.

"I didn't make the reservation," I said quickly as she stared at the book in wild-eyed terror. "And I hope Sylvia Babcock thought to do so. Because from the looks of it, you have close to a full house."

"Then you're not here for an impetuous lunch with your husband?" Ben quirked a wistful smile as he continued to hold my hands and look deep into my eyes. Never had he looked more uncompromisingly handsome. His dark, elegant looks appeared to particular advantage against the early-nineteenth-century ambience of Abigail's foyer, and I felt like a worm for disappointing him.

"I've brought Sylvia's wedding present." I tapped the gift-wrapped package under my arm. "But I think she wanted to have lunch in hopes of persuading me to take Heathcliff back."

"That dog?" The love light flickered out of Ben's eyes. "Or should I say that *horse*? Ellie, if he moves into the house, I move into the stables."

"Babcock . . . Babcock," the receptionist muttered as she ran her finger down the reservation page. "I don't see the name here; could the lady have used . . . ?"

"An alias? I don't think so." I shook my head. "But perhaps you wrote her down under 'Sylvia.' "

"I don't see that either, but then, sometimes I have trouble reading my writing, particularly when I've used my left hand because I was holding the telephone in my right." This admission was made in fear and trembling because the temperature in Ben's vicinity had dropped dramatically. "Oh, yes . . . here's a reservation beginning with an *S* . . . but I can't read the rest of the name."

"We could have a glass of wine together before your friend gets here." Thoughtful Ben unknit the ravelled brow of care and placed an arm around my shoulders, but I had to go and spoil things.

"Darling, I wish we could, but it's twelve o'clock already. . . ."

Whereupon Ben bowed stiffly as if releasing me from my promise to dance the minuet with him and retreated into the dining room to make sure a table was ready and waiting.

I stood looking after him, consumed by a ridiculous wave of remorse and of something irrevocably lost, when I heard footsteps entering the foyer. I turned to see a pink-haired lady, past the first bloom of middle age, coming towards me with a broad smile on her face and her feather boa fluttering. And at that moment I realized with a sinking heart that I wasn't meeting Sylvia Babcock for lunch.

The person with whom I would be sharing a meal was none other than Mrs. Swabucher of Eligibility Escorts.

Chapter

11

"Giselle Haskell, we meet again at last!"

The woman responsible for bringing Ben and me together through the rent-a-gent business swooped towards me in a flurry of pink-feather boa. "You're shocked to see me. What in the world has brought me to Chitterton Fells, you're asking. But all will be explained in the twinkling of an eye when that lovely husband of yours finds us a table for two in some nice, quiet corner. My telephone message didn't catch you too much on the hop, I hope?" Her eyes sparkled and dimples appeared in her cheeks. For a moment she looked more like a girl than someone's granny.

"It's lovely to see you. . . ." I forced a smile while my eyes strayed shiftily towards the dining room where, thank God, I didn't see anyone I recognized except my husband, who turned from speaking to one of his waiters and hurried towards us.

"Mrs. Swabucher, what a pleasure!" he exclaimed in a voice better suited to a medieval town crier. "This is quite a moment, Ellie"—arching an eloquent eyebrow— "our very own Cupid, here at Abigail's."

"Dear Bentley." The lady enveloped his hands in her pudgy paws and studied him impishly. "Still as handsome as ever, no crow's-feet or silver threads among the ebony, I'm glad to see. Marriage suits you, as I knew it would.

The moment Giselle walked into my office—why, it seems like yesterday—I took mental inventory of my male escorts and instantly decided that Bentley Haskell was just the man to waken this sleeping beauty with her first kiss." Mrs. Swabucher beamed in my direction. "And from that moment on, neither one of you, dear young things, had a hope in heaven of escaping your destiny. Not with Aunty Evie waving the magic wand."

"We're very happy," I said, switching Sylvia Babcock's present from one hand to the other and doing a sort of Charleston shuffle with my feet. Luckily the receptionist had vanished from immediate earshot in response to a waiter's beckoning finger, but I could not rid myself of the feeling that the secret of my wild past was out and that by nightfall everyone within reach of a hearing aid would have heard how Ellie Haskell met her man. I would be a laughingstock and Ben—my breath faltered as he laid a husbandly arm around my shoulders—would be regarded in many quarters as a gigolo. It was all so unfair! The name without the game! For months into our relationship, my fiancé-for-rent had treated me with the most demoralizing propriety.

"We very much appreciate your looking us up, Mrs. Swabucher." Ben spoke with all the enthusiasm I lacked. "And I would like to think one of the reasons is that word of Abigail's delectable cuisine has reached you even in London."

"I've kept abreast of your success, you may be sure of that, dear boy. You have a fine establishment, no doubt about that." The lady's glance took admiring note of the Regency ambience and returned immediately to our faces. "But the truth is, my sweet young things . . ."

"That you came to see us," I said in hollow accents, "for a more specific reason."

"Exactly!" Mrs. Swabucher nodded her powder-pink head. "At the risk of bursting Bentley's bubble, my mission on this occasion is to have a chat with you, darling Ellie, in regard to a business matter. Which isn't to say, dear boy"—she waggled the feather boa at my beloved—"that I wouldn't be delighted for you to join us for a glass of white wine before lunch."

"Thank you, but I wouldn't dream of intruding," Ben

responded at his most suave. "I'm sure you have been looking forward to spending quality time with my wife, and I—at the risk of sounding like Martha in the Bible—am needed in the kitchen." He offered his arm to Mrs. Swabucher and a quizzical look to yours truly. "If you will allow me the honour of escorting two lovely ladies, I will see you seated at the best table in the house, before making myself scarce."

The journey into the dining room could not have seemed longer had I been crossing the Sahara on a camel that decided to lie down and die every third step. *A business matter?* What could that mean, other than Mrs. Swabucher wished to use my name and—God help me—my photo in an advertising campaign for Eligibility Escorts? My face plastered in every tube station in London! To be gawked at by every man, woman, and child going up and down the escalators! It was too horrible to contemplate! Veering off the path between the linen-clad tables, I collided with a chair and mumbled an incoherent apology to the gentleman who got soup all down his shirt. And he thought *he* had problems! If the campaign was a success, what hope was there that I wouldn't show up, large as life, on buses and billboards in Chitterton Fells?

My knees gave out at the moment that Ben pulled out a chair for me at a table in the window nook overlooking Market Street. I was afraid to lift my eyes beyond the pink blur that comprised Mrs. Swabucher lest I see a man on a ladder, propped against a warehouse building across the way, pasting down the first giant poster.

Ben and I were ruined. Our lives as pillars of the community in rubble. But in typical male fashion, he failed to get the point. Through lowered lids I could see him moving Mrs. Swabucher's wineglass an inch or two closer to her bread and butter plate, adjusting her dessert spoon and fork, and shifting the bud vase so that it did not crowd the salt and pepper shakers. I could hear the rich murmur of his voice as he extolled the virtues of an exemplary white burgundy, recommended the chestnut mousse, the curried eel, and the roasted pheasant. And then he was gone. Never had I felt more alone than in that crowded room, with Mrs. Swabucher seated across the table. I wanted to rise up from my chair, toss my serviette in her face to throw her off balance, and rush out to the kitchen into Ben's arms. "Please," I would beg him, "take me and our adored babies far, far from the madding crowd and the wagging tongues to an uncharted island where no one has heard of Eligibility Escorts!" But, alas, this was the 1990s and the helpless female had gone the way of lead pots and button boots. Besides which, Mrs. Swabucher did not deserve to be treated like the Black Death.

"Excuse me!" I shot from my chair and clutched my throat. "I think I dropped my grandmother's pearl brooch by the reception desk, and I won't be able to enjoy my lunch for fear of someone trampling on it. If the waiter comes while I'm gone, please go ahead and order for me."

"Don't rush, Giselle dear."

"I won't," I said, stepping on Sylvia Babcock's wedding present and catching my heel in the strap of my handbag before making my getaway. Luckily, Abigail's other patrons had taken care to confine their belongings so that they did not constitute a danger to anyone jaywalking between tables. And I succeeded in exiting the dining room without further incident, if one discounted my sending a waiter into a spin that would have won him top marks in an Olympic figure-skating competition.

Mercifully, Ben was alone when I barged into the kitchen whose stainless-steel majesty demanded that each and every saucepan be always on its mettle whether suspended from the chef's rack or on duty on the cooker. The most indomitable fly would take one look at the gleaming white surfaces and get the hint to buzz off. A sauce simmering in a coddle cup gave a couple of small, tasteful burps, but otherwise all was serene despite this being the lunch-hour rush. A master of organization, that was my husband. And as I breathed deeply of the air ripe with the aromatic memory of sun-drenched olive gardens and cottage kitchens in Provence, I felt the panic occasioned by the arrival of Mrs. Swabucher drop from my shoulders like . . . a pink-feather boa.

"Ellie! You came, my darling one." His arms were around me and his lips came down on mine in a kiss of utmost tenderness. I reached up to touch the smooth plane of his cheek. It was a moment to be treasured, had the timing been right.

"Ben, we have a problem—"

"So that's it." He stepped back from me but maintained hold of my hand. "You came here to toy with me, but your conscience won out. Foolish female, don't you know that I am the ultimate cad? Married women have long been my specialty."

"Ben—" I began again.

"Now I begin to see the light!" His black brows drew together in a mock scowl and he tossed my hand aside, then wiped his on a handkerchief plucked from his pocket. "You've discovered you left your purse at home and find yourself in the embarrassing position of having to make a deal with me in return for a free lunch for you and Mrs. Swabucher. Tough luck, Ellie. I can be a hard man when pushed to the brink, and I've always found it an incredible turn-on to watch a tearful woman slogging through a mountain of washing up. Of course"—his eyes narrowed and his lip curled—"dessert would be extra, but I am sure we can come up with some arrangement to suit my male appetites. . . ."

"Please"—I grabbed the hankie away from him and threw it in his face—"don't be an idiot! You know perfectly well that the first time I'm asked to pay for a meal at Abigail's I'll burn the kitchen down. And don't tell me," I continued as he opened his mouth, "that my doing so would add a few sparks to our relationship. I need you to be serious and tell me what to do about Mrs. Swabucher."

"I don't get your point, Ellie." Ben leaned against the working surface, ankles crossed, the picture of a man without a fear in the world.

"You heard her!" I pushed my hair back from my beaded brow. "She said she was here to discuss a matter of business with me, and that can mean only one thing. Mrs. Swabucher intends to make hay out of your . . . my . . . *our* involvement with Eligibility Escorts. Oh, I don't mean she's going to blackmail us or anything like that, but . . ."

"I should think not." Ben's eyes had darkened from turquoise to emerald. "We have nothing to be ashamed of—or do you feel differently on that subject, Ellie?"

"No, of course not," I said, "but I don't think either of us would wish to show up on a billboard for E.E."

"Think what the neighbours would say!"

"Exactly!" He understood. I breathed a sigh of relief.

"Or the members of the Library League," he continued in the most silken of tones. "Heaven forbid that we should shock the brigadier or the pompous Lord Pomeroy. Yes, my darling, I do see that my past employment, if leaked to the population of Chitterton Fells, could be an insupportable embarrassment to you."

"You're making me sound quite horrid," I flared. "And you're completely off the mark: It's not that I'm ashamed of how we met, it's just that people, not knowing that you worked for Eligibility only because you were trying to write a spy novel at the time, might misinterpret the situation."

"That wouldn't bother me."

"You don't care that in addition to the nasty things people might say about you, they might conclude I was desperate to get a man, whatever the price?"

"I've never viewed our marriage as anyone's business but our own, and I'm rather surprised to discover you would rather we had met at a vicarage tea party." Ben retreated to the cooker and began stirring the sauce in the coddle cup. "One of the things I always loved about you, Ellie, was your willingness to let the world be damned."

"We have the children to consider."

"True enough, and I wouldn't worry even if Mrs. Swabucher does spill the beans. No one who knows you, sweetheart, would believe you ever did anything so preposterous as to rent a man for a weekend and end up marrying the renegade."

"Thanks a lot!" Wiping my eyes with the back of my hand, I banged open the door into the foyer, putting a dent in the forehead of the luckless waiter about to enter the kitchen, and plowed forward towards the dining room, where I was brought up short. Just inside the entryway stood Brigadier Lester-Smith, briefcase in hand, engaged in conversation with a tall, broad-shouldered man, the town's foremost solicitor, my friend Bunty's ex-husband, Lionel Wiseman. Both men expressed pleasure at seeing me, and the brigadier added the information that they were meeting for lunch to discuss some minor details of Miss Bunch's will.

"Mrs. Haskell is going to refurbish the house for me," he cheerfully advised his legal advisor.

"Excellent!" Mr. Wiseman inclined his handsome silver head in my direction. "That, coupled with your family obligations, should keep you busy. Too busy, I imagine"— he cleared his throat—"to see much of Bunty."

"Oh, no." I tried to steady my breathing and keep my gaze from flickering to Mrs. Swabucher. "I plan to keep in touch with Bunty."

"Mrs. Wiseman is a valued member of the Library League," supplied Brigadier Lester-Smith.

"Splendid!" Mr. Wiseman spoke to the room at large. "I'm pleased to know my ex-wife is keeping herself occupied. Do you happen to know, Mrs. Haskell, if she is seeing anyone special?"

"You mean a man?" I asked.

"One tries not to be a dog in the manger." Avoiding my gaze, Lionel Wiseman looked straight at Mrs. Swabucher, and the brigadier followed suit.

"That woman in pink," the latter said from the floor, where he was scrambling to pick up his dropped briefcase, "she's . . . a remarkable-looking woman, if you'll pardon the observation, Mrs. Haskell. I'm not up on ladies' fashions, but that feather boa does attract the eye."

It had obviously taken his breath away. The brigadier was wheezing heavily as he got to his feet, and I wondered if I might be witnessing that trademark of romantic fiction—love at first sight. Personally, I felt as if a cannon ball were lodged in my chest as I realized that he might react with starry eyes to the discovery that I was lunching with Mrs. Swabucher and request diffidently that I introduce him to the Venus in Pink. Thank God for Mr. Wiseman. He intercepted a waiter, and after a few moments of murmured conversation, imparted the news that there wasn't a spare table to be had in the next thirty minutes, and suggested to Brigadier Lester-Smith that they try their luck at the nearest pub, The Dark Horse.

"We'd better hurry so as not to make you late back to your office, Lionel." This response contained a definite note of relief, causing me to suspect, as the two men bade me good afternoon and made their departure, that the brigadier's courage had failed him and he preferred to moon upon the lady's charms from a safe distance rather than risk his hopes being forever blighted by her indifferent response to his impassioned gaze.

Mrs. Swabucher was studying the leather-bound menu and looked up only when I sat down at the table and spread my serviette across my knees. If she had seen me talking with the two men, she gave no sign of it, and I forgot all about the brigadier as I contemplated her cheerful face.

"You're back, Giselle." She lifted her water glass and took a sip. "Did you find the brooch?"

"The what? Oh, you mean . . . ?"

"The one that belonged to your grandmother."

"Oh, that one." My hand moved to the neck of my blouse. "It wasn't in the foyer and I'm beginning to think I didn't wear it after all."

"Very likely, but you're still worrying about it, aren't you, dear? You're all flushed, and who can wonder in this warm weather. What you need is to have a nice cold drink. The waiter, such a nice young man—very handsome in an Italian sort of way—came to take our order, and I told him we would have the pheasant, roast potatoes, and parsnip fritters. No counting calories on such a special occasion, those are Aunty Evie's orders. If Ben had wanted a skinny wife, he wouldn't have married you, would he, dear?"

"I suppose not," I muttered, staring at the table.

"He loves you just the way you are. Always remember that and don't try to change; time will take over that job for you. One day before you know it, you will look at Ben and discover that seemingly overnight you have both grown old and wrinkled—"

"Mrs. Swabucher!" Desperation drove me to interrupt the flow of her voice. "I will always be grateful to you and Eligibility Escorts, but—to be completely blunt—I'm not interested in participating in a national advertising campaign!"

For a moment I thought she was choking. Then I realized I was hearing a chuckle. "Silly me! I should have known, Giselle, you were bound to think I was talking about Eligibility when I spoke of a business matter, but in fact I sold that business a couple of years ago, for a very tidy profit, when I decided to embark on my new adventure."

"Really?" I was dimly aware of the waiter setting our luncheon plates before us.

"I had grown disenchanted with Eligibility." Mrs. Swabucher broke her roll apart and spread butter with a liberal hand. "Except in rare situations such as yours and dear Bentley's, I found the element of romance lacking in the escort business and, as I am sure you realized at our first meeting, I am a romantic to the core." She pressed a hand to the breast of her powder-pink suit. "Leafing through my files day after day to find the right gentleman to escort a sad little widow to a West End play failed after a time to make my heart sing." She smiled impishly at me. "Would you please pass the salt and pepper?"

Struggling to overcome my astonishment, I pushed the little pots towards her and picked up my knife and fork without any immediate plans of using them. "Do . . . tell me about your new venture."

"As my late husband, Reginald, used to say"—Mrs. Swabucher cut into her pheasant with enthusiasm—"we learn far more from our successes than our failures. And Eligibility taught me how to assess masculine potential for extraordinary romantic appeal at the commercial level. I became the business agent for a young man who had ambitions of working as a cover model for novels. The rest, as they say, is history. And I know you will agree with me, Ellie, that no one has ever added such luster to romantic fiction as the heroically handsome—"

"Karisma!"

"So now you know why I am here, Giselle." Mrs. Swabucher had managed to polish off most of her pheasant while I sat gawking at the woman who had guided the dream lover to the pinnacle of fame and fantasy. "When my secretary took your phone call yesterday, asking if Karisma would come to Chitterton Fells for a benefit, I was not present. But later, when she told me, I was most upset that I had missed speaking to you. Because a request from you, or dear Bentley, makes for a very special circumstance."

"I'm a member of the Library League . . ."

"A worthy organization, I'm sure." Mrs. Swabucher

laid down her knife and fork. "And of course I also thought immediately that in addition to my desire to be of service to you, Giselle, you do live in that delightful little castle, which would be the perfect background for a series of photos of Karisma. We could use one for next year's Dream Lover Calendar, or even put together an entire book of them. So what I am proposing, dear, is that Karisma, accompanied by myself, his hair designer, his athletic trainer, and his photographer, stay at Merlin's Court for a couple of nights when coming down for your little library's benefit. You don't have to concern yourself, or dear Bentley, with preparing meals. Karisma eats only high-fibre, protein-sparing, vitamin-enriched meals prepared for him by his personal chef. Did I say that Emanuel will be coming too? Now, tell me, dear, are these acceptable terms, Giselle?"

Acceptable? Karisma, the realization of every female fantasy, a guest in my home? The concept of being able to gaze at will upon his breathtakingly handsome visage and unparalleled physique was so incredible that I dug my nails into my sweaty palms and welcomed the pain as proof that I was not dreaming.

Belatedly, I realized I wasn't breathing either. "Mrs. Swabucher . . . Ben and I will be honoured. . . . Do you have some dates in mind, ones that would not coincide with Karisma's really important commitments, that I could present to the Library League? And of course they will also need to know what fee he will charge for appearing at the benefit."

"Karisma and I have discussed the matter and, in consideration of my relationship with you and dear Bentley, Karisma is pleased to forgo the customary honorarium. I won't mention the amount because you would fall off your chair, Ellie. But we are talking about a national treasure." Mrs. Swabucher adjusted her feather boa about her shoulders and smiled benignly at the waiter as he bent to remove her plate. "You haven't taken a bite, Giselle," she said as I indicated to the man that I had finished eating. "Still worrying about your weight, aren't you, dear? So silly, because as my beloved Karisma will tell you when you meet him, he sees beauty in all women no matter what shape, size, or age." Her eyes grew misty. "He is truly a man for all seasons of the heart."

"He sounds wonderful," I opined with a quiver in my voice.

"The man is unique." Mrs. Swabucher's eyes shone with pride. "As you will see for yourself, Giselle, this coming Saturday."

"That's tomorrow!"

She was unruffled. "I know it's short notice. But I am afraid Karisma is booked up with engagements for decades ahead and it is quite a fluke that he is available this weekend. The plan is for him to spend Saturday at Merlin's Court for the photograph sessions and then make his appearance at your quaint little library on Sunday afternoon. After attending morning service at the Anglican church," Mrs. Swabucher added, settling her handbag on her lap. "Karisma is a deeply spiritual man, Giselle."

"That won't present any problem," I said. "St. Anselm's is just a stone's throw from Merlin's Court. But I am concerned there won't be time for us to publicize the benefit and attract a decent-sized crowd. Which would be unfair to Karisma and"—I hesitated to sound mercenary— "we would like to raise as much money as possible for the commemorative statue of Miss Bunch, our recently deceased librarian."

But Mrs. Swabucher waved a genial hand at me. "Don't worry about that. Word of Karisma's appearances spreads like wildfire. My suggestion is that you arrange a meeting of your library group for this evening and you'll see, dear, everything will fall into place. If you like, I will delay my return to London and accompany you . . ."

Before she could finish speaking, a waiter appeared at her side with a portable phone, ascertained that she was Mrs. Swabucher, and informed her that a gentleman was on the line, waiting to speak to her. She thanked him with a smile that promised a handsome tip as she lifted the receiver to her ear. "Karisma, is that you, my impetuous one?"

She chuckled softly, winked at me, and listened intently. "Yes, yes, everything is arranged. Giselle is delighted, positively *thrilled* to bits. We are to stay at Merlin's Court; what could be more convenient! . . . No,

I haven't got round to talking with her about who's who in Chitterton Fells, but I am *sure* we will meet some sparkling personalities, and—who knows?—we may even be invited to tea on the vicarage lawn. It's that sort of Victorian little place. Good-bye, my . . . oh, yes, she is, sitting across the table from me, just a moment." Mrs. Swabucher handed me the telephone. "Karisma would like a word with you, dear."

"He wants to talk to *me*?" I clung to the receiver for dear life, nearly slid off my chair, and croaked, "Hello?!?"

"Giselle . . . such a beautiful name!" The husky voice throbbed with emotion. "Already I am counting the hours until we meet, for I do not doubt you are as lovely as you are kind. Until Saturday I keep you as a dream in my heart."

It was too much: I could picture him so clearly, kissing the tips of his fingers into the receiver. My head spun, and before I could unstick my tongue from the roof of my mind, I heard a click and I was left listening to the dial tone.

I set the phone reverently down and endeavoured to bring Mrs. Swabucher's face back into focus. "Amazing . . . that Karisma should care enough about a small-town library benefit to track you down in order to find out what arrangements have been made."

"I told him I planned to have lunch with you at Abigail's, and that's just the way he is, dear, always so considerate. A heart of gold."

"I'm sure he's devoted to you." I was still starry-eyed. "And that you've become just like a mother to him."

"Well, I wouldn't say that." Mrs. Swabucher was occupied in opening up her handbag. "I'm not really the maternal sort. Reginald and I never had children together, although I helped raise his three by his first marriage and there's a bond between us, as you might imagine. Reggie, the eldest one, named for his father, is always looking over my shoulder when it comes to my business affairs. A nice, kind man, but being a worrywart has aged the poor boy beyond his years and I'm concerned that he'll end up with the health problems that plagued my Reginald's last years." She didn't wait for me to respond, but swept on.

"Growing old can be pitiful, but believe me, Giselle, I'm fighting the erosion of time every inch of the way." Mrs. Swabucher touched a couple of fingers to her pink-tinted head and put a dent in the beehive. "But I don't plan on doing anything so childish as marrying yet again. End of subject on boring old me! Here"—she reached into her handbag and brought forth a handful of goodies—"these are for you, a few little gifts from Karisma—one of his Build-a-Body-Beautiful exercise tapes, an autographed photo in a heart-shaped frame, a calendar, and a sixteen-ounce bottle of his Desire perfume."

"I'm overwhelmed," I said, trying to get a grip on my emotions *and* the loot. And who was that dark-browed stranger approaching our table? Not surprisingly, given the amount of emotional overload to which I had been subjected, I had forgotten all about my tiff with Ben in the kitchen.

Unfortunately the evening was taken if I could arrange an emergency meeting of the Library League, but as I got to my feet, I vowed that as soon as this celebrity weekend was through, I would spend quality time with my husband. His smile was somewhat cool around the edges when he asked how we had enjoyed our lunch. Something kept me from bursting out with an announcement of Karisma's impending visit. There would be time enough later when we were conveniently alone to discover Ben hadn't a clue as to the magnitude of the honour being bestowed upon us and our humble abode. Being of the male persuasion, he probably wouldn't respond enthusiastically to my demands that we redecorate overnight.

"Do you have to rush back to town, Mrs. Swabucher?" he asked pleasantly enough as he walked us out into the foyer.

"Not until this evening, dear boy." The woman who brought us together resembled a bird of rare pink plumage as she took three steps to every one of his in keeping up with his long stride. "Giselle and I have a dozen plans to make for—"

"This afternoon," I interjected hastily. "Oh, bother! I left Sylvia Babcock's wedding present under the table! Would you be a dear, Ben, and fetch it for me?"

"I live to serve," he replied, and while he was fetching the package I quickly explained to Mrs. Swabucher that Sylvia was a newlywed member of the Library League and that it would be killing three birds with one stone to stop at her house, give her the present before I lost it for good, and tell her about Karisma's visit and the library meeting.

My husband did not delay our departure by engaging me in a three-minute round of kissing which necessitated a referee's bell to break us apart. Indeed, as Mrs. Swabucher and I drove away from Abigail's in my car, it occurred to me that Ben's behaviour that day reminded me of someone, an extremely irritating someone, but I couldn't think who it could be or why I experienced a sensation of discomfort bordering on foreboding.

The penny didn't drop until we reached the Babcocks' street of identical semi-detached houses, with their lace curtains, handkerchief-size front gardens, and names such as Dun-Romin or Myshatow. It was hot. Beastly, baking hot. The inside of the car was like an oven set at 450 degrees and I could feel myself crisping up like Yorkshire pudding.

A typical English summer, one solitary day of unmerciful heat to justify the purchase of shorts and T-shirts. Tomorrow we would be back to good old grey skies and drizzle. The sun had bleached the sky with its savage glare, the leaves on the trees were perspiring heavily, and the rosebushes in the Babcocks' garden, at number forty-one, looked ready to pull up stakes and crawl over to the porch for some shade. The newspaper headlines would surely read *Hottest Day in Twenty-five Years,* just as they did at least once a summer, to prevent ninety percent of the population from climbing in leaky little boats and sailing for Florida.

Tellingly, Mrs. Swabucher abandoned her feather boa before getting out of the car and we staggered up the path like a pair of firemen in dire need of wet cloths to wrap around our faces. It took all my strength to press the doorbell before sagging against my companion, who also looked ready to expire.

But not for long. A wild barking shook the house walls and sent a couple of tiles scudding off the roof, missing our heads by inches. A black, furry form lunged at the door's side window, and the creature's talons shredded the glass. A pitiful squeal was followed by the faint promise: "I'm being as quick as I can! Don't move, or he'll turn on me, I know he will!"

Sylvia Babcock presented a sad picture as she opened the door. She was immaculate as always in a crisp print frock, with every pin-curl hair in place and her lipstick on straight, but her hands were shaking and her eyes looked like the glass ones sewn on teddy bears. And a teddy bear is what my canine friend Heathcliff became upon seeing me. Dropping down on his haunches, huge pink tongue lolling, he cocked his massive head and grinned broadly, as if to say "Ah, the nice lady who rescued me from my orphan state and found me this loving home, come in, do, and bring your friend. My hacienda is your hacienda!"

"Hello, Sylvia," I said in some doubt that she was thrilled to see me. "This is Mrs. Swabucher who, wonder of wonders, is the business agent for Karisma. She has graciously persuaded him to participate in our benefit for Miss Bunch. Can you believe our good fortune?"

"How nice," came the faint reply. "Albert and I just got back from getting the groceries, or you would have missed us." Sylvia jumped and her glass eyes almost popped off as Heathcliff swished his tail, giving her the nudge that it was only proper etiquette to invite us in. "Won't you?" She opened the door a further inch. Feeling I had to put my best foot forward as I crossed the threshold, Mrs. Swabucher on my heels, I held out the gift-wrapped package. Bother! I failed to explain quickly enough that it was a wedding present and with a grateful woof Heathcliff leapt up, snatched it from my nerveless grasp, and bounded off down the hall.

"You need to take him to obedience school, dear." Mrs. Swabucher spoke the obvious. "Happiness is a well-trained pet."

"Happiness is a *dead* pet," Sylvia spat out with an unusual burst of ire. "But I'm afraid to let him out in the road to get run over because Albert is tickled to bits with him." Poor Sylvia, she truly was afraid of everything from spiders to the pages of a book being turned too quickly. On one regrettable occasion, when Lord Pomeroy had let wind at a library meeting, she had dived for cover as if in the thick of a hurricane. And because of me, meddlesome Millie, her hopes of wedded bliss with the likable Mr. Babcock were being sorely put to the test.

"You have to put your man's happiness before your own, dear." Mrs. Swabucher, still feeling the heat, was fanning her cheeks with a gloved hand. "As I've learned, at times to my cost, a woman must be prepared to make *any* sacrifice for the good of the one she loves."

Far from taking offence at a stranger butting in on her personal affairs, Sylvia's impeccably made-up face brightened. "You're right, I do have to remember that Albert is a gift from God, the salt of the earth, the man I've been waiting for all my life. I shouldn't get worked into a froth because he sometimes forgets to take off his shoes when he comes in, or hangs the toilet paper the wrong way, or doesn't remember to give the soap a rinse and a pat dry after he washes his hands. His heart is in the right place . . . even if his clothes aren't always hung up."

"Speaking of things not being where they are supposed to be," I said, "perhaps we should get that wedding present away from Heathcliff, seeing as I failed to purchase breakage insurance."

"And then we can have a word or two about my wonderful Karisma and how a visit from him will not only raise money for your memorial fund, but put Chitterton Fells on the map. Now, doesn't that sound a cheery prospect!" Mrs. Swabucher, ever the businesswoman, gushed. And Sylvia, further heartened by the suggestion that we did not plan to make an entire afternoon of our visit, led the way into her kitchen. This room, which was not much bigger than a garden shed, was as implacably pristine as the rest of the house. Heathcliff was under the table thriftily unknotting the ribbon decorating the wedding present, and the only eyesore, to put it unkindly, was Mr. Babcock. He, from the looks of him, had just made his fourteenth heavily laden journey from the car parked a few yards from the open door.

His arms were loaded with shopping bags bursting forth with boxes of Weetabix and packages of Tide. His hair was matted to his brow and his florid face was dripping with sweat as he set one load down on the table and rested another on the bridge of his stomach. Sylvia was right, he was a perfect dear. Between explaining to her that he had put all the other groceries away in the pantry or fridge, he greeted me with pleasure and expressed himself delighted to meet Mrs. Swabucher.

"Can you believe this weather?" He mopped his red face with his shirt-sleeve and knocked a shopping bag, which toppled over the one already on the table so that the contents of both, including a joint of beef and an enormous cauliflower, spilled out, sending tins of baked beans and oxtail soup rolling over to the edge to land in a series of thumps on the floor.

Sylvia had been nervously trying to coax Heathcliff into handing over the wedding gift. Now she let out a piercing scream. The dog, no doubt interpreting this as a call to action, bounded out from under the table in pursuit of a tin of pineapple, knocked Mrs. Swabucher sideways, and skidded to a halt only when the joint of beef took a flying leap off the table.

"Here, Cliffy!" Mr. Babcock patted his broad thigh without much conviction. "Nice doggy, come to Daddy."

To his credit, Heathcliff did cock an ear, but his hunting blood was up, and before his beleaguered mistress could emit another scream, he had seized up the joint of beef in his mighty jaws and raced with it out into the raging heat of the garden.

"Go after him, Albert!" Sylvia shrilled. She was understandably beside herself, given the dents in her once-perfect kitchen floor. "That's our Sunday dinner! Albert!" she wailed.

Mr. Babcock needed no further prodding. I doubt that he saw me as I held out the chewed-upon gift package or heard me suggest that he offer to trade it with Heathcliff for the roast. Huffing and puffing, he disappeared through the doorway, and as Mrs. Swabucher and I peered through the window above the sink, we saw him engage in heroic battle, man against beast under the gruelling sun. It was an awe-inspiring sight, a hard-fought tussle in which neither combatant appeared to give an inch of rump roast, and then . . . yes, it really seemed that victory would belong to Mr. Babcock. I was about to cheer, when he released his hold, staggered backwards a few paces, and collapsed in slow motion on the lawn.

My horrified eyes met Mrs. Swabucher's. I knew exactly what she was thinking: Poor man, what a ridiculous, wasteful way to die.

Chapter

12

"Another one added to the death roll." Vanessa swatted a fly with a cushion and stood back to savour her kill. She and I were in the wainscotted study at Merlin's Court. Gerta was in the kitchen making potato kuchen like a woman possessed while the twins took their naps. And Mrs. Swabucher, who had taken the abrupt demise of my friendly milkman harder than might be expected, given their five-minute acquaintance, was resting upstairs in one of the spare bedrooms.

I was pretty much done in myself. Keeping the hysterical Sylvia propped up in my arms so she did not keel over and do herself or the kitchen floor an injury had kept me occupied until the ambulance and assorted fire engines arrived. But when the professionals took over I was enormously relieved to give a quick account of what I had witnessed, promise to be available if needed for further questions, and escape with Mrs. Swabucher back to the comparative calm of my own home.

"Here." Vanessa dropped the cushion used to kill the fly onto the easy chair by the fireplace. "Sit yourself down, Ellie, and pull yourself together. Anyone would think by the way you're carrying on that you were married to the man. How about a sherry?" Her favourite drink because it matched her eyes. Rooting around among the decanters on the butler's tray, she poured a sizable jolt into a glass.

"No thanks." I waved it away, leaned my aching head back, and stared gloomily at the latticed windows. The sun, having caused enough trouble for a month of Sundays, had called it a day and was hiding out behind clouds that had popped up out of nowhere during the last half-hour.

"Drink it." My cousin pushed the glass under my nose. Her unexpected solicitousness puzzled me until I noticed a sparkle on her finger that put the crystal glass in my hand to shame. Her engagement ring. It had grown at least a couple of carats since I last saw it on her finger. That poor fly. Vanessa had killed it, with her left hand I now realized, as an excuse to dazzle me into commenting on her ring. "What do you think?" She perched on the edge of a chair, her titian head tipped to one side and the Hope diamond resting on her crossed knee. "Darling George took me out this afternoon while you were gone and bought it for me at that really pricey jeweler's in Market Street."

"But you already had a ring. . . ."

"True." Vanessa blew on the new gem and buffed it with the hem of her olive-green skirt. "But you know how men are! George got this bee in his bonnet that I deserved something twice, three times as good. And you know me, sweetie, I strive to be the dutiful fiancée. He's going to have the first little stone made into a pendant for me to wear on our wedding day. Isn't he a dear?"

"The salt of the earth," I muttered, and went back to thinking about the late Mr. Babcock.

"There you go, always casting a blight on my happiness." Vanessa slipped off the chair and went to stand by the desk littered with all the comforting signs of Ben's industrious use of it. His handwritten recipes, the litter of pens and pencils, and the stacks of gourmet journals were all arrayed on the desktop.

"I only said—" I began.

"Yes, but it's *how* you said it." My cousin closed her eyes so that her lashes fanned out on her damask cheeks. "I know what you are thinking, Ellie—ashes to ashes and all that dreary stuff. But it's not my fault, is it"—she flashed me a petulant glance—"that this Babcock man kicked the bucket? And, loath as I am to pour oil on troubled waters, you're not to blame either."

"Oh, yes, I am!" I swallowed the sherry in one gulp and set the glass down on the side table. "If I hadn't pushed the man into taking Miss Bunch's dog, he wouldn't be dead."

"Rubbish." Vanessa refilled my glass and handed it to me. "I expect he had a heart condition or some other health problem and wouldn't have lasted long in any case."

"You could be right," I conceded. "I remember how on the day he came into the house and ended up taking Heathcliff, Mr. Babcock had a nasty turn—he attempted to make light of it, but it was apparent there was something wrong with him."

"There you are! And if you ask me"—Vanessa refilled my glass once again and poured one for herself—"it's his wife who should be suffering the torture of the damned." Her eyes lit up with mischievous malice. "Unless your friend Sylvia married the old goat for his insurance policy and being fully aware that he was a prime candidate for a stroke or heart attack sent him charging out into the broiling heat after the dog. Think about it—it could be she's laughing on the inside, the sly vixen, while sobbing up a storm."

"You've got an evil mind." I sipped my third sherry and sat up straighter in my chair. "I'm sure Sylvia adored her husband."

"Even when it became a case of love-me-love-my-dog? Really, darling"—Vanessa disposed herself gracefully on the low stool in front of the fireplace—"you're *such* an innocent. Next you'll be telling me you believe that I'm in love with George. And you know something? Crazily enough, for once you'd be right. It's not the same sort of thing that you have with Ben, or at least did at the beginning, all soft eyes and violins playing in the background. But it works for me. We fit together somehow and, weird as it sounds, when I'm with George I really don't mind when we don't devote every minute to talking about me."

"I'm pleased for you, Vanessa."

She cupped her left hand in her right one and studied

her ring. "Honestly, I wasn't the one pushing for a bigger diamond. I think George gets a bit insecure at times on account of his humble origins and then I suppose it's only natural that he worries about some gorgeous guy coming along out of the blue and sweeping me off my feet. But I can't see that happening in Chitterton Fells, can you?"

"Not unless . . ."

"And even if Mr. Tall, Dark, and Handsome did show up on the doorstep, I've decided, Ellie, to embark on a new personality; in fact, I've made up my mind to make a career of being *nice*. After all, how bad can it be? I figure I'll get my weekends off, a couple of holidays a year, and I'll retire when I'm sixty-five or so and spend my golden years being a bitch." Vanessa sat on her stool, gazing mistily into the future for a few moments before adding, "Did I rudely interrupt you just now? Forgive my gross insensitivity, darling, and proceed with whatever you have to say, no matter *how* vacuous."

"It wasn't anything earth-shattering." I stood and was pleased to discover that my legs were no longer wobbly. "It was just that when you mentioned the possibility of a mind-bogglingly handsome man showing up at Merlin's Court, I realized that with the Babcock tragedy I hadn't told you why Mrs. Swabucher is here. And given your modeling career, I imagine you'll be interested to know she is the business agent for Karisma, the—"

"I know who he is. Who hasn't seen him, stripped to his loincloth, flexing his muscles, and otherwise flaunting his bronzed bod on the covers of those dippy romance novels?" Vanessa wrinkled her nose. I fought down the urge to swat her with a cushion.

"Well, he's coming down here at great personal sacrifice, considering his myriad of engagements, to aid in our raising money for Miss Bunch's memorial statue."

"Who?"

"The librarian who recently dropped dead while on the job after decades of devoted service to the members of the reading community, some of whom—like me—occasionally enjoy reading romantic fiction. Heathcliff was Miss Bunch's dog and"—I sat down with a wallop that set my head spinning and my powers of rational thought flying out the window—"I don't know why I didn't think about the Rigglesworth curse when, today, tragedy struck again."

"You've lost me, darling!" Vanessa put the stopper back in the sherry decanter, signalling she'd decided I'd already imbibed more than was good for me.

"Poor Sylvia Babcock is a member of the Library League, and when I went to see her, I planned to discuss plans for Karisma's visit. How could I have allowed my excitement at the prospect of meeting God's gift to womankind to blind me to the realization that we are courting disaster in having him here? I told the other members of the league yesterday that old Hector is not the sort of ghost to fade into the woodwork, and I was dead right."

"Don't be silly, Ellie," said my cousin. "You always look like a corpse when your makeup wears off, but take my word for it, *you're* still in the land of the living."

"But the same can't be said for the late Mr. Babcock," I said grimly, "and God alone knows who is fated to become Hector Rigglesworth's *next* victim."

Seemingly Vanessa was genuinely intent on developing the human side of her personality because she urged me in a voice similar to the one I might have used with Abbey and Tam to calm down and tell her the whole story, however boring. So I gave her an unabridged account of Hector and his seven daughters, his deathbed curse, and the chilling coincidence, if you could call it that, of Miss Bunch meeting her end on the hundred-year anniversary of his demise. Talking it out helped. By the time I finished, I decided I should have titled my spiel the Rigglesworth Rigmarole, and I couldn't feel miffed at my cousin when she made her pronouncement.

"I don't know about the sherry," she declared, "but you've definitely been overdosing on Gothic novels. The headless woman haunting the north tower by day and clanking her chains by night while bodies continue to stack up in the butler's pantry. I'm not saying those books aren't good for a giggle, especially if Karisma's on the cover. But honestly, darling, I'm surprised at you taking such superstitious rot seriously. Whatever would the vicar say? Oh, don't sit there hanging your head"—she gave that part of my anatomy a bracing pat—"trust me, Ellie, I won't breathe a word to her. I wouldn't want you to be excommunicated and find the doors of St. Anselm's barred against you on my wedding day. It would be too *awful* for words to be married without having you there so that people can make odious comparisons, in whose favour we need not ask." She twirled a tendril of silken hair around one finger and gazed dreamily into a white-satin-and-lace future. "I must practice blushing and work on my self-deprecating smile." She sighed. "Does the list of bridal responsibilities have no end?" Vanessa had not changed out of all recognition.

The sun peeped out from behind the clouds. I decided to take it as an omen. Mr. Babcock's death was indeed a tragedy. My heart ached for Sylvia, and I even had sympathy for the re-orphaned Heathcliff, who had escaped through a two-inch crack in the fence before the breath had left his master's body, and was no doubt roaming the streets. A dog without a country. But such is the way of this world, without any assistance from the unseen forces of the Beyond.

"Thanks for the pep talk, Van," I said.

"Why don't we celebrate and go out for dinner?" She was back at redefining her personality. "We could go to Abigail's and tell Ben we're having a surprise party for him. George will treat if I promise him dessert. And I suppose we could even include his mother and that pink-haired friend of yours along with the little tots."

"I can't." Looking at the clock, I discovered it was gone five o'clock. "I have to get on the phone, set up a meeting at the library, and then drive over there with Mrs. Swabucher."

Vanessa shrugged. "Suit yourself. But I don't intend to die from lead poisoning eating Gerta's dumplings. If you ask me, that woman is a curse if ever there was one. Apart from her cooking, I don't think she's right in the head. Oh, don't look like that, Ellie! I'm not suggesting that if you don't watch her every minute the kiddies will end up in the soup, but she certainly is . . ."

"A pressure cooker about to explode?" I bit my lip. "You may be right and, God help me, I can't afford to take any risks with Abbey and Tam, even though I feel sorry for Gerta with her marital problems. Perhaps . . . yes, that's it! I'll tell her tomorrow morning that with Karisma and his entourage arriving for the weekend, it would be best for her to move into Freddy's cottage and spend the next few days getting herself settled in. That will give me a little time to come up with a long-term plan that would not put her out in the mean streets along with poor Heathcliff."

"You're such a softie"—Vanessa shook her head—"and to show you I too can be sweetness and light, I'll let the woman come out to dinner with the rest of the gang, so long as she doesn't bring a doggy bag with her."

I thanked my cousin and, hearing footsteps just beyond the door, I went out into the hall to find Mrs. Swabucher looking much better and eager for a cup of tea and perhaps a slice of toast before we set out for the library. Shamefacedly I confessed that I had not got round to ringing up the other members of the league.

"You had a nasty shock, Giselle," Mrs. S. soothed, "and I had to go and make things worse by carrying on like I had lost someone near and dear to me. Reginald, bless him, always said I was too sensitive to live, and the truth is, dear, seeing that man die this afternoon brought the memories of my husband's passing flooding back. But even if," she rallied bravely, "Mr. . . . ?"

"Babcock," I supplied.

"That's right. As I was saying, even if his wasn't a dignified end, he went quickly. Reginald's last months were an endless round of bedpans and throwing-up bowls. He had so many hoses going in one end and out the other, he looked like a fire extinguisher."

"I'm so sorry." I put a sympathetic arm around her powder-pink shoulders.

"Silly of me to go on like this, Giselle, but I don't think I could go through that hell again. Seeing Mr. Babcock turn blue reminded me I'm not a tough old bird. Death is usually an ugly business. And the thought of someone I loved being so rudely taken from me . . . it was—shall I say"—she fingered the downy pink-feather stole—"as if a goose had walked on my grave. But enough of my ramblings, dear. You have to phone the library and I need to repair my makeup so that I don't appear looking like I'm a hundred and two."

While Mrs. Swabucher was in the cloakroom applying lipstick and wielding the mascara brush, I rang up Mrs.

Dovedale at her corner grocery shop and was lucky enough to catch her before she pulled down the shade on the door and trotted off home. She voiced delight that Karisma was coming, expressed amazement that the notice was so short, did not question why Mrs. Swabucher had chosen to communicate in person with me, and kindly offered to notify the other Library League members that there would be an unscheduled meeting at seven o'clock that evening.

It was not until I hung up the phone that I realized I had not said a word about the Babcock tragedy. But when I rang back several times in the course of the next half hour, Mrs. Dovedale's line was engaged. And by the time I had cuddled the twins, got Mrs. Swabucher her tea and toast, admired Vanessa's prowess at setting out the crockery, and had spoken to Gerta, it seemed pointless to ring back. Mrs. Dovedale would surely have left the shop by then to have a bite to eat and freshen up before setting out for the library.

During the drive into Chitterton Fells I was preoccupied and failed to point out to Mrs. Swabucher any trees or fence posts of interest along the way. Gerta had taken my suggestion that she move into the cottage at the gates for the weekend with commendable restraint. No exclamations of "You get rid of me!" No unbridled sobbing. She had promptly agreed that the house would be bursting at the seams with Karisma and his minions and admitted it would be nice to have a little place of her own. Shame on me. I ended up feeling like the royal executioner.

I was still wondering if I had allowed Vanessa to make me paranoid where the au pair was concerned when I parked the car and led Mrs. Swabucher up the steps and into the library. My preference would have been to go in the back way and thus avoid seeing Miss Bunch's successor presiding at the desk. But it seemed only right to introduce Karisma's business agent and explain the reason for her presence. Unfortunately, Mrs. Harris was a woman after Hector Rigglesworth's heart. The new librarian confessed without a blush that she had never heard of the world's foremost romance cover model, never read fiction except of the literary sort, and voiced the hope that during her tenure readers could be steered towards books of an *uplifting* nature.

Given this reception, Mrs. Swabucher was not inclined to waste her sweetness on the musty air and, with only the briefest dawdling to find books featuring Karisma on the cover, we went through the door into the narrow hall with the loo to our right and the stairs to our left and saw Mrs. Dovedale coming in through the back entrance. Her pleasant, homespun face lit up when I introduced her to Mrs. Swabucher, but she did not have the best of news to report.

"I'm ever so sorry, Ellie, but I had terrible luck getting a full group here tonight. Gladstone Spike said he had a lot of baking to do this evening because he and his wife are expecting company this weekend. And I never did reach the brigadier, although I left a message with his landlady. As for Sylvia Babcock"—Mrs. Dovedale drew a ragged breath—"I'm afraid I've saved the worst for last in her case. I had trouble getting hold of her too, but when I finally got through, I couldn't believe my ears when she told me. The most terrible news! It seems her husband dropped dead this afternoon." The kind grey eyes brimmed with distress.

"I should have told you," I murmured guiltily.

"You were in shock," put in Mrs. Swabucher, "and at such times the mind puts up a wall." She addressed Mrs. Dovedale. "We were both at the Babcock home and witnessed the whole appalling scene. The dog bolted outside with the Sunday joint and Mr. Babcock made the fatal mistake of chasing after him on a day hot enough to roast him along with the beef."

"Dog?" said Mrs. Dovedale. "I can't picture Sylvia having a dog. She's so house proud and animals, even the best of them, as well I know from having half a dozen cats, do get hair and paw prints all over the place and scratch the furniture."

Right on cue, in validation of this statement, something clawed with frenetic purpose at the back entrance. Stepping backwards, I trod on the tail end of Mrs. Swabucher's boa, which had slid off one shoulder when she, clearly alarmed, had bumped into the wall. By the time I had straightened her, the boa, and myself out, Mrs.

Dovedale had braved the unknown by opening the door. Heathcliff bounded into our midst like the Grim Reaper's intermediary. At once the narrow hall was reduced to the size of a shoe box. And the oxygen supply went on wartime rations.

"He ran away from the death scene," I said as I tried to harden my heart against the dog, who sprawled on the floor and, being an animal of very little brain, adopted the guise of a hairy black rug. "Probably he went first to Miss Bunch's house and then followed his nose here. Goodness knows what is to become of him."

"I'd take him," Mrs. Dovedale sounded sincere, "but my cats are all getting along in years, so it wouldn't be fair to them, or to Heathcliff here. Perhaps Sir Robert would give him a home." At the mention of his name, her eyes turned misty and I was more than ever convinced she had a girlish crush on our fellow league member. "That man is such a softie— Are you feeling all right, Mrs. Swabucher? Your face has gone all pale."

"It's nothing, dear." This response was not borne out by the pink hair having lost some of its hue. "Silly me, I had the oddest feeling seconds before this dog started scratching at the door that someone was standing in the shadows laughing at us. It threw me right off balance; you saw me bang into the wall, Giselle"—she rubbed her right shoulder—"but I've got my sea legs back now."

If not for Vanessa's recent pep talk, I would have undoubtedly introduced Mrs. Swabucher to the legend of Hector Rigglesworth, while deluding myself that I too had sensed something untoward lurking on the outskirts of my peripheral vision. Being of renewed common sense, however, I suggested instead that we go upstairs to the reading room and get the percolator going so Mrs. S. could have a reviving cup of coffee before the meeting commenced. The question of what to do about Heathcliff in the immediate future was solved by his signalling, with a wag of his tail, that he would follow where we led and would not make any objection to a ginger biscuit tossed his way.

"It does seem odd getting here before the brigadier," Mrs. Dovedale remarked as we reached the top of the stairs and crossed the strip of Persian carpet into the reading room. "He's always such a sport about seeing everything, including the coffee, is ready by the time the rest of us arrive. I do hope he's all right. His landlady mentioned he'd looked a bit off-colour when she saw him this afternoon."

"Well, it wasn't anything he'd eaten at Abigail's," I said jokingly as I stepped over Heathcliff, who had abruptly lain down without a woof as if we were hiding out from the Nazis and our lives depended on his silence. "I saw him there with Lionel Wiseman at lunchtime, but the wait for a table was too long and they went somewhere else. Maybe that's him now," I said as footsteps mounted the stairs and the dog came to life with a swish of the tail. But it wasn't Brigadier Lester-Smith.

The person who joined us in the paneled room was the hale and hearty Sir Robert Pomeroy. By the time I had introduced him to Mrs. Swabucher, Heathcliff had nosed his way behind the cupboard containing the coffee supplies and Bunty Wiseman had joined us.

"I can't believe this!" Her blond curls were tousled as if she had just raced out of the shower and her eyes sparkled with impish delight as she stood surveying us, her hands on the hips of her ultra-tight jeans. "*Karisma* is going to be here in living colour! I tell you I'm a basket case. Will he fall in love with me on sight and ravish me on the spot, do you think? My mother always told me to put on clean underwear on the chance I ever found myself in that sort of emergency, but up until now I've never got back what I spent on soap powder and fabric softener." Bunty batted her eyes, moistened her lips, and pranced on tiptoe around the table, where Mrs. Dovedale and Sir Robert were setting out the coffee cups, to extend her hand to Mrs. Swabucher.

"I'm the ex Mrs. Wiseman and you must be the woman behind the incredible hunk, pleased to meet you. Crikey, what a gorgeous feather boa! Don't leave it lying around or I could be tempted to steal it to remind myself of the one I used to wear doing striptease before I hooked up with Li."

"You can borrow it anytime, dear."

"We were just talking about Lionel," I broke in. "I saw him and the brigadier at Abigail's today and he made a point of asking about you, Bunty."

"Well, bully for him." The eyes flashed but her mouth had softened. "How did he look?"

"Handsome as always."

"Not riddled with remorse?"

"He seemed a bit down," I said, aware the coffee was cooling in the cups and Mrs. Swabucher must have been eager to get on with the meeting—with or without Mr. Poucher. Neither he nor Brigadier Lester-Smith had yet arrived.

"But you wouldn't describe Li as racked with regret?" Bunty's lips hardened. "Oh, never mind! The man ditches me for the church organist, and because that little fling didn't work out he thinks he'll pick up where he left off with me! Like bloody hell he will! The world's a stage and every bloke a player. I'm getting on with my life."

"Speaking about getting a move on," I said, "perhaps we should conclude that the brigadier and Mr. Poucher aren't able to join us and have Sir Robert call the meeting to order." Upon glancing down the length of the table, I beheld our peerless peer engaged in a discussion with Mrs. Dovedale which, despite its being about who of the group took sugar, was as intimate as an embrace. It took several repetitions of their names for me to bring them back to their surroundings.

Watching nice Mrs. Dovedale try to hide her blushing confusion by rearranging the spoons on the saucers, I wondered if, now that she and Sir Robert were both conveniently widowed, they would be able to forget their different stations in life and act upon the thwarted passion of their youth. Or was it, as seemed to be the case with the Wisemans, too late for second chances?

"What! What! Am I wanted on the bridge?" Sir Robert blew out his ruddy cheeks, patted the dome of his waistcoat, and assumed his chair. "Bloody bad show, this business of Sylvia Babcock's husband," he said as the rest of us seated ourselves. "Getting past a joke, all this dropping dead. First Miss Bunch, and now this milkman chap. A drain on the old cash box, that's what it is, but I suppose we'll have to send a wreath."

"I hadn't noticed that Sylvia wasn't here," said Bunty. "She's not exactly the life and soul of the group, is she?

But gosh, she hasn't been married a month. When did all this happen?"

By now I should have had the story down pat. But fifteen minutes ticked away, partly due to asides from Mrs. Swabucher that included her late lamented husband, before I finished delivering all the details of that afternoon's tragedy. And when I'd concluded, no one mentioned Hector Rigglesworth or indicated he was in their thoughts by indulging in a convulsive shiver. None too soon we were ready to get down to the serious business of planning Karisma's appearance at the memorial benefit.

"Rather short notice, what! what!" Sir Robert took the lead with this assessment and in so doing ruffled Mrs. Swabucher's pink feathers.

"I'm afraid that can't be helped. As I explained to Giselle while we were having lunch, it was a miracle that Karisma had this one weekend free."

"Lucky us!" Bunty beamed. "Yesterday he wasn't coming. Now we are counting the hours until he arrives. Anyone would think someone had pulled a few strings." She gurgled a laugh. "Like Ellie, for instance, had the inside track."

Mrs. Swabucher ignored my beseeching eyes. "As a matter of fact I met Giselle and dear Bentley some years ago in London and I knew they had come down here to live at Merlin's Court. So when my secretary told me she had taken a phone call from a Mrs. Haskell at the Chitterton Fells library, asking if Karisma could do a benefit, I immediately rearranged our schedule to help out a very special young lady."

How neatly explained. What did it matter that Mrs. Swabucher hadn't mentioned the attraction of Merlin's Court as a photographic background for Karisma? I didn't mind her coming off like a philanthropist. She had protected my good name and earned me the gratitude of my fellow Library League members.

"So, Ellie, we owe this golden opportunity to you." Mrs. Dovedale came around the table to reward me with a refill of coffee. "In years to come, when people hereabout talk about Miss Bunch's memorial benefit, your name will be upon everyone's lips."

"Thank you," I said, particularly appreciative of the

hot beverage because the room had grown chilly, a sign that evening had made more headway than could be said of our well-intentioned but dilatory little group. Catching my eye, Sir Robert blew out his moustache and proceeded to make several excellent suggestions for getting word out on the double in hopes of bringing the crowds out in force to pay five pounds apiece for the pleasure of meeting Karisma.

Sir Robert would personally phone the radio station and also arrange for an announcement to appear in tomorrow's evening edition of *The Tittle Tattle.* "And if it wasn't asking too much, what! what!" Here tender glances were exchanged; he hoped Mrs. Dovedale would put up a notice advertising the event in her grocery shop window.

"I will gladly." His reward was a heartfelt smile.

"And if Gladstone Spike would do up a flyer"—Bunty was bubbling with enthusiasm—"and give me a list of St. Anselm's parishioners, I'd be pleased to deliver them. We want to make him feel part of this, don't we?" Perhaps she had forgotten that Gladstone had not been in favour of inviting Karisma to participate in our benefit, and I didn't feel it would be right to mention the man might have more pressing concerns on his mind. Instead, I offered to have Ben put a notice in Abigail's window and to ask my hairdresser to do likewise. And I might even have come up with some other brilliant ideas if Mr. Poucher hadn't broken my train of thought by coming into the room.

"Ha!" He stood at the end of the table, rubbing his hands together and looking, as Mrs. Malloy would have said, like a wet week of Mondays. "I'm not late, can't be, if the brigadier's not here. And don't suppose I've missed much anyway—just a lot of jawing about nothing much to the purpose." His gloomy eyes seized upon Mrs. Swabucher as the cause of his being dragged away from home. "My mother had one of her queer turns and it took forever to get her off to sleep, even after I doctored her milk. Blast the woman, she'll still be alive and kicking in the morning. And from what I hear tell, that's something Sylvia Babcock's husband won't be doing."

I had forgotten all about Heathcliff. Having retreated behind the coffee cupboard, he hadn't made a sound until now, when—his master's name invoked—he came bolting out of the shadows in a black, hairy rush. I will say this for him: He did remember that libraries frown on raised voices. But in keeping his woofs to a minimum, his pent-up energy found release in knocking Mr. Poucher down like a skittle and sitting on his chest.

"Nice doggy!" Mrs. Dovedale tried to coax him away with a ginger biscuit. "He turned up here tonight just after Ellie and I arrived, and we couldn't bring ourselves to turn him out into the streets."

"You always had a heart of gold." Sir Robert's voice was muffled by emotion, and in hopes that he might be moved to offer the orphan a home, I started to explain Heathcliff's sad history. Obviously I did a heartrendingly good job, because Mr. Poucher, still flat out on the floor, made the startling announcement that *he* would take the animal.

"He won't be the first to chew my ear off," he said, patting the furry weight on his chest, "and what's more, he won't want to marry me, so Mother shouldn't have any objection to me bringing him home. Off you get, boy; we'll borrow the coffeepot cord for tonight and tomorrow I'll get you a proper lead."

"Does this mean the meeting's over?" Mrs. Swabucher whispered in my ear as the rest of the group gathered around the new pet owner, offering tips on feeding, play-time, and the advantages of regular walks.

"I'm not sure," I said. "As a rule the brigadier makes a motion to conclude and someone seconds it, but with him not here, we haven't been sticking to the bylaws."

And in the scheme of things I don't suppose it mattered much. While Mrs. Dovedale was assisting Mr. Poucher in knotting the makeshift lead to Heathcliff's collar, she promised to deliver several caseloads of soft drinks and fancy cakes to the library on Sunday morning. Notice-ably moved, Sir Robert gallantly offered to provide paper serviettes, cups, and plates. Bunty said she would help where needed and, as she suspected the dragon at the desk would not take kindly to sticky fingers and cake crumbs, wouldn't it be best to serve the eats and drinky-poos up here? Finally it was left to Mr. Poucher to ask the all-important question.

"Is anyone going to tell us what time this jolly roundup starts?"

Mrs. Swabucher and I looked at each other and said with one voice: "Two o'clock." Almost everyone agreed that this would sandwich in well between mealtimes, and within seconds the room began to thin out. Heathcliff set things in motion by lifting his leg against the table and his new master led him away with promises of stopping at every streetlight on the walk home. They were followed by Sir Robert and Mrs. Dovedale, Bunty only a few steps behind them. An equally speedy exit seemed to be in store for myself and Mrs. Swabucher, until I realized that in the process of making major decisions no one had thought to empty the coffeepot, or wash up the cups and saucers.

Oh, well! The two of us buckled down to business and within five minutes the table was cleared and I was emerging from the cubbyhole-size kitchen, when we heard footsteps on the stairs. Was it Miss Bunch's successor coming to warn us we were over our time limit? Or had one of the group come back for something they had forgotten? Mrs. Swabucher was rearranging the feather boa—which she had taken off while helping me—around her shoulders, when who should walk in upon us but the brigadier.

He stood in the doorway and I sensed at once that something was wrong. His briefcase, always an integral part of him, was missing. And his eyes looked straight through me as if I were the ghost of Hector Rigglesworth. They fixed wistfully on Mrs. Swabucher.

"It's nice to see you again, Evangeline," he said.

"You'll have to refresh my memory"—a smile lifted her plump face but her eyes were puzzled—"I'm afraid I don't remember where I've met you."

"That's odd," said Brigadier Lester-Smith with a painful twist of the lips. "I recognized you the moment I looked across a crowded room at Abigail's today and saw the girl I once loved seated by the window."

"You can't be . . ." The boa slipped from Mrs. Swabucher's shoulders to lie in a heap of once-rosy dreams upon the floor.

"But I am," came the choked reply. "I'm the man you married, Evangeline, long ago."

Chapter

13

"The woman didn't recognize her own husband?"

Ben and I were in the drawing room, where the windows stood open, letting in the warm evening air, and he was sprawled on the sofa across from me. My husband's exhaustion after a long day was apparent in the fact he obviously hadn't been paying close attention to my detailed account of the fateful reunion.

"I told you, twice," I said, "the marriage was annulled donkey's years ago."

"But that hardly makes him a casual acquaintance, for God's sake! They lived together, slept in the same bed, made love!"

"No, they didn't." I was becoming impatient. "Evangeline—now Mrs. Swabucher—and the brigadier never consummated their marriage. She freaked out on the wedding night and fled from the bridal bed, never to return."

"The woman must be nuttier than a fruitcake. I'm surprised you let her go back to London on her own."

"That's unfair!" I bridled at this male viewpoint. "Her marriage to the brigadier took place over thirty years ago. It was a different era. She was a sheltered girl who didn't have a clue about the facts of life."

"Neither did I"—Ben folded his hands and assumed a

reflective pose—"but you didn't have me bursting into tears on our wedding night and sobbing that I wanted my mummy."

"I don't know how you can sneer; the brigadier was a lot kinder. He understood that his bride had come to him thinking that intimacy meant a kiss on the lips while wearing only one's night attire and marriage was sharing the same pot of marmalade."

"Poor devil, I'm not surprised he never remarried after such a hellish experience." Ben began to pace in front of the fireplace. "Is there any justice in this world? He meets up with the frightened virgin after all these years and discovers she found herself another husband and somehow managed to stick it out for the long haul. Or"—he raised a sardonic eyebrow—"are you about to tell me the *Swabucher* marriage was never consummated either?"

"Of course it was." I settled a cushion behind my head and curled up in the chair. "But from what Mrs. Swabucher told me after Brigadier Lester-Smith left us, Reginald, having been married before, was mostly interested in companionship. He was a kind, sensitive man who took things slowly at the beginning and never made excessive demands."

"What a champ!"

"I think he sounds a dear."

"The sort of man *you* should have married?" Ben was now standing with one arm resting on the mantelpiece and I resented his tone of voice.

"We're not talking about us."

"Sorry, that was uncalled-for, wasn't it? What I find curious is that Mrs. Swabucher ended up running an escort service. I wouldn't have thought that was the business for a Victorian-minded woman."

"As you should know from having worked for her," I responded as gently as I could, "there was never anything seamy about Eligibility Escorts; I think she saw herself as a sort of fairy godmother, making sure no one had to go to the ball, the theatre, or the office party alone. She's a very sweet woman and I always thought you were rather fond of her."

"So I am; she brought us together." Ben rubbed his forehead. "I'm sorry, Ellie, for being such a grouch. Sometimes the long hours at Abigail's catch up with me, but that's no reason for me to snip at you. Your day can't have been much fun. Vanessa mentioned this evening at Abigail's that your friend Sylvia's husband had died. There wasn't time for her to give me any details because Abigail's was so busy, but I understand he was our milkman. Did Mrs. Swabucher seem all right when she took off for London?"

"She was still a bit dazed."

"Perhaps you should have asked her to spend the night."

"I did suggest it, but she had to get back to discuss the weekend arrangements with Karisma."

"Who?"

"Oh, cripes!" I bounced out of the chair and guiltily faced my husband. "I haven't told you anything about that, have I? You don't even know why Mrs. Swabucher came to see me."

"You were afraid she wanted to rope you into some advertising campaign for Eligibility Escorts."

"I was mistaken and I'm sorry, darling, for carrying on the way I did at Abigail's. What it comes down to is that Mrs. S. is no longer in the escort business. She's the business agent for—"

"The bloke with the funny name?"

"Exactly," I said, and proceeded to explain the sequence of events that had ensured Miss Bunch's memorial benefit would be an unqualified success.

"And we're to entertain this Adonis for the weekend!" Ben did not sound particularly enthusiastic at being given the rare opportunity to host a celebrity who might be persuaded to give him some pointers on muscle-building. "Well, you'd better let me know what I'm to expect. For instance, does he wear regular clothes or just a G-string?"

"Don't be silly!" I turned away to hide the blush that fired up my face. "If you are worried that having Karisma here will turn the house upside down, you're mistaken. We don't even have to cook for him. He's bringing his own chef, along with his trainer, hairdresser, and I'm not sure who else."

"You're right, sweetheart, sounds hassle-free to me." Ben crossed the room to lay a supportive hand on my shoulder. "I should go outside and practice my Tarzan swing through the trees so I can compare notes with our guest when he arrives, but I think I'll go upstairs to make sure Abbey and Tam are snug in their beds. Vanessa helped Gerta get them settled down and waited until I got home before she went out again with her fiancé, but I miss saying good night to the children." He paused at the door and smiled rather wistfully. "Do you suppose that in addition to all his other attributes Karisma is the sensitive-male type?"

Something twisted deep inside me; but before I could answer, Ben was gone, and even as I took steps to follow him I heard a murmur of voices and Gerta came through the door. She looked cozy and completely wholesome in her wooly dressing gown, her braided hair coiled tidily around her head. Surely, I was the wacky one for listening to Vanessa's snide suggestions that we had been harbouring a demented nanny in our midst.

"Frau Haskell," she began, and her quiet voice and gentle manner did not make me feel any better about myself, "I am sorry to come in on you so late. I was in the hall on my way to make some hot milk, and I see Herr Haskell, who tells me you are in here alone."

"My cousin is still out with George Malloy," I said, wishing the guilt I felt did not make me sound so stiff. "Please come and sit down, Gerta, and tell me how the dinner at Abigail's went."

"It was very good." Gerta sat down on the sofa, hands on her knees and a smile on her face. "Abbey and Tam they have a nice time and eat all on their plate. Mrs. Mop, she came too and she looked pleased. I think she gets to like your cousin, who is very nice even to me. Mr. Malloy made lots of jokes about me thinking he was a crazy man and telephoning the police station. We all laughed a lot and for a little while I forgot my troubles."

"I'm glad," I said, sitting beside her.

"But the pain is still here"—Gerta placed a hand over her heart—"that I am so glad you get me out of the house before that man arrives."

"Karisma?"

"That's him, Frau Haskell." The plaits slipped from their anchors and plopped over her slumped shoulders.

"And now I see clear as daytime why you acted to save me."

"You do?"

"Mrs. Mop had a book with that most-naked man on the cover. In her handbag at the restaurant. And when your cousin told her he was coming to this house, she showed him to me. It was almost more than I could bear without the tears landing on my face."

"Oh, dear," I murmured.

"He is so much like my husband."

"Really?"

"The hair it is much longer and my Ernst always wears his trousers up to where they are supposed to be, not down around his personal parts, but otherwise they are the same man."

"Good heavens!" I was beginning to wonder if Vanessa had been right after all. "You never said anything about this when you saw Karisma on television the other morning."

"I was too upset that Mrs. Mop would let the children watch such a person, instead of the dinosaurs, to see what was in front of my face. And I have you to thank, Frau Haskell, for saving me from going wacky."

"You do?"

"Yes." Gerta picked up my hand and planted an impassioned kiss upon it. "You remembered what I had told you about my Ernst and knew I could not be in the house with this unclad man. All that talk you made about him bringing lots of servant people and it being nice for me to have a quiet place of my own, it was your kind heart speaking. And I can never make enough strudel and dumplings to repay you."

I was at a loss for words, but even had I attempted to say anything, my voice would have been drowned out when Gerta jerked her head towards the open window and let out a scream that threatened to shred the curtains end to end.

"He is here!" She was on her feet, hiding her face in her hands. "I must go to the cottage before he comes in and my mind is never the same again."

"Karisma isn't due here until tomorrow night," I assured her, somewhat bewildered by her panic. "You must have seen a shadow cast by one of the trees, or even more likely Ben went outside for a minute. It's getting dark, so it's not surprising you would confuse him with someone we were just talking about."

This was not Ellie Haskell's evening. At that very moment my husband came charging into the room with his eyebrows elevated to the middle of his forehead and steam coming out of his nostrils. "Who gave that bloody awful screech? I was all the way upstairs and it sounded as though a siren was going off inside my head." So much for Ben being the lurker in the shadows. Gerta and I had both opened our mouths to explain, when the doorbell rang.

"That must be Vanessa and George," I said even as my heart began to hop, skip, and jump. "Who else could it be?" There would have been no point in my saying that Gerta's hypothesis was rubbish, because suddenly I was alone in the room. She had escaped, in fear and trembling, through the French windows into the courtyard and Ben had gone to open the front door.

"Good evening, I do not arrive too late at night I hope."

The masculine voice of incredible sexiness was as recognizable to me as my own face in the mirror above the bookcase as I made frantic, futile attempts to smooth my hair and lick my lips into some semblance of desirability. Not only had I heard that voice on the television, I had known it always in some secret corner of my heart, possibly from time immemorial and certainly from the time I stopped reading *School Girl Annual* and walked the Yorkshire moors with Heathcliff's namesake.

"Ellie, guess who just arrived?" My husband sounded politely enthused, but how he looked as he came back into the room is anyone's guess. My eyes saw past my spouse to the embodiment of all my girlish dreams. Karisma! Here in the glorious flesh. He crowded out every sane thought with his magnificent height, powerful breadth of shoulders, flowing mane of hair, and those eyes that looked deep into my soul as if he too had been waiting a dozen lifetimes for this moment. He was indeed virility personified and—my heart slowed to an even thud—inhumanly handsome.

"Hello," I said, amazingly still on my feet and able to

extend my hand. Only now did I focus on his clothes—
blue jeans and a black leather jacket opened to the waist
with not a stitch of shirt underneath. He wore them like a
second skin.

"Giselle . . ." His smile would have melted the ice
age as he bent and kissed the tips of each of my fingers. "It
is so good of you and your husband to make me a guest in
your home. But I have goofed"—the word sat enchant-
ingly on his lips, given his deep-timbred continental accent—"I arrive on your doorstep before I am expected."

"He and Mrs. Swabucher got their wires crossed."
With this interruption, Ben reminded me of *his* presence.
"But I told Mr. Karisma there's no problem. It won't take
more than half an hour to get a room ready for him, and I
wasn't going to bed for another five minutes anyway."

"I intrude . . ." Karisma's eyes darkened with anguish.

"Nonsense. Whatever gave you that idea?" Ben
strolled between me and our guest to wave a hand at the
sofas and chairs. "You can ring Mrs. Swabucher when
she's had time to reach home and let her know you're here.
In the meantime, why don't you and Ellie sit down and I'll
fix you both a drink? A sherry for you, darling?" The voice
was that of the devoted spouse, but the glance he gave me
was inscrutable. "And what's your pleasure, sir?"

Karisma had paused before the mirror to stand
rumpling the tawny strands of his hair through his hand.
His expression was perplexed as he turned around. "Forgive me, I did not catch what you said to me."

"A drink?" Ben held up the crystal decanter from
which he had been pouring my sherry. "I can offer you a
fairly decent brandy, or would you prefer Scotch?"

"You are so kind, but if it is no problem I would
prefer a glass of vegetable juice if you have some freshly
made, or . . ." Taking the silence as a negative, he suggested, "I will take a mineral water."

"From our very own springs." My husband's little
joke bounced off Karisma, who in accepting the Perrier
and lime pronounced it better than anything currently
available on the market. Or was he being polite? The
world's most beautiful man was a mystery, I reminded
myself, except on one subject.

"I *lorve* women," he said.

Ben, not appreciating such exquisite sensitivity, merely raised an eyebrow.

"They are my intoxicating beverage." Karisma leaned forward so that his classic features and incomparable bone structure made every other object, inanimate or otherwise, fade into the walls. He opened the room up to the sky. He *was* the room. "To me all women are beautiful. They feed my spirit, fuel my masculinity, and make music in my heart."

"Excuse me if I get myself another drink."

It was inexcusable of Ben to sound as if he were being driven to overindulgence, but Karisma did not appear to notice. He was looking at me as if I were an entire orchestra.

"Women have something that we men lack." His expression became one of utmost tenderness, which only served to emphasize the sheer physical power of the man. "They have the gift of friendship. I know from looking into your eyes . . . Giselle . . . that you have many people in Chitterton Fells who turn to you when they need desperately for someone to make them feel part of the human race."

"*She* has *me*." The sound of Ben replacing the stopper exploded into the air like a gunshot, forcing me at last to find my voice.

"I think Karisma was speaking of social friends," I said as kindly as I was able. "And we are lucky there, aren't we, dear? Since coming to live here we've been fortunate in meeting some wonderful people, including the members of the Library League, all of whom are *so* grateful, Karisma, that you have spared some of your valuable time to be the drawing card for our fund-raiser."

"It is no problem." He modestly shied away from further expressions of my gratitude. "This is a beautiful house you live in. It is quite like a fairy tale castle, just as Mrs. Swabucher told me."

"You know the old adage," Ben said with an eloquent shrug, "an Englishman's castle is his home."

"Yes, I have heard that saying." Karisma walked towards the windows that still revealed something of the grounds in the amethyst light. "Such beautiful trees and you are so privately situated. You do not have any other houses pressing up close to you."

"The vicarage is quite near." I addressed his broad back while admiring the feral grace with which he rested his hand against the open window.

"And the people who live there are your great friends?"

"Eudora and Gladstone Spike are special people. She is a very caring clergywoman—"

"And he is a splendid cook." Ben drained his brandy glass and set it down by the decanters. "Of course, some people may not consider whipping up a cake to be the height of masculinity, but being a chef myself, Mr. Karisma—although I don't suppose that counts for much in the glamorous world you inhabit—I'm inclined to cheer for the bloke who can separate the white from the yolk of an egg."

If my husband had been the age of the twins, I would have sent him up to bed with a flea in his ear. But being stuck with his dampening presence, I put a bright face on the situation.

"Gladstone also writes the *Clarion Call*, which is the St. Anselm's Church bulletin," I said. "He manages to make it a real page-turner; last week I couldn't wait for it to arrive so I could read the latest thrilling installment of the discovery of church records in a biscuit tin in the vestry. . . ." My voice petered out as I realized how boring all this must be to Karisma.

"I would *lorve* to meet your friends, Giselle." He turned from the window and stood cloaked in twilight as if having just leapt through it after being hounded along the cliffs by the king's excise men who suspected him of supplying us with contraband brandy. "Perhaps tomorrow we can go and visit them. I will take them a life-size photo from my swimsuit calendar."

"The Spikes won't believe their good fortune." Ben managed to sound passably sincere.

"Speaking of photographs, Karisma," I said, "Mrs. Swabucher told me you would be bringing your own cameraman along with members of your staff. But you came alone."

"Not entirely"—again my husband stuck in his oar—
"he must have fifty pieces of luggage in the hall."

"We had an upset at my home." Karisma shook the
tousled locks back from his noble brow. "A stomach upset. The chef prepared a midday meal for himself, my
trainer, and my hairstylist while I was gone on a photo
shoot. And when I got back, it was too great a shock. They
were all crawling around on the dining room floor. It was
horrible, the moans and the groans. Poor Wu Ling, he says
if he gets better he will have to kill himself. Nothing like
this has ever happened to him before. He says he must
have offended the kitchen-god's wife and she has put a
curse on my house."

"Giselle doesn't believe in curses." Vanessa's voice
floated in upon us from the doorway before I could ask if
something untoward had happened to the photographer.
Moving into the room with George Malloy in her wake,
Vanessa had never looked more lovely. Her amber silk
frock was cut high at the thigh and low at the neck. She
was barefoot and flushed as a June rose, and I realized I
was really delighted to see her.

"You told me he was coming tomorrow, Ellie!" Stepping within two inches of Karisma, she tilted her face up to
his and touched his fingers with a pearly fingernail. "How
interesting, our hair is almost the same colour. Mine's natural"—her lips parted in a pensive smile—"what about
yours?"

"Nessie!" George expressed his consternation by
dropping one of the sandals he had been carrying for her.
Even Ben looked mildly embarrassed when he saw Karisma stiffen into a sculpture of himself. My heart ached for
the man even though he was enough to knock Geronimo
off his bronze pedestal.

"My cousin Vanessa is such a tease." I attempted a
laugh, but it got tangled up in my vocal cords. "And she's
particularly giddy just now, Karisma, because she recently
became engaged to George Malloy, whose mother has to
be one of your most devoted fans here in Chitterton Fells."
Leading the redheaded, red-faced fiancé forward with the
result that he dropped the second sandal, I kept right on
gabbling. "George manufactures exercise equipment and
Vanessa is doing some modeling for his television spots."

"So she and I are in the same business. Could it be that one day we will work together, like this?" Karisma came back to life with a flourish. Sweeping the undeserving Vanessa to him in one fluid motion, he held her draped over his arm. Her hair spilled almost to the floor and her bosom swelled above the neckline of her frock. It was a pose straight from the cover of a Zinnia Parrish novel, and my heart almost stopped when I tore my eyes away from it and glanced at George. He was also a picture—of utter despondency. How could he not see himself as anything but overweight, blunt-featured, and dull as ditch-water in the face of such sizzling competition? He wasn't like Ben, who though he might not be of romance-cover calibre, was certainly handsome enough on the everyday scene and had no reason to get his ego out of whack.

Being a first-rate coward, I escaped George's wounded eyes by saying I must go and check on the children. Ben followed me out with such speed that when I closed the door he was right on my heels.

"Vanessa really is the limit," I raged, "and you weren't any better."

"The fellow's a royal pain in the rear."

"Shush! he'll hear you."

"Good! What an egocentric ninny! The man doesn't talk—he *emotes*! And don't tell me he went over to the window to look at the view! He was making love to himself in the glass."

"How can you be so hateful?" I had trouble keeping my outrage down to a whisper. "He's a *celebrity*. People like that aren't like you and me. They have flair, spontaneity, and—"

"*Karisma?*" Ben growled. "Did you ever hear such a stupid name? I felt a complete idiot every time I said it. And what does anyone—man or woman—need with all that *hair*? We'll be vacuuming it up for days and tearing up the drains at God knows what expense."

"He's here on a mission of mercy."

"Because he *lorves* libraries? Give me a break, Ellie."

"Exactly what are you getting at?"

"Do I have to spell it out? The man has an ulterior motive."

"You're right." I bared my teeth in a smile. "Mrs.

Swabucher must have shown Karisma my photo and raved about how men drop like flies when I enter a room. Whereupon he knew he could not live another day without me in his life."

"My idea"—Ben stepped back and knocked over two suitcases—"is that he had to leave town in a hurry because the law is after him for dressing in a manner that undermines the morality of this nation. Consider the facts, Ellie! He doesn't give you enough time to properly prepare for his visit, and then he arrives the evening before he is expected. And take a look at this luggage! I'll have to empty his room of furniture before I can get this lot inside the door!"

"He'll need to change his clothes any number of times for the photo sessions." I righted the toppled suitcases with a couple of thumps. "From the way Mrs. Swabucher spoke, I'm sure he plans to spend the best part of a day in front of the camera."

"*If* the photographer turns up."

"Of course he'll be here," I said coldly. "I expect he'll arrive tomorrow morning with Mrs. Swabucher. And now, if you've nothing else nasty to say, I'll go back and see how our guest is doing."

Ben's savage glare faded. "I'm sorry." He reached out a hand, then dropped it to his side. "I don't know why I'm being such a lout, Ellie. This library thing is important to you, and it's not going to kill me to be pleasant to the bloke for your sake. Tomorrow you'll get the new and improved me; that's a promise."

I watched him tuck an overnight bag under one arm and pick up three of the larger suitcases, then start up the stairs. For a moment I was tempted to run after him, but when he said, "I'll even serve him freshly made vegetable juice for breakfast," I had to strain to catch the words because he had reached the upper gallery. And as I crossed the hall I had the feeling that he might as well be on the moon.

It was when I stumbled over Tobias, who came out from under the trestle table, that I knew I had to get out of the house for ten minutes. Gathering my furry friend up in my arms, I opened the drawing room door and stuck in my head. The scene presented would have been quite ordinary if Karisma and Vanessa had been two other people. They were doing nothing more scintillating than standing talking to each other by the window. But the juxtaposition of his supreme machismo and her vivid beauty provided enough drama for a three-act play. And there was George Malloy. He was by the mantelpiece, and it was woefully evident his was a walk-on part.

"Hello!" My overly cheery voice made even me jump. "I have to take the cat for his evening walk, but I won't be long."

"You go alone, so late?" Karisma took two strides towards me. "I shall come with you and we will talk, how is that?"

Vanessa clapped her hands and gurgled a laugh. "What a treat for you, Ellie, walking with Mr. Romance himself in the moonlight and sheltered from any threat of rain by the cape of his hair."

At that, poor George came unexpectedly to life. "Nessie, she's a married woman."

"I'll be fine on my own, thanks, Karisma." I ducked back into the hall while Tobias tried to claw his way out of my arms. He had never been a cat who enjoyed organized activity, and no sooner were we out of the house than he let me know, with a fierce meow, what he thought of me and my bright ideas. Setting him down in the courtyard, I crossed the moat bridge and made my way down the gravel drive to pause at the cottage by the gates. For the first time since she had vanished through the French windows I remembered Gerta. Should I knock and see if she was all right? No, better not. She was probably getting ready for bed.

What, I wondered as I made my way out onto the road, was wrong with me? Why did I feel as though I would have liked to haul up a boulder and send it rumbling over the cliffs? Why was I not beside myself with joy? I was a woman to be envied by every member of my sex with enough breath in her body to pant Karisma's name. He was a guest in my house. He had spoken to me, kissed my hand, looked at me with fire enough to singe his eyelashes. The easy answer was that I was furious with Ben for dampening my innocent enthusiasm. But as I drew level with the vicarage, which showed no sign of life, I decided the problem was Vanessa. I resented her making a play for Karisma's attention, because in doing so she had upset George. And it wasn't in me to rejoice in the face of another's suffering.

Then there was Gerta, I thought crossly. How could I let my spirits glow when she was holed up at the cottage? She would be afraid to come up to the house tomorrow for fear of meeting Karisma, who surely no one else but she could possibly think resembled her husband in the least. Marching on down the hill that became darker with every step, I knew I had more than sufficient reason to be upset; but wasn't there something else, some half-formed realization lurking just below the surface of my mind that was the real root of my distress?

A cat leapt over a hedge, then streaked into the shadows. Had Tobias followed me? Sometimes he showed an uncanny propensity for listening in on my most private thoughts. But not tonight. The animal I now saw crouching under a tree was less portly than my friend and black as a witch's cape.

"Here, puss puss!" In my jumbled state of mind I thought I was doing the coaxing, until I saw a figure step through a gate in the hedge and wander towards me with a hand outstretched as if proffering a tidbit. It wasn't until we were almost nose to nose that I was able to determine the person was a woman. She, like the cat, was dressed all in black, was thin as a fence post, and gave off a familiar . . . slightly mildewed smell. I blinked.

"Miss Tunbridge . . . Fancy meeting you for the second time in one day."

"Mrs. Haskell?" She stepped back to get a better squint at me, thus providing me a glimpse of jet-black hair that had to be dyed, done up in a frizz of curls on top of her head. "So you did decide to come and visit me. How nice. If you'll wait just a moment, my dear, for me to find my naughty pussy, I'll take you inside for a nice cup of tea. Or should we have elderberry wine, as this is such a special occasion?"

"Oh, but it's so late . . . And really, I was just out for a walk . . ." Belatedly I realized the house peering out at us from between the trees was Tall Chimneys. Once the residence of Hector Rigglesworth and now home to Miss

Ione Tunbridge. "I'll come and have tea with you another time," I promised as she bent down to pick up the cat, who had been about to leap once again over the hedge.

"But I want you to come in now." I could hear the pout in her voice and there were no two ways about it—I *was* dying to see inside the house that figured so prominently in local legend. "Don't disappoint me, Mrs. Haskell"—she was already heading back to the gate—"I don't like it when I don't get my way." Her chuckle happened to coincide with a shiver of wind that made its way down my back. "We were always fated to meet. I've known that ever since I watched you going into the church on your wedding day. You looked so frightened and I wept for you, my dear."

"That was only because I was late for the ceremony," I said just as I had that morning when Vanessa and I had met the Lady in Black at St. Anselm's.

"Your husband is very handsome." The quickening breeze may have distorted her voice, because what should have been a compliment sounded more like an accusation. We were by this time halfway down the path to the front door of Tall Chimneys. And the way the trees crowded in upon us from all angles, obscuring all but the faintest patches of sky, made it easy to believe this place, as well as the library, was haunted. I remembered, as Miss Tunbridge stepped up to a porch overgrown with creeper, my picnic with Ben on the open green to the right of the house. What was it I had felt then on looking over here? I couldn't put one name to it even when the sensation came flooding back. There were too many ingredients all mixed up together: oppression, spite, bitterness, and, perhaps worst of all, boredom.

"Here we are!" Miss Tunbridge opened the door into a narrow hall with very dark paper and a staircase twisting its way up one wall. There was a strong smell of cat; but even so I doubted that Puss Puss, for all his posturing as his mistress put him down, would be able to keep the mice holed up when they decided to cut loose and have a dinner dance. I pictured hundreds of beady eyes peering at us from under the skirting boards.

Dust and decay was the decorating theme of the smallish sitting room into which my hostess led me. Every inch was crammed with enough furniture to fill a junk shop, making it a squeeze to pick my way towards a chair. Sitting down meant taking the risk of breaking one of its legs or my own. The paper was peeling off the walls and the curtains hung in tatters at the windows; but surprisingly I began to feel better about the house.

"This is such a treat." Miss Tunbridge skimmed between a couple of tables to lift a dusty bottle of wine from the top of a pair of library steps. And immediately I could see one of Hector Rigglesworth's seven daughters bunching up her long skirts as she trod nimbly up the rungs to search the bookshelves for her favourite Brontë novel. *The Tenant of Wildfell Hall*—that would be the one, I decided. Page after page of long-suffering womanhood and unimpeded virtue. But, horror of horrors, one of the other sisters would have absconded to the back parlour with the book and Hector Rigglesworth must be turned out into the blustery wind to go down to the library to borrow a copy.

Miss Tunbridge's voice broke into my reverie. "I don't know what I did with the wineglasses. Could you make do with this little bud vase?"

"That would be perfect," I said.

"And I'll empty out this aspirin bottle and use it." Sounding pleased as a child, she did the honours, then sat down on a lumpy chair a couple of tables away from me. "Oh, it is such fun to entertain again. When my parents were alive we always did things in such style. I was an only child and indulged in everything, Mrs. Haskell."

"Please call me Ellie."

"You are such a poppet." Miss Tunbridge dropped her vial of wine onto the lap of her rusty black frock without appearing to notice, and clapped her wizened hands. "I didn't like the woman you were with this morning. She is a great beauty, just as I once was, and even this late in my life, dear Ellie, I don't invite competition."

"Vanessa is getting married; that's why she wanted to take a look inside the church." I almost added, "Remember?" But that would have been rude and probably futile. Miss Tunbridge did not have a strong grip on reality. Nonetheless, I felt compelled to ask her about the former inhabitants of her home.

"The Rigglesworths?" She screwed up her face pettishly, adding deep wrinkles to the ones already there. "I don't know why people make such a fuss about them. I've seen photographs of the daughters and not one was anything in the looks department. Old Hector gave a ball for them when the youngest turned seventeen, but I've heard it was a very shabby affair." Miss Tunbridge smiled. "*My* parents gave me a dance that was the talk of the county."

"How lovely!"

"I was"—she stood and preened garishly—"very, very lovely! Everyone said so. I had four proposals of marriage that very night. All from extremely eligible men, but"—her voice fell away to a whisper—"I made the fatal mistake of accepting Hugh."

"You must have felt so betrayed when Hugh didn't show up on your wedding day." Sympathy made me forget I had been hoping to steer her into showing me the house. And her reply made me realize it would be insensitive to prolong my visit.

"Ah, but Hugh did come, an hour before the ceremony—to tell me he had fallen in love with one of my bridesmaids. He said he hoped I would take it like a lady, and really I was very well behaved. I didn't shed a tear when I hit him over the head with the poker and saw that he was dead. My parents were so dear about it. They buried him in the copse and said we would never, ever talk about it again. But of course that was silly of them, wasn't it?" Miss Tunbridge smiled delightedly at me. "How could I possibly keep something like that to myself without going quite mad?"

Chapter

14

"Where is he?" Mrs. Malloy came clattering into the kitchen the next morning just as I was finishing giving Abbey and Tam their breakfast.

"Who?" I asked, dropping a spoon when she slammed the door behind her.

"Karisma, who else!"

"He went down to the station with Ben to meet Mrs. Swabucher, who's coming in by train." I washed off the spoon in the sink and returned it to Abbey, who was ready to start bawling from frustration at seeing her brother about to win the egg-and-spoon race. "I'm sorry, Mrs. Malloy, but you'll have to wait awhile for the privilege of throwing yourself in Karisma's arms."

"I'll throw meself at him all right, I'm going to *kill* him, that's what I'm going to do."

What was wrong with the woman? Had she been sniffing glue or, perish the thought, inhaled too much face powder? She certainly would appear to have flung her makeup on in a hurry. Her rouge was all over the place, and her eyebrows had been crayoned in with ultraviolet lipstick.

"Here"—I pulled out a chair—"you look as though you need to sit down." The twins stopped eating to listen with open, eggy mouths to the conversation.

"I'm better on me feet." Mrs. Malloy looked down at her high-heeled shoes, one of which was brown and the other blue. "If I sit down, I'll never get up." Her expression became even more grim. "When a woman of my age has been up all night, Mrs. H., something has to give—and it's not me corsets. I was in that much of a state, let me tell you, that I put on the pair that belonged to me third husband, and there wasn't much of him"—derisive snort—"in any department."

"Why were you up all night?" I rescued Tam's bowl before he could upend it on his head like a combat helmet.

"I wonder you can ask me that, Mrs. H., seeing as you had to know what went on in this very house last night. My sonny boy came home and talked me head off till the sun came up."

"Oh," I said, light finally dawning in the kitchen, "George was upset because Vanessa did rather ignore him once she got chatting with Karisma."

"*Upset?*" Mrs. Malloy's bosom threatened to explode through her purple blouse. "The poor lamb sobbed in me arms for hours!" She caught my eye and switched her gaze to the ceiling. "All right, so he got a bit misty-eyed, but a mother knows when her baby's heart is breaking. And it may come as a surprise to you, Mrs. H."—she pressed a hand to her forehead, taking off an eyebrow—"I'm not blaming your cousin."

"You're not?" I tried not to sound disappointed.

"I think I've misjudged her." Mrs. Malloy's tone of voice made clear who was to blame for that state of affairs. "She was as nice as ninepence when we was out for dinner last night and said if ever she'd been a bit cool, she was no end sorry. From the sound of it, someone had given her the idea I'm a bit uppity and inclined to look down me nose at people who don't measure up to my intellectual level."

"Did Vanessa sob in your arms too?"

"No need to be sarcastic, Mrs. H. The long and the short of it is she promised to toe the line as a daughter-in-law and I could see she was very fond of my George. It shouldn't need me to tell you he's over the moon over her, which is why I could slice that Karisma up one side and down the other for causing trouble between them."

"Well, this is a change. I thought you were crazy about the man. You almost climbed inside the TV when he came on the other day."

"We all have our moments of acting silly." Mrs. Malloy watched me wipe off the twins' faces and get them out of their chairs. "And I suppose I shouldn't be surprised at you going on about your business as if it's all right for Karisma to break my lad's heart. If you'd cared two hoots, you would have sent the bugger packing last night."

"He didn't do anything the least offensive." I gathered up the breakfast things, stepped around Abbey and Tam, who were engaged in a tug-of-war, and went over to the sink. "He can't help being gorgeous beyond belief. Even Ben got his nose out of joint and I certainly wasn't fawning all over the man. In my opinion"—I squeezed Fairy Liquid into the washing-up bowl—"Karisma wasn't particularly taken with Vanessa. She made a joke about his hair that was in extremely bad taste. But your future daughter-in-law is still in the Land of Nod, and I can't speak for what went on while I was gone from the house last night. When I got back, George had left and, apart from the hall, the house was in darkness."

"Just what time did you come rolling home?" Mrs. Malloy spoke from the depths of her newly-fired maternal instinct.

"Late." I left a bowl bobbing on the soapy water, dried off my hands, and sat down in the nearest chair. The memory of my scurry home from Tall Chimneys brought back all the creepy feelings that had accompanied me around every tortuous twist and turn of Cliff Road.

"Well, there's no need to snap me head off."

"I'm sorry. I didn't get much sleep either."

"Oh, like that, was it?" Mrs. Malloy overcame her reluctance to take a load off her feet and availed herself of a pew. "Mr. H. was showing you all the tricks up his pajama sleeve so you'd know he's twice the man Karisma could ever be when it comes time for some how's-your-father."

"It wasn't anything like that," I said hastily, hoping Abbey and Tam were too preoccupied with setting up camp inside the pantry to pay attention to Mrs. Malloy's risqué talk. "Ben was dead to the world when I got into bed. And talking about D-E-A-D people—the reason I hardly slept . . ." My voice trailed off as I wondered if I should be bringing up the subject.

"I think I know what you're about to say, and we'll be here till next week if you're going to spell out every other word." Mrs. Malloy had brightened visibly. "It's all over the village about Mr. Babcock, and if you ask me, it's more than a bit fishy him getting called up to the pearly gates when he hasn't been married a month. Think about it, Mrs. H.: That middle-aged bride of his turned up here out of nowhere a year or so back, and for all we know, she could be a regular Bluebeard."

"Rubbish," I said, putting no stock in Vanessa's having said something along the same lines. "Mr. Babcock had a bad heart."

But Mrs. Malloy shook her head at my naïveté. "Use your noggin. Talk about eligible bachelors: The poor sod already had one foot in the grave, so no one bats an eye when she gives him a shove from the rear. Mark my words, she'll deck herself out in black from head to toe, with a veil, no less. A sure sign of guilt if ever there was one . . . now, why are you looking at me like that, Mrs. H.?"

"Because," I said, "the reason I hardly slept is that when I went for a walk last night I met Ione Tunbridge, the Virgin Bride, otherwise identifiable as the Lady in Black, and when she took me into her house for a glass of elderberry wine—"

"She told you she'd bumped off her feller on what was supposed to be their wedding day because he'd been up to high jinks with one of the bridesmaids, and the good-for-nothing lies a-mouldering under one of the fir trees in the garden?" Mrs. Malloy raised her remaining purple eyebrow and added a knowing smirk for good measure.

"You mean it's no secret?"

"And there was you, Mrs. H., thinking you'd been singled out to hear the woman's true confessions because you've got such a nice kind face or whatever. Well, sorry to burst your bubble, my duck! Ione Tunbridge has been telling that story for years and she's still walking around free as a dicky bird. So what does that tell you?"

"The police are too busy with traffic duty to have her in for questioning?"

"No need to get all defensive." Mrs. Malloy assumed her most condescending expression. "Word is they did have a poke around her place with their little buckets and spades. But I don't reckon they had high hopes of hitting the jackpot, seeing as the old crone has to my knowledge told at least three versions of what happened to the missing bridegroom."

"That doesn't mean she didn't kill him."

"If my opinion counts for peanuts"—Mrs. M. could have been St. Paul addressing the Corinthians—"I say the young man did a bunk with the bridesmaid, they changed their names and went into hiding because in them days jilting a woman, on her wedding day no less, meant you didn't get invited to tea at the vicarage never again. And Ione Tunbridge has spent all these years wishing she could have got her hands round his throat."

"She told me she hit him with the poker."

"That's my point, Mrs. H." Her smile was complacent. "It's never the same story twice. So if the police aren't lying awake nights wondering if they should dig up every tree within a mile of Tall Chimneys, I don't for the life of me know why you're all worked up over the ramblings of a batty old woman."

"There was something . . ." I rose in order to get a better view of the twins. "Something bleak and oppressive about the garden and outlying woods even in daylight when Ben and I went on that picnic. Now, I suppose"—bending to pick up a toy fire engine that shot across the floor and threatened to cut me off at the ankles—"that could be because the house belonged to Hector Rigglesworth and his bevy of spinster daughters. Although I really had made up my mind that all that ghost business was a load of superstitious bunk." I handed the toy back to Tam.

"It won't do to let our imaginations run away with us." Mrs. Malloy got to her feet and smoothed down the bosom of her taffeta frock. "But there's no call to hang your head, my duck, seeing you're not the only one who could be guilty on that score."

"You mean you've been indulging in your own fantasies when it comes to Sylvia Babcock?"

"I wasn't thinking about her, Mrs. H., but I stand by me suspicions. Mark my words, all that nervy business and squealing if a speck of dust shows up in her kitchen is a put-up job. Hard as nails, that's what she is underneath them soppy pin curls of hers. Stuffing her victims with cream buns and suet puddings against doctors' orders, saying they need to keep their strength up for sex until, whoopsy daisy, they drop dead. I read about a woman in the papers once who switched her hubby's heart tablets for some other kind that wouldn't do diddle for him. Trust a man not to notice. And I wouldn't put it past that Sylvia Babcock to do the same thing, so she gets to collect the insurance money with tears in her wicked eyes. I tell you it don't bear thinking about."

"Then let's not think about it." I settled Abbey in the rocking chair alongside Tobias, who was industriously taking a nap, and ordered Tam not to step on the runners and send his earthly companions hurtling towards the ceiling. "Let's just forget about Sylvia Babcock, Mrs. Malloy."

"Who brought up the woman's name?" She sounded seriously miffed. "What I was about to say—before *someone* got us off track—is that perhaps my George let his imagination run away with him about Karisma making advances to Vanessa. I don't suppose there was nothing personal, seeing as the man's made a career for himself turning women's knees to jelly."

"He kissed my hand," I said. (I had to tell someone.)

"Well, there you are!" Mrs. Malloy need not have made it abundantly clear there could be no further doubt that Karisma was just fulfilling his professional obligations the previous evening. "I'll bet you went all fluttery inside. And if he'd unbuttoned his shirt, Mrs. H., you'd have thought he was proposing marriage."

I was about to argue that point, when the garden door opened and in came the Love God himself, followed by Ben and Mrs. Swabucher. Immediately the kitchen shrank to half its size. The curtains quivered at the open windows, and they weren't the only ones. Neither the book jackets on which he had appeared nor my meeting with him the night before had fully prepared me for the man in broad daylight. He was an awesome vision of masculine perfection. Mesmerizing eyes and magnificent jaw. To put it bluntly: six-foot-plus of raw sexual power.

"Me insides are doing flip-flops," Mrs. Malloy hissed in my ear.

"You shouldn't skip breakfast," I said, and realized the same could be said of me. Obviously the reason I felt as though a major void had just opened up in my life was that, with everything I had to do that morning, I'd made do with only one slice of toast and hadn't bothered to put sugar in my tea. But this wasn't the moment to focus on my state of being. Even allowing for the fact that standing next to Karisma made Ben's tan look like a pallor in comparison, Mrs. Swabucher, despite being clad in her signature colour, was not looking in the pink.

"You have been on the go making two trips down here." If I sounded breathless as I shuffled towards her, it was because I was holding Mrs. M. up by the armpits.

"I had a snooze on the train"—her smile was lacking in sparkle—"and it was lovely to be met by Karisma and . . ." She blinked in an effort to recall Ben's name.

"Let's not stand here making small talk," said my co-host with a regrettable lack of savoir faire as he stuffed Abbey into my arms, forcing me to abandon Mrs. Malloy to her own two legs. "I'll bolt the door while someone barricades the windows. It's a pity we don't have a rifle or two stashed in the cupboard under the stairs, but I suppose we can try and make do with Tam's water pistol."

"Whatever is he talking about?" My eyes went to Karisma, whose eyes had darkened to convey deep emotional perplexity.

"I think he is joking."

"Then you and I have a different sense of humour," Ben told him crisply. "Personally I see nothing the least amusing in having hordes of your female fans run sobbing and screaming alongside the car as we left the station. I thought at least two of them would throw themselves under the wheels, but I wasn't prepared for the ones who leapt into their own vehicles, or grabbed some luckless person's ignition keys and continued the chase all the way to our gates."

"I *lorve* these women." Karisma tossed back his wealth of flowing hair and spoke into an invisible microphone. "Always it is my wish to bring joy into their lives, but my guardian angel"—here he looked with a softening of the eyes and mouth at Mrs. Swabucher—"my dear Evangeline had said not to do autographs before tomorrow at the library."

"That's right." Ben hoisted Tam, who had been clamouring for attention, onto his shoulder. "Let the woman who wanted you to sign her underwear pay her five quid and get in the queue with the rest of Chitterton Fells' female contingent."

"I wonder . . ." Mrs. Malloy came back to life with a fluttering of the eyelashes. For a dreadful moment I thought she would peel off her corsets and present them with a bashful smile for the coveted signature. But I wronged her. "I wonder if I should nip outside and see if any of those hussies have had the bloody nerve to break into the garden."

"You are a brave woman!" Her hand was seized and pressed to Karisma's incomparable lips before I could properly introduce them and, afraid that she would collapse once outside the house, I followed her through the door and down the steps to the courtyard, where we had an excellent view of a row of faces peering over the hedge that separated the grounds from the road.

"They look like the beheaded wives of Henry the Eighth," I commented, only to have my voice drowned out by Mrs. Malloy yelling at the top of her lungs that if the lot of them didn't scarper, she'd let the dogs off their chains and then there would be no doubt in anyone's mind about who was man-hungry.

"We don't have a dog," I protested as the hedge cleared in a trice.

"And whose fault is that?" Mrs. M. pulled out the neck of her dress and blew down it to cool off. "I heard from Mrs. Dovedale on me way to the bus stop that you gave the librarian's woof-woof away for the second time last night to Mr. Poucher, and speak of the devil . . ."

"Heathcliff?"

"No. Mr. Poucher. That's him coming through the gate, and if me eyes don't deceive me, he's got his mother with him. Cantankerous old biddy. In her mid-eighties and up until recently there didn't seem to be no hope in sight of her calling it a day. But I've heard she's begun to fail, so maybe"—Mrs. Malloy looked positively maternal—"Mr. Poucher will have a bit of young life at last."

Considering that the gentleman in question was past sixty, it was difficult to imagine him nipping off to discos when he no longer had to worry about being home on time or risk having his pocket money stopped. But before I could say as much, mother and son were within hearing distance. Not that this consideration inhibited Mrs. Malloy.

"See what I mean?" She elbowed me in the ribs. "Got a face like a hatchet, hasn't she?" Regrettably this was true. Mrs. Poucher's facial features had enough sharp edges to do serious bodily harm. "And just wait till the old bat opens her mouth." Mrs. M. was not about to close her own. "That voice of hers makes a dentist's drill sound like a canary."

"Shush," I said, and had to immediately convert my glower into a welcoming smile as the Pouchers reached us and greetings were exchanged. My guess was that I owed this visit to Heathcliff and I was going to be told exactly what I could do with my dog. But I was way off the mark. When I tentatively broached the subject, Mrs. Poucher actually worked her pinched lips into a smile. And if her son's look of surprise was anything to go by, this was at most an annual event.

"Don't you fret your head none," she croaked. "I didn't say more than a couple of cross words when my lad here brought that dog home without a by-your-leave last night. He's a nice enough beastie, and with all the break-ins you read about in the papers it don't hurt for a sick old woman to have a bit of protection. And I got to thinking as I was mixing up my morning enema, we can always put him out to stud and raise a tidy amount, leastways enough to pay for his keep."

"He's nowt but a mongrel, Ma." Mr. Poucher spoke up with bleak fortitude and received a flinty-eyed stare that did not bode well for his being allowed to stay up and watch telly that evening. No wonder the man always looked so down at the mouth. Probably the only time he got away from home without being made to feel like an undutiful son was to the library meetings. And even then there were occasions when he arrived late. Had he been joking last night when he had said he'd been driven to slipping something in his mother's hot milk to knock her out? My eyes met Mrs. Malloy's and read the message loud and clear. But surely it was one thing to think Mr. Poucher would have been justified in bumping his mother off years ago and quite another to surmise that an eighty-year-old woman's failing health was due to his finally having decided to cut the apron strings once and for all?

"I'm sorry." I blinked at him. "I didn't catch what you were saying. . . ."

"That's because he mumbles," supplied Mrs. Poucher in a voice that threatened to take the roof off the house. "Never could break him of the habit, even after I went out cleaning and wore out my insides so he could have elocution lessons from a proper teacher." A couple of chimney pots shifted sideways. "The money I've spent on the lad don't bear thinking about—false teeth the moment he asked for them—and you'd have thought I was asking for the dome of St. Paul's when I said I wanted to come and meet this celebrity that's got everyone going in circles."

"You came to meet Karisma?" I did not dare look at Mrs. Malloy.

"That's what I was saying," growled Mr. Poucher. "Ma's been in bed the better part of a month, but she couldn't get out of the house fast enough this morning to scurry over here. I had to leave Heathcliff behind because I was afeared he'd get winded trying to keep up on the way to the bus stop."

"Come into the house." I tried to sound enthusiastic. "Karisma will be delighted to meet both of you."

"I'm off home," announced Mrs. Malloy. "George will be ready for a bite of lunch and I need to put me feet up. And if you ask me, it's indecent for a woman beyond a certain age to get all worked up over a sex symbol." Having delivered this thrust at Mrs. Poucher with the aplomb of someone who had not brazenly ogled Karisma fifteen minutes earlier, Mrs. M. took off down the drive. And I led the way across the courtyard into the kitchen, which we found occupied only by the man for whom millions of women would have killed to have as a guest.

Between kissing the old lady's hand and expressing

vast enthusiasm at meeting her son, Karisma relayed the information that Mrs. Swabucher, having admitted to not feeling well, had gone to lie down and Ben was upstairs with the twins.

"Mr. Poucher is a member of the Library League," I was saying as the garden door opened and in tripped Bunty Wiseman wearing an unbelievably short mini-skirt, a camera strung over one shoulder and a pad of paper in her hands.

"Sorry to burst in uninvited," she caroled with blatant untruthfulness, and received a stony look from Mrs. Poucher, who understandably saw more competition in the blond intruder than I provided. Poor Karisma! It was unnerving to discover I felt sorry for him. Just how long could he go on tossing his hair and gazing deep into yet another woman's eyes without feeling he was chopping out chunks of his soul and autographing them on request? Could the fame and money be worth the price? Did he wish for a moment that he could change places with Mr. Poucher, who stood ignored in shadows of his own making?

"I'm speechless!" Bunty was anything but as she pranced around Karisma, eyeing him up one side and down the other, eliciting enchanted smiles from him and venomous glances from old Mrs. Poucher. "Honest, Kris, you're even more luscious in person than on the book covers or even the telly. And it's a damn good thing I'm divorced, because I think we should get married. Just kidding!" Her giggles floated in the air like sunbeams set to music. "Although if you insist"—she moved in even closer—"we *could* have a word with the vicar and see when the church is available."

"I would *lorve* that very much." Karisma spoke with a throb in his voice and fire in his eyes, so that Bunty, having checked her brain at the door, might be excused for assuming that she had succeeded where millions had failed.

"Ellie"—she backed smack into me—"I want you to be my bridesmaid, but don't spend a lot of money on a frock. At this wedding nobody will have eyes for anyone but the groom."

"Don't be a ninny," I said before Mrs. Poucher could snatch up a carving knife. "Karisma does not want to marry you. He wants to take a look at St. Anselm's Church and meet the Spikes."

"Oh!" Bunty pouted adorably. "I suppose I can accept that, seeing Gladstone is a member of the Library League and it's only a few steps to the vicarage. It would be harder to take, Kris, if I thought you were a religious fanatic. Hairy chests are okay, but I do draw the line at hair shirts." She studied Karisma's face, apparently groping for confirmation that any marriage between them would be doomed to failure. I did not feel it appropriate to mention that Mrs. Swabucher had described her client as a deeply spiritual man who would wish to attend a church service while in Chitterton Fells. At this moment Mrs. Poucher unblushingly croaked out the revelation that she found God-fearing men incredibly sexy. Mr. Poucher growled something incomprehensible. And Karisma, who, it need hardly be said, dealt with people every bit as brash as Bunty on a routine basis, appeared for a full minute to be robbed of speech.

"On the way to pick up Evangeline at the station, Giselle, your husband was so kind as to stop at the vicarage." His marvelous eyes singled me out from the others, but the intensity that promised to stand time on its head was missing. "I rang the bell and knocked on the door, but there was no answer."

"Not used to being turned away, are you, my bonny lad?" Mr. Poucher chewed down on the words with relish and paid no heed to the scorching glare he got from his mother.

"The Spikes were expecting company this weekend," I said, and instantly wished I had kept my mouth shut. I might be wrong in assuming the visitor was in any way connected to Gladstone's operation, but under the circumstances the less said the better.

"It's a nice day, so they probably went for a drive or a walk along the beach." Having dismissed the Spikes and their houseguest, Bunty recovered much of her perkiness. "Now, down to business." She jiggled her camera on its shoulder strap and brandished her notepad under Karisma's incomparable nose. "I didn't come here just to gawk, honest I didn't, Kris! I need to interview you for the flyer I'm going to put in my hairdresser's window and other places."

"It is my utmost pleasure."

"Now, let me think"—Bunty produced a pencil from the camera case—"what do my readers want to know?"

"Ask him if he wears pajamas!" Mrs. Poucher screeched, managing by dint of foaming lips and a reddened face to make this rather lackluster suggestion sound incredibly lascivious.

Bunty, the quintessential professional, ignored her. "Tell me, Kris, a little about your political views."

"I *lorve* women." With infinite finesse Karisma undid a couple of shirt buttons.

"And you would like to see more of us in key governmental positions?"

"I *lorve* women to be happy."

"Excuse me, Bunty," I said, "this is a flyer you're doing, not an article for *Woman's Own,* and it really isn't fair to waste Karisma's time when all you need to cover is the time and place of his appearance at Miss Bunch's benefit. On the other hand"—I noted her quivering lip—"it might be a big help if you took some photos, especially ones outdoors."

"That would be marvelous." Karisma radiated enthusiasm.

I smiled back at him. "We mustn't forget one of the reasons you came down here. Mrs. Swabucher made it very clear that a primary consideration was using the exterior of the house as a background in photographs."

"Yes, that is so."

"It's a pity about the cameraman not getting here. You've lost the whole morning, but until he turns up, I'm sure Bunty will be happy to take some potshots at you."

"She can take a picture of me in his arms." Mrs. Poucher spoke with a grisly determination that brooked no argument from her long-suffering son. Without much further ado, the garden door opened and closed and I had the kitchen to myself for at least thirty seconds before the telephone rang. My expectation was that Ben would answer on the upstairs receiver. However, when silence did not prevail, I had to assume the twins were holding him prisoner in the nursery. I went out into the hall to pick up the phone.

"Ellie"—Eudora Spike spoke in a breathless rush in my ear—"I really need to talk to you, if you have a free minute."

"Of course. Is it about the redecorating?"

"No, nothing about that."

"That's good, because I'm afraid that what with one thing and another this week, I haven't settled down to mapping out ideas for your bedroom or—"

"Yes, I realize you've a lot on your plate, especially now you've got that man staying with you." There was a pause in which I pictured Eudora gnawing her lower lip. "He came to the house this morning; Gladstone happened to catch a glimpse of him from the window and I'm ashamed to say we didn't answer the door."

"I'm sure you had your reasons" was all I could say.

"And I'd like to tell you about them, Ellie, but not over the phone. Could you come here, just for half an hour?"

"I'll be there in a couple of minutes," I promised, and replaced the receiver in time to see Ben coming down the stairs with the twins at his heels.

"Sorry I couldn't get that," he told me. "Abbey was on the pot and Tam was hopping up and down waiting his turn."

"It was Eudora. For me."

"Anything wrong?"

"I'm not sure." I leaned up against him, thinking how good such ordinary moments were. "I said I'd go round and have a chat with her."

"Go on, then." He touched my face and I knew he understood that Eudora, who spent a big part of her life listening to other people's problems, sometimes needed to be on the talking end of the conversation. By going out the front door, I avoided interrupting Karisma's photograph session or having to explain where I was going and being put in the awkward position of not offering to take him with me. It was such a shame when he was so keen on church that the Spikes' particular circumstances prevented them from being up to welcoming him to the vicarage.

Passing the cottage at the gates, I stared up at the

windows and wondered guiltily if Gerta had recovered from last night's terrors which, while they might seem far-fetched to me, had been very real to her. I'd been dread-fully neglectful in not going down to see how she was doing. It was no excuse that I'd hardly had a free moment to breathe. I vowed that on my way back from the vicar-age I would knock on the door, and if there was no an-swer, I'd go in through a window.

Eudora saved me from opting for that form of entry at the vicarage by opening the door before I rang the bell.

"It's so good of you to come, Ellie. I don't know when I've been more in need of a friend." She gave me a hug and bustled me into the comfortably old-fashioned sitting room. "You must have noticed I wasn't myself the other day when you came over to talk about the redecorating."

"I did sense that something was a little off kilter, but I hoped there wasn't anything seriously wrong. We are . . . that is," I stammered, "Ben and I are so very fond of you and Gladstone."

"Thank you, dear." Eudora gave a wan smile as she gestured for me to sit next to the table set out with coffee for two and one of her husband's sponge cakes. "It's about Gladstone that I wish to speak to you." She took the chair across from mine and stared into the empty fireplace.

"I thought that might be it," I said.

"I'm usually a very private person, Ellie, but this does involve you."

"It does?" My hand set down the coffee cup it had just picked up.

"In that it involves your husband." Eudora turned to-wards me with a determinedly cheerful look on her face. "You see, Ellie, Gladstone has always admired Ben very much, they share the same interest in cooking, and that's a special bond between two men. Then, when your cousin Vanessa fainted in church and Ben picked her up so effort-lessly, Gladstone told me he realized for the first time how incredibly handsome Ben was and that there were no two ways about it, this was the man he wanted. And he wasn't going to settle for anyone else."

"Well, he can't have Ben!" I flashed back without a thought for poor Eudora's anguish.

"And there was me thinking"—she gave an embarrassed laugh—"that you'd be rather tickled by the idea."

"Oh, really?" I was growing just the least bit annoyed. Surely it was one thing for a woman to support her husband in his decision to have a sex-change operation, and quite another to encourage him to latch on to a friend's husband.

"You're not a fuddy-duddy like me, Ellie, and I know you love romance novels, so please forgive me if I mistakenly thought you'd enjoy seeing Ben on the cover of what Gladstone's publishers believe will be a runaway best seller." She smiled benignly at me.

"I'm very confused," I said, and proved the point by starting to stand up just as I went to sit down. "Could you please start at the beginning, Eudora, and tell me who your husband is when he isn't baking the perfect sponge cake or putting together the parish bulletin?"

Chapter

15

"Zinnia Parrish!" Ben was sitting on the edge of the bed the next morning, pulling on his socks. "What sort of name is that for a man?"

"One with lots of sales appeal." I gave up on brushing my hair, which wasn't any great sacrifice seeing I had been slacking off on this exercise routine recently and was so badly out of shape that fifty strokes would have done me in. "She—er—Gladstone Spike is one of today's most popular romance writers. His—*her* books sell by the ton."

"We're talking about paperbacks, right?" Ben took my place at the dressing table and proceeded to comb his hair without breaking a sweat. Neither of us had to rush what we were doing, because Vanessa, intent on changing her image, had volunteered to take care of the twins until we came downstairs.

"There's no need to turn up your nose," I told the man in the mirror crossly.

"I wasn't doing anything of the sort."

"Yes, you were. People do that all the time. They dismiss romances as not being real books and carry on as though the definition of a literary masterpiece is a novel written in the present tense about people who spend six hundred pages contemplating their navels and that sells all of three copies because only the supremely intelligent can get through the bloody title."

"Ellie"—my husband came up behind me and pressed his hands over my mouth—"I was not belittling Gladstone Spike's writing career. When you and I first met I was trying to write a spy novel, remember? And we know how that turned out."

"You sold a cookery book"—I wriggled away from him—"and a very good one it was too."

"Thanks, sweetheart, but I seriously doubt it kept anyone up all night turning the pages to see if the beef Wellington made it out of the oven unscathed. To be honest, I'm quite jealous of old Gladstone."

Now was the moment to inform Ben that if he couldn't have his name on a novel of his own creation, he might have the opportunity to show up on the cover of the next Zinnia Parrish blockbuster. But something held me back. And I rattled on instead about how amazed I'd been to discover that one of my favourite writers was our friend and neighbour.

"What amazes me"—Ben stood, buttoning his shirt cuffs—"is that you didn't tell me about this yesterday; I would have expected you to rush home bursting to spill the beans."

"On the way back from the vicarage"—I turned away from him and started spreading up the bed—"I stopped at the cottage to look in on Gerta. And she was so down in the boots that I spent the better part of an hour trying to persuade her to come up to the house for lunch. But she kept saying she couldn't risk seeing Karisma because he looks so like her husband she'd immediately have a nervous breakdown."

"It sounds to me as though she's already having one." Ben hung up his black silk dressing gown.

"I'm worried about her." I finished tucking in my side of the bed. "When Gerta showed me a snapshot of Ernst I saw a heavyset bald man with a moustache and not a glimmer of resemblance to Karisma, whichever way I turned the photo; but that's love for you. And it got me thinking. Maybe the frog didn't turn into Prince Charming when the girl in the fairy story kissed him—except in her eyes, that is. So that for fifty years of domestic bliss, until the day he finally croaked, he slept on a lily pad in the bathroom basin. And everywhere they went she introduced him as her tall, handsome husband to women who were petrified he would hop up their skirts and to men who vowed never to touch another drop of Scotch as long as they lived."

"Rrribit-rrribit" was Ben's juvenile response to my insightful outpourings.

"I wasn't talking about you. People are forever telling me how handsome you are." After plumping up the last of the pillows I sat down on the bed. "If anyone's the frog in our relationship, it's me."

"Now who's displaying false modesty?"

"Well, nobody's ever suggested putting me on the cov—"

"What's that?"

"Nothing." I smiled up at him. "I've gone off on a tangent, but back to why I didn't tell you about Gladstone Spike yesterday. If you think about it, Ben, you'll realize we never had a moment alone after I got back to the house. Luckily, Bunty Wiseman and the Pouchers had gone. But either Vanessa was in the room, or I was talking to Mrs. Swabucher, who couldn't hide that she was down in the dumps over her meeting with Brigadier Lester-Smith. The twins constantly required attention from one or the other of us. And of course there was Karisma, who couldn't be expected to stand around tossing his hair all day. It all proved to be rather exhausting, and by the time we came up to bed, I was practically sleepwalking."

"It's interesting about the photographer." Ben's voice was muffled by his pulling a sweater over his head.

"You mean that he never showed up?"

"Precisely. As I understand it, Mrs. Swabucher told you at Abigail's that a camera session, using the exterior of Merlin's Court as a background, was a major objective in Karisma's coming down here. Lancelot valiantly defending the castle against the enemies of the realm. But lo and behold—no photographer. And I didn't sense any major disappointment on either of their parts, did you?"

"No, but as I've said, Mrs. Swabucher hasn't been herself and that would affect Karisma, who seems very fond of her. What's your point, Ben?"

"That the photography angle was a smokescreen."

Ben flopped down on the bed, placed his hands behind his head, and crossed his legs at the ankles. "I'm wondering if Karisma's willingness to do your library benefit has anything to do with Gladstone and his books."

The obvious question. My moment of truth was at hand, and I wished now that I hadn't dragged my feet. Excuses! Excuses! I could have made time yesterday to put Ben in the picture had I been ready to deal with the realization that I had been hoodwinked.

"It never crossed my mind"—I sat winding the edge of the bedspread through my fingers—"that there was anything odd in Mrs. Swabucher's insistence that Karisma could make an appearance at the library only this weekend. I was just grateful that he was willing to come at all, particularly after we had received a refusal over the phone. The short notice did make it impossible to advertise the event in a big way, but in a place as small as Chitterton Fells, word spreads like wildfire." I paused to draw a shaky breath. "Gullible me! I was touched when Mrs. Swabucher said Karisma would want to go to church. No sirens went off inside my head when he asked if we had any close neighbours. But I realize now he often led the conversation around to Gladstone Spike, hoping you or I would offer to make the introduction. And the reason he came down a day early must have been to allow himself extra time to set up the acquaintance."

"So why did it have to be this weekend?" Ben shifted closer to the edge of the bed and reached for my hand.

"Because, so Eudora told me, Gladstone's editor had arranged to visit the vicarage to discuss the book in progress. It's a sequel to a smash best seller by the late Azalea Twilight and there's been a lot of speculation, mounting almost to a frenzy in the press, owing to the publisher having refused to say who landed the plum job of writing *A Knight to Remember*. It is also a closely guarded secret that Gladstone is Zinnia Parrish."

"Then how did Karisma get his information?"

"He was approached about doing the cover."

"By a woman, may we suppose?" Ben lay back and flickered a glance at me from under his lashes. "One who was so overcome by the fame and fascination of the man that she told him everything he needed to know without realizing she had even opened her mouth. But what I don't understand, Ellie, is why if Karisma had the cover assignment for *A Knight to Remember* in his pocket did he go to such lengths to meet Gladstone?"

"There could be all sorts of reasons." Bouncing off the bed, I marched over to the window and back again.

"Agreed, but what was Eudora's take on the situation?"

"That Karisma knew that Gladstone was horrified at the prospect of having him do the cover, on the grounds that Karisma bears no physical resemblance to the hero of *A Knight to Remember* and that such a misrepresentation would violate the integrity of the book. Apparently, Gladstone has created a character whose good looks are defined by elegance rather than untamed magnificence. He is of medium height, with dark curly hair cut to a conventional length, and his eyes are by turns emerald green or midnight blue."

"So"—practical Ben did not bat an emerald-green eye—"have Karisma put on a wig, a three-piece suit, and bend at the knees."

"Don't be silly," I said crossly, "he couldn't do that to his image, and Gladstone would never have agreed. Eudora said her husband spent hours—no, days—going through his contract with the publisher, hoping to find a loophole. But he couldn't find any way round the fact that he had no power of veto where the cover was concerned." Upon taking a well-earned breath, I remembered the documents I had seen on the coffee table in the vicarage sitting room and how, having let my stupid imagination take over, I had thought they were medical consent forms.

"Eudora explained this has all taken a terrible toll on Gladstone," I continued. "He must have thought there was some sort of curse on him when the Library League decided to invite Karisma to do the benefit. What rotten timing to have all this going on when he has to go into hospital shortly."

"Anything serious?"

"He has to be circumcised."

"Ouch," said Ben.

"Apparently he should have had it done years ago and

Eudora has been feeling extremely frustrated—with the situation, I mean."

"Are you telling me"—Ben sat up and swung his legs over the side of the bed—"that Karisma came hot-footing down here because—being such a sensitive bloke—he's been losing his beauty sleep over Gladstone's negative reaction to having him on the cover of a novel?"

"No, it's not like that. It's because a couple of days ago Karisma was notified that he wasn't getting the job after all."

"I'm not tracking, Ellie."

"It's all quite straightforward," I said. "Gladstone was so royally upset—he couldn't knit, he couldn't bake sponge cakes—that he informed his editor he no longer felt obliged to keep his identity a secret. He threatened to go public with the announcement that he was Zinnia Parrish. And immediately that put a whole new spin on the situation."

"A clever move on our friend's part."

"The editor begged Gladstone to reconsider, saying that sales of *A Knight to Remember* would be drastically reduced were it known to have been written by a man, let alone one who wears grey cardigans and puts out the parish bulletin. But Gladstone stuck to his guns even after his editor sent an enormous bunch of flowers and said he would come down to the vicarage this weekend to discuss a very lucrative deal for the next Zinnia Parrish book. And the day before yesterday Gladstone got word that in return for his agreeing to keep his identity from becoming public knowledge, Karisma would not do the cover."

"At which time"—Ben stood looking at me from under locked brows—"Mrs. Swabucher got in her car and came buzzing down here to meet you for lunch at Abigail's. Tell me, sweetheart, don't you feel that she and her mesmerizing client pulled a pretty dirty stunt?"

"I don't blame Karisma."

"No, I suppose not."

"He couldn't be expected to tamely walk away from what must have seemed like a professional slap in the face. He's the most celebrated cover model in the world, and *A Knight to Remember* is a major book. But . . ." Turning away from Ben, I fiddled with the candlesticks on the mantelpiece. "I am a little hurt that Mrs. Swabucher used her relationship with us to try and get to Gladstone."

"You could take some satisfaction," Ben responded gently, "knowing the plan failed."

"Lots of things went wrong from the beginning," I said, "such as his staff being taken ill. And I really do think he wanted a photographer here, because Eudora told me Gladstone modeled the home of the hero in *A Knight to Remember* on Merlin's Court. So for Karisma to produce photos of himself posing with such authenticity of background would have been a real plus."

"He was again out of luck when he insisted on knocking at the vicarage yesterday." Ben did not evince sympathy. "It did strike me he was not nearly so keen on looking in on choir practice last night after you mentioned the Spikes would be gone for the evening."

"He intends to go to church this morning," I said, "but Eudora told me Gladstone would be taking a miss this once because the editor is arriving before lunch, and that's something we have to talk about, Ben."

"Lunch?"

"No, the editor." I dropped down in a chair, stretched out my legs, and studied my feet. "Gladstone wants you to meet this man and overwhelm him with your photogenic possibilities. Now why are you looking so blank?" I said as kindly as possible. "Surely you grasp what I'm telling you. The editor in his present conciliatory mood wants to make Gladstone happy. And Gladstone wants you on the cover of *A Knight to Remember*."

"You're joking?"

"According to Eudora, you are the hero made flesh."

"I am?" Ben studied his reflection in the dressing table mirror with a disturbingly self-satisfied smile on his face.

"Gladstone came to this startling revelation when Vanessa fainted in the church and you swept her up in your manly arms."

"Really?"

"So"—my eyes were closed but I could hear him arching his eyebrows—"do you think you'll take the job?"

"I'll have to think about it." Ben came up behind me and deposited a kiss on the top of my head. "What do you know about the character?"

"At the beginning he is away from Merlin's Court or whatever it is called in the book, valiantly making the most of being shipwrecked on a coconut island, with no supplies other than a stunningly beautiful woman."

"Would I have to pose in the nude?"

"No . . . I'm sure you'd get to wear an eyepatch."

"This is all very flattering. But I have to consider your feelings, sweetheart. How would you feel knowing that millions of women were ogling my brawny chest and taking me to bed with them at night?"

"I'd be thrilled," I lied. "You'd probably make a lot of money, and it's not"—I forced a bright smile—"as though you'd have to make a career out of being a cover model."

"You're right"—he drew me to him—"and even if I did, I don't believe I would give up the restaurant. One has to be realistic, Ellie, and face the fact that the demand for my services would slack off when my youthful vigor begins to wane. Although"—he released me abruptly, turned back towards the mirror, and sucked in his cheeks—"I guess when the time comes I could extend my longevity by colouring my hair and having a face-lift."

"Why stop there?" I pressed my hands to my hips to stop them from shaking. "You could go all out—have liposuction and a tummy tuck. But let's not get ahead of ourselves; you still have to meet Gladstone's editor, even though from what Eudora said, that sounds like a formality. You're to be at the vicarage for lunch at one and—"

"That's not going to work out." Ben stopped making love to the mirror and swung around to face me. "I'd be late getting to the library benefit—if I managed to put in an appearance at all."

"You don't have to come." I held up my hand as he started to speak. "Really, I wouldn't mind a bit. Gladstone is under more of an obligation to be there than you; but it's understandable he would wish to avoid Karisma, even if he did not have a more pressing obligation. Eudora's going to fill in for him, and this way I'll be able to keep her company. The only problem is the twins. I had thought of asking Vanessa to watch them, but that won't work out."

"Why not?"

"Because"—I somehow managed to speak cheerily—"Eudora said Gladstone would like Vanessa to accompany you on the interview. That way the two of you can re-create the pose that won you this golden opportunity. She's a professional model and, who knows, perhaps she will be offered the job of the heroine. I'm sure my lovely cousin would find a book-cover assignment infinitely more glamorous than doing stints for George Malloy's exercise equipment."

Before Ben could answer, the bedroom door opened and, talk of the devil, Vanessa glided into the room—a vision to restore breath to a shipwrecked hero if ever I saw one.

"Oh, I'm sorry," she purred, "I was hoping I might be interrupting a truly decadent moment."

"You are"—I smiled at her—"we were talking about you."

"Now, I do *hate* to break things up"—Vanessa gave a sigh that set her silky apricot skirts fluttering—"but there's a phone call for you, Ellie. A Brigadier Lester-Smith. And he sounded quite upset, so you'd better run along and calm him down while Ben tells me how I came to be the fascinating topic of conversation. Don't worry about the kiddies"—she held the door open for me and executed a mock curtsy—"they've got plenty of people fussing over them. George just arrived with his mother, and Karisma came downstairs ten minutes ago."

"Ellie, I think we need to continue our talk," said Ben.

"And I think"—I looked back over my shoulder at him—"that you need to discuss matters with Vanessa. I'm sure she'll make you see that it would be wrong to disappoint Gladstone."

How thoroughly noble of me, I thought as I went along the gallery to the phone at the top of the stairs. The trouble was, I wasn't at all sure why I got to feel noble. Ben had been offered the opportunity of a lifetime. There was no reason in the world to hope—let alone expect—him to turn it down. And I wasn't even entitled, damn it, to take mental jabs at Vanessa. If she did end up on the cover of *A Knight to Remember,* it wouldn't be because she had gone after the job. Dear, sweet Nessie couldn't help it if she fainted extremely well and looked sublime in my husband's arms. Telling myself that if they were practicing their parts in the bedroom right this minute I would be a beast not to applaud their work ethic, I picked up the receiver.

"Hello," I chirped, ever the noble, self-sacrificing wife.

"I'm sorry, Mrs. Haskell, if I took you away from something important. A man on his own tends to forget that other people have real lives."

Brigadier Lester-Smith sounded utterly despondent and I wished I could have cheered him up by going into exciting detail about plaid sofa cushions for the house he had inherited from Miss Bunch. Instead, I told him I would get busy on the project in the next few days.

"I'm not phoning about the house, Mrs. Haskell."

"No, I didn't think you were."

"It was a bit of a facer seeing Evangeline after all these years. I'm glad that she went on to have a full life. She's done very well for herself. Marriage to a decent chap, by the sound of it. And now managing the career of a world-famous celebrity. She's obviously extremely fond of him."

"Yes," I said.

"I shouldn't have been surprised."

"About Karisma?"

"That Evangeline looked at me"—the break in the brigadier's voice tore at my heart—"as if she didn't know who I was. Of course we were married for only a very short time. And the marriage wasn't a proper one at that—it ended with a whimper in annulment, not even the bang of divorce."

"You had a little time to prepare before coming face-to-face with Mrs. Swabucher." I floundered around, hoping to make him feel better without implying he was being a crybaby. "She must have been thrown for a loop when you showed up at the library. We had talked about you quite a bit that evening as 'the brigadier,' but I don't know that your surname was ever mentioned. Please don't make too much out of it if she looked blank for the first few seconds when you spoke to her. I'm sure that was from shock, not because she couldn't . . ."

"Exactly place where she had seen me before?" Brigadier Lester-Smith's attempt at sounding matter-of-fact failed miserably. "I'm sorry, Mrs. Haskell, if I'm not taking this on the chin, but—and this is what I rang to say—I don't think I can be at Miss Bunch's benefit today. I'm ashamed to admit this, but I'm not sure I could conduct myself as an officer and a gentleman."

"You're understandably upset."

"What I am"—the brigadier sounded surprised—"is, if you'll pardon the language, bloody annoyed. It occurs to me, Mrs. Haskell, that if I had behaved like a wild boar on our wedding night instead of minding my P's and Q's, Evangeline might have had an easier time remembering that she had met me at the altar."

"I think you're making a mistake in not coming to the benefit." My heart ached for him. "For one thing, none of the other Library League members knows how to handle the coffee percolator the way you do and, more important, I believe you need to see Mrs. Swabucher again in order to work through your feelings. Promise me you'll at least reconsider?"

Saying a quick good-bye so that the brigadier would not think I was trying to pressure him, I hung up. My timing proved excellent because, before I could start down the stairs, Mrs. Swabucher came out of her bedroom wearing a powder-pink dressing gown and a matching hairnet. Truth be told, I hadn't been feeling particularly kindly towards her, even before the brigadier's anguished phone call; but she had dark circles under her eyes, indicating she hadn't slept well. And she looked older without any makeup except a scrape of lipstick. So I caved in and acted like a hostess first and a friend to the wounded second.

"Did the phone wake you?" I asked.

"The ringing made me realize, Giselle, that it was time for this lazybones to crawl out of bed." Mrs. Swabucher looked down at her fluffy pink slippers. "I'm sure Karisma will want me to go to church with him on this lovely morning."

"What a pity," I said as the ice re-formed in my veins, "that the vicar's husband, Gladstone Spike, won't be in church this morning. And I really don't think"—looking her squarely on the top of her head because she was still looking squarely at her slippers—"that it would do any good for you to abandon the backhanded approach and pay Gladstone an official visit. He's busy today, very busy."

"Giselle"—Mrs. Swabucher looked every bit as fluttery as if she had been wearing her feather boa—"how did you find out about my little ruse?"

"Why don't we just call a scam a scam?" I managed to keep my voice steady by wrapping my hands around the throat of the banister knob and squeezing hard. "Gladstone's wife told me all about *A Knight to Remember*. She's a friend of mine, which is why you used me and Ben in hopes of weaseling Karisma into the author's"—hysterical edge to my laugh—"good books, isn't it?"

"I'm sorry, Giselle." Mrs. Swabucher sounded appropriately stricken. "I'm fond of you and I really don't enjoy the cutthroat side of this business. As Brigadier Lester-Smith could tell you, I'm fragile by nature. I respond to situations instinctively rather than acting upon them in a cool-headed fashion."

"Fascinating," I said.

"That's been both my strength and my weakness in business dealings. It's what told me after meeting you for five minutes that you and Ben were perfect for one another. A Cinderella story come to life if ever there was one. And you must see that in this instance my first obligation was to my darling boy. If he is done out of this assignment, some other upcoming cover model may eclipse him by being signed up as the Starfire Man for the new Moonstruck line. Even so, Karisma, bless his heart"—Mrs. Swabucher's eyes grew misty—"had qualms about my course of action."

"I'm sure you're being truthful about that." My voice rose and I couldn't drag it back down because my hands were still squeezing the life out of the banister. "Karisma wouldn't be the man of every woman's dreams if he were not the epitome of exquisite sensitivity under that phenomenal male exterior."

"You have to look at it from both sides, Giselle dear." Mrs. Swabucher was recovering command of herself. "It's true I hoped your friendship with the Spikes would pave the way, in a seemingly natural and congenial fashion, to reopen negotiations with Zinnia Parrish. But it most certainly was not all take and no give. Karisma squeezed this fund-raiser into his extremely busy schedule because he was deeply moved when I told him about how your little

community wanted to raise money for a statue to commemorate a librarian who died on the job."

"And because it seemed like an excellent way to put
pressure on Gladstone Spike to reconsider his position."

"That's not kind, Giselle."

"No, I don't suppose it is."

"And I don't see why, now that I've explained matters"—Mrs. Swabucher's tone was briskly chiding—"you
can't put in a good word for Karisma with the author."

"It wouldn't do any good. Gladstone knows what
Karisma looks like and," I said bravely, "his wife told me
he has his heart set on someone else for the cover."

Mrs. Swabucher's face flushed a darker shade than her
dressing gown. "Who?" she demanded.

"An unknown." I drew a ragged breath. "Does this
mean Karisma will be backing out from his appearance at
the library?" My heart quaked at the thought, but Gladstone was not expendable, and if Miss Bunch were not to
be cast in bronze for posterity, so be it. The woman who
had never caved in when it came to collecting library fines
from people who claimed she was forcing them into the
gutter would understand.

"Karisma will fulfill his commitment." Mrs. Swabucher now wore her hairnet like a crown. The thought
crossed my mind that she was counting on Gladstone being at the library and, knowing that he would be otherwise
engaged with his editor, Ben, and Vanessa, I felt sufficient
compassion to back off from my righteous resentment for
the moment.

"If you're worried about meeting Brigadier Lester-
Smith, that was him on the phone a few minutes ago and,
although he may change his mind, he was saying he didn't
plan to be at the benefit."

"That would make things easier, Giselle. When I saw
how time had taken away all his good looks and turned
him into a walking briefcase, I was so shocked"—Mrs.
Swabucher brought her hands up to her shoulders—"that I
dropped my feather boa and didn't remember to pick it up
when we left the library."

"I'm sure it's still in the meeting room." I didn't add
that the new resident dragon might exact a heavy fine in
exchange for its return. Hoping that Brigadier Lester-

Smith did not change his mind about the meeting on my account, I mumbled something semi-coherent about needing to check on the twins and left Mrs. Swabucher to get ready to face the downstairs world.

Entering the kitchen, I found the dragon who could have taught the one at the library a thing or two installed at the table, having a cuppa.

"Good morning, Mrs. H." She turned her head in the sequined hat and gave me the once up, twice down. "Or should I say good afternoon?"

"Where's everybody else, Mrs. Malloy?"

"A spaceship landed on the cooker not two minutes ago." She stood up and smoothed down her crushed-velvet hips. "Without a word of good-bye George climbed aboard with the kiddies, and wouldn't you know, Karisma, Mr. Wonderful himself, had to go tagging along? It was all so quick, Mrs. H., by the time I blinked they was gone in a puff of green smoke."

"Is that tea you're drinking?"

"I was trying to spare your feelings."

"Why?" I grabbed the back of a chair. "Is something wrong with Tam or Abbey?"

"Only that you scared them half out of their little wits." Mrs. Malloy looked at me severely from under her neon lids. "Shouting at the top of your lungs like you was doing at whoever you had it in for upstairs."

"I was not shouting."

"Well, you wasn't whispering, that's for sure. I told the two men to take the kiddies outside before the plates came down off the Welsh dresser and somebody got hurt. Who was it"—enticing smile—"set you off like that, Mrs. H.? Don't tell me it was my George's Nessie; I've got right fond of the girl since she promised to give me her last year's fur coat. Seems she gone right off mink. And I don't like to think of you having words with your hubby. Men get their feelings bruised so easy. Can you believe it, Karisma got all embarrassed when I caught him looking at himself in the toaster and I told him it wouldn't cost him a train fare to go and look in the hall mirror."

"I was having words, as you call it," I said stiffly, "with Mrs. Swabucher."

"What about, ducky?" The purple lips positively

quivered with interest; but before I could decide whether or not to satisfy Mrs. Malloy's unwholesome curiosity, her son came in through the garden door. His ruddy face made his hair pale to ginger in comparison as he posed an intriguing question.

"Either of you two ladies want to come out and watch the duel?"

"The what?"

"It's all just a bit of fun between him and Karisma." His mother beamed at him with fatuous pride. "They're going to put on a bit of a show, like you see in Errol Flynn films, for the kiddies. No harm in that, is there? I was telling George last night about the set of swords—"

"They're called foils, Mum."

Mrs. Malloy nudged me in the ribs. "That's education for you. No doubt about it, my sonny boy's got brains to spare."

"You won't think that," I said crossly, "when he misses his step and gets them sliced out."

"Rubbish!" Mrs. Malloy was very much on her high heels. "As I was saying"—she gave me a quelling look—"I was talking to George about the foils—"

"You was rinsing off some carrots in the colander at the time, Mum," supplied the child of her substantial bosom.

"That's right, I was." Mrs. M.'s inflection gave warning that maternal pride drew the line at interruptions when she was talking. "It got me to thinking about them mesh fencing masks Mr. H. bought at St. Anselm's fête along with the foils. You remember, we was discussing them the other day, Mrs. H. Anyway, the long and the short of it is, when Karisma came downstairs this morning, I said it was a shame for two young lads to be cooped up on such a nice morning and why didn't they go outdoors and play pirates."

"You told me," I said frostily, "that everybody went outside just now for a bit of peace and quiet."

"And never was a truer word spoken." Mrs. Malloy hustled her son out the garden door with promises that Mummy would be out to watch in a minute. "All I left out was the bit about George and Karisma taking the swords and the other gear with them. And I was going to get round to that," she added with a virtuous purse of the lips, "when you got over your tiff with Mrs. Swabucher and stopped looking like you was sorry you hadn't murdered the woman."

"Talking about unhealthy impulses"—I strode over to the window and peered outside without getting a view of the swordsmen or my children—"are you sure you didn't come up with this bright idea in hopes that George will pink Karisma where it hurts most as a means for your son to get his jealousy of a supposed rival for Vanessa's affections out of his system?"

"The thought never crossed me mind." Mrs. Malloy succeeded in looking outraged. "I'm not one to harbour a grudge, leastways not against a man who makes me quiver in unmentionable places."

Her voice followed me out into the courtyard and a second later she was close on my heels. The sky was very blue—showing its false colours was my interpretation, because this was definitely not a good morning. It hadn't begun well and now I was weighed down by the feeling that something unspeakable was about to happen. The oppression I had felt on my picnic with Ben or in the garden of Tall Chimneys was nothing compared to this. I wished that black clouds would roll in and put an end to the cruel mockery of all that unrelenting blue.

Abbey and Tam came toddling towards me across the flagstones, and I would have scooped them both up in my arms if Mrs. Malloy hadn't done the honours with my daughter. What a rotten mother I was in not immediately rushing to them! Who knew if George planned to fight to the death in defending his beloved Nessie's honour! And two men doing the washing up, let alone on the brink of a duel, could not be trusted to keep a proper eye on my children. And there was the moat to consider. There wasn't any danger of my darlings drowning because we had put in drains before they were born. And being the ornamental variety of moat, there wasn't a horrendous drop. But even so, the thought of one of them tumbling over the stone rim was enough for me to clutch Tam's sturdy little body close to my palpitating heart.

Clearly Mrs. Malloy did not share my fears. Seating herself on a sarcophagus-style bench with Abbey on her knees, she offered up the observation, "A sight for sore eyes, if ever there was one, Mrs. H." She wasn't talking about the glories of nature, the sun in its heaven, the heady perfume of the flowers, or the green haze of the trees. Her eyes were focused on the two men standing with crossed sword blades at the far end of the courtyard. One born to dance the deadly minuet, invincible in his heroic good looks, his hair lifting around him in a triumphal banner before a blow was yet struck. The other, an uncouth yokel doomed to be speared like an over-ripe tomato and brandished on high by his opponent before being tossed through the air into the arms of his disappointed mother.

"What do you think, Mum?" George shouted. "Isn't it time to say ready, set, go?"

"Mrs. Haskell, will you do me the immense honour of acting as my second?" Karisma bowed with masterful grace over his sword.

"This is silly." My words were muffled by Tam's hair.

"Oh, get on with it, do," Mrs. Malloy instructed the combatants.

"Yes, I do not want to be late for church." Karisma's voice sang out as he held his blade at arm's length and executed a series of dazzling dance steps.

"Did you say late for church?" George guffawed. "Or the churchyard, old cock?"

"En garde!" came the reply, and before I had time to catch my breath, the duel was in progress. The flash of gleaming steel hurt my eyes, but I couldn't look away. Common sense had returned in dribs and drabs, and I was busily telling myself that Mrs. Malloy was right, that this was just a bit of harmless fun, when George's feet skidded out from under him and he yelped *"Tooch"* as he went down smack on his back within inches of the moat.

But before his mother could finish turning pale, he had bounded back onto his feet, his sword still in his hand, ready to resume thrusting where he had left off. It became apparent to me as I watched that George's willingness to test-pedal his own exercise equipment had paid off in muscle development, but whether he would have overwhelmed Karisma under his own steam is neither here nor there. For who should come wafting out into the courtyard like a summer breeze at the critical stage of the duel but Vanessa!

Did she pause to take note of the fact that her fiancé was occupied in a manly endeavour? Of course not. Without a glance at Mrs. Malloy and Abbey, she brushed past me and Tam and crossed the courtyard to tap George on the shoulder for all the world as though he were having a chat over the fence with a neighbour instead of being engaged in a fencing match.

"Darling, you won't believe what I have to tell you!"

"Not now, Nessie." George parried a thrust with commendable presence of mind. "I'm busy—"

"But it's *so* exciting," cooed my cousin as the blades flashed. "I've got the most *marvelous* piece of news. It turns out that the old stick who's married to the lady vicar writes romance novels and he wants Ben to pose for the cover of a book called *A Knight to Remember* and there's a very good chance I'll get to model for the heroine."

"What's that?" George froze and dropped his sword, but luckily this didn't present a problem for him. Karisma, understandably distracted, had taken a step backwards and fallen with a sickening thud into the empty moat.

Chapter

16

"Don't say it, Eudora," I said.

"Say what?"

"That you trust it was nothing trivial."

"Ellie, how can you possibly think I would be . . ."

"So unchristian?" I laughed. My friend and clergy-woman was looking particularly nice in a soft pink blouse with a matching cardigan. "Easy—you're only human and you don't like the man because he's been a thorn in Gladstone's flesh."

"But that doesn't mean I'd rejoice if he'd been badly hurt in that fall."

"Just a bump on the back of the head and a red line where he brought the foil up against his own throat when he tripped."

"That's all?" Eudora leaned closer and whispered with endearing naughtiness in my ear, "Not a chance of any major bruising to his ego?"

We were in the library, hemmed in against the leaded windows overlooking Market Street by the press of people, ninety-nine percent of them women, waiting for the King of the Cover Models to arrive. Upstairs in the reading room, Bunty Wiseman and Mrs. Dovedale were setting out refreshments of little cakes and lemonade. There had been a minor panic when the cord for the percolator could not be found. Then it had been remembered that Mr. Poucher had used it as a lead when taking Heathcliff home. And Sir Robert Pomeroy had pointed out, with remarkable acuity, that a coffeepot that made at most ten cups would not be much use given the size of the crowd, with people still squeezing in through the library doors. Not that there was any excuse for Mr. Poucher's failure to return a vital piece of library property, Sir Robert had concluded, "What! what!"

Had Miss Bunch still been in charge, she would doubtless have imposed a heavy fine, coupled with thirty days of stacking books. And it seemed likely her successor would take an equally grim view. Mrs. Harris now came up to Eudora and me, using her razor-sharp elbows to part the crowd. There was a glitter to her spectacles that boded ill for anyone intending to withhold knowledge of the purloined percolator cord.

"It has come to my attention that a serious breach of policy has taken place." She made this pronouncement in ringing tones that violated the prominently posted notice that no one speak above a whisper, even should the library be on fire or an armed robbery in progress. "If this sort of thing continues"—the dragon lady wagged her accusing nose at me—"I shall have no choice but to deny the Library League continued access to these premises."

"What sort of thing?" Eudora bit down on a smile.

"A *boa* was left on the meeting room floor the other night."

Two women inches away from us let out piercing squeals. Envisioning the room erupting into a panic that would result in most of the female population of Chitterton Fells being trampled to death, I hastily explained for the benefit of anyone within earshot that we were talking about the feather variety of boa.

"It belongs," I added, "to Karisma's business agent, Mrs. Swabucher."

"I don't care if it belongs to the Queen Mother," persisted the dragon lady. "Tell the woman, Mrs. Haskell, that I am running a library here, not a lost-and-found booth. It is to be hoped I shall have no further reason for complaint after this afternoon's indoor picnic. Is anyone monitoring who comes through the door so that we will have a checklist should any books go missing?"

"Sir Robert Pomeroy is collecting the entry money," I answered.

"And just when do we expect Mr. Karisma to arrive?"

"In about fifteen minutes."

"Let it be clearly understood, Mrs. Haskell, that the man is not welcome to take over the reception desk. Should he wish to sign autographs, he may avail himself of one of the reading tables. And I do trust he will bring his own pen rather than expecting to borrow one of ours and running it out of ink. The library operates on a strict budget, Mrs. Haskell."

"She certainly has mastered the knack of being unpleasant," I said to Eudora when the dragon lady disappeared into the crowd of bobbing heads.

"Perhaps she's intimidated at having to fill Miss Bunch's shoes." My friend smoothed a hand over her grey hair. "While we've got a few moments, Ellie, I'd appreciate your telling me how you feel about the possibility of your very own husband appearing on the cover of *A Knight to Remember*."

"If it makes Ben happy," I smiled brightly, "I'm happy."

"Oh, I do wish that had been my attitude when Gladstone decided, in the face of his publisher's determination to have Karisma do the cover, that he would reveal his identity as Zinnia Parrish." Eudora tugged at the sleeves of her cardigan. "But I thought only about myself and how I would feel having people know Gladstone had written those books with their vividly descriptive sex scenes. You saw how disagreeable I was when you came over to the vicarage to talk about the redecorating. And I'm ashamed to say, I'd been in the same kind of mood for days beforehand. Picking on Gladstone for leaving his knitting lying around. As if the bishop couldn't have looked before he sat down. Grumbling at my dear one for, of all things, putting off"—Eudora lowered her voice—"having the circumcision done. Acting as if he hadn't been considering my feelings when he moved into another bedroom, the intimate side of our married life being an impossibility until he is put right . . . down below."

"Quite," I said.

"I only hope and pray, Ellie, that I can make things up to Gladstone."

I put my arm around her, which wasn't easy, given the size of the crowd. "Don't you think you're being a little hard on yourself? I can understand your concern that some narrow-minded people, including your bishop perhaps, might take a dim view of a clergywoman's husband writing torrid romances."

"That wasn't the problem." Eudora stared out into the sea of faces. "What bothered me was the prospect of standing in the pulpit at St. Anselm's being ogled by my parishioners, all of whom would know that Gladstone hadn't made up all that steamy stuff inside his head. No man, Ellie, has *that* much imagination."

"I see your point," I said, trying without success to banish the picture of Eudora surrendering her virginity on a billiard table, in transports of unclerical abandon. "But the good news is that the publisher has agreed not to use Karisma for the cover art of *A Knight to Remember,* and in return Gladstone has promised not to reveal that he is Zinnia Parrish."

"I'd like to think, Ellie, that my secret is safe."

"I remembered, a bit belatedly, to warn Ben and Vanessa to be discreet. Mrs. Malloy and her son do know," I admitted. "It would be practically impossible to keep them in the dark, seeing that Vanessa is going to marry George. But he and his mother both gave me their word that they won't say anything to anyone. And I'm certain you can trust them."

Eudora's eyes narrowed. "I wish that I could feel as sure of Karisma. Don't mistake me, I don't believe he would risk running afoul of Gladstone's publishers by a public announcement, but I wouldn't put it past him to leak word as to the true identity of Zinnia Parrish while he's here in Chitterton Fells."

"You could be misjudging him," I told her.

"The man's a snake, Ellie."

This last word was picked up by a woman standing two feet in front of us, and it was buzzed on to another, who said she had previously heard mutterings about a boa constrictor left loose in the upstairs reading room, but she had believed this to be an unfounded rumour started by one of Karisma's more fanatical fans as a ploy to thin out the mob of autograph hounds.

"Hello, you two!" Bunty Wiseman appeared out of nowhere to dazzle Eudora and me with her sunbeam smile. "We're taking our lives in our hands being here. Most of this lot would kill to be first in the queue. That doesn't include my ex-husband, I need hardly say. Li has made it one hundred percent clear he showed up only to pay his five quid for the good of the cause. A regular philanthropist, that's him." Bunty opened her china-blue eyes wide and batted her lashes. "Not a bloody chance he took me seriously when I told him Karisma was so thrilled at having me take photos of him yesterday that he offered me the job on a permanent basis, with all fringe benefits included." She wiggled her hips, knocking the unfortunate woman standing next to her sideways and creating a domino effect with half a dozen others.

"Did Karisma really ask you to be his photographer?" Eudora asked her.

"Not on your Nellie." Bunty grinned impishly. "Every time I snapped a picture, old Mrs. Poucher had to get in the act, swooning and mooning in his arms like a bloody schoolgirl. Honestly! I could have killed her; but you know me—always the good sport. I told our pal Mr. Poucher, who at this late stage of the game probably can't find any way out of being her son, that he got first dibs on pushing her into the moat. Now, why are you looking at me with that funny expression on your face, Ellie?"

"We had an accident this morning at Merlin's Court."

"Blimey!" Bunty looked stricken. "And here's me rattling on about a lot of nonsense. Did something happen to Ben? Is that why he's not here?"

"No, he's fine," I said.

Eudora spoke up. "My husband and Ben are having a meeting. It's about Parrish"—and I had no doubt that being a truthful woman, she added the extra *r*—"business."

"Something that cropped up at the last minute," I hastened to contribute.

"Gladstone is not one to lightly shirk his responsibilities to the Library League." His loyal spouse had to raise her voice to be heard over the animated conversation taking place among a group of people to our right. "I'm here as his proxy and will be only too pleased to take over any responsibilities assigned to him."

Bunty gave her a cheeky grin. "That's awfully nice of you, Eudora. I'm sure Mrs. Dovedale will let you pour the lemonade. And if you make a success of that job, there's a good chance you can progress to something more challenging, like helping Sir Robert count up the money we've collected. But don't think"—she tossed her blond curls—"you can have the job of being Karisma's assistant for the day, because I've already offered to stand next to him when he signs autographs and blot his fingers if his pen leaks."

"Speaking of our celebrity"—I deemed it time to get this conversation back on track—"he's the one who had the accident—but don't worry, he wasn't badly hurt."

Bunty's blue eyes grew big. "What happened?"

"He fell in the moat."

"It wasn't Karisma's fault," Eudora interjected, then surprised me by adding with uncharacteristic snideness, "believe it or not, he wasn't attempting to walk on water."

"There isn't any water in the moat," I said. "And if I have anything to say about it, there won't be any more duels taking place at Merlin's Court."

"Any more *what*?" Bunty's voice shot above the babble going on all around us and I explained what had happened as concisely as possible, adding that George Malloy had made it difficult for me to remain cross with him because he had insisted upon doing penance by baby-sitting Tam and Abbey until Ben or I got home.

"To be fair to George," I added, "his mother was the main culprit. She put him up to the idea of the duel because she thought he needed to get his jealousy of Karisma out of his system."

"Sort of like fighting it out on the school playground?"

I nodded at Bunty. "According to Mrs. Malloy, George got his underpants in a twist because he's engaged to Vanessa and he thought Karisma fancied her."

"Oh, surely not," exclaimed Eudora. "I can't believe Mr. Magnificent would be unfaithful when he's already heavily involved."

"Don't tell me that! How did I miss reading about it in the tabloids?" Bunty's lower lip protruded and she dug her knuckles into her eyes.

"I was talking about Karisma's long-term love affair with himself." Eudora did not hang her head even when she added, "Please forgive me for my uncharitable attitude."

"I get it"—Bunty winked at me—"being in the church—and married to boot—our friend here is in bloody torment trying to come to terms with her intense physical feelings for a sex object. It's all clear as could be now."

"What is?" I asked.

"Why Gladstone wasn't gung ho when the Library League talked about inviting Karisma to make an appearance, and why he's now at a parish meeting with Ben instead of being here asking people if they want a big or a little piece of cake. The man has to be riddled with jealousy, just like George Malloy." Bunty heaved a sympathetic sigh. "But you mustn't blame yourself, Eudora, if you've been talking in your sleep about the love god. You're a woman. And it won't do a bit of good telling yourself you're too old for emotional high jinks. You should have seen Mrs. Poucher yesterday." A flutter of the eyelashes. "There's a woman who should be in a museum as an archaeological exhibit! Instead, she was all over Karisma. And I'll bet money that when the old bat finally dragged herself away from him, she hopped on the bus and went shopping for a vibrator."

"Bunty!" I glanced around, fervently hoping that no one in the ever-swelling crowd was listening in on this exchange.

"I bet the old bird said she needed the latest model to help relieve muscle tension or a pinched nerve in her neck," came the irrepressible reply. "You see them advertised in magazines all the time as life-savers for sufferers of chronic neuralgia."

"I must bone up on my reading," said Eudora with a half-smile.

"You're a busy woman," Bunty excused her. "Honestly, I'm amazed you have time to get your nose stuck in anything except the Bible. I've been meaning to read it myself"—here she looked momentarily virtuous—"but someone kind of spoiled it for me by telling me how it ends. And I must say, Eudora, I'd never have figured you— no offence meant—for a person who reads romances. What are your favourites? Regencies? Or the doctor-and-nurse ones—where she's the junior on the ward, forever running afoul of Matron for not pinning her cap on straight, and he is Sir Somebody-or-Other, whiz pathologist, who drives a grey Rolls-Royce and has a dear old nanny who keeps house for him."

Eudora opened her mouth, but before she could get a word out, Bunty giggled mischievously.

"Don't tell me you go for the hot and heavy ones by authors like Zinnia Parrish? I'm not what you'd call naïve by a long shot, but let me tell you, I've learned a thing or two from reading *that* woman's books."

I think it occurred to Eudora and me at the same moment that we had been slacking off long enough. And this was particularly naughty given the fact that we were short so many Library League members. I had yet to see Mr. Poucher. No one could expect poor widowed Sylvia to show up. And I did not have any great hopes that Brigadier Lester-Smith would change his mind about not coming.

It was time to elbow our way through the panting press of humanity and assist Sir Robert and Mrs. Dovedale in any last-minute preparations for Karisma's imminent arrival. When we reached the reception desk, Bunty left us to go upstairs to the reading room to make sure, she informed us, that the lemonade had not gone off. I was tempted to offer my services in sampling the cream cakes, for the purpose of determining that they did not pose a health risk to the unwary. But just as Eudora left me and headed for the main door to offer to spell Sir Robert at collecting the admission fees, I turned and collided with Mr. Poucher.

He did not seem overly enthused to see me. Indeed, I had never seen him look more like a wet washday in November. His raincoat was too big for him, suggesting he had dropped a couple of sizes since yesterday. His eyes were sunk in his head and he shuffled his feet as he went to move past me as if I were invisible to him in the fog that swirled around him.

"Hello, Mr. Poucher!" I caught hold of his elbow as he was about to incur the ire of the tyrannous lady librarian by bumping into the desk and sending her Overdue stamp flying.

"Oh, it's you," he responded in a voice that was devoid of inflection and stared through me into the bleak beyond. "I'm late, but I don't guess everyone's been breaking their hearts. . . ."

"What's the matter?" I matched my tread to his halting steps while leading him towards a gap in the crowd. "Something has happened. Is Heathcliff"—my mind conjured up the unsettling image of an entire roomful of furniture being devoured in a single lip-smacking gulp, to be followed shortly thereafter by a request for a canine indigestion tablet—"is Heathcliff the problem?"

"Nothing's wrong with the dog; he's the one comfort left to me." Mr. Poucher trod on a woman's foot and vouchsafed no reaction to her yelp of pain. "The problem, if you must know, Mrs. Haskell, is my mother."

"She's been taken ill?"

"Worse than that!"

"Oh, Mr. Poucher!" I pressed a hand to my throat. "You have my deepest sympathy."

"I'm going to need it, right enough." His eyes suddenly snapped to life. And while I was still thinking rigor mortis, he enlightened me. "Mother's suffered a serious setback. She's relapsed into good health."

"What?"

"She bounded out of bed this morning like she was a slip of a girl and she's been on the go ever since. Singing like a lark all the time she was scrubbing the kitchen floor. Then, when she was done with that, she turned out the front room, took down the curtains to wash, polished the brass, made a batch of potato scones, milked the cows, and dug over the patch of garden I'd given over to weeds. All before I was done shaving."

"That's amazing!"

"Then, when we sat down to our midday meal, Ma made some very ugly threats." Mr. Poucher's face clouded over to the extent that I expected it to start raining inside the library. And I'm almost sure I saw the glimmer of tears in his eyes. "She told me she'd changed her mind about dying anytime in the near future. And if I didn't do like she told me, when she told me, she may up and decide not to die at all."

I was speechless.

"And we know, don't we, Mrs. Haskell, who's to blame?"

"Her doctor?"

Mr. Poucher's weary shake of head suggested I was the one in need of medical attention. "That buggering chap Karisma, he had to make over Mother, didn't he? Fussing and cooing at her like she was the first rose of summer. Going on, fit to make you spit, about how he loves all women irregardless of whether they was nineteen or ninety-two. He brought her back to life with a kiss on the lips, she says, like she was Sleeping Beauty and he was Prince Charming. Can you believe such vile talk?" Mr. Poucher drew an ugly breath. "Just wait till I set eyes on the interfering bounder!"

The hot words had not cooled on his lips, when a frenzied roar of *"Karisma!"* went through the room like a gale-force wind, and the mob surged forward intent, I thought with a flicker of alarm, on all the excesses of idolatry. My eyes sought out Mrs. Swabucher without success. In the process I lost sight of Mr. Poucher, and anyway I forgot about him instantly in the shock of seeing Sylvia Babcock, just two women away from me. I didn't get to speak to her there and then because the Nazi librarian rose to the occasion. Mounting the reception desk, she stood feet apart and gave three blasts of the whistle Miss Bunch had been known to keep handy for the purpose of scaring a book thief into dropping his stash. The crowd hushed, though eyes everywhere gleamed with lust.

Order being peremptorily restored and a warning delivered that no further outbursts would be tolerated, Mrs. Harris resumed her seat. With creditable aplomb Sir Robert Pomeroy paraded Karisma down the aisle formed between rows of people lined up like trees, to the desk where he was going to sign books. The desk was to the right of the arch, the one that led into Nonfiction. And above that arch was the bust of Shakespeare. It suddenly struck me as funny that William Shakespeare should be looking over Karisma's muscled shoulders while he was autographing.

Funny and . . . I never got to decide what else, because a heavily made-up woman in a sequined hat and a crushed-velvet frock glared at me from under pencilled brows and told me that if I was thinking of jumping the queue, I had another think coming.

"Mrs. Malloy!" I stepped backwards in case she decided to make her position clearer yet by bopping me on the head with her armload of paperbacks. "I thought you might have decided not to come."

"Am I to take that as meaning you'd just as soon I'd stayed away, Mrs. H.?" Bridling, so that a button popped off the front of her frock and scored a hit. The woman in front of us nipped smartly out of the queue, making for only forty-five heads currently in front of us.

"Of course I wanted you to come," I said.

"Well, that does ease me mind." A sigh that produced another bull's-eye, moving us up yet again. "For a moment there I thought I'd become something of an embarrassment to you, on account of my George winning that sword fight all fair and square. I suppose, Mrs. H., you think I should have told him it was only good manners to let his opponent win, seeing as the other lad didn't have his mother there to buck him up."

"The only reason I thought you might stay away," I said, "was that it occurred to me you would possibly prefer to spend the afternoon with George; especially as Vanessa was going to be gone for a while and he had kindly volunteered to look after the twins."

"What, and miss me outing?" Mrs. Malloy looked suitably shocked. "Just what sort of a parent would I be, when all's said and done, if I didn't know the difference between mother love and smother love? The day comes, Mrs. H., when it's time for mummy bird to fly the nest."

"And not leave a forwarding address? You're absolutely right, Mrs. Malloy. Believe me, I'm getting ready to cut the bib strings any day now." We were now close enough to the front of the queue to see a woman in a strident orange frock lunge across the desk to grab at a handful of Karisma's flowing tresses and press them to her cheek.

"I can't believe I'm seeing you in the flesh!" Her voice was choked with emotion . . . and possibly a hank of hair. "You're even more fabulous than in your pictures. I've read every book you've ever been on. Miss Bunch used to phone me whenever the library got a new one in. A friend gave me your exercise tape for Christmas and I'm going to splurge and buy your calendar."

"When it comes out in paperback, I'll bet." Mrs. Malloy nudged me with her elbow.

"I *lorve* women." Karisma was beginning to sound as if he were rubber-stamping the words. But who could blame him? Certainly not the woman in orange, who told him (at considerable length) that he had helped her through a bad marriage, the death of a beloved Pekingese, and a rift with her next-door neighbour. Finally, in all likelihood after getting a kick in the shins, she was supplanted by an equally loquacious fan.

"I'm beginning to think I've got it easy scrubbing other people's toilets for a living," sighed Mrs. Malloy. "This celebrity business isn't all it's cracked up to be. In fact, I'm on the brink of changing me mind about going on the stage. Strictly between you and me, Mrs. H., because I wouldn't want George upsetting himself, it was a shock when Karisma went flying into that ditch."

"It's a blessing he wasn't badly hurt."

"Well, *I* was!" Mrs. Malloy's glower told me what she thought of my gross lack of sensitivity. "Something in me died at that moment, but I don't suppose you've got a clue what I'm talking about."

"Yes, I have!" I fired back at her. "I'd been working up to the realization ever since he arrived at the house; but until the moat incident, I hadn't fully acknowledged that in meeting Karisma I'd lost"—I blinked back tears—"my first true love. Being me, I had a little more trouble than some getting over him, even after I married my wonderful Ben. The great thing about the dream lover is there's no emotional risk. Should you ever get angry with him, or heaven forbid momentarily bored, you can close the book on him whenever you choose. Face it: You're committed to the relationship only for several hundred pages."

"And now here's me wondering if Karisma has a mother who understands him." Mrs. Malloy inched forward in the queue. "Oh, I know he's got his Mrs.

Swabucher, but that's not the same, is it? By the way, where is she?"

"Somewhere around." I peered into the crowd, but my only glimpse of pink was Eudora's cardigan. Just as I was about to say that perhaps Mrs. Swabucher made a point of keeping in the background at these events, Mrs. Malloy gave me another of her nudges.

"Now, this is a surprise!"

"What is?"

"Use your eyes, Mrs. H.!" Exasperated snort. "That's Ione Tunbridge, all in black as usual, about a dozen places ahead of us. Imagine her showing up in broad daylight! Could be that little talk with you the other night, Mrs. H., helped her clear away some of the cobwebs from that spooky old attic she calls a mind."

"One legend meets another." I watched as Miss Tunbridge stepped up to the desk and inclined her black-bonneted head to speak to Karisma.

"She does look like a bloody bird of prey." Mrs. Malloy shifted the load of books in her arms. "I'll bet she's got talons six inches long under those crocheted gloves of hers, but I don't see as why you've got that look on your face, like she just walked over your grave."

"I think I'm ready for a cream cake," I told her, not wishing to dwell on the point, even in my own mind, that Miss Tunbridge who lived at Tall Chimneys might have brought something of its disturbing past into the library with her. Surprisingly, I hadn't thought about Hector Rigglesworth until now. And there was a reason for that, I realized. When Karisma had gone crashing into the moat, I'd had no doubt that he was dead. But when he was found to have suffered no injuries beyond the bump on the head and the mark on his throat, my reaction was more than straightforward relief on his behalf. I was able to tell myself that the deaths of Miss Bunch and Mr. Babcock were an unhappy fact of life and in no way related to a century-old curse. But here I was, suffering a setback. What I had to do, I decided, was get out of this queue before I began wondering if Miss Tunbridge had been telling the truth the other night about murdering her bridegroom-to-be and burying him on what had once been Hector Rigglesworth's property. Although, I brightened up, if one were to go by the old adage that the third time is the charm, it would be reasonable to suppose that with the death of Mr. Babcock, Hector Rigglesworth would be ready to set aside old grudges and vanish permanently into the next world.

I explained to Mrs. Malloy that I had merely been keeping her company in the queue and that it was time for me to assist my fellow library members in seeing that the refreshments would be ready when Karisma finished autographing. Far from begging me not to leave her, she displayed no emotion whatsoever, which is more than could be said of me when I bumped into Sylvia Babcock a couple of seconds later and saw who was standing next to her.

"Gerta! What made you decide to come?"

"This morning I am making strudel in the kitchen at the cottage, Frau Haskell"—she stood with her braided head held high and a glow on her face that could not be purchased at any cosmetics counter—"and I know there has to be more to life than standing in one place. The tears they are all used up. I have to accept the truth that my marriage is over and put Ernst behind me. But before that is possible, I must to face the memory of him one last time. To see him in his new life"—she spread her hands—"that is too hard, and looking at photographs is not enough."

"So you decided to take a close-up look at Karisma who," I added for Sylvia's benefit in case she wasn't in the know, "reminds you so much of your husband. That was very brave of you."

"It is not so hard after all." Gerta smiled, showing dimples I had never before seen. "Not nearly so bad as what Frau Babcock suffers, and yet she is here."

"I had to get out of the house!" Not one of Sylvia's pin curls was out of place, and there wasn't a crease in her green-and-white-striped frock despite the crush of people, but her voice trembled on the brink of hysteria. "I thought I'd feel better if I was around people, but half the time I can't stop shaking. I keep hearing people talking about it—how Albert died so soon after we got married . . . I don't know how much more I can take without going completely to pieces and shouting at them to shut up!"

"People can be insensitive. Why don't I go and get you a glass of lemonade?" I suggested, and hurried towards the door that opened into the little corridor with its staircase leading up to the meeting room. In my haste I barely acknowledged handsome, silver-haired Lionel Wiseman's greeting. Nor did I waste much time on a double take when I noticed Mrs. Swabucher, looking quite smart in a pale rose suit, standing up against the fiction stacks in conversation with Brigadier Lester-Smith. So he had changed his mind about coming! Splendid. But knowing him to be a man who would strive to do his duty under the most difficult of circumstances, I wasn't greatly surprised.

When I was halfway up the stairs I saw Mr. Poucher start down from the top and in passing him—something that Mrs. Malloy, who was given to her superstitious moments, had told me brought the worst of bad luck—I asked him if he had remembered to bring back the coffee-pot cord.

"It's in my raincoat pocket," he muttered as he rushed down the last of the steps. "I don't have time to dilly-dally, Mrs. Haskell, I just looked out the window and saw Heathcliff sitting next to the dustbins outside the back door."

"You mean he followed you here?" My knees trembled out of all proportion to this latest doggy escapade as I leaned over the banister. And in a weak attempt at hiding my ridiculous fear that Heathcliff had all along been an emissary from beyond the grave, I said I hoped Mrs. Poucher had put him in a taxi rather than let him make the long walk from the farm.

"I reckon she purposely forgot to feed the old lad." Her son's bitterness wafted up to me in almost tangible form, rather like stale air released from a room that has been locked up for too many years. But seconds later sunlight—along with Heathcliff—rushed into the corridor when Mr. Poucher opened the door. To give credit where due, the dog restrained himself from raucous barking. Indeed, he did no more than whimper piteously as he wound himself around his master's legs.

"Do I have your solemn promise to behave yourself if I let you come upstairs with me?" Upon receiving a woof of acquiescence from the black beast, Mr. Poucher's glum expression softened. He looked up at me. "If you'll agree to keep mum, Mrs. Haskell, there's none as will be the wiser if I tuck him away behind that little cupboard in the corner of the reading room."

"My lips are sealed," I assured him, having fought off my attack of silliness. "But if Mrs. Harris finds him, we'll all be in the soup."

Fortunately for Heathcliff, we encountered no problem in spiriting him upstairs. Sir Robert and Mrs. Dovedale were positioned squarely in front of the long table that was laid out as if in readiness for a wedding banquet. But they posed no problem, being locked in an embrace that showed no sign of unclenching as Mr. Poucher and Heathcliff tiptoed across the reading room. It was as well, however, that they acted speedily. Within seconds of the dog disappearing behind the cabinet, on the top of which lay Mrs. Swabucher's feather boa, the kissing couple was jolted apart by the sound of footsteps thundering up the stairs. Before Mr. Poucher and I had finished exchanging a relieved glance, people poured into the room as if eager to seize it for king and country. And I could see that the corridor was jampacked with those who had not made the first rush to the stairs.

For at least ten minutes I was kept occupied alongside Mrs. Dovedale pouring lemonade until the last jug ran dry. The first person to whom I handed a cup was Mrs. Swabucher. I asked her if she would like an extra one for Karisma.

"Better not, Giselle; I'm not sure where he is." She attempted a smile. "And by the time I find him, I expect I would have spilled it in this tight squeeze."

"The turnout has been spectacular and"—I lowered my voice—"despite what I said this morning, I am still very grateful to you and Karisma for making it possible to raise the money for Miss Bunch's statue."

"That's nice to know, dear." There was a constraint to her manner, but it was for Mrs. Swabucher to know and me to guess whether that was due to my failure to live up to expectation in bringing off a meeting with Gladstone Spike, or because she remained uncomfortable at having been thrust into another meeting with Brigadier Lester-Smith. As she was about to depart with her cup of lemonade, I told her that her feather boa was on the cabinet in the corner.

"I don't see it, Giselle"—her eyes followed my gaze—"perhaps someone moved it out of the way; I'll go and look."

"Good luck!" I called after her, and slipped in a silent prayer, while pouring more lemonade for women who could only gasp "Karisma!", that Heathcliff had not reared up from behind the cabinet to snatch up the downy pink boa in his capacious jaws and retreat with it into his lair. But I was probably worrying unnecessarily. Mrs. Swabucher would find her prized piece of apparel safe and sound. Poor visibility was the problem. With the room ready to burst at the seams, I got the feeling that I was looking through a kaleidoscope. Objects and people became triangular quivers of stained glass colours that shifted by the split second into different patterns. I found myself straining to piece together a familiar face, but after a few minutes even the people standing right in front of me, with their hands out for lemonade, became the nose or the eye of some patchwork entity.

Ben suffers from claustrophobia. We don't talk about it very often and it took me several minutes to realize what was wrong with me. Just at the moment when I decided it was time to escape to a place where oxygen was not in critically short supply, the room exploded into a cacophony of undeniably canine barks. And two life forms came simultaneously into focus. One was Heathcliff, who leapt onto the table, knocking the lemonade jug out of my hands and trampling cream cakes and sandwiches under his giant paws. The other was Mrs. Harris, the kamikaze librarian, who demanded in a voice that rose above the dog's unearthly howls to know who was responsible for this outrage.

I was surprised that Mr. Poucher had not rushed forward to soothe his pet and the furious woman. Was it possible that he was out in the corridor, so engrossed in conversation that he had failed to hear the uproar? Feeling it incumbent on me, as his accomplice, to find him before Heathcliff took a chunk out of the dragon lady or vice versa, I edged away from her glare and slipped through cracks in the crowd to reach the doorway. There I ran smack into Sylvia Babcock. And after apologizing for not looking where I was going, I felt compelled to chew up another moment or two telling her I was sorry I had forgotten to bring her the glass of lemonade I had promised.

Sounding painfully out of breath, she grabbed at my arm. "It doesn't matter, oh, God, my heart's beating so fast, I'm scared it's going to explode. That horrible dog! I never wanted to see him again, but here he is—appearing out of nowhere and howling in that bone-chilling way as if . . . as if he's seen a ghost!"

"Sylvia," I said with all the conviction I could muster, "the dog must have heard something—an ordinary, everyday sound that scared him, perhaps a door slamming or a floorboard creaking. An animal's ears are so much sharper than ours. Listen! He's quieting down and he'll be even better when I find Mr. Poucher, who very kindly gave him a home."

"Gave him a home after I killed my husband, that's what you're thinking, isn't it?" Sylvia's voice faded into a whimper. "It's what everybody is thinking?"

"That's rubbish," I assured her. "You've got to stop blaming yourself for getting upset when the dog raced out of the house with the roast beef. If the same thing had happened to me and Ben was in the house, I would have yelled at him to chase down our Sunday dinner. But I do see it's not a good idea for you to be anywhere near Heathcliff; so why don't you come out into the corridor with me while I look for Mr. Poucher?"

Sylvia did trail after me for a few yards, but when I saw no sign of my quarry and said I would go downstairs to look for him, she huddled up next to Gerta, who was standing under a picture of the librarian whom Miss Bunch had replaced decades ago. What had caused Heathcliff to practically leap out of his fur? I wondered. Was it possible he had seen something—or *someone*—who was not of our time? Sylvia, I was certain, had been thinking of the late Mr. Babcock, but . . . no, I resolutely set my foot on the bottom step, I would not allow myself to sink back into the bog of superstitious folly.

A courageous decision which did not save me from leaping a foot in the air when Eudora came out from the toilet to the left of the staircase. Our vicar was as white as the walls and her eyes had a glassy stare as she stood plucking at a loose thread on her pink cardigan. She was trembling.

"What's wrong?" I asked. "Did you hear all that noise upstairs and panic that something was dreadfully afoul? It was nothing," I assured her. "Mr. Poucher smuggled Heathcliff into the reading room and the dog went a bit wild, that's all."

"No, that isn't all." My friend drew a ragged breath. "Please give me a moment, I've been having trouble getting air into my lungs. I suppose it's the shock, although a crisis doesn't usually take me this way. Ellie, there's been a terrible accident. And I can't think of any way to break the news to you gently. *Karisma is dead!*"

"That can't be!" I staggered backwards and leaned against the wall facing her.

"He's lying on the library floor."

"Then he'll be meditating." My voice spiralled around my head. "People who are really good at it go into a deep trance state."

"There is no mistake." Eudora pressed a hand to her forehead. "I came downstairs after looking for Karisma and not finding him in the reading room or in the upper corridor. I intended to tell him in a straightforward manner why Gladstone had not wanted him to do the cover for *A Knight to Remember* and that I resented his attempt to put pressure on my dear and gentle husband. But I didn't get to speak to him. I found him sprawled within a few feet of the desk where he had been signing books. That bust of Shakespeare was also on the floor. It must have fallen off the wall bracket and struck him on the head."

"You're saying it was an accident?" I stammered.

"Ellie"—Eudora took a halting step towards me— "what else could it have been?"

"Murder!!!"

The voice rained bitter anguish down upon us, and we looked up to see Mrs. Swabucher sway in slow motion against the banister before crumbling into a merciful swoon.

Chapter

17

Mrs. Malloy said that even in death Karisma posed like a dream and someone should take a photo to make sure he got to be on one final book cover." My voice broke as I looked up at my husband, and he pressed a glass of brandy into my hand. "He did look incredibly fabulous, Ben. It was hard to believe he had not been told to lie on the floor with his hair spread around him like a river soaking up sunlight while the camera closed in for an adoring farewell."

"Drink up, sweetheart." Ben joined me on the sofa. I had cried so much since getting home that my face was damp from forehead to chin. It was seven o'clock in the evening, but I couldn't face the thought of food, even though I knew a sandwich or two would do more than a brandy to buck me up.

"I'm sorry to be carrying on like this." I risked spilling the glass when I leaned back against the cushions and closed my eyes. "Perhaps I should go and telephone Mrs. Swabucher at the Hollywood Hotel, the one that opened recently after being converted from the Wisemans' former home. I keep thinking that had I tried a little harder, I might have been able to persuade her to come back here for the night."

"Obviously"—Ben smoothed the hair back from my brow—"Mrs. Swabucher felt a need to be on her own."

"Then I'll go upstairs and look in on the twins."

"They're sound asleep," Ben assured me, "and Vanessa promised to make periodic checks on them."

"She's been wonderful."

"Our leopardess would seem to have changed her spots."

The enthusiasm with which he said this did not settle well on my empty stomach. For a moment I forgot about Karisma's sad fate and wondered how Ben and Vanessa's afternoon at the vicarage had gone. Naturally the subject had not come up, given the bad news I had brought home. But I thought an inquiry might be appropriate now, to let my husband know that even in times of tragedy I was first and foremost a considerate wife.

"Are you and Vanessa going to do the cover of *A Knight to Remember*?" I put down my glass and reached towards the plate of salmon and tomato sandwiches on the coffee table.

"Gladstone's editor was very enthusiastic, but we've plenty of time to talk about that later. Unlike poor Karisma"—Ben went back to stroking my hair—"we have our whole lives ahead of us."

"That's true." I withdrew my hand from the sandwiches without taking one. "It does seem incredible to realize he's dead."

"Is it equally hard, Ellie, to believe Mrs. Swabucher's accusation that he was murdered?"

"I don't know." I shook my head. "Everything happened so quickly after she passed out on the stairs. Mr. Poucher appeared on the scene and carried her to one of the sofas in the library. And while Eudora was trying to get her to drink some water, Brigadier Lester-Smith was suddenly there, insisting on taking over Mrs. Swabucher's care. Then the scene became wall-to-wall people, with so much screaming and wailing that I thought the ambulance had arrived before it did. Sir Robert Pomeroy did the telephoning, and the new librarian did a great job of keeping the crowd back from . . . the body. That's pretty much all I'm clear about. Everything became a major blur with men rushing in with a stretcher and lots of questions being asked, particularly of Eudora, because she was the one who found him. It seemed hours before we all got to leave. There's to be an autopsy, of course, but I'm pretty sure Karisma's death is being officially viewed as accidental."

"But you don't think it is?" Ben put a sandwich in my hand and told me to finish it before answering him.

"I'm not sure." I swallowed dutifully. "Under different circumstances it would seem unlikely for that big marble bust of Shakespeare to take a flying leap off the wall, but despite all my determination to be sensible on the subject, I can't completely dismiss the possibility that Hector Rigglesworth was involved."

"The ghost?"

"He is said to have vowed to haunt the Chitterton Fells library until he was finally avenged for a life spent in slavish attention to his daughters' obsession with romantic fiction. And Karisma is . . . *was* the living representation of the heroes in those books."

"Ellie"—Ben shook his head—"you've suffered a nasty shock and you're not thinking straight."

"I'm trying to look at the facts objectively," I told him. "This year is the centenary of Mr. Rigglesworth's death. And think about this, Ben: On the actual anniversary date, Miss Bunch, an apparently healthy woman, dropped dead in the library with a copy of a book titled *The Dream Lover* lying beside her. Then Mr. Babcock, the newly-married husband of a Library League member, meets his end. And"—I fortified myself with another sandwich—"there are other odd happenings to be taken into account, such as the members of Karisma's staff being struck down by food poisoning, which prevented them from coming down here and keeping a protective eye on him."

"He had Mrs. Swabucher in attendance."

"Agreed," I said, "but she wasn't her usual redoubtable self because she was distressed at meeting the man she'd abandoned on their wedding night years ago. And that upset caused her to leave her prized feather boa at the library."

"What does that have to do with anything?" Ben went to pour himself a glass of brandy.

"She was in the reading room"—I tried not to sound exasperated—"looking for that boa, perhaps at that very moment when she should have been downstairs with Karisma and able to throw herself between him and that bust of Shakespeare when it came off the wall. I haven't a doubt in the world that she would have given her life to save his. But Mrs. Swabucher wasn't the one Hector Rigglesworth wanted today. It had to be Karisma."

"If any of this were to make sense"—Ben resumed his seat beside me—"it would seem to me your ghost had equally good, if not better, reason to strike down Gladstone Spike. After all, he writes the very kind of book the Rigglesworth daughters spent their lives reading."

"I had thought of that," I admitted. "But it could be old Hector means to exact a different kind of vengeance on our friend Gladstone. One which would be worse than death." I had difficulty continuing. "If Eudora were to be accused of Karisma's murder and—incredible as it sounds—found guilty, I don't know that Gladstone would want to live."

"Now you are looking for trouble." Ben spoke in his most soothing voice. "You're the one who said that it seems rather improbable that Shakespeare just took it into his marble head to leap off the wall and land on Karisma's skull."

"But that doesn't mean I'd think for a moment that Eudora lent a helping hand."

I rubbed my forehead to ease away the beginning of a headache. "I'm sure she didn't. But I don't know how the police, who have such nasty, suspicious minds, might view the fact that I found her close to the scene of the body, when everyone else—to the best of my knowledge—was upstairs. And she was in such a state that she'd gone into the loo to recover rather than immediately reporting the bad news."

Ben studied my face closely. "I find that entirely understandable. And I don't know why you're so worried."

"Because something could be made out of the fact that Eudora and I discussed the moat accident earlier at the library and she made a couple of joking remarks that could be misconstrued if they were overheard. Also, she would readily admit if questioned by the police that she went looking for Karisma to tell him off for pressuring Gladstone about the cover of *A Knight to Remember*."

"So she had a grudge against him," Ben said. "I don't suppose for one minute she was the only one."

"Not by a long shot," I answered in a low voice.

"Don't tell me, Ellie, that you're worried about coming under suspicion should it turn out that Karisma's death was not accidental?"

"It's bound to come out that I had an argument with Mrs. Swabucher this morning over my feeling that I had been used by her and Karisma. Mrs. Malloy heard my raised voice and wanted to know what had been going on. And . . . the whole thing could be blown out of proportion so that it would sound as if I'd had a major crush on Karisma and had gone berserk at the thought of his betraying me."

"Did you?" asked Ben in a neutral voice.

"Go berserk and kill him?"

"No—have feelings for the man?"

"How could I, when I hardly knew Karisma?"

"And are a happily married woman."

"I don't suppose that I would have thought about the possibility of my becoming a suspect if Mrs. Swabucher hadn't made her accusation. She looked right into my eyes when she said Karisma had been murdered, and I felt such a chill go through me that I wanted to turn and run."

"Come here, my silly one." Ben drew me into his arms and I rested my aching head against the comfort of his shoulder.

"Believe me, I don't want Eudora to be dragged down to the police station," I whispered, "but the thought of my being locked up for life, away from you and the twins, is at the front of my mind. It's awful to admit that the reason I couldn't stop crying when I got home didn't have nearly as much to do with Karisma's death as with not being able to forget that look Mrs. Swabucher gave me."

"You can't make much out of that," Ben said reasonably. "The woman was in shock."

"That's true." But I sounded uncertain.

"My guess, Ellie, is that if she were thinking of anyone in particular, it would be Brigadier Lester-Smith. The man has to harbour feelings of bitterness; and she may have leapt to the conclusion that he'd found a way of punishing her for the blow she had inflicted years ago on his male ego."

I sat up straight. "Oh, but he's such a dear, it's difficult to imagine him resorting to brutality."

"If you don't want it to be him," said Ben obligingly, "then how about Mrs. Malloy? She was on the spot. And Vanessa was telling me on the way to the vicarage that her future mother-in-law had gone off Karisma a bit when she thought he might be trying to cut George out of the picture."

"Oh, we're starting to talk nonsense!" I stood up and immediately sat down again.

"I disagree. It seems to me that I'm making a valid point, Ellie. When someone is murdered, and we don't even know that is the case here, almost everybody who has any connection—however remote—with the victim can be found to have some reason for committing the crime."

"It did cross my mind," I admitted, "that Mr. Poucher might be the guilty party, if, as you say, there is one. He was extremely upset when he told me his crotchety mother had rebounded back to top-notch health after meeting Karisma yesterday and doing a photo session with him. And he was decidedly evasive about where he was when Heathcliff practically tore the reading room apart."

"You see." Ben smiled fondly at me. "The list of people with motives is infinite. But we won't explore them all. I think you should go upstairs and have a nice relaxing bath, sweetheart, while I heat you up some soup. And afterwards you might like to get into bed and take things off your mind."

This suggestion was not without appeal, but I had jumped to the wrong conclusion. Ben went on to suggest that I take some of my interior decorating books with me and snuggle down with them under the blankets.

"That's not a bad idea," I said. "It would be relaxing to browse through catalogs of duvets for Eudora's bed"— my mind went blank for a second—"and . . . and try to find possible curtain material for Brigadier Lester-Smith's house." I was expressing my appreciation for Ben's thoughtfulness with a kiss, when the drawing room door opened and in floated Vanessa.

"Sorry, lovebirds," she cooed as we broke apart, "but you're wanted on the telephone, Ellie. It's your friend Eudora Spike, and she was so rattled when I answered that she never mentioned my wedding, let alone my modelling career. But"—Vanessa was still talking as I hurried out into the hall—"I'm not about to criticize this once, because I've just remembered that in the excitement of my own life I forgot to report to either of you on Gerta, the priceless nanny. She came up to the house and asked me to tell you she's going to London this evening to pick up some of her things from home, so not to set off the alarm if you couldn't find her."

My cousin's voice faded into a hum as I grabbed up the receiver and breathlessly asked Eudora how she was doing.

"I've had a rather disturbing telephone call from Sir Robert," she told me. "He'd stopped by Mr. Poucher's house on the way home from the library to ask him if he still had the coffeepot cord, and got the news that old Mrs. Poucher had passed away during the afternoon, apparently between the time her son left and arrived home. The doctor was there and said it was an open-and-shut case of old age. And from the sound of things, the old lady did rather overdo things earlier in the day."

"Another death . . ." I said.

"Yes, they do seem to be coming in droves," Eudora replied evenly, "and that's why Sir Robert rang me up. He'd been talking to Mrs. Dovedale, who in turn had a word with Bunty Wiseman, and they are all convinced that an evil force is at work in Chitterton Fells. So Sir Robert has asked me to perform an emergency exorcism immediately at the library, to rid it of Hector Rigglesworth's ghost."

"What? This evening?"

"Ellie, I really should talk to my bishop, but he's unavailable and Gladstone's feeling is that if I don't do something, a panic may set in that could spread throughout Chitterton Fells. So I think the best thing I can do is go down at once to the library and conduct a prayer service, invoking God's blessing on the repose of Mr. Rigglesworth's soul."

"Will all the Library League members be in attendance?"

"Gladstone, of course, will accompany me," Eudora replied, "and I imagine most of the others will be there. Can you manage to join us, Ellie? I'd feel more comfortable if you were present."

"I'll leave immediately," I promised, and as an afterthought said I would bring a bottle of holy water my mother-in-law had brought with her on one of her visits. We might as well avail ourselves of all the help we could get.

When I went back into the drawing room and told Ben about the latest development, he said it sounded like utter nonsense to him, but offered to accompany me to the library. Vanessa said with a sweetly self-sacrificing smile that she'd stay and watch Abbey and Tam, even though she had made plans to go out to dinner with George, who was still a little down because he was afraid he'd blotted his copybook with the moat incident and would no longer be made welcome at Merlin's Court. Having thanked them both, I said I would just as soon go on my own, as I could do with the time alone in the car to think things through.

Luckily, Ben understood how I felt. He came out to watch me drive off without offering any advice except not to offer anyone—friend or stranger—a lift home and insisting I promise to give him a ring if anything occurred to make me nervous. I could tell he didn't believe for one second that the exorcism would produce any terrifying results. No vile substances hurtling out of the mouths of luckless persons possessed by demonic invasion, the kind that are manifested in films dealing with excursions into the occult. As for me, I wasn't sure what to expect when I walked into the library through the back entrance and once again mounted the stairs to the reading room.

Just outside its door I was a little taken aback to see Mrs. Malloy about to enter ahead of me with Mrs. Dovedale, but she explained they met up at the bus stop outside the grocery store and she had decided to come along and provide me with moral support.

"You was looking very peaky this afternoon when you went home," Mrs. M. told me, "so after I sat for a bit and had a cup of tea, I said to George as how I would put on me hat and coat and pop up to Merlin's Court to see how you was doing. And a good thing I saw Mrs. Dovedale at the bus stop, or I'd have wasted a fare."

"That's very kind of you, Mrs. Malloy," I said as we entered the room to find Sir Robert Pomeroy in conversation with Bunty Wiseman, deciding whether or not it would be appropriate to serve ginger biscuits on this occasion. Mrs. Dovedale accepted their congratulations on the nice job she had done of cleaning up after the ill-fated benefit. And I took the opportunity to tell Mrs. Malloy that I didn't think she was looking particularly perky herself.

"Must be me new rouge," she said. "I should have stuck to me usual Coral Reef instead of trying the one Vanessa recommended, not that I'm trying to suggest she was attempting to make me look old enough to be George's mother. The girl's been nice to me after her fashion, Mrs. H., and I do believe as how she loves my boy. So I'd just as soon you didn't say a word to her about what's been worrying me silly."

"I knew there was something wrong!"

"I'm sure I'm working myself up over nothing." Mrs. Malloy gave me a look that dared me to say otherwise. "It's just that I can't stop wondering if that fall Karisma took into the moat didn't put him in a weakened state, so to speak. Meaning, Mrs. H., that he already had a crack in his noggin when that statue fell on him. You know what I'm getting at: My George could end up taking the blame, and visiting a son in prison has never been my idea of a good time."

"You're looking for trouble," I told her even though I was thinking that she might be on to something. And, I'm ashamed to say, I latched on to the possibility with a feeling of relief. Dreadful as was the thought that Karisma had died as a result of suffering one blow to the head too many that day, it was preferable in my mind to the possibility that he was a victim of Hector Rigglesworth's ghostly machinations. Or, even worse, had been murdered by someone I knew.

"Karisma fell into the moat because he misjudged his step," I told Mrs. Malloy firmly. "No one could blame George for what happened."

"Don't you believe it, ducky!" She dabbed at her eyes with a hankie. "There's millions of women out there who'll be looking for a scapegoat when they hear about the death of their idol. And word will spread like measles that my boy was jealous of him because of Vanessa." Mrs. Malloy drew a shaky breath. "There's only one thing for it, we'll have to plant the blame fair and square on someone else."

I didn't relish the way she was looking at me but, before anything else could be said, Eudora and Gladstone came into the room with Sylvia Babcock at their heels. No sign yet of Brigadier Lester-Smith, and I was wondering if he feared Mrs. Swabucher might be joining us, when Mr. Poucher appeared on the scene, wearing a black armband in deference, one would assume, to his mother's passing.

"Just the man I want to see, what! what!" Sir Robert's moustache bristled with authority as he strode forward with a hand extended. "If you'd be so good, my man, I and our fellow members of the Library League would appreciate the return of the coffeepot cord."

"Here—take the dratted thing." Mr. Poucher produced it from his raincoat pocket and stood with a scowl deepening the habitual gloom of his face. "I know what the pack of you are thinking. I'm not so daft I didn't realize right off the bat as all that rubbish about an exorcism was just a way to get me here so I'd break down and confess. But it wasn't me put that red mark on the dead man's throat. I can swear on my mother's grave"—a sour smile twisted his lips—"that I didn't use this here cord to choke the life out of Karisma."

"Of course you didn't, dear." Mrs. Dovedale spoke in her gentle voice. "I noticed that mark when he got here, same as you all did."

Mrs. Malloy and I exchanged looks, but it was Eudora who staunchly proclaimed that there was absolutely no connection between the mark on Karisma's throat and his death. Gladstone added kindly that he harboured no suspicions of Mr. Poucher. And Bunty piped in with the information that she had been too busy looking at other parts of Karisma's anatomy to focus on his neck.

"Well, then"—Sir Robert assumed a more jocular expression—"I say we plug in the coffeepot and all have a

cup before we get going with the exorcism, what! what!"
This suggestion met with mixed degrees of enthusiasm.
Eudora smiled wanly at me as I took the bottle of holy
water from my bag and handed it to her. Mrs. Malloy did
brighten up when Sylvia Babcock sidled towards her and
started up a conversation. But Bunty was not her usual
sunshine self when she headed over to me.

"This is a rum go, Ellie."

"I don't know what to expect of an exorcism," I
agreed.

"That's not what I meant." She ran an agitated hand
through her blond curls. "I heard what Mrs. Swabucher
said about Karisma being murdered and I've got this awful
feeling that my ex might have done it."

"Lionel? But he's a respected solicitor."

"What difference does that make?" Bunty choked
back a sob. "He's still in love with me, don't tell me he
isn't, because I know him like the back of my hand, and if
he were here, I'd slap him silly for scaring me this way.
He's been nosing around ever since the divorce to see if I
was knocking around with anyone else and, like a bloody
fool, I had to go and tell him this afternoon when he
showed up here that Karisma had fallen for me on sight
like a ton of bricks."

"Oh, for heaven's sake, Bunty," I exclaimed, "you're
working yourself into a froth over nothing. Lionel isn't a
fool. He'd have known you were making that up."

"Thanks a lot, chum."

Trust Mrs. Malloy to come clattering on her high
heels into our conversation. In a stage whisper that would
have carried to the back row of a theatre she announced
she knew how and why Karisma had croaked. Regrettably, before she could satisfy our avid curiosity, Sir Robert
clanged on the coffeepot with a spoon and suggested that
we all help ourselves to a spot of brew and, if the idea did
not offend, make free of the ginger biscuits before taking
our places around the table. "Or is an old duffer like me
confusing an exorcism with a séance?"

Mrs. Dovedale, with a tender look, attempted to clar-
ify matters for him by explaining that as she understood it,
the point of an exorcism was to tell evil spirits to scram,
whereas a séance invited them to pop in for a visit.

Gladstone had been seated at the table, knitting placidly. Now he said mildly, "Well, all I can hope is that should Hector Rigglesworth get the signals confused and show himself, he will at least exercise the good manners not to help himself to a couple of ginger biscuits. There are barely enough to go round as it is. I did mention to Eudora"—Gladstone smiled fondly at his wife—"that I was uncertain about the protocol of bringing a sponge cake to an exorcism, and she agreed with me that it would not do to make a social event out of the evening. Which is not to imply, Sir Robert"—needles still clicking along—"any criticism of your ginger biscuits."

"They are not his biscuits." Mrs. Dovedale's face flushed becomingly as she spoke up on behalf of the man by her side. "The brigadier brought them a couple of meetings ago, and very nice of him too."

"By the way," I asked, "are we going to wait for him to arrive before we get started at casting Hector Rigglesworth into someplace beyond reach of library fines?"

"Honestly, I don't think Brigadier Lester-Smith will be coming." Bunty handed me a cup of coffee. "I think he'd feel funny about leaving Mrs. Swabucher."

"You mean she's staying with him?"

"That's what I understood." Bunty looked at Mrs. Dovedale, who nodded agreement.

"I thought she was staying at the Hollywood Hotel." I was having a little trouble grasping this turn of events. "Mrs. Swabucher must have changed her mind after I spoke to her. But why on earth would she choose to go to Brigadier Lester-Smith's lodgings?"

"I heard them talking," Sylvia Babcock said from a corner of the room, where she had been standing as if oblivious to what was going on around her. "He was quite persistent in his invitation. It looked to me as if he wore the woman down in the end, and she was in a bad way to begin with, wasn't she?"

"Wouldn't it be lovely"—Mrs. Dovedale smiled up at Sir Robert—"if something good came out of this terrible business and two people ended up finding happiness in each other's arms?" It wasn't clear to me whom she was talking about, but being of a romantically susceptible nature, I found myself hoping that Mrs. Swabucher and the brigadier might find the way, if not back to the golden days of their courtship, to somewhere equally heart-warming and magical. Surely, I thought, looking over at Gladstone in his grey cardigan, if this man could exist as Zinnia Parrish, author of the world's steamiest romances, nothing was beyond the realm of possibility.

By the time I had gathered my wits about me, Sir Robert was closing the curtains, on the advice of Mrs. Dovedale, who said that as she remembered it from watching a program on the telly, the exorcist had to enter the world of darkness to wage war with the evil one on its own turf. As the room descended into dense shadow, everyone scrambled for a seat at the table and I was made aware that my companion to the right was Eudora only when her voice practically jumped into my right ear.

"My dear friends, in your names and my own I offer a prayer to our Heavenly Father that He look with favour upon all His servants and through the gift of His abiding love bring peace to the soul of Hector Rigglesworth."

"That's not going to scare off the bugger," Mrs. Malloy muttered into my left ear. And the screech that came from the far end of the table did not emanate from Hector Rigglesworth, unless he had developed a feminine voice from living with all those daughters. My money was on Sylvia Babcock.

"How about trying the holy water, dear?" That was Gladstone speaking, and Eudora said that it was right in front of her if she could only find it.

"Ah, here it is!" Her voice sounded distinctly strained as she intoned, "Depart, Hector Rigglesworth, from this earthly domain, and leave the Chitterton Fells library to the service of its community." This really wasn't fair, I thought. Eudora might well find herself without a job should her bishop learn of this escapade. A splash of water landed on my cheek. Another squeal was heard from—now I was certain—Sylvia Babcock. And I gave way to a nervous start myself which was imitated by Mrs. Malloy as if we had previously choreographed the movement together.

A draft had swept in upon our backs in what I took to be a venomous rush and the darkness peeled back into shadows that revealed pale globs of faces all staring towards the door.

"Is it him?" Mrs. Dovedale asked in a quaking voice that immediately drew the reassuring arm of Sir Robert around her shoulders.

"He's come for *me!*" Sylvia rose up like a splash of moonlight from her chair. "He's come to take me with him into hell because I murdered my husband for the insurance money."

"Oh, for goodness' sake, shut up, woman, do!" Mr. Poucher growled as he stumbled to his feet.

"I did it! I gave Albert saccharin tablets instead of the ones for his heart. It didn't seem like murder what with him having one foot in the grave already. But I knew the devil was after me when he showed up disguised as that black dog. And he came back today to gloat in my face." Sylvia was sobbing hysterically by the time Sir Robert and Mr. Poucher wrenched back the curtains so that the room lightened sufficiently to reveal a black-clad figure standing in the doorway.

"Good evening," said Ione Tunbridge. "Forgive me for the interruption, but I did so enjoy my visit to the library and all the accompanying excitement that I decided I may have overindulged my taste for solitude. Thus I came back this evening to borrow a book and was told by that sweet little librarian that a meeting was being held in the reading room and I would certainly be welcomed with cries of delight were I to present myself in your midst."

"A pleasure, madam." Sir Robert strove to act the genial host.

"Now, don't tell stories, you enchanting jackanapes!" Miss Tunbridge giggled archly and wagged a black crochet finger at him. "It is abundantly clear that I interrupted this lovely young woman's woeful tale"—she fixed her black eyes on Sylvia, who was sobbing heartily—"before she had time to relate all the distressing details. Having committed murder myself, although only once—which I realize does not make me an expert—I do know that it is imperative to tell people what you have done. Otherwise you go through life burdened by a nasty secret." She drifted over and placed her bony hands on either side of Sylvia's face, effectively compressing a scream. "It doesn't matter whether or not you are believed, dear. The police don't seem to have taken my story seriously. But that's their problem, isn't it, my sweet?"

"I told you she bumped him off!" Mrs. Malloy told me triumphantly as the babble of voices swamped the room. "Oh, I admit I thought Miss Tunbridge was telling tall tales—and I may have to rethink that one—but I was right on the button about Sylvia B. As a matter of fact, Mrs. H., that's what I meant when I said I'd figured out how Karisma came to die. And you have to agree that it's as plain as the nose on your face!"

"What is?"

"Come on." Her elbow dug my ribs painfully. "Use the brains God gave you. Our Mrs. Babcock got in a right tizz thinking she'd been found out, so she bumped off Karisma to make it look like there was one of them serial killers on the loose. Are you listening to me, Mrs. H.?"

"Yes," I said. The coldness in my voice astounded me.

"Well then, what's to be done?"

"Someone will ring up the police." I turned towards the door. "Sir Robert is taking charge tonight, so I think you can safely leave it up to him."

"And where do you think you're going?" Mrs. Malloy called after me as I hurried out into the corridor.

"To see a friend," I called back, but she may not have heard me, because by that time I was halfway down the stairs.

It was chilly when I reached the street, and the shiver that wormed its way down my spine made me hesitate for a second or two under the lamppost. Perhaps I should have told Mrs. Malloy where I was going and that if I didn't return within fifteen minutes, she should phone the police on my account. But if I'd done that, she would have insisted on coming with me. And I wouldn't want that on the off chance there was any risk involved. The same was true of Ben, much as I wished I could turn and find him standing beside me. As for my ringing up the police station and spilling out my suspicions, there would have been no point in that. I knew, especially now that I played them over in my mind, that they were much too threadbare to constitute anything approaching legal evidence. But if I did nothing, someone I knew might be in terrible danger without knowing it.

I heard my feet running down Market Street towards Barberry Road and realized that I had only to turn the corner and cross an alley and I would be there. The tall, narrow house with its front door only inches from the street came towards me at a fast clip, and before I knew it I was standing on the scrubbed stone step and ringing the bell.

It was probably only thirty seconds, although it seemed like a year, before the door was opened by a woman in a print apron. Grey hair poked out from the rim of her knotted scarf.

"Hello . . ." I tried not to sound too breathless. "Is Brigadier Lester-Smith at home?"

She looked me up and down warily. "He is."

"May I come in and speak to him for a minute?"

"Well, I don't know . . ." She sounded as though this were anything but a run-of-the-mill question. "He pays his rent regular as clockwork and isn't one to cause any sort of rumpus. But he's already got a lady upstairs with him, and that's not like the brigadier, let me tell you."

"Well, actually it's her I wanted to see," I said.

"Oh, that's different, then. You're not likely to make a habit of showing up on the doorstep." She stepped back and pointed to the stairs. "His rooms are first on the right, and I'd appreciate you not making a lot of noise going up because my other lodger will give me an earful if you do."

"Thank you," I told her, and conscientiously endeavoured to keep my heart from thumping too loudly as I tiptoed up to the small landing. My hand felt like a five-pound bag of flour when I raised it to knock on Brigadier Lester-Smith's door. He opened up before I managed to bring it back down to my side and peered out at me with an expression of mild surprise on his face.

"Why, good evening, Mrs. Haskell!"

"I'd like to talk to you," I said.

"Certainly." He ushered me into an immaculate sitting room which managed to look inviting even though every piece of furniture was arranged with military precision. "Is it about the decorating for the house?"

"No." I took the chair he offered me. "It's about Karisma's death. I'm sorry to say this, Brigadier Lester-Smith, but I'm inclined to agree with Mrs. Swabucher that it wasn't an accident."

"I see." He sat down across from me and adjusted the knees of his trousers with great care. "Evangeline is in the bedroom." He nodded towards a door to the left of the fireplace. "She's been resting for the past few hours. And I doubt she'll hear us."

"That's good." I held on to my handbag with both hands.

"Are you here to tell me"—he smiled with infinite sadness—"that you think I murdered the lad?"

"No." I blinked back tears. "I think Mrs. Swabucher ended Karisma's life. When she stood on the stairs and said that he had been murdered, I thought she was making an accusation. But a little while ago at the library, Ione Tunbridge turned up and said that when people . . . do something like this they have an intense need to confess. She's a very odd woman, and I don't believe her theory holds water most of the time, but I found myself thinking about what Mrs. Swabucher said in a new light. I remembered the look in her eyes when she said 'He was murdered,' and I have this feeling that she wanted me to know the truth because holding it inside—being all alone with the terrible knowledge of what she has done—was anguish."

"Evangeline loved him."

"That's why she did it," I told Brigadier Lester-Smith. "She was afraid for him. She had watched him lose the opportunity of doing the cover for *A Knight to Remember* and I think all of a sudden she looked ahead to the day when he would no longer be the man of so many women's dreams. And she couldn't bear that to happen to him. She had watched her husband die a slow, undignified death, she told me so the other day."

"So you think"—the brigadier stared into the sootless grate—"that Evangeline picked up that bust of Shakespeare and hit him over the head?"

"No, she wouldn't have done that." I shifted in my chair. "I've been putting other bits and pieces together, such as Eudora saying, after breaking the news to me that Karisma was dead, that when she found his body she had trouble breathing. And tonight, just before I left home for the exorcism, I was about to look through books on duvets to find one with a good synthetic filling, because when I talked to Eudora about redoing her bedroom she mentioned that she was allergic to feathers. Do you see what I'm getting at, Brigadier?"

"Evangeline's feather boa."

"Eudora was wearing a pink cardigan this afternoon and I remember that as she stood telling me about Karisma, she was pulling at what I supposed was a loose thread, but what if it were a piece of down, one of several that may have been in the air when she bent over the body, and that her breathlessness was not due to hock but to an allergic reaction? Mrs. Swabucher wasn't wearing her boa while Karisma was autographing. She had left it in the reading room the other night and I told her where it was when I was pouring lemonade for the refreshment part of the benefit."

"So you are saying, Mrs. Haskell, that Evangeline must have come downstairs wearing the boa *after* she had spoken to you." Brigadier Lester-Smith straightened himself in his chair. "But that is hardly evidence that she smothered him with it."

"I don't think she did," I said slowly. "I think she . . ." It was difficult to get out the word. "*Strangled* him with it, because he already had a red mark on his throat. And, not thinking at all rationally, she hoped that the new injury would be taken for the old one."

"Did he look like a man who had been strangled?" Brigadier Lester-Smith asked with a wistful mockery.

"He looked like Apollo resting up for the sunrise, but I don't suppose Mrs. Swabucher had to do more than pull the ends of that boa tight for a few seconds if he were already unconscious from being struck on the head by Shakespeare. And that is what happened, isn't it, Brigadier? You were there and you saw it all, didn't you? That's why you begged her to come home with you and finally persuaded her to agree."

"I wanted to protect her." Brigadier Lester-Smith walked over to the window and continued speaking with his back to me. "I knew it could be for only a little while, but I felt I owed her that because she was once my wife, for one day at least. I went upstairs for a while after the autograph session, but I kept seeing Evangeline, from wherever I was standing. We'd talked a bit earlier, and I'd thought I'd overcome my distress at meeting her again, but I realized I was fooling myself. I went back down into the library. Karisma was still sitting at the desk, looking through the books with himself on the cover. But as I crossed in front of the reception desk he got to his feet. He took a couple of steps before that bust of Shakespeare came flying off the wall and hit him on the head. Maybe the bracket on which it had been sitting had been knocked loose. But that would seem unlikely because it always looked a very solid piece. The sound of the crash was blotted out by the howling of the dog."

"Yes," I said, "he did make the most unearthly racket."

Brigadier Lester-Smith continued as if he hadn't heard me. "For a moment Karisma stood absolutely still. Then he staggered before falling backwards. I was about to go over to him, Mrs. Haskell, when I saw Evangeline hurrying towards him with her arms outstretched. And immediately the bitterness stuck in my throat again, and I thought she's going to blame me for this, it would be my fault just as it was on our wedding night. She'll accuse me of attacking the lad as a way of getting even with her. So I hid in the stacks, Mrs. Haskell, like the coward I am. And I saw her kneel beside him and touch his cheek. It was too much! I closed my eyes. And when I could bring myself to look again, she was lifting that feather boa from his face."

"Perhaps she believed that's what he would have wanted. Suppose she knew he dreaded growing old? I've heard those snide remarks about him being the only man in the world to look at his reflection in his dinner plate. If it's true, maybe the reason was that he felt a need to keep checking that his looks weren't beginning to dim."

"What she did was terribly wrong"—the brigadier came slowly towards me—"but she wasn't a wicked woman. She was a girl who never completely grew up, just like the Rigglesworth daughters, so that the only man she could ever love with her whole heart and soul was one who would never destroy the magic by making himself attainable."

"What's going to happen now?" I asked.

"Why don't we go in and take a look at her?" Gently, Brigadier Lester-Smith led me towards the bedroom door. "Evangeline told me she was going to take something to help her sleep for a hundred years until her Prince Charming wakens her with a kiss."

EPILOGUE

It was a couple of months later and another meeting of the Library League was taking place in the reading room. Sylvia Babcock was no longer with us, for reasons we rarely discussed these days. Mrs. Malloy, however, had joined our little group, and the mood was cheerful that evening. Brigadier Lester-Smith presided over the coffeepot, whose cord was now flagged with a bright red label proclaiming it to be Library Property. Mr. Poucher had not hidden Heathcliff behind the corner cupboard this evening, but we heard news of him on this occasion, as we always did. Far from bringing doom and gloom to his current master, the dog had acted as a matchmaker. One day when Mr. Poucher was taking him for a walk in the pet cemetery— Heathcliff having professed an interest in searching out the graves of his illustrious forebears—they had met a woman who was mourning the recent demise of her beloved corgi. Heathcliff in actual fact made the introduction by absconding with the wreath recently laid beside dear Toffee's tombstone, and romance had bloomed for Mr. Poucher. Sir Robert and Mrs. Dovedale still kept me hopeful that they would one day tie the knot. Bunty Wiseman was talking about giving Lionel another chance. Gladstone Spike continued his secret writing career as Zinnia Parrish. So, all in all, Romance flourished in the Chitterton Fells library environment.

With the murder of Karisma, the ghost of Hector Rigglesworth would seem to have been laid to rest. Some of us believed he had felt himself sufficiently avenged against the library and had taken himself off of his own accord. Others thought that the exorcism had done the trick. Mr. Poucher maintained that he had never believed in the Rigglesworth rubbish. It was an opinion that was put to the test on the evening in question when Brigadier Lester-Smith rose to make his presentation to the members.

"As the treasurer's records will show"—he opened his briefcase and produced a sheaf of official-looking papers— "we were successful in raising a substantial sum of money with which to commemorate the memory of our late lamented librarian. The original plan was to commission a bronze statue of Miss Bunch. But it has recently been brought to the league's attention that the library has serious problems with dry rot and woodworm, which have caused some shifting of the building. With the result that"—the brigadier paused and lowered his head— "books have fallen off the shelves and one heavy object is known to have tumbled off its pedestal. It is, therefore, my proposal we would do best to honour the memory of Miss Bunch by righting structural decay. Shall we vote on the matter?"

It was unanimously agreed that Miss Bunch would wish to sacrifice her bronze statue for a better cause, but before we went on to other matters of business, Mrs. Dovedale whispered audibly to Sir Robert, "Dry rot and woodworm, that's what Hector Rigglesworth promised when he laid the curse on the library!"

"I didn't leave my dog home to see to his own dinner," growled Mr. Poucher, "so as to come here and listen to a load of tripe."

"I won't voice me opinion on Mr. Rigglesworth"— Mrs. Malloy leaned her black taffeta elbows on the table— "because I haven't been a member long enough to know much about him except what I've heard from Mrs. H., and it wouldn't do to take that as gospel. But as sure as I'm sitting here, there is something, a presence, if you like, as I feel every time I come into the library these days."

"I agree!" Bunty opened wide her cornflower-blue eyes. "I feel it too, but I'm sure it's not old Hector, because it gives me such a warm tingle all over, like I'm glowing from the inside out, and I always go out of here feeling absolutely beautiful."

"Worshipped, that's the feeling I get," said Mrs. Dovedale.

Sir Robert, not surprisingly, tugged at his moustache, said "What! what!" several times, and suggested we proceed with the matters at hand. Brigadier Lester-Smith hastily produced another batch of closely typed papers, and the meeting proceeded smoothly until it was time to call it an evening. When I reached the bottom of the stairs I hesitated for a moment to see if I felt anything such as the other women had described. But nothing brushed up against my soul. And after saying good night to those of the group who had straggled down with me, I headed for my car.

"I've been wanting to have a word with you for some time," Mr. Poucher said, appearing out of the shadows. "It's about the day of Miss Bunch's benefit and me not being around when Heathcliff misbehaved himself in the reading room."

"Dogs are said to howl at the moment of death," I said.

"Yes"—Mr. Poucher looked bleakly pleased at hearing his pet had done something right—"but the reason I wasn't around to quiet him down was I'd gone down to the toilet. And when I found it locked—Mrs. Spike, as we found out, being inside—I went out into the alley to relieve myself of all that rotten lemonade."

"I appreciate your tying up that loose end," I told him.

"Mother would have properly given me what-for if she'd known." Mr. Poucher sounded almost fondly reminiscent as he made this admission before trudging off home to Heathcliff and his new lady-love. And I drove home to Merlin's Court.

Ben was waiting for me in the drawing room. We had planned a rather special evening of conversation and cappuccino. I had become quite accomplished at the frothing part after watching the video. After running upstairs to look in on Abbey and Tam and coming back down again, I told Ben that I'd had a letter from Gerta that morning. She was very happy in her new job, working in a coffee shop very similar to the one she and her husband had operated, and particularly wanted to tell Ben that getting to know him had convinced her there were still some decent men left in this world.

He and I then spoke about Vanessa's upcoming marriage to George Malloy. And probably because being at the library in Gladstone's company had brought back the recent past, I asked Ben if he had any regrets about deciding not to do the cover for *A Knight to Remember*.

"None," he said as he joined me on the sofa, "and I gather Vanessa feels the same way. It sounded glamorous to her at first, but when it came down to it, she didn't want to take any time away from modelling for George's company." He grinned. "Also, there was the fact that her fainting spell in the church was due to her being pregnant."

"I'm afraid you're not being honest with me about your feelings," I told him. "Didn't you really want to be on the cover of a steamy best seller?"

"I was tempted for one reason only."

"Which was?"

"That you'd see me as the man of your dreams." Ben turned and cupped my face in his hands. "Am I that, Ellie?"

"No," I said softly. "You're the man I want next to me when I wake up in the morning, because every day with you is like a new page of my favourite love story of all time."

If you enjoyed Dorothy Cannell's

HOW TO MURDER THE MAN OF YOUR DREAMS

you'll want to read

GOD SAVE THE QUEEN!

the first book in her new mystery series.

Look for it at your favorite bookstore.

When she was three years old, Flora Hutchins went to live at Gossinger Hall in the village of Nether Woodcock, Lincolnshire. Upon first seeing the gray stone house with its turrets sprouting up all over the place, Flora had decided it was bigger than the cottage hospital where her mother had died, so it had to be Buckingham Palace. And when her grandfather came down the steps to meet her, looking so distinguished in his pin-striped suit, she was surprised he wasn't wearing a crown because she was so certain he had to be the King of England.

It took the little girl a few days to learn the true state of affairs. Grandpa was not the King, but Sir Henry Gossinger's butler. But that didn't mean Flora turned into a downtrodden little thing kept hidden away behind the broom cupboard door. When she got bigger she liked helping the series of housekeepers, who came and went as regularly as the seasons, to make the beds, dust the furniture, and peel vegetables for dinner. Grandpa wouldn't let her help him make up the special recipe he used to clean Sir Henry's prized collection of eighteenth-century silver, but Flora loved sitting with him at such times because then he would tell her stories about Gossinger Hall.

"Start at the very beginning," she would beg.

"Very well," Grandpa would reply. "The original part of this house was built in the twelfth century by Thomas Short Shanks, a henpecked baron whose wife, Lady Normina, agreed to let him go off and fight in the Crusades on one minor concession. He had to build her a house that would turn her eleven sisters green with envy.

"Lady Normina doesn't sound a particularly nice person, does she, Grandpa?"

"That's not for the likes of us to say, Flora," he would reply firmly as his hands kept polishing away at a piece of silver. "The story goes that Lady Normina was tired of the way her less-than-loving kin looked down their knobby noses at her. All because her husband had provided fodder for every second-rate town crier in England, by being disqualified from a major jousting tournament (plus fined a purse of gold) for galloping into the arena before Queen Eleanor had time to drop her hanky."

"Poor Thomas." Flora's tender young heart was always touched at this juncture of the story.

"Sir Thomas to you and me," Grandpa would say reprovingly. "He may have been dead for close on a thousand years but that's no reason not to pay him due respect."

"I'm sorry."

"Then we will continue." This would be said with a smile. "Truth be told, Flora, Lady Normina's sisters weren't the only ones she wished to outdo. In those days, kitchens weren't part of the main house. And, bent on keeping up with the Ostaffs who lived two castles away, Lady Normina insisted her kitchen be within easy distance of the house in order that she might spy on the shiftless cook; but not so close that were a leg of mutton to catch on fire her dream house would go up in smoke with it."

"I think I would have been scared of Lady Normina." Flora always hoped this did not sound too much like a criticism.

"By all accounts she was a masterful woman." Grandpa had usually finished polishing two or three pieces of silver by this time. "She didn't mind that the other ladies in the vicinity called her nouveau riche and terribly standoffish! Lady Normina thought them all pathetic creatures and understandably jealous that the rushes on her floors always stayed so nice and fresh. Her Ladyship had made a vow to her patron saint, Flora, that she would put a dent in the armor of any knight who didn't remove his shoes before setting foot inside her abode. And anyone who wanted to spit had to go outside."

"Did Sir Henry tell you all this, Grandpa?"

"Quite a bit has been written down, my dear. The Gossingers have always been great ones for keeping journals. But don't keep interrupting me, Flora, or I'll never be finished before it's time for Sir Henry's tea." Grandpa often picked up a clean polishing cloth about now. "It isn't hard to believe that Lady Normina's pride and joy was the garderobe."

"What's that?"

"An indoor toilet, something most people—even very rich ones—didn't have in those days, and so called because it doubled as a storage room for clothing, on account of the felicitous chemical composition of the fumes doing a bang-up job of keeping out moths. The word *wardrobe,* Flora, comes down to us from the garderobe."

"That's interesting," Flora would say dutifully, trying not to wrinkle up her nose.

"The sisters were beside themselves—with happiness we must hope—at their dear Normina's good fortune."

"Is the garderobe still here, Grandpa?"

"Of course it is," he would reply as he glanced up at the clock. "But it's locked up now. Do get down off that stool, there's a good child, and fetch the chocolate cake from the pantry for Sir Henry's tea."

Flora understood from listening to Grandpa that Gossinger Hall had once been the last word in luxury, by the standards of its time. John of Gaunt was said to have visited there on several occasions with his mistress Catherine Swinford. And, in this latter part of the twentieth century, the Hall still made for an interesting place to view on the days it was open to the public. The price of admission was modest, only two pounds per adult and fifty pence for any juvenile who made a sincere attempt to look short and sufficiently bored to pass for under the age of twelve.

Making even better value for the money was the inclusion in the tour of a pair of headphones and a hand cassette, which provided an audio guide to points of historical and architectural interest. However, the sad truth is that whilst it wasn't a bad place to visit, especially on early closing day at the shops, very few people who appreciated the comforts provided by even the most modest semidetached house would have wanted to *live* at Gossinger Hall.

Little Flora, with the ghost of the twelfth century Lady Normina looming larger than life over her shoulder, was very glad that Sir Henry, at nearly sixty, remained unmarried. She quite liked Mrs. Warren who worked in the tearoom-cum-gift-shop. She was fond of Mr. Tipp, whose job description was stable boy even though he was close to the same age as his master, Sir Henry. And she adored her grandfather, even though she sometimes thought crossly that he loved the Queen better than anyone else in the world.

Her childhood had seemed to pass through her fingers like an enchanted daisy chain, all pastel colors and gentle fragrances. School in the village. Sir Henry giving her toffees and patting her on the head. Sunny afternoons spent rummaging for cast-off finery in attic trunks, so she could dress up and pretend to be one of Lady Normina's handmaidens. And Grandpa telling her other stories about earlier times at Gossinger.

There was the one about Queen Charlotte paying an afternoon visit that ended with a terrible stain upon the family honor, when it was discovered that the silver tea strainer Her Majesty had brought with her was missing. The Gossinger heir at that time was a wild young man, up to his powdered wig in gambling debts, and it was naturally suspected that he had pocketed the tea strainer to sell at the first opportunity.

Flora spent countless hours hunting for the strainer in all the nooks and crannies she could discover. It would have been so wonderful to have gone running in to Grandpa with her hands behind her back and say "Guess what I've found? Sir Rowland didn't steal the tea strainer after all! It was here all the time!" It would have been Flora's small way of repaying her grandfather for making up to her all the love she had missed by her mother's untimely death. And for the fact she never seemed to have had a father.

Grandpa, she knew, would have been immensely pleased to have the Gossinger honor thus restored. But that wasn't all. Holding the tea strainer in his hands would have been a magical moment for him. His great passion was the silver he polished for Sir Henry, which made it surprising, Flora always thought, that there was one story he would never tell her even though she was sure he knew all about it: how the superbly crafted silver collection he loved so much had come into the Gossinger family's possession in the first place.

Flora never did find that tea strainer. And suddenly, as if she had gone to bed one night a child and awakened the next morning a young woman, Flora was seventeen. And before she had time to turn around, a big change occurred at Gossinger Hall. Mabel Bowser appeared on the scene.

On the fateful day in question, Flora had been looking out the window of the sitting room she shared with her grandfather when she saw a woman in brown tweeds get off the sightseeing coach and set foot inside the gift-shop-cum-tearoom that served as the public entrance to Gossinger. Why, she looks just like the reincarnation of Lady Normina, Flora thought, and a strange little pang of fear quivered up her spine.

Miss Mabel Bowser certainly had the iron-clad look of a woman who would send her man off to the Crusades without first packing him a lunch. And no one, including Flora, could ever have suspected that her heart was beating fast under her forty-five-year-old bosom as she entered the gift shop/tearoom. It was a chilly day in October, and Mrs. Warren took her entry fee money by dint of inching the tips of her fingernails out of the sleeve of her cardigan. Or, to be accurate, cardigans. Mrs. Warren was bundled up in at least three, and did not appear to be joking when she declared the radiators that lined the walls were for neither use nor ornament. Unless, that is, you happened to be a "bally" dancer and wished to practice your arabesque.

Undaunted, Mabel Bowser embraced the chill of centuries bearing down on her from the towering stone walls of the great hall. However, two women schoolteachers from her sightseeing coach were less than enthusiastic. They groused that their headphones would have to do double duty as earmuffs. Mabel was able to hear their petty complaints because she had declined Mrs. Warren's offer of a personal electronic guide. She hadn't wanted any encumbrance to bring her down to earth. Being a woman of substantial build, she walked on air somewhat at her own risk. Besides, the device would have stamped her as a visitor, and Mabel Bowser wanted to pretend for one glorious hour that she dwelt in the musty splendor that was Gossinger Hall.

From her childhood days in the flat above her parents' secondhand shop, Mabel had yearned to be part of Britain's upper crust. With this commendable goal in mind she had taken to wearing dowdy tweeds, lisle stockings, and pudding-basin hats. She had applied herself to elocution lessons with a dedication that would have pleased Henry Higgins no end and gave her sister Edna, who still lived in Bethnal Green, a sad little pang. But what does a woman whose idea of personal fulfillment is an evening spent at the dog races know about bettering oneself? Shortsighted Edna would not have bet a fiver that on that visit to Gossinger her sister's schoolgirl dreams of moving up a class would be amply rewarded. But fate has been known to pull a few strings. For outside the garderobe, which was locked and had a "Keep Out" sign posted on the door, Mabel Bowser collided with Sir Henry Gossinger himself.

With a somewhat awkward bow, the baronet introduced himself. Sir Henry wasn't a man designed by nature to bend at the middle. And being a true aristocrat, he spoke to her in a voice that sounded as though he had mouthful of hot plum tart.

"Frightfully sorry, m'dear. Shouldn't be let out on m'own without a seeing eye dog."

What address! What savoir faire! Mabel couldn't make head nor tail of what Sir Henry was saying, but she knew instantly that he was everything she had ever wanted in a man. Stout, balding, and three inches shorter than herself.

"It was my fault," she assured him. "I wasn't looking where I was going." A simple apology, but one elevated to operatic proportions by the throb of passion in her voice.

Sir Henry said something she couldn't follow, to which she responded with a series of heartfelt nods. Within moments Mabel discovered that if she watched his lips closely she could understand his every other word. It was miraculous! Like going to France and realizing you didn't need the phrase book to get off the ferry.

Smiling kindly at her, Sir Henry explained that the garderobe was kept locked because a shift in Gossinger's foundation had enlarged the (Sir Henry got extra-mumbley here) seating area to the point of making it dangerous. A toilet by any other name is not the same. Mabel Bowser was captivated by Sir Henry's chitchat on the subject of his twelfth-century loo.

Perspiration bathed her face in dewy luminosity. For all she was a sizable woman, she felt herself grow fragile. Was she dreaming, or had Sir Henry just offered to personally escort her around his historic abode? She didn't go so far as to imagine he had fallen in love with her at first sight, but she did wonder if the baronet recognized in her a person of his own kind. Mabel Bowser trembled in her brogue shoes when Sir Henry put his hand on her elbow to guide her across the great hall.

Less than half an hour later, Sir Henry showed her Gossinger's remarkably fine collection of eighteenth-century silver, which was displayed in glass cases in the former buttery. He assured her that Hutchins, the butler, was responsible for the silver's cleaning and of course she would not be expected to so much as dust this room were she to accept his offer and make Gossinger her permanent abode.

Admittedly, it wasn't a lengthy courtship. But times have changed since Lady Normina was betrothed before she was fully out of the womb (she was a breech birth) to Thomas Short Shanks in 1172. Emotion may have wrought Sir Henry more than usually indistinct, but Mabel Bowser had no trouble making it crystal clear that she would marry him without waiting to get her best frock back from the cleaners.

The wedding took place several weeks later at St. Mary's Stowe. It was a tastefully small affair with only Sir Henry's nephew Vivian and Miss Sophie Doffit, a third cousin who strongly resembled the Queen Mother, in attendance. It didn't do, of course, to count Hutchins, his seventeen-year-old granddaughter Flora, and Mrs. Johnson, the current housekeeper, seated respectfully at the back of the church. Mr. Tipp, the elderly stable lad, didn't come because someone had to stay behind in case burglars stopped by and took the huff at the lack of hospitality. And Edna couldn't come up from Bethnal Green to witness her sister's triumphal walk down the aisle, because she was in hospital having an operation for piles, as she insisted on calling them. But that was all for the best. Edna would have had trouble saying the minimum and trying to look educated.

With nothing to cast a blight except a fleeting regret that she had not married Sir Henry when she was of an age to provide him with a son and heir, the fledgling Lady Gossinger had every anticipation of living happily ever after. In the ensuing years she grew ever more tweedy. No one would stamp her as nouveau riche, thank you very much! Lady Gossinger's concept of life as lived by the gentry was based on certain novels written in the 1930's and 1940's—in particular, those by Dame Agatha Christie.

To the former Mabel Bowser, the Golden Age meant a time when breakfast was laid out in a grand parade of silver-domed dishes on a twelve-foot sideboard. Gentlemen went fox hunting, or busied themselves doing nothing in their libraries, while their wives concentrated on their herbaceous borders. And the discovery of a corpse on the premises was not permitted to delay mealtimes by more than one hour, even though the cook's favorite carving knife was stuck up to its handle in the victim's back.

It goes without saying that Lady Gossinger, née Bowser, never seriously expected anyone to be murdered under her nose. Her married life moved contentedly forward until came that ill-fated day seven years later when Sir Henry dropped his bombshell and the rose-colored scales fell from her eyes. Afterward, Mabel was to remember with bitter clarity how very chipper she had been feeling only an hour before her brave new world was blown utterly to smithereens. And she would reflect with a pinched and sour smile, very much like the one worn by Lady Normina on her marble tombstone, that she would never have guessed in a thousand years that a girl as seemingly unimportant as Flora Hutchins would have to be dealt with, one way or the other.

BANTAM MYSTERY COLLECTION

____57204-0 **KILLER PANCAKE** Davidson • • • • • • • • • • • • • • • $6.50

____56860-4 **THE GRASS WIDOW** Peitso • • • • • • • • • • • • • • • $5.50

____57235-0 **MURDER AT MONTICELLO** Brown • • • • • • • • • $6.50

____57300-4 **STUD RITES** Conant • • • • • • • • • • • • • • • • • $5.99

____29684-1 **FEMMES FATAL** Cannell • • • • • • • • • • • • • • • $5.50

____56448-X **AND ONE TO DIE ON** Haddam • • • • • • • • • • • $5.99

____57192-3 **BREAKHEART HILL** Cook • • • • • • • • • • • • • • $5.99

____56020-4 **THE LESSON OF HER DEATH** Deaver • • • • • • • • $6.50

____56239-8 **REST IN PIECES** Brown • • • • • • • • • • • • • • • • • $6.50

____57456-6 **MONSTROUS REGIMENT OF WOMEN** King • • • • • $5.99

____57458-2 **WITH CHILD** King • • • • • • • • • • • • • • • • • • $5.99

____57251-2 **PLAYING FOR THE ASHES** George • • • • • • • • • • • $6.99

____57173-7 **UNDER THE BEETLE'S CELLAR** Walker • • • • • • • $5.99

____56793-4 **THE LAST HOUSEWIFE** Katz • • • • • • • • • • • • • $5.99

____57205-9 **THE MUSIC OF WHAT HAPPENS** Straley • • • • • • $5.99

____57477-9 **DEATH AT SANDRINGHAM HOUSE** Benison • • • • • $5.50

____56969-4 **THE KILLING OF MONDAY BROWN** Prowell • • • • • • $5.99

____57191-5 **HANGING TIME** Glass • • • • • • • • • • • • • • • • • $5.99

____57579-1 **SIMEON'S BRIDE** Taylor • • • • • • • • • • • • • • • • $5.50

Ask for these books at your local bookstore or use this page to order.

Please send me the books I have checked above. I am enclosing $_____ (add $2.50 to cover postage and handling). Send check or money order, no cash or C.O.D.'s, please.

Name _____

Address _____

City/State/Zip _____

Send order to: Bantam Books, Dept. MC, 2451 S. Wolf Rd., Des Plaines, IL 60018
Allow four to six weeks for delivery.
Prices and availability subject to change without notice.   MC 10/98